Contents

PREFACE 3

INTRODUCTION 4

1814-1819 5

CHAPTER II 1819-1820 12

CHAPTER III 1820-1825 18

CHAPTER IV 1825-1827 28

CHAPTER V 1827-1828 38

CHAPTER VI 1828-1829 45

CHAPTER VII 1829-1830 50

CHAPTER VIII 1830-1831 54

CHAPTER IX 1831-1835 60

CHAPTER X 1835-1837 70

CHAPTER XI 1837-1840 78

CHAPTER XII 1840-1842 88

CHAPTER XIII 1842-1849 99

CHAPTER XIV 1849-1863 104

PREFACE

IT is difficult to express one's gratitude. Mine I owe to my brother, R. E. Dickinson, to Mrs. Ernest Farquhar (granddaughter of Lady Theresa Lewis), to Sir Guy Campbell, Mrs. W. Rendel, and Sir Arthur Stanley, for the loan of letters in this book. I also thank Mr. Claud Paget and Mr. W. Barclay Squire for the help they have given me.

Doubtless, through want of experience, I have been guilty of leaving out much that might have been left in, and leaving in much that might not be of interest.

The pleasure of knowing Lady Campbell through her letters has been doubled by the kindness I have met with from her daughters, Mrs. Ellis and Mrs. Percy Wyndham.

Lord Cromer before his death in 1917 had been interested in reading these letters. It is due solely to his encouragement that they are now published, though lacking the Introduction he was good enough to offer to write.

A friend of mine read some of the proofs. I found on three occasions they induced sound sleep within a few minutes, which leads me to hope perhaps other readers may find them equally soothing.

V. D.

July 1919.

INTRODUCTION

IN the autumn of 1913 a Life of Lord Clarendon was published, and among many of his letters were a few written to him by an old friend, Miss Eden. It was thought that a further selection of Emily Eden's letters might be of interest.

She was a keen politician of the Whig order, clever, amusing, critical, an excellent friend and a devoted sister. Her father, William Eden, was the third son of Sir Robert Eden, Bart., of West Auckland, Durham, and he married in 1776 Eleanor Elliot, a sister of the 1st Earl of Minto. Two years later, Eden went as a Commissioner to America. He was Chief Secretary in Ireland under Lord Carlisle; Minister-Plenipotentiary in 1785 to the Court of Versailles; in 1788 Ambassador to Spain, and in the following year Ambassador to Holland; he was given a peerage in 1789 (Baron Auckland). Mrs. Eden, from her own account, was evidently a first-rate traveller; she took great interest in her husband's work, and she had a child, often amidst much discomfort, in every country to which they were sent.

Emily was born in 1797. Her parents were settled at Eden Farm, Beckenham, Kent, and her father now devoted his time to politics. Her mother took great trouble to rear and educate her family of fourteen, leaving a detailed account in her Diary of their upbringing, diseases and marriages. Evidently her sense of humour and cheerfulness helped her through much misery.

"Out of fourteen I suckled thirteen. Eleven of the children had smallpox during their wanderings, also cow-pox, whooping-cough, measles and scarlet fever."

In 1786, Eden, who was then in Paris, wrote to his friend Lord Sheffield: "Mrs. Eden is just returned from passing nearly a week in the Circle and Society of the whole Court of Versailles without feeling a moment's discomposure. It is impossible to describe to you all the glorious attentions with which she is honoured by the Queen of France, not only in presents, but in what she values more, in admiration of her children. She and the little Frenchman are both well, and we have now as many nations in our Nursery as were assembled at the Tower of Babel." Another friend also wrote:

"Every report says Mrs. Eden's Nursery is the admiration of the Court and the Town, that they make parties to see it, that she had made domestic life quite fashionable"; and there are constant allusions to the Brattery, the Light Infantry, and the little Parisians.

By her contemporaries Lady Auckland was known later in life as Haughty Nell, and the Judicious Hooker. Her eldest girl, Eleanor, was Pitt's only love, but for various reasons, after a long correspondence between Pitt and Lord Auckland, the affair came to an end, and Eleanor in 1799 married Lord Hobart, who became Secretary of State for War and the Colonies in 1801, and succeeded his father as Earl of Buckinghamshire in 1804.

Lord Auckland died suddenly at Eden Farm in 1814. Lady Auckland only survived him four years. Six of their daughters had married, and the remaining two, Emily and Fanny, lived with their elder brother George, and went with him to India when he became Governor-General in 1835.

From an account given of herself in a letter to one of her friends, Emily had profited by the education she received from her mother. She had read Boswell's *Life of Johnson*, the *Memoires du Cardinal de Retz*, Shakespeare, and knew a great part of the Bible almost by heart before she was eleven.

She took a strong interest in politics, but she was never happier than when living quietly at Greenwich with her brother, sketching, reading and gardening, and in 1835 the prospect of a five months' sea journey to India, and being obliged to leave her sisters, friends, and interests, depressed and worried her.

On her return to England in 1842 she published her *Portraits of the People and Princes of India*. She also wrote *Up the Country; Letters from India*, edited by her niece; and two novels, *The Semi-Detached House* and *The Semi-Attached Couple*.

Three large volumes of her Water-colour Sketches were sold at Christie's in 1907 and are now in the Victoria Memorial Hall, Calcutta.

The year 1849 proved to be one of the greatest sorrow to Miss Eden. Her brother, Lord Auckland, died quite suddenly in January, and three months later she lost her sister Fanny. For the next twenty years she divided her time between Eden Lodge, Kensington Gore, and a little cottage at Broadstairs, writing her books, and seeing many of her friends. Though she had become quite an invalid, her house still remained a centre of political interest. One of her nieces, Lena Eden, lived with her.

Among her most intimate friends were Mr. George Villiers (Lord Clarendon) and his sister Theresa, who married Mr. Lister of Armitage Park in 1830. He died twelve years later, and in 1844 she married George Cornewall Lewis, M.P.

Unfortunately, none of Lady Theresa's letters to Miss Eden can be found. She had a most attractive and gifted nature; her family and friends were devoted to her. Kent House, Knightsbridge, in which she lived nearly all her life, was within a short walk of Eden Lodge.

Another great friend was Pamela, daughter of Lord and Lady Edward FitzGerald. Her father, the chief figure in the Irish Rebellion of '98, had married her mother, the beautiful and fascinating Pamela, six years previously. He died in Newgate Prison, Dublin, leaving three children, Edward, Pamela, and Lucy.

After his death a bill of attainder was passed against his estate, and his wife had to leave Ireland. Edward was left to the care of his grandmother the Duchess of Leinster; Lucy went to Lady Sophia FitzGerald (Aunt Soph), at Thames Ditton. Pamela lived abroad with Lady Edward till 1811, when she returned to her grandmother; three years later the Duchess died; Pamela was then sent to Thames Ditton to be brought up with her sister; she married Sir Guy Campbell in 1820. Her correspondence with Emily Eden covered a period of thirty years. Her letters describe her life with all its Irish and English fun and misery, her adventures and difficulties, the bringing into the world her eleven children, and her efforts to educate them on a dwindling income.

Sir Guy Campbell and Lord Auckland both died in 1849. Pamela lived to be seventy-three, and Emily to be seventy-two; they died in 1869. Emily's letters began in 1814, and were written to her elder sister, Eleanor Lady Buckinghamshire, who lived at Eastcombe, near Greenwich, within driving distance of Eden Farm, the Edens' home till their mother's death in 1818.

17.i.21

Miss Eden's Letters

by Emily Eden

1814-1819

Hon. Emily Eden (aged 17) to her Sister the Countess of Buckinghamshire (aged 37).
EDEN FARM, BECKENHAM, KENT,
Monday, September 26, 1814.

WE have been very much surprised by a letter from Miss Milbanke to Mary informing her she was engaged to marry Lord Byron, a "person of whose character she has had the best opportunity of judging, and who, as he merits her greatest esteem, possesses her strongest attachment." That last sentence certainly sounds very well, but, that she does not seem to be acting with her usual good sense is Mama's opinion, as by all accounts Lord Byron is not likely to make any woman very happy. It is particularly unlucky, at present, as Mary's letters to her about "Lara," the "Corsair," etc., have not expressed much admiration for their author....

September 30.

Mr. Van. came here to dinner to-day and goes away to-morrow. I wish you would tell me what to say to him just now, for he looks as if he wanted some one to talk to him. Mary and George are so busy at chess, and Mama is so interested in the *Anarchie de Pologne*, and I am so tormented by a real, large, green, crawling caterpillar which has found its way to the table and keeps hunting me round it, I have not presence of mind enough left to make out one topic.

Mary has just received Sarah's letter. You perhaps may not know that she is going to change her character to that of a good-natured shilly-shally fellow. She is also thoroughly to understand politics, and is studying Junius, and for want of better society is to get into great habits of intimacy with me. If we were not to change our characters sometimes, there would be rather a sameness in our lives.

George is going to Dropmore and Shottesbrook, but will return home to receive the Colviles, stay here a week longer, and then go for six weeks to Melbury.

He will be a great loss to us, and I cannot but look forward with dread to the long evenings, which used to be so happy, and which will seem so lonely without *Him*, who enlivened them so much.

Good-bye, my dearest Sister. Do not trouble yourself to answer my letters, as a letter to any part of this family does as well for the rest.

Miss Eden to Lady Buckinghamshire.
EDEN FARM,
October 25.

MY DEAR SISTER, Charlotte has had a good night by the account we received this morning. The baby is wonderfully well.

Lord Francis goes to Newmarket on Sunday, and I am to go to Earl's Court for a week, and George and Willy Osborne come here. It sounds as if we were going to play Puss in the Corner on a grand scale, but I shall be glad to get back to my corner again....

George writes me word that one story about Lady Caroline Lamb is, that the separation had been agreed upon, and the articles ready; that Lady Melbourne set out one morning from London to try and arrange matters, and on her arrival she found the happy couple at breakfast, and Lady Caroline drawling out—"William, some more muffin?"—and everything made up.

Mary has grown so fat she can scarcely waddle about, and flatters herself she is looking very well. I remain ever your aff. sister,
EMILY EDEN.

(*Quite private*)

I must just mention that the tucker Ingram made is considered as the most beautiful, elegant, decent, well-behaved, unassuming good sort of tucker in His Majesty's dominion, and is quite the rage. I am in a fever, which should be called the *decent* fever, till I can get four dozen made just exactly like it.

Mary has been very busy preparing for her journey, and desires her love to you, and is very much obliged to you for the use of your necklace, bracelet, etc., which she will take great care of.

She has not heard from Miss Milbanke lately, but we hear that Lord Byron is going to be a good boy, and will never be naughty no more, and he is really and truly writing a new version of the Psalms!

Lord Auckland to Miss Eden.
MELBURY,
November 12.

MY DEAR EMILY, I must write one line though it is past midnight, and that because nobody writes to poor Emily. Well, I am glad you have got a little gaiety at last.

As for us here, we are as merry as grigs, and as active as flies, and as chatty as the maids. We eat and drink, and work and walk, and shoot and hunt, and talk and laugh, all day long—and I expect my pretty master, you would like the eating and drinking the best of all. Such luncheons! a roast turkey, and hash and potatoes, and apple pudding, and what not, and I stand by and abuse them all for eating, and eat with the best of them.

We have been trying the new experiment of burning clay for manure, and have not above half succeeded—and we have just found an old book, 80 years old, which gives a full and detailed account of what all the wiseacres are all making an outcry about as a new discovery, and as the practice has not been adopted, we are beginning to suspect that its merits are a little exaggerated.

We have a house brimful.

Give my love to all, Vansittart and all, and so good-night, my old boy, for I must go to bed. Your affec. brother,

AD.

Miss Eden to her Sister, Lady Buckinghamshire.

EDEN FARM,
December 1814.

MY DEAREST SISTER, Mary's first letter is arrived, so I must begin copying and extracting, and abridging, as if I had never done anything else all my life.

But I must begin by observing that we all parted most heroically on Wednesday morning, not the least in the O'Neil style, but we were all as cool as cucumbers, and as hard-hearted as rocks. (What beautiful similes!) Mary looked very smart, her coat was covered with grey vandykes, which does not sound pretty, but looked very well, and her hat of course matched it exactly. She says they did not arrive at Shottesbrook till late, as they went round and round the place several times before the postboy could find the entrance....

We heard from Morton the other day, a long account of his gaieties. He has been showing Oxford to the Feildings, and the Meerveldts (what a difficult word to spell), and then was invited to go to Middleton with them, where he met the Worcesters, Cowpers, Eustons, and the Duke of Devonshire. We are rather in dread of his return, and to find him grown very fine, which will be an unlucky turn to take....

Mrs. Percival's marriage shocked us all, as we had not heard of it before, but Mrs. Moore sent in word of it, and of the gentleman's name afterwards. Ever your affec. sister,

EMILY EDEN.

Miss Eden to her Sister, Lady Buckinghamshire.

EDEN FARM,
December 23, 1814.

MY DEAREST SISTER, We have had two such long letters from Mary (at Bowood). You must be contented with some extracts. She says: "We have almost as few events here as at Eden Farm; in the morning we walk four or five miles, and in the evening everybody reads a little except Lady E. Feilding, who walks about disturbing us all. She brought down a great book full of verses and epigrams, that she is collecting all over the world and gathered chiefly at Middleton; she let few of them be read, and screamed and pulled away the book every three minutes in case we should see more than we ought.

There were some pretty things of Lady Cowper's composing, one addressed to her sleeping baby, and another on an Infant that is one of the most beautiful things possible. It seems to be the fashion collecting these things, for Captain Feilding says it was quite ridiculous to see Lady Jersey and Lady Cowper, and Lady E. Feilding and two or three others coming down of an evening at Middleton with their great books in satchells like so many schoolboys, and showing each other their 'little treasures,' and one saying, 'May I copy this?'—'No; not unless you will let me copy that.'—'Very well, but you won't turn over the page?'—'No.'—'Then you must not go further than that line.' And then the books are all locked up again, for they each have keys, and Lady Elizabeth says everybody wore the key of her manuscript book at her side, in case the others should get it by fair means or foul.

Lady Elizabeth's maid is also making a collection. Lady Lansdowne looked prettier than ever last night, and is the kindest, most pleasing-mannered person I ever saw. She has got some receipts for dyeing muslins, sattins and silks any colours, and has been all this morning up to the elbows in soap-suds, starch and blue, and then on her knees for an hour ironing on the floor,—the work of the morning. I saw her little girl for a moment, and it seems to be a pretty little thing; the boy is exactly like Lord Lansdowne, but is never to be seen, and I only met the little Feildings once on the stairs since I came here. We are much too learned to think of children."

So much for Mary's first letter. George says, "Mary behaves like an angel. She walks with Lansdowne and talks learnedly—I do not know what about. The only words I could hear were, *And be hanged to you*, and *Slip-gibbit*, and *Betty Martin*."

Mary says in her second letter: "We had a tremendous fit of Crambo again last night from eight to eleven without stopping. Lord Lansdowne gives his whole heart and mind to any little game, or whatever he is about, and it is really quite amusing to see him fretting and arguing, and reasoning and labouring, at this Crambo, as if it was a matter of the greatest importance. It is certainly rather fretting, but it is as good a way of passing a long evening as another. Lady Lansdowne takes a great deal of charge of me, and is a person I really cannot find one fault in...."

I had advanced so far in copying, and was just thinking how nicely and quickly I had done it, when the post arrived, and brought a letter from Mary of nine quarto pages thickly written, and so amusing. But you must not see it to-day—you little thing—this is quite enough for once. Your affectionate sister,

EMILY EDEN.

Lord Auckland to his Sister, Miss Eden.

MELBURY,
December 31, 1814.

MY DEAR EMILY, I am living in a state of great fright about the event of my message by the last post, and if the key is not found, you must not be much astonished at seeing me arrive either with or without Mary on Tuesday; but I do not like to settle anything about this fussy, provoking scrapey piece of business till I hear from you and from Dyer to-morrow.

We have been doing nothing particular to-day except going in a large party after some woodcocks.

I am as pleased as Punch with the American peace. We shall get rid of the property tax, and the 3 per cents will be up in the skies. We have nothing yet to succeed Whishaw. Sir George Paul is near seventy, but he is a fine old beau, and has one of the prettiest places in England, so that if the Dowager Lady Ilchester does not snap him up, something may yet be done.

To console us for not having you, we have an Emily here who has something of the fooley in her, but she unluckily is a dullfooley.

I have in leisure hours been looking over a good many old letters which are here, written by the Fox's and Pelhams and Sir Charles Hanbury Williams, etc., etc., in the reign of George II., some of which are very entertaining. I send you a copy of verses written by Sir C. H. Williams to one of Ilchester's aunts, Lady Susan O'Brien.

Sweeter than the sweetest Manna,
Lovely, lively, dear Susannah,
You're the girl that I must muse on,
Pretty little smiling Susan.
Oh! if verses could amuse ye,
Fairest, gentlest, laughing Susey,
I'll write to you, but ne'er rebuke ye,
Handsome and good-natured Sukey.
Every rhyme should flatter you
Trifling, dimpling, tender Sue.
I've sung my song and so adieu! adieu!
Susannah, Susan, Susey, Sukey, Sue!

Mary is quite reviving to-night, and is making a deuce of a noise, and be hanged to her. My love to my Mother and all. Yours very affectionately,

AUCKLAND.

Miss Eden to Lady Buckinghamshire.

Monday, January 1815.

MY DEAR SISTER, I have not a guess how far Mary's journal has been continued to you. She says, "The great amusement here seems to be eating, which goes on from morning till night. There is an immense breakfast for people to go in and out to, a large luncheon which stands two hours on the table, a very long dinner, and a regular supper, which altogether takes up half the day. To-day, by way of amusement, and keeping up an old custom, we have all been baking, that is, spoiling an enormous quantity of good things in the housekeeper's room, making some uneatable gingerbread and cakes, and ourselves very dirty. There are a quantity of children here, and all very nice ones seemingly. Lady Theresa Strangways would be really a dear little thing, if Lady G. Murray would not talk and teaze one so about her stomach and teeth.

...Lady G. Murray is in greater beauty than ever, and happier than anybody I ever saw. She has two sons here."

Tuesday.

...I was so cross and stupid with a pain in my ear which I have had this week, and in such a fury with Willy Osborne who made a point of dropping his shuttlecock on my paper every minute, that I was obliged to leave off writing in order to fight with him, and when that battle was ended, he insisted on playing at Blind Man's Buff....

Mary seems quite delighted with her visit to Melbury, and even nearly reconciled to quitting Bowood, which she was very sorry to do. Sir George Paul, nearly eighty years old, is very much struck with her, she says, and when she goes to the pianoforte puts on his spectacles, and sits opposite her, gazing on her beautiful countenance with great satisfaction.

He drank two glasses of wine with her at dinner, and all the other ladies insisted on his drinking one with them, that they might at least have half as much done for them as was done for Mary.

We are all in doubt whether to like Sir G. Paul best or Mr. Whishaw, a lawyer, about ten years younger, but with only one leg. But the poor man, George says, was terribly smitten, and if they had staid but two days longer at Bowood, it would have come to a happy conclusion.

I myself should prefer somebody rather older and steadier.

Lady Ilchester wrote to Mamma, to know whether she was to let this flirtation go on, as it does at present....

George writes in good spirits, and seems delighted with his tour and with Melbury, which is the pleasantest place he knows. He says Mary is in very good spirits and makes a deuce of a noise and that she is a great favourite wherever she goes, and he believes *deservedly* so.

They neither of them seem to have any idea that they must ever come home again; but if ever they do I will let you know. Yours affectionately,

EMILY EDEN.

Miss Eden to her Brother, Lord Auckland.

EDEN FARM,

Monday, January 1815.

POOR DEAR LITTLE GEORGY, I am quite sorry it has been in such a fuss about the key, and I am afraid my last letter will not have set it's little heart at ease, but on Sunday morning Morton and I hunted for an hour, and at last found the key tied with a *yellow* ribbon, and not a blue one, and when we had found it and made Bob ride to Greenwich as fast as he could, he found Mr. Dyer laughing by himself at the fuss you and Morton were in. He said the chest was broken open at a quarter past twelve and is now broken up for life. Which of your brothers-in-law do you like best? because I cannot make up my mind quite to either, though I believe I like lame Whishaw better than the venerable Paul. Mama is really fidgetty about them; and if you write again, will you let us know whether Mary is really as pleasant as she pretends to be and whether she did not make you underline the words "*deservedly liked*" in your last letter? Because it looked very suspicious.... Talking of Fooleys, by the bye, Mr. and Miss Vansittart come here this afternoon, and I am grown duller than ever. Thank you for your verses, which we liked very much. Ever your affectionate sister,

EMILY EDEN.

Lord Auckland to Miss Eden.

DROPMORE,
January 13, 1815.

MY DEAR EMILY, Here we are once more within 30 miles of home, came here late yesterday, everybody at dinner—Mary in such a fright you never saw—such a silence you never heard—room so hot you never felt—dinner so cold you never tasted—dogs so tiresome you never smelt. So we must go to Shottesbrook *bon gré, mal gré*. Hang labels round your necks when we arrive on Wednesday or Thursday with your names on them (like the decanters) for do what we will, Mary and I cannot recollect your faces. Are you the one with the long nose?

Lady Riversdale's maid has had an offer of marriage, and she has refused it, because she "had not that attachment that ought to subside between man and wife."

Mind that, girls, and don't marry rashly. Yours, and a day no more foolish than yourself,

AUCKLAND.

Miss Eden to Lady Buckinghamshire.

EDEN FARM,
March 9 .

MY DEAREST SISTER, As the Queen has been so uncivil and even spiteful to me and my sattin gown, as to put off the drawing-room, our three letters per day upon dress may now cease, and this is merely a letter of thanks for all the trouble you have taken with Wynne, Pontet, lace, notes, hoops, drapery, sattin, carriers, feathers, jewels, etc., and which have unluckily, by this strange and unaccountable spitefulness of H.M., all proved useless.

Poor Beckenham is gone mad about the corn laws, and have revenged themselves on poor innocent harmless out-of-the-way George, by drawing him on the walls hanging as comfortably as possible, and Mr. Cator on another gibbet opposite to him. Mr. Colvile is also hanging somewhere else.... Every house and wall is covered with mottoes, and "No corn laws" in every direction. Ever your affectionate,

E. EDEN.

Miss Eden to Lady Buckinghamshire.

EDEN FARM,
June 24 .

MY DEAREST SISTER, We had not expected the satisfaction of two letters from you to-day.... A letter that condescends to speak of two housemaids, without talking of battles and Bonaparte, is a very delightful novelty, as I am quite tired of rejoicing and lamenting over this news which, upon the whole, strikes me as very melancholy, though I know that is a very wrong feeling.

There have yet been no accounts of poor Lady Delancey! She must have had a horrible shock at first, as Sir William, believing himself to be dying, refused at first to be removed from the field of battle, which gave rise to the report of his death. Poor Lady I. Hay quitted London at six yesterday morning to inform her father, who was in the country, of Lord Hay's death. He was not more than nineteen, and was a friend of Bob's at Eton.

The George Elliots came here to dinner yesterday, with their youngest child, who is a very fine child, and as a baby, I thought its name might be interesting to you, though it was not very different from other children, except that it had, on its cap a lilac satin cockade, which is naturally a very pretty thing, though a baby sewed to it does not add to its beauty.

That is, however, a mere matter of taste.

Mrs. G. Elliot we all like, and she has full as much sense as the rest of the world, and would be as pleasant, if her manner was not rather hurried and rough, evidently from shyness and a fear of being thought dull.

Except these, we have not seen anybody, not even a neighbour, nor do I believe there are such things as neighbours left in the world, and it is much too hot to go and look for them if they are yet alive.

Mrs. Green, poor woman, seems to think you a little dull, but I always told you how it would be when you lost me, and I am glad to see Mrs. Green has so much penetration. Ever your affectionate sister,

E. EDEN.

Miss Eden to Lady Buckinghamshire.

July 3, 1815.

We heard yesterday from the Selkirks a certain account of poor Sir W. Delancey's death, and we heard it also from several other good authorities. The Selkirks have been in town every day in hopes of hearing either of or from Lady Delancey, but without success. Her situation is most dreadful, as he died at Waterloo, so she is not near any acquaintance she might have made at Brussels. She is but eighteen, and literally just out of the nursery. She has with her only a new maid, whom Lady Selkirk procured for her but three weeks ago. It appears very shocking that none of her relations should have gone to her on hearing of his wound, as she will now have every detail to manage for herself, and her return to Penge, which she quitted in such violent spirits not a month ago, will be dreadful. The Selkirks expect her every hour.

I have just been interrupted by the arrival of the Lansdowne children, who are come here for the afternoon to make Lady Lansdowne's excuse for not coming to take leave before she goes out of town. The little girl is the prettiest little thing I ever saw—the smallest child—looking like a fairy *for all the world*.

July 6, 1815.

We were all very sorry to hear of poor Comte Meerveldt's death, for *her* distress must be very great. Little Rodolphe will now be a great consolation to her. Lady Selkirk has had one very short note from poor Lady Delancey. It was almost too composed to be comfortable to her friends. She said her husband had died at Waterloo, and was buried the morning she wrote, at Brussels, and she wished Lady Selkirk would have his picture done immediately by Heaphy, as that was the only thing she could now live for. She made no complaint, except saying that she had had but one very happy week at Brussels, which was over, and that she was sure Lady Selkirk, at least, would feel for such a very wretched creature. She is expected at Penge to-morrow. There is an odd mixture of joy and sorrow in that house, as Lady K. Douglas is married there to-day, which is rather astonishing, considering the state her family is in....

Miss Eden to Lord Auckland.

EDEN FARM,
August 11.

MY DEAREST GEORGE, I put a most excellent joke in these two first lines, but was obliged to efface them from my fear of the police, but it is inserted in sympathetic Ink, and if you will hold it for ¾ of an hour by a very hot fire, rubbing it violently the whole time without intermission, with the back of your hat and one hand, I daresay you will find it.

We are much as you left us. I cannot buy any sheep yet, for the price has risen in the market prodigiously, and we must wait a little, but Walsh is to go to Smithfield this week to see how things are. In your directions you left out a very important word, whether the ferrule should be fixed in the bottom, or the seat of the Tilbury. I say the former, and Mama the latter. One makes the umbrella too low, the other too high, but by a little arrangement of mine, too long to explain, I have made it the right height for myself, bonnet, feathers, and all, and it will altogether be very comfortable.

There is to be a meeting of all the Sunday Schools in the district next week at Bromley, and a collection, and a collation. We mean to eat up the collation, and give all our old clipped sixpences to the collection, which we think is a plan you would approve if you were here.

Madden has given us so much to do, we have not a minute's spare time. We are duller than a hundred posts about Astronomy, and if you can find any planets for us in Paris, we shall be obliged to you, as we cannot find one on the globe, and Madden only laughs at us. There! Good-bye, my dearest George. Take care of your little self. Your affectionate

EMILY EDEN.

Miss Eden to Lady Buckinghamshire.

EDEN FARM,
Thursday, August 31, 1815.

MY DEAREST SISTER, Did Mama write to you yesterday? I wish I knew, but she is unluckily upstairs, and indeed I must say is hardly ever in the way when I want her.

I had meant to have answered your letter yesterday, but Mary, Miss Vansittart, and I went a-pleasuring, so that I had not time.

We went in the morning to Greenwich, where Mr. Van. met us in the Admiralty barge, and took us to the steamboat.

We found there Lord and Lady Liverpool, my dear Letitia Taylor, Lady Georgina, and Lady Emily Bathurst, Lord Bathurst, Lord Harrowby, Sir G. Hope, Sir George Warrender, Mr. Lushington, etc. Lady Liverpool still retains the notion that I am Miss Eden in the country, as well as in town, and introduced Mary as Miss E. Eden, and me as Miss Eden to all the company, and Mr. Van. insisted on calling Miss Taylor—Miss Rickets, so that the most curious effect steam has had yet was making a large company answer to wrong names.

The Invention itself, I believe, was supposed to succeed perfectly. We had a very pleasant row, or steaming, or whatever else it may be called, beyond Woolwich, and back to Greenwich again in three hours, during which time we also contrived to eat a large breakfast, and a larger dinner and dessert.

Lord Liverpool had some very improper purring scenes, and Lady Liverpool was very good-natured....

It must be an amusing sight to see Sarah scolding the post-boy for not driving fast enough, or calling to the hostler for "a pair of horses to St. Albans immediately," or adding up the innkeeper's account, and giving him something over for the scoundrel that drove.

That is the style she must now adopt. Ever your affect. sister,

E. EDEN.

Miss Eden to Lady Buckinghamshire.

August 19.

MY DEAREST SISTER, The reason I am in such a state of ignorance about the letter is, that Mama and Louisa went to meet them in *their* way to London; that we were behind them in the poney-cart; and George behind us in the gig. We all fell in with each other and the letters in the middle of Penge Common, where we each took what belonged to us. I met immediately with the dreadful intelligence that you were going actually to take May Place, and on our recommendation, which dreadful intelligence I communicated to George, who immediately fainted away, and was driven off by his servant. I fainted away, and was driven off by Mary, and Mama and Louisa went on in hysterics to London. I really am quite in a fright about it, and cannot think what beauties I ever saw in it. The house is nothing but a pile of old bricks, the rooms cold, damp, dirty, inconvenient cells, the view cheerless and bleak, the offices large and decaying, the garden unproductive and expensive, the neighbours impertinent and intrusive, the gardener impudent, the housemaids idle, the landlord exacting, and the tenant in a terrible scrape indeed—and so is the tenant's sister too, as far as I can make out.... The only thing I know for certain is that I am to send our bricklayer there early to-morrow to look at the house, and to meet George, who goes there at break of day; and if I can bribe him, as he is a very clever person, to pull the whole thing down, I will. It is past letter-time, and I have not time to read over what nonsense I have written. Lady Byron and her child come here the 27th. Most affectionately yours,

E. E.

There is a rheumatic headache attached to the place, and let with it.

Miss Eden's Letters

Miss Eden to Lady Buckinghamshire.
TONBRIDGE,
October 10.

MY DEAREST SISTER, The "Eden Farmots" have kept me in such profound ignorance with respect to you that I had some doubts whether you were not settled at Charlton, or whether you were not tired of the name of house, and had fitted up a nice hollow tree for yourself with some little hollow trees round it for your sisters and friends. It looks rather pretty and attentive though, in me, that I should answer your questions two days before you ask them.

This weather is particularly provoking in a house where there are but few books, but the last week we have contrived to be out nearly ten hours every day, beginning at seven in the morning. Getting up at that time and swimming through the fog to drink the coldest of all cold water is the least pleasant part of the day, but otherwise I have lost all hatred to exercise, from the circumstance of never being fatigued with any quantity of it.

The Vyners are so close to us that we are always together.... I wish somebody would just have the kindness to marry Miss Vyner. She would be such an excellent chaperon-general to all young ladies.

We had on Sunday morning the finest sermon I ever heard from Mr. Benson—so fine that we went in the dark and in the rain to hear another. He began by preaching at the Opposition, which gave me a fit of the sullens; then he went on to smugglers, then to brandy merchants; and, lastly, laid the sins of the whole set and all the other misfortunes of the country upon "ladies who wore fancy dresses" and encouraged smuggling by example and money.

It is a very odd fashion now, I think, to abuse women for everything, but, however, there were so few gentlemen at Church that we all bore it tolerably well. People's French bonnets sat tottering on their heads, and if it had not been for some sense of decency and a want of pockets, many a French shawl was preparing to step itself quietly out of the way. Your most affect. sister,

E. E.

Miss Eden to Lady Buckinghamshire.
November 16.

MY DEAREST SISTER, You seemed by your last letter to be so overcome by the communications of your friends, that I burnt a long composition of mine. Indeed, nobody but an excellent sister could be induced to write on such a gloomy, dispiriting afternoon, but I have put the table close by the fire, with one leg (belonging to the table, not to me) in the fender, to prevent it from slipping away, the arm-chair close behind the table, and me supported by them both, holding a pen in one hand and the poker in the other, and now, have at you.

Yesterday was not a flourishing day by any means, but this is to be different, as the Osbornes and their five noisy, unmanageable, provoking, tiresome and dear children are coming, so we have all collected whatever health and strength we possess to answer the demands of the day.

I called on Lady Grantham last week. The Baby is a remarkably pretty child, immensely fat and very nice-looking for its age, but still I could not come up quite to her raptures on the subject, and I thought it still looked red like other babies, and I never should of my own accord have thought of coaxing it so much as she expected. Ever, my dearest Sister, most affect. yours,

E. EDEN.

Miss Eden to Lady Buckinghamshire.
NEWBY HALL,
Sunday Ev. September 13, 1818.

MY DEAREST SISTER, Your account of Mary agrees very much with her own. I do not know if you have heard from her since she has settled to pay a little visit at Frognal, but, if so, you must have thought with me that Lord Sydney will be a very pleasant brother-in-law for us. Such a great addition, in every sense of the word, to our society, and when the Miss Townshends have been turned out of doors, upon any slight pretence, it will really be a very nice establishment.

I am going on here just as was expected, very unhappy at first for about three days, without any particular place in the room, or any particular rule about being in the library, or my own room, or Lady Grantham's, and then, you know, my trunk and all my worldly possessions were missing and lost, which was a cruel blow, at my first setting out, but at last my dear trunk reappeared unexpectedly, and from that time I got comfortabler and comfortabler, till I could get no further.

Miss Wynn I like very much, probably because I expected to dislike her. The rest of the family are perfectly inoffensive, with nothing particularly agreeable or disagreeable in them, except indeed I have the pleasure of beating Mr. Wynn at chess every evening, till the tears almost course one another down his innocent cheeks, but I go on beating him for all that.

Lady Grantham is much better than she was during the journey; we go out every day in the pony-cart together, and call on the farmers and cottagers. I do not understand one word in ten the people say, and should be glad to take a Yorkshire master if I could find one. I hope, for your sake, Gog Magog is not as green as this place is, else you will be more angry than ever with the dusty trees and brown grass of Eastcombe. The grass was quite dazzling when I first came here, and the green is a bad colour for the eyes, after the nice quiet brown we have been accustomed to, but green peas agree remarkably well with me, and sometimes I give a little passing thought to you, when I am packing up a great forkfull of them, and again when the children bring me in immense nosegays of mignonette, sweet peas, jessamine, which are to be put out at night because they smell so very sweet.

Lady Grantham's garden is beautiful, and full of every sort of flower, but then it is generally locked. The house is excessively comfortable, with a stove in every passage, and a fire in every room, servants' and all, an excellent library, and a very pretty statue gallery, heaps of amusing books, and an arm-chair for every limb. I foresee a great probability of my being very happy here, as my love of Lady Grantham does not diminish by any means, and he and I are great friends, and he likes to be played to for hours together. Your most affec.

E. EDEN.

Miss Eden to her Brother, Lord Auckland.
NEWBY,
Monday.

MY DEAREST GEORGE, Having in our former letters nearly settled all our business matters, I may venture this time to indulge you with a few lighter topics.... This house is what Bob would call *chuck full*, but I do not think you know any of the company except the Markhams and Mrs. Graham. I think all the Markhams pleasant in their way. Anne is rather an odd fellow, but very amusing, and Frederica is very pleasant. Cecilia desires me to give you her kind remembrance. As for your friend Mr. Graham, though I would not wish to be severe, yet I cannot think a man who wears a light sort of mulberry-coloured "don't mentions," from a wish to look *waspish*, can be any great shakes. The rest of his character may be very good perhaps, but I can hardly think so under these circumstances.

Your Bess has been making sad work of it indeed, and I wish she had not been promised to Sister, for the Granthams are enquiring everywhere for a dog of that description, and I think Bess would find this place pleasanter than Eastcombe. Your most affectionate

E. E.

Miss Eden to Lady Buckinghamshire.
NEWBY HALL.

MY DEAREST SISTER, Your pride must be getting up again, I should imagine, and I must give it a little epistolary pat on the back (what a remarkably odd clever expression) to keep it all smooth.

My illness was remarkably opportune, inasmuch as it began at Studley, and which was so uncommonly dull, that the impossibility of dining down was an immense advantage that I had over the rest of society. We were nineteen at dinner every day. We were all immensely formal in the evening.

The house is but a bad one in the old-fashioned way, and my room was peculiarly liable to murder and that sort of accident, a large dark green bed with black feathers on the top, stuck in a deep alcove, and on one side of it an enormous dark closet, quite full of banditti I fancy, and all the rest of the room actually swarming with ghosts I know, only I was much too sleepy to lay awake and look at them.

Mrs. Lawrence has an unhappy turn for music without any very remarkable genius, and we played 150 pages of the dryest Duetts in the Dussek and Pleyel style without even changing our time, or rising into a forte, or sinking into a piano, and minding every Repeat and Da Capo in the book.

On Wednesday Lord Grantham and Mr. Graham went on some Yeomanry business to Leeds, on Thursday we came home to my great joy. Adieu, my dearest sister; this has been written in a confusion of tongues, and I cannot make it any longer by any means. Ever your most affec.

E. EDEN.

P.S.—I have got a beautiful black cloth gown for two guineas, so fine you never saw the like.

Emily Eden to Lady Buckinghamshire.
NEWBY HALL,
November.

MY DEAREST SISTER, We are now quite alone for the first time since I came—that is, the Wynns are here still, but they are part of being alone, and we have never before been so few, and I must say that it is uncommonly pleasant after so much company. The mere comfort of being able to go about the house with *rough* hair, or a *tumbled* frill, and in an old black gown, is not to be despised, and there is some pleasure in taking up a book in the evening and yawning over it, and then saying anything that comes uppermost, without thinking. We are very busy, dressing little dolls for Lord Grantham's Theatre, which is one of the most ingenious pieces of mechanism I ever saw, and one of the prettiest things altogether. There is to be a grand representation to-night, and we have been rehearsing all the last week. It takes nine people to manage the scenery, figures, and music, and we all of us lose our tempers at it regularly every morning. I act the orchestra, and whilst I am playing away to the best of my power the music belonging to any particular scene, Anne and Lady Grantham, who manage the figures, get into some hobble, and the music is finished before the action to which it belongs is begun, so that Harlequin and Columbine have to dance out without any time to assist them. I believe nothing in the world could ruffle Lord Grantham's temper; but these theatrical difficulties go nearer to it than anything else, and while he is explaining to Lady Grantham that the figures will move if she takes pains, and to me that the music is quite long enough if I will but play slower, it may be rather provoking that Freddy should let down the wrong trap-door, Anne set her sleeves on fire in one of the lamps, Mary turn the cascade the wrong way, so that the water runs up instead of down; Thomas the footman should let down a light blue sky to a dark moonlight scene, and Shaw should forget the back scene altogether, so that his coat and buttons and white waistcoat are figuring away in the distance of the Fire King's Palace. However, patience and scolding have overcome these little difficulties, and our last rehearsal was perfect.

Lady Melville and her children were here for five days last week. I do not know exactly what I thought of her. She is too clever not to be rather pleasant, and too argumentative not to be very tiresome, and altogether I do not think I liked her. But her visit took place very soon after I had heard of poor Sir S. Romilly, and I was too much shocked and too unhappy really to like anybody, particularly a person who insisted upon discussing the whole thing constantly, and in a *political* way. I think I have never been more shocked by anything that was not a private calamity—I mean, that did not concern one's family or one's self—than I was by this, and poor Captain Feilding who was here, and who was a private friend of his, was so completely overcome that I was very sorry for him too. Altogether it is a horrible history, and only shows how very little we can know what is good for man in this life, when we were all saying some months ago that this would be the proudest year of Sir S. Romilly's life. Your most affectionate

E. E.

Lord Auckland to Miss Eden.

BRUTON STREET,
Monday, November 1818.

MY DEAR EMILY, I have this moment seen an agent of Mrs. Wildman, a rich Kentish widow, and she has agreed to take Eden Farm on my own terms, which gives us a prospect of being a little more settled and comfortable.

She is to have it for seven years and pay £600 a year. And now I must look out for a house in town, which you will find pretty near ready for you when you arrive. I am in a great bustle and hurry, for we are all alive with this election, though with the melancholy impression of poor Romilly's death it is difficult to rouse people. Hobhouse has behaved so ill that it is right to try to beat him, but I fear that Lamb is too late. He will certainly be low on the poll for the first week, but it is possible that afterwards he may recover. In the meantime, people are very busy, and none of our friends are sanguine. Your affectionate brother,

AD.

Lord Auckland to Miss Eden.

1818.

MY DEAR EMILY, Lamb carried his election to-day by 604, and made a sort of a speech saying that now he was their member, and they were his constituents, and that they would soon learn to be friends. He was a little hooted, but not much more than usual; but all our foolish friends appeared to cheer him with cockades in their hats, and all was uproar and riot and confusion and pelting and brickbats and mud, and it is lucky none of them were very seriously hurt. They all arrived covered with dirt to the west end of the town, and the mob at their heels, for they were too gallant not to stop to be occasionally pelted.

I never saw such a scene. Your friend Graham looked as if he had just come out from the pillory; Sefton, Morton, and twenty others in the same plight.

Report says that one servant is nearly killed; I hope it is not true. Ferguson had a blow on his head, and Mr. Charlton another more serious one; but I hear of nothing worse. It makes but an ugly triumph for our great *victory*. What a glorious debate was yesterday's!

You will live at No. 30 Lower Grosvenor Street, the only house I can get, small but convenient, and I think we shall make it do well enough. Ever affectionately yours,

AD.

Miss Eden to Lady Buckinghamshire.

NEWBY HALL.

MY DEAREST SISTER, ...Mr. Ellis left this place yesterday, so I could not give him your message. I think he enjoyed the latter part of his visit here very much, as there was a very pleasant set of gentlemen, and Mr. Douglas, who is more amusing than ever. We had besides them, two Mr. Lascelles's, one "a cunning hunter" and the other very gentlemanlike and pleasant; Mr. Duncombe, a *pretty* little London Dandy, rather clever in his way; Captain Cust, a soldierly sort of person, and a kind of *Lusus Naturae* (is that sense do you think?), because he is pleasant and well-looking though he is a Cust, and Mr. Petre, very rich and very stupid, so that we had a very proper mixture of character....

We are all hunting mad in these parts, and I am afraid that when I come to Eastcombe I shall be a great expense to you with my hunters and grooms. I have already made great progress in the language of the art.

I have heard a new name for the Miss Custs, in case you are tired of the Dusty Camels; by uniting their names of Brownlow and Cust, they become Brown Locusts, which is a very expressive title I think. I remain, ever yr. very affec. sister,

E. EDEN.

CHAPTER II

1819-1820

Miss Eden to the Dowager Lady Buckinghamshire.
NEWBY HALL,
Sunday, February 14.

MY DEAREST SISTER, I was very sorry to hear of the unfortunate state in which you have been, and in which Sarah is, as I have a sufficient recollection of the Mumps to know what a very disagreeable disorder they are, or they is.

We have had a *spirt* of company for the last three days, but they all very kindly walked off yesterday, and as it is wrong to dwell upon past evils, I spare you an account of most of them.

There were a Mr. and Mrs. Winyard amongst them, who were very pleasant. He was in the army, and is now in the Church, and though they are the sort of people who have a child every year, and talk about their governess, and though she very naturally imagined, that because she was absent, the high wind would blow away the little tittupy parsonage, and the ten precious children, yet they really were very agreeable.

He sang so very beautifully though, that it made all his other good qualities quite superfluous, and I am convinced it would have touched your unmusical heart to hear him sing some of the Irish Melodies.

I have some thoughts of writing an Essay on Education for the good of my country, and I think the little Robinsons will in most cases serve for example, and I must say that, tho' children, they are very nice things, and uncommonly well managed.

If at any time you will let me know how you are going on, the smallest intelligence will be thankfully received. Ever, my dear Sister, your very affect.

E. EDEN.

Miss Eden to Lady Buckinghamshire.

LONGLEAT,
Monday, March 15, 1819.

MY DEAREST SISTER, This place affords so very little to say, that if this prove to be a long letter, of which at present I do not see much chance, I pity from my heart your feelings of weariness at the end of it. There is nobody here but the Campbells, but I imagine that the family of Thynne are much pleasanter out of a crowd. At least, we are not the least formal or dull, which from the account Mary and Fanny used to give I thought would have been the case.

The magnificence of the house far surpasses anything I have ever seen, and with all that, it is one of the most comfortable abodes possible. It is inconvenient too in some respects, at least to me, who have an unfortunate knack of losing my way even in a house that may consist of only ten rooms, so that I cannot stir without Fanny or some other guide.

There are several roads to our rooms. The servants make it, I think, about five and twenty minutes' walk, a little more than a mile and a quarter; but then that is a very intricate way.

Lady Bath is very much out of spirits at times about Lord Weymouth, who is going on very ill; but she is always very pleasant and very good-humoured....

Lady Elizabeth and Lady Louisa both make themselves very pleasant.

We leave this place Saturday night, probably, which I am very sorry for, but George must be in town Monday, and therefore it is necessary to be there Saturday. However, he is first going to see poor Lord Ilchester at Weymouth, and is to rejoin me on the road, so our plans depend a little on Lord Ilchester's. London will be a little dark and dismal-looking this weather, but the FitzGeralds are coming up to be at the Meeting of Parliament, and I shall be rather glad to meet Pam. Your most affectionate

E. EDEN.

Miss Pamela FitzGerald to Miss Eden.

So you are not dead at all, Emmy! I am very glad, for I can't spare you. I have been what the people call in a great deal of trouble. Aunt frightened me, she chose to neglect her cough so long, that when at last on her complaining of pain in her side I bullied her, and sent for Dundas, he found she has a considerable degree of inflammation on her chest, and she was to be bled directly; the Apothecary out of the way, never came home till night. Aunt made a monstrous piece of work between fright and fever, and cried out, and the candles flared, and Baker stamped, and I who thought myself so courageous, I was turned upside down with the whole business.

Lucy is staying at Mrs. Seymour's, luckily out of the mess; she went over for a ball Monday, and Mrs. Seymour has kept her on there.

I had a letter from Edward a few days ago, written from the Slough of Despond; he has joined his regiment at Lichfield, and you may imagine the transition from Paris, poor darling. I would give the whole world to go and comfort him.

Emmy, don't you know what I mean? But when anything one loves is unhappy, it seems more particularly to belong to one.

He comes to us the 11th, for a few days, which I look to with some anxiety, after that taste, or rather distaste, we had of each other in London.

I am looking about for a conveyance to Town, because I want to buy a hat; at present I am all shaven and shorn, and shall be reduced to wear a paper cap, if I don't take care.

I am obliged to write with this pen, which is like a Chinese chop stick, because I am in Aunt's room, and she is asleep, and I dare not begin that quick rustle, which disturbs and wakes a Patient as much as the roar of a cannon, and which would be unavoidable in a hunt for quill or knife; as it is I have some trouble to keep the paper from crackling, and the few books *d'alentour* from throwing themselves head-long off the table, which is the way of all books the moment one drops asleep.

I have had sad fits of low spirits. Spring makes one languid to a degree, that the air is a weight upon one.

The Assizes were delightful. I don't think it right to carve out futurity for oneself, or else I really think I should like never to marry anybody who does not wear a Lawyer's Wig. It is proper, it adorneth the outward and visible man; those thin terrier faces, those hollow cheeks and deep eyes, are precious and lovely.

I was amused at the younglings, whose callow smooth faces look all the younger for the wig. Seriously, the interest of the most important cases to me was inexpressible. It is the reality which presses on one's heart, and makes an impression far deeper than the utmost stretch of imaginary sorrow can ever produce.

I have seen no creature, and have established my character Bearish in the neighbourhood, so they are content to let me alone....

Mr. Peel could not help marrying that girl who is silly; those things fit, and are so far satisfactory they establish some sort of system in the goings on of the world, and give body to speculation. Wise men love fools.

I had done writing, and then as usual a whole heap of things came lumbering about my head. I had a high letter from poor Eliza Fitz. She has given up her dearest hopes on earth, and if she should be obliged to marry any one else, miserable, wretched, homeless, she trusts she will do her duty and be a good wife; that's the résumé of four criss-cross sheets of paper. I wrote her a very reasonable letter to comfort her, for she is painfully ashamed of herself, poor girl, and there is no use in that, so I turned her over to the bright side. She has only fallen in that common error of whipping up her feelings with words, and they never can keep pace *even*, one will always be before the other.

Miss Eden to Lady Buckinghamshire.
June 4 .

MY DEAREST SISTER, Mary went out last night to Mrs. Baring's ball, which was not likely to do her much good, and is completely "frappée en haut" (Sir W. Wynn's translation of "knocked up") with headache and fatigue this morning. Dissipation is not likely to agree with her, certainly, but then, Sister, think of the pineapples and strawberries and ices and temporary rooms and magnificent hangings and beautiful flowers at Mrs. Baring's.

I wish I was a rich old banker; but then I would not have, or *own*, so many fellow-creatures as the Barings do. I keep my comforts a little more to myself.... We have had a most alarming visit from Rogers the Poet this morning, the very recollection of which would make my hair, black pins, combs and all, stand on end, if they had ever subsided since his first appearance. I never saw such a satirical, odious wretch, and I was calculating the whole time, from what he was saying of other people, what he could find ill-natured enough to say of us. I had never seen him before, and trust I never shall again. Your most affectionate

E. EDEN.

Miss Eden to Lady Buckinghamshire.
June 10, 1819.

MY DEAREST SISTER, You will, I hope, have more pleasure or rather happiness than *I* can yet teach myself to feel, in hearing that our dearest Mary is going to be married to Charles Drummond. It cannot be a surprise, of course, to any one, as he has certainly taken no pains to conceal his attachment; but the objections arising from want of fortune, we had not hoped could have been so well overcome as they are, quite to the satisfaction of his friends and hers also. It was almost settled at Lady Darnley's fancy ball on Monday, and concluded by letter (such a very pretty letter!) on Tuesday morning. Mary and I went down to Langley for an hour for a little advice, as George was gone to his Committee; then we saw George; then Mr. D.; and, in short, everything went on smoothly, and as such things usually do go on. George has seen the old Drummonds, who were very good-humoured and quite agreeable. In short, I should believe we were all amazingly happy, only I *know* I have seldom felt so wretched. She will be such a dreadful loss to me! But I will only think of the advantages of the case; and George is so pleased, and it is altogether a very desirable thing for all of us, besides the real chief point of her happiness, which she ought to find, and of which she has so reasonable a prospect. The Post Bell is ringing. Mary would have written herself, but *he* is here, and this is their first real conversation. Sarah will excuse my not writing to her to-day, I hope, and I really have had great difficulty in making out this one letter, and we have told nobody else yet. Your most affectionate

E. E.

Miss FitzGerald to Miss Eden.
THAMES DITTON,
Friday, August 13, 1819.

MY DEAREST EMILY, I was really sorry not to be able to accept Lady Buckinghamshire's invitation, but you see it could not be, for Lucy sets off Tuesday morning, and as Aunt Soph never parted with her before in her life, I must stay and comfort her....

Think of Sister liking me! I know of few phenomena that ever more surprised me, for I concluded she had set me down as wild and scapegracish. However, it was certainly reciprocal, for she certainly took my fancy very much.

Mary is very much changed since she has gone to live with that Drummond; however, you must get the better of that awkwardness, my poor dear Emmy, which for some time will hang over you. Besides, when Mary's mind settles again, you will get on better, and no longer miss her. In short, make haste and come, for I cannot write, but I want to talk to you.

Mary gave a sad account of that comical Dog, I trust he is better....

It was a very foolish thing of Mary marrying, but let us hope that, as a cook once said to me when I represented that she had not married prudently, "It was very foolish. The only thing is never to do so again, Ma'am, let us hope." I say she will look upon it as warning....

I have bought me some ducks, Emily, which I have to dill-dill myself. As yet I hold out, but as I may think dill a bore, I must hope Providence or instinct, that instinct, Emily, which does "Blush in the rose, and in the diamond blaze," that wonderful instinct I do hope will teach them their solitary way to the back yard.

I am going to get me a Pig too, which I mean to farm upon speculation and make monies.

Have you heard from that comical Dogge? By the bye, I hear that a man was bit by a comical dog at Kingston, and is very bad. Sad times, bread is dear, reformers meeting, dogs mad, and such a harvest the farmers must be ruined.... Ever your affect.

PAM.

Miss Eden to Lady Buckinghamshire.
BURGH,
Friday, September 10, 1819.

MY DEAREST SISTER, My visit to Thames Ditton I liked of all things. Poor Aunty was confined to her room with a bad sore throat till the last two days of my stay, so that Pam and I had it all to ourselves. We lived from breakfast time till seven at Boyle Farm, a beautiful place of Lord H. FitzGerald's by the river. I drew a great deal (what an odd word drew is! I mean, I drawed a great deal) and Pam read loud a very little, and I played and she sang, and the talking and laughing we divided in two equal large shares. I was very sorry to leave her, but I should have missed Mary altogether if I had not come here this week. There is an immense party in the house, but as everybody does what they like that is rather an advantage than otherwise. We set off after breakfast yesterday in *seven pairs* to take a walk, Mr. D. and Mary leading the way like Noah and his wife. Then came Mr. and Mrs. Shem, Ham and Japhet, and two or three odd pairs of beasts, the remainder here I suppose. I was set upon a horse, too, after luncheon, which was a Mazeppa-ish sensation—but there are beautiful rides about here, and if I was not as stiff as a poker to-day, I should have enjoyed that ride yesterday particularly.

Any little shyness that change of circumstance may have made, and indeed must have made at first, is quite over, and we are as comfortable as ever, which is satisfactory, considering that I love nothing in the world so well as her—tho' I should be sorry that she should say the same of me *now*. I am quite contented to be second. Her happiness is not the least surprising, as it must be pleasant in the first place, to be *considered* as she is by all the Drummonds, and Mr. Drummond's merits open upon me every day. He is much superior to all his family, I think, and as Mary thinks him superior to everything else, it all is as it should be. Adieu, dearest Sister. Your ever affectionate

E. E.

Miss FitzGerald to Miss Eden.
THAMES DITTON,
September 23, 1819.

...You must tell Mr. Drummond I never thank him enough for having blessed me with Bess, for some days she pondered on the vicissitudes of sties, but she has recovered herself, and enjoys existence with all the buoyancy and exuberance of youthful spirits. Her beauty is remarkable, and she possesses much of that *piquant* and *espièglerie*, which so seldom is allied to regularity of feature. Her disposition is very engaging, her heart mild and tender, and so affectionate she will eat out of my hand. In short, her perfections are such, I defy the bosom of a Jew to resist the fascination of them.

Your Uncle Henry went away last Thursday; he went without bidding us good-bye, but wrote a very quiet touching note, saying parting gave him such a squeeze about the heart, he could not bear the idea of taking leave. Poor Aunt did not like it at all—by the bye, that's one of the topics that are spoiling in my mind, for want of you to discuss them. I think one don't escape the squeeze at the heart by avoiding a parting, and that one has in addition a very unpleasant jar, besides having one's mind all over in a litter of things one still had to say, and odd ends of topics (the pig just stepped into the room to see what I was about; it must have some Irish blood in it, for it seems quite at home in the house).

Lucy comes back next Saturday. She met, she tells me in her last letter, Lady Harrowby, and Newman the Russian, and Pahlen the Prussian, and Lady Ebrington behind her parasol and Lord Ebrington, and Lady Mary Ryder, and Ed. Montagu; in short, as she says, the whole cavalcade of Click.

We have just now my cousins Cootes staying with us, I have always a sort of nervous fear of seeing them vanish, they seem so like bad visions.

Miss FitzGerald to Miss Eden.
October 3, 1819.

I cannot say how much your long satisfactory letter delighted me, that's something like a letter. I ought not to have been surprised at the tidings you give of dearest Mary, for when people marry there is nothing we may not expect them to do, and it is our own fault if we allow ourselves to be astonished at anything.

Lucy came back yesterday week, fat, well, in high force, delighted with all she has seen and done; in short, for you can bear with my obliquities, her spirits were a peg or two higher than my own, which trod me down very much at first....

I have been spending a day at Bushy with the Mansfields. I like her infinitely the best of the two, she really is sensible, amiable, and as clever as need be. He seems to have a cloudy unhappy temper, and some pretensions which he has not ability enough to either disguise or excuse.

Mr. Rose was there (the Court of Beasts Rose), and I like him much better on acquaintance. With wretched health he manages to keep up an even flow of spirits. He appears to indulge himself in his whims and oddities for his own amusement, and to divert his mind from dwelling upon the sufferings of his body, which makes one very lenient towards his jokes, poor man! even when they are not good. He seems amiable, and when one can get him to speak seriously his conversation is very charming, for with great information he is perfectly natural and easy; it is very odd he should like dirty jokes. I wonder whether it is inherent, or merely the consequence of bad health which catches at anything for relief and distraction.

What are your plans? When do you go your travels, or has not the Comical Dog told you anything about it, but means to have you off at a moment's warning, bundled into the carriage, with one arm in your sleeve, and only one shoe on?

What do you think? Is there any hope of your going to Bowood? Are you to live all October in the papered up rooms in Grosvenor St. with brown paper draperies?

Miss Eden to Lady Buckinghamshire.
GROSVENOR STREET,
October 7.

MY DEAREST SISTER, I am going to write you a long letter, and I shall be like a ginger-beer bottle now, if once the cork is drawn. I shall spirtle you all over—not that I have anything to say, but just a few remarks to make.

In the first place, I am eternally obliged to you for your just and proper appreciation of Autumn; nobody cares about it enough but you and me, and it is so pretty and so good, and gives itself such nice airs, and has such a touching way of its own, that it is impossible to pet it enough.

I tried some cool admiration of it upon Louisa, but she said she did not like it, as it led to Winter, and the children wanted new coats, and she must write to Grimes of Ludgate Hill for patterns of cloth, etc.

However, London is a very pretty check to enthusiasm; there are no trees to look brown and yellow, and the autumn air only blows against poor Lord Glengall's hatchment, and the few people that wander about the streets seem to think it cold and uncomfortable. Except the Drummonds and ourselves, I believe there is nobody here but the actors who act to us, and the bricklayers who are mending the homes of all the rest of the world. I have seen when I go sneaking down to Charing-Cross two or three official people, who think I suppose, that they govern us and the bricklayers.

Fanny and I shall end by being very accomplished, if we lead this life long. We breakfast at a little before ten, and from that time till a little after three are very busy at our lessons.

We have just finished Mrs. H. More, which I like very much, particularly the latter part.

We have foolishly begun *Modern Europe* for our history book, which I think much too tiresome to be endured, and then we take a peep at what the Huns and Vandals are about. My only hope is that fifteen hundred years hence we shall be boring some young lady in the back Settlement of Canada with our Manchester Riots. That is the only thought which supports me under the present dulness of the newspaper.

George brought us such a quantity of Confitures from Paris, that it is a mercy we are not in bilious fevers before this. I enclose you some Fleur d'Orange because it is so genteel. Pray remark when it is going down, whether your sensations are not remarkably lady-like? Your most affect.

E. EDEN.

Miss FitzGerald to Miss Eden.
THAMES DITTON,
Tuesday, October 1819.

Very pleasant, but not correct, as our immortal Monkey said when he kissed the Cat, my going to see you in town! It would indeed be a case for Hannah More, as that very comical Dog said; why it would make the few pious hairs she still preserves rear up, like quills upon the fretful Porcupine; to say I should like it is saying very little indeed.

Next to Hannah More, that Chancellor is the greatest Beast and Bore to prevent our going up; I won't have my oath trifled with no more than my affections, and since he coquets with my conscience, I have a great mind not to swear at all, and keep myself disengaged for some little *Lèse-Majesté*. This letter seems copied out of Buffon or "The Book of Beasts," for I find honourable mention made of cat, dog, monkey, beast, bore, porcupine.

I will try and let you know what day I come, if I can get it out of old Sullivan, and if it is soon I will take the duck to you. I suppose Hannah More will not be shocked at the dead duck spending the night under the roof with you; the duck being dead must remove all impropriety attendant on such a step.

Your account of your bonnet diverted me highly; it certainly is much more difficult to find a congenial bonnet than a congenial soul, and after all they don't last one so long. Sullivan talks of Thursday as the most likely day I shall land at your house, and I may from there branch out into all other ramifications of business. I send you some three or four violets to sweeten you in London.

Miss FitzGerald to Miss Eden.
November 7, 1819.

DEAREST EMMY, I meant every day to have written to you whilst you were at Shottesbrook, but I never could hit the right temperature; when I felt dull, I thought it was not fair writing to you, making "confusion worse confounded," and when I was merry, I imagined the shock might be too much for you, and only serve to make your "darkness visible." This is a very deeply Miltonic apology, the truth I daresay may turn out to be a severe fit of laziness, which has incapacitated me from doing anything beyond reading, which delights me, and swallows up all my duties.

Your sister Caroline seems an admirable Brood Mare. I admire her exertions, but, Emmy, it is lucky we are not put to the test, we never could imitate them. However brilliant and liberal our views, we should fail in the plodding perseverance, which is the necessary ingredient to fill up the gaps and make it all solid.

I have of late been driven by Aunt in the Chaise, to try a Mule, which a man wants us to buy. In my life I never was on service of such danger. She holds her reins so very loose, that she puts me in mind of the picture of Phaeton when he is in the act of *culbute* from Heaven, and I find myself humming a Te Deum for my safety as I get out, for she has no manner of power over the beast, and throws herself upon its generosity with wonderful philosophy. I, who have not this reliance upon its honour, really suffer greatly from terror.... My dear Emmy, the Ogress's dereliction from the sober paths of temperance was a shock I have not yet recovered from. Our cook has taken to drinking too, but she certainly boasts some originality in her tastes; she ruins herself in Antimonial Wine and emetics of the strongest nature; no remonstrance can deter her from pouring every species of quackery down her unhappy throat. It is very remarkable how the lower classes love physic.

Your anticipated fondness for your powder'd Friend quite enchanted us. I have an extinguisher on my mind to-day, so good-bye. I write just to show you I can make an effort for you. Good-bye. I am your own

PAM.

Miss FitzGerald to Miss Eden.
Sunday, November 14, 1819.

What are you about? Write to me directly. Yesterday I was stirred up by one of those hubbubs that vanish into smoke. Mr. Ogilvie wrote to say he was coming to us for a few hours previous to his going to Paris for a fortnight on business, upon which Lucy went mad; she would and should go with him, raved and tore about, wrung from the hard hands of Aunt her vile consent, and so far infected me with her fuss that I was all of a twitter.

Her cloaths were preparing, in short, she was far on the road to France. Ogilvie arrives, Lucy downs upon her knees, to beg he will take her to Paris, and lo! he would have been delighted to take her, but he had given up the journey!

We all dropt in spirit like so many sacks, after the excitation of the morning.

We go to Town positively on the 27th of this month, God willing. Let me know whether the master of your destiny, your fate, George, brings you to Town. We shall be in Stratford Place, and about the beginning of next month I suppose the Chancellor will have us up. Pray how do you think we ought to dress the character, something of the sackcloth and ash nature?...

How do Fanny and Edward Drummond go on? I hope she still thinks him pleasant. Don't rob her of those comfortable illusions, any bulwark against bore is a blessing.

Aunt has had the white Cock, the pride of the Dunghill killed, and Lucy has replaced him by a pair of stinking red-eyed rabbits. We have robberies going on on all sides. The thieving establishment is put upon the most liberal footing; they drive their cart, and keep their saddle-horses, and nobody seems inclined to disturb them.

I understand Stocks? Emmy, I have been making Mr. Ogilvie give me a lecture on Finance, but to-morrow I shall relapse into darkness. Nature has done much for you and me, but we are not organised for Stocks.

Miss FitzGerald to Miss Eden.

November 26, 1819.

We go to Town to-morrow, but too late to see you. I am so unhappy, my snug own home so clean, so warm, my life so humdrum, to-day walking in the footsteps of yesterday, all thrown over by going to that Babylon. If it was not for you, I should hang myself previous to my departure. Conceive my situation on finding myself to-morrow night, amidst the smoke and stir of that dim spot which men call Stratford Place, Nr. 2....

I had a kind note from Lady Lansdowne, I love her. Emmy, if you desire to keep a Grantham and four horses, I surely may have my Lansdowne and two!

I feel walking against the wind, which is the only way I can express the feeling one has in parts of one's life when matters go contrary. We are coming up in truly Scriptural style, for we know not where we shall eat, and where we shall drink, nor wherewithal we shall be clothed.

December 17, 1819.—Emmy, the moon whistles, but why don't you write? My trunk is gone forth and is now on its remote, unfriended, melancholy, and slow journey to Bowood, and drags at each remove a lengthening chain, and the weather is so bad, and so we are all very unhappy. Isn't (I never know how to tittle that abbreviation, but to you my meaning is palpable) well to go on. Isn't this a day for Crack-skull Common?

Miss FitzGerald to Miss Eden.
BOWOOD,
Thursday, a great deal p.m., December 23, 1819.

MY DEAREST EMMY, I am safely arrived into this country, and as you have never peregrined into these parts, a few remarks, peradventure, a few remarks upon the nation Wiltshire may give you satisfaction. The Wilt is generally of noble disposition, kind of heart and of sound understanding. In person short of stature, thick set, square built, hath straight hair, and a pleasing aspect. In civility most laborious, insomuch there seems a wall of politeness which keepeth off better acquaintance in this tribe. The Wilt woman liveth bounden in subjection and loving obedience unto the husband, and filleth her time duly in catering and ordering for her household. The Wilt when young is ill-favoured, given unto the asking of questions, eager for food, and hath a harsh and unmusical voice. It is the custom to *déjeune* at the hour Ten. The Wilt doth eat, and read the signs of a large leaf showing the contests of the Two Tribes—the one having power that doth act foolishness, and the other which hath no power—speaking wisdom; and after breathing a word or two at intervals when the meal is ended, the Wilt will go unto his avocations and work with his brains, and then at about the hour Two, he eateth of a mixture of flour and water like unto cakes, and then doth go forth unto the exercising of his body in the way of quick walking, or managing of a small horse. At dinner the Wilt ordereth himself seemly, eateth of all things freely and slow, drinking moderately. He then adjourneth unto another part of the Habitation and doth talk of divers matters good and well spoken, rubbing his hands withal exceedingly; and after he hath drunk of a hot brown liquor, the women take their tools and do sew wearing apparel and are still, and the Wilt taketh a volume and doth lift up his voice and read. I do mention this because the custom is after the manner of this tribe peculiarly, and is regarded upon by other tribes as an abomination, inasmuch that one of the tribe of Dumont has been known to cover his countenance with a cloth when the same has been practical. I have been at some pains to get particulars of this form of idolatry to the god Bore, and have collected thus much: Bore is an evil spirit that, they reckon, commonly doth haunt empty places, but is more terrible when he doth infest crowded places. He doth possess people after the fashion of the Devils in Judaea, and hath, besides, a contagious property, it having been noted that one possessed will generally infect others. What a fool I am, Emmy dear! but I was so full of nonsense I was obliged to come and write you, and such an ill-tempered pen too, that would go no way, not even its own. I am sure it came out of Lady Holland or the Dss of Bedford's Wing!

I am very snug here as to my body, but I do want you to talk to beyond expression, and I cannot bear to think Lucy is missing me all this while. I have been over all my old walks here, and remembering all the corners and rooms and chairs and tables, so that I feel two years the younger. But I wonder how I got on at all without knowing you. Lady Lansdowne is in high favour with me. There is so much to like in her. Him of old I have always doated on, but I have sat with my extinguisher upon my head ever since I arrived, so that I fear, pleased as I am with them, the feeling is not reciprocal. I always shall love this place for having brought me acquainted with old *Mary*, for my liking to her was a sort of halfway-house to my affection for you.

I have not an idea who or when anybody is to come. I don't care. You have lost the art of writing me good long letters. I desire you will mend. Goodbye, Dearie, God bless you. Tell me more. And believe me ever your own
PAM.

Emmy now, don't let all my stupid jokes lay about, and don't because you have nothing ready to say to Mary and Mr. Drummond, in an evil hour go and shew my letter. You know you have done such things, you animal. Remember, I will never write again if you play me this trick. I pour my nonsense into your trusty bosom only in confidence. If I must restrain my nonsense, what a bond of Friendship will be broken!

Miss FitzGerald to Miss Eden.
BOWOOD .

That One Pound Bill is for the liquidation of the debt I contracted that morning in Town with you at a shop in Regent Street for value received of silk handkerchiefs, ribbons, etc.... I am fallen in love with Mr. Abercromby. He is quite a darling, mouth and all. The first day I saw him I thought of your face and laughed; but we are now inseparable. He is so natural, so good-natured, and does love nonsense. You would delight in him. The Macdonalds have been here, and they are no loss. She is so very dull, oh dear!—and they are much too newly married to be fit for society.... I take long walks with my dear Lord Lansdowne. Emmy, he is so good, and so knowledgeful, and so liberal, I think he is the most liberal man I ever met with at all, in taste as well as principle. And that is a great merit, for one knows where to have him. Emmy, don't New Year's days and all those milestones in one's life make you very melancholy? They do me to a degree. I take some time shaking off the weight. Of course I won't say a word of the Dromedaries to any one, but I don't see that you have any duty laying in that quarter, particularly as the more you see of them and go to Charing Cross, the more obligations they will imagine themselves bestowing on you.

CHAPTER III

1820-1825

Miss FitzGerald to Miss Eden.
BOWOOD,
February, 1820.

HUSH, hush, Emmy, the King *is* dead, and we have entered a new reign, yes, yes, and George IV. *has* been proclaimed, and I *have* wondered what he'll do with his wife, and Henry VII. would not let his Queen be crowned for two years, and Hume says so, and all the newspapers are very black, and the *Times* blacker than any, and there is an end of the topics and we know it all. Now to our old channel.

My hair is on tip-toe. I have heard with my outward ears to-day, that there hangs a possibility in Fate of my not getting home for a month. Not that I am uncomfortable here, but only I do so wish to see you again, my dearie, and poor dear Lu! It quite amounts to longing, or craving, or hunger, or thirst. It is so long since I have done out my heart and mind, it is all in a litter.

I enjoyed myself so very much indeed while your brother and Mr. Fazakerly were here. As for the others, I wished them hanged, for I had to make company to them, and they did not make amusement for *me*.

We are quite alone, and have been ever since Wednesday. After I have made breakfast, and Lord Lansdowne has engulphed as much Tea as he can carry, I take my mornings to myself and bask in the Library. I do not mean this as a figurative allusion to the sunshine of the mind, but that the room stands South, as all rooms should stand, or walk off. I then at about two, lunch, and see Lady Lansdowne for half-an-hour, take my walk till five, come in, and write an empty line to Lucy to while away her time.

Lady Lansdowne dines with us, goes to bed before eleven, and I stay on talking till near one with the Wilt. I do, I *will* like him, tho' I have run very near hating him, that Wilt wise man! He goes next Monday to Woburn and Middleton on his way to Town, and Lord knows when it will please Providence we should follow.

Tell me something of Mary, and above all, tell me about yourself. Your last letter made me laugh so much! Do it again. I ever remain, your affectionate old

PAM.

Miss FitzGerald to Miss Eden.
BOWOOD,
February 10, 1820.

It is now settled we are to be in Town the 20th.... We do not mean to be in London this year at all to remain, Emmy; it is not worth while. I need not say it to you, for we compared notes last year upon the emptiness of existence in that Town—gaiety as it is called. You will come to Thames Ditton, where we have the certainty of being comfortable together.

Lord Lansdowne set off to-day for Middleton. I miss him shockingly. He has crept into my affections in a wonderful degree these last ten days; I have pounded a little nonsense into him. Twice I made him laugh at jokes not worth repeating, and once at his own matter-of-fact method of understanding Fun: in short, our intimacy grew so thick he committed himself far enough to say that he was quite in a childish fidget to see his new Gallery and ceiling—much more anxious about that than about the Meeting of Parliament. And last night the agony he got into fancying he should want all the identical books in this library in Town, and which to take, and the sort of goodbye he bid the volumes, gave me hopes of him.

Emmy, you know the brother, William Strangways? He is a curious specimen. He certainly will pack himself up by mistake and send himself as a Fossil to the Geological Society some fine day. I rather like him, he is so good-natured, and so cram full of out of the way information. Another Brother arrived to-day, y-clept Giles. I know nothing of him, and am likely to remain in ignorance, as they go away to-morrow.

She and I get on charmingly. I like her more than I ever did, more than I ever thought I could love anybody who has the misfortune of not being one of us.

Miss FitzGerald to Miss Eden.

March, 1820.

Your letter gave me such delight, the laugh of other days came o'er my soul.

My dear, rums is ris, and sugars is fell. My cold is gone, but Aunt is sick, in short, barring myself who am very well thank you, the house is an Hospital.

Aunt has been quite ill, shut up, and the Apothecary busy, all over pocket handkerchiefs and Ipecacuanha.

All my neighbours far gone in liver complaints and buried in bile, so that I have kept aloof from all, when they did not want me, and we are so very, very quiet here, I almost fancy I must be grown deaf, for I suppose the world is still in a bustle, and going on. No letters, no murder, no crimes.

What a *retention* of correspondence this cessation of franks seems to have caused: when shall we see our wholesome days again?

Emkins, Holland will never do. Why? When, shall I see you? Why can't you stay where you are? Your brother George is like an *âme en peine*; he can't abide nowhere. I suppose you will like the junket, you Beast.... So you have your Grantham. It is all very well we should allow those sort of people to love us, etc. but they must be kept in their place. How little I saw you in Town, and then you think it my fault and that I won't dine with you. You don't know, you cannot know, how I have been bothered about it, not by Aunt alone. In short, there is a bother in our celibacy, that as there is no one to speak as one having authority, the whole herd think they have a right to have a pull at one's tether, and pin one down to their own fancies....

Emmy, only think Danford is going to-day! A woeful day that such a Dan should go.

There's been a grand inventory to do, and glass and china, etc. Aunt was aghast at the mortalities among the rummer glasses. He denied having crackt their noble hearts, when, oh Providence! oh, *juste ciel!* their glassy relics rose in judgment, and from the cupboard called for vengeance. There lay their bottoms, which, like the scalps of his enemies, had accumulated in evidence of his deeds. His wen grew pale when he thought of his wages. "Conceive his situation!" What a climacteric! Good-bye, write to me much and often, but if you don't, never mind, for I know what London is.

I do long to see Matthews, so provoking the animal won't begin his pranks before we leave London.

April, 1820.

...Poor Aunt gets no worse, but I see no great amendment.... I assure you, Emmy, I take great care of myself; we only sit up every other night, and my spirits are quite good. I am screwed up like a machine, and get through day and night very quickly indeed. I eat and drink and laugh and don't let myself think.

You must come again, when you can, to see me, Emmy. I have no scruple in asking you to come and see me in the fullness of my dullness, out of the fullness of your gaiety, because when we get together, we get into our element, my darling. Your visit quite refreshed me the other day. I send you some flowers to brighten up your room, and you will put them into the Christening bowls, which lie about your tables.

April 30, 1820.

I have given up the hopes of seeing you, nobody is going to Town, unless I take a cling to some carriage footboard as the beggar boys do. I have given up all prospects of bonnets for the future, and so have ordered one at Kingston.

I had an obliquity the other day, and awful longing to be in London for a *leetle*, a very *leetle* while. I tried and tried what you call to reason myself out of it, and I partly succeeded, but the getting out of that folly cost me a great deal, and made me rather rough and uncomfortable. Brushing up one's reason is just as disagreeable as having one's teeth cleaned, it sets one on edge for the while....

I am sure you will be obliged to me for telling you, that in a shower in London, a man was running along with an umbrella, and ran against another man, this latter offended man snatched the offending umbrella, out of the umbrell*ee's* hands, and throwing it away said, "Where are you running to like a mad mushroom?"

If Aunt gets better soon, I will go up in a week or two, and have a look at you, and get a hat. Your Leghorn sounds well, but I never yet found home brewed bonnets answer, they are always ill-disposed, full of bad habits, and get awkward crics about them. Good-bye.

Miss FitzGerald to Miss Eden.

May, 1820.

I should have written directly to wish you joy of Mary's job being so prosperously accomplished, but I have been keeping my bed. My cough has got such a grip of me, nothing does me good.... What a fuss you must have been in I can but think. Was Mr. Drummond in a fuss? Well, it must be a great relief off your mind, and off hers too, poor dear. I suppose she is already doatingly fond of the little brute as if she had known it all her life.... I have got a horrid cold and cough, and I look a beast of the first water, and of course, Edward has fixed this moment to come and see us. I expect him in two days, and he expects me in my present haggard, worn, water-gruel state of mind to amuse him and be *sémillante*. I, who am so low in words, I have not one to throw at a small dog.

Miss FitzGerald to Miss Eden.

June, 1820.

I am quite so much better to-day, I entertain some hopes of prolonging my precarious existence a little longer. Company to dinner yesterday. Humbug and Bore kissed each other without truth or mercy. Why didn't you come to me to-day? Come to-morrow for I have such a piece of nonsense for you.

EDINBURGH,

August 12, 1820.

We sailed Tuesday and arrived this morning by 5 o'clock at Leith. Our journey was most prosperous and very amusing. Our Society of Passengers also kept me in great amusement. I must just mention that their meals amused me as much as any part of their proceedings. One poured whisky over cold pie for sauce, and one ate raspberry jam with bread and butter, all ate peas with their knives. We shall see the sights between this and Tuesday, when we go to Bonnington. Write to me my own Emmy, and direct at Lady Mary Ross, Bonnington, Lanark.

BONNINGTON,
October 9, 1820.

...Your letter amused me. The geographical happiness which has befallen us in being born near one another is indeed inestimable. That horrible supposition of my being the amiable Laplander made me shudder. You always do hit the funniest ideas in the world. You darling, I require something to keep up my spirits, for if I don't laugh I shall cry when I tell you it is more than probable I shall not see you till next May.

Mary Ross has put it into Aunt's head that it would be the best plan in the world for us to pass the winter in the Isle of Bute. Living is for nothing. As this is a plan of economy I dare say nothing, but I am very unhappy, I am very unhappy indeed, for I feel my heart sink into my shoes when I think how long it may be before I again see you or any of you.... We shall stay here till November, when we shall go to our little Bute. Our society there is likely to be confined to Mrs. Muir, the factor's wife, a quick, lively, little body, I am told, which sounds awfully bustling and pert, an occasional King's officer in search of smugglers, and the master of the steam-boat. I have liked Scotland upon the whole, in short I had determined to make the best of it, and one always partly succeeds in those cases, yet I don't like the people; they are very hospitable, but *du reste*, they appear to me stubborn, opinionated, cold, and prejudiced. The women are either see-saw and dismal, or bustling and pert, and appear to me to be generally ignorant, which I did not expect, and the minute gossip they keep us is something I cannot describe.

Miss Eden to Miss Villiers.
GROSVENOR STREET,
Monday .

DEAREST THERESA, Please to write again directly to say how you are going on. I take your Grove to be equal to my Nocton in matter of bore, and that being the case, if one is to have an illness, one may as well have it at those houses. It fills up the time. My ague is subsiding, but I have fits of it occasionally and hate it very much. I had one yesterday, which even moved George's strong heart to pity, though he has such a contempt for illness that I keep it all very snug. I am going to Langley to-day, and that is another thing which makes him so *scrapey* that I am writing in his room in order to talk him over in my most insinuating and winning manner between the sentences of my letter.

He and I go on such different tacks about town and country, that we make our plans, and talk them over for half-an-hour before I recollect that we are working for different aims. He thinks every day spent in the country by anybody who does not shoot is so much time wasted, and I happen to think every day spent in London is a mistake, and I was roused to the sense of our different views by his saying, "Well, but I want you to gain another day in London, and you can write to Louisa that you were not well yesterday, and then stay here, and I will go to the play with you to-night." Such an iniquitous plot! And I am about as fit to go to the play as to go in a balloon.

George liked Middleton very much. Lady Jersey was going, as soon as the present party was all gone, to turn unhappy for the poor Duke of York, and as far as I can make out, she was going to show it by putting off all the *ladies* of the party she was to have had this week, and to keep up just enough to receive all the gentlemen. She and Lady Granville seem to have had a fine *tracasserie* at Paris. George is so charmed with Lady Jersey's children. He says he never saw such a fine pleasant set of boys, and the girls are very pretty.

I have not been out of the house, except once, to see Elizabeth Cawdor, and with that wonderful quickness of observation that I possess I discovered that she will probably soon add to her family, and that the addition will be very considerable—three or four at least.

Lady Bath is at Rome again and not the least anxious to come home, which is odd. One of Elizabeth's children is so pretty. I have no news to tell you, as it does not come of itself. One must go to look for it.

Before you read thro' this letter call your maid, and get the smelling bottle, for you will certainly faint away with surprise and wonder. Who would have thought it! I don't believe it myself so I cannot expect you to believe it, but I am going to be married perfectly true in about a month or six weeks.

I am going to be married to Sir Guy Campbell.... What I would have given to have had you with me all this time, and at this moment, I miss you beyond expression. He is uncommonly right-headed, of course it follows he is liberal, *wide*-minded and indulgent, at the same time I see he can take violent dislikes, as you do at times, my best one. He is very tact to a degree, and that you know, Dearest, is a corner-stone in happiness, for there is no fitting two minds without it.

Just like you, and quite tactful not to cool our affection for each other by sending me a wet blanket in the shape of a congratulation. I like Sir Guy more and more, he understands me so well, he knows my faults, which is a great relief, for I have no silent obliquity to smother, or no good behaviour to act up to more than is comfortable. He is doing a set of sketches of the Highlands for you, which I am sure you will like. However, tho' he is of a Highland family, let me take from your mind any impression that he is at all Scotch in obstinacy, cunning cheek-bones, or twang. He has not been in Scotland for the last six and twenty years. You need not tell dear Mrs. Colvile this, who has built all my hopes of future happiness on his being Scotch to the bone. Hers was the first letter I received with Lady Campbell on it....

I cannot say how pretty it was of you to send that pretty cap, which I think the prettiest cap that ever was prettied. Pat your Grantham for she did that commission well. So she was very brimful of London and the ways and means of the place? You wonder at her liking it so much after having had so much of it; but it grows upon them like a description I read somewhere of some part of the Infernal Regions, where the damned were condemned to misery and dirt, wallowing in mire and sand, but they were so degraded they had lost the sense of misery, and had no wish to leave the darkness for light.

I wear your dear cap often and often, and occasionally Sir Guy wears it when he is not very well. He says he is sure you will be gratified by the attention.

I have had a very neat silk pelisse trimmed with fur, sent without the donor's name, and as the poor thing is a very pretty pelisse, but can't tell me its business or where it comes from, I have a silent great-coat here, and thanks I can't impart. I believe it comes from those Lady Hills, those bosom friends I never could bear, and if I have thanked the Gods amiss, I can't help it.

Have you seen your Elliots? for I am anxious to know what India has done for them. It is a dangerous experiment, they get so stuffed with otto of roses, sandal-wood and sentiment, they never come quite right....

Aunty is in the grumps with the rheumatism, and the winds and draughts. You know the sort of silent-victim appearance of suffering innocence some people take and wear, which increases when the meat is tough, and the pudding burnt, and which is all more or less aimed at me, till I feel so *culprit*, as if I blew the winds, and made the cold, and toughed the meat, and burnt the dish. However, I don't mind it now and go on doing my best for all of them, particularly as she desired not to be troubled with housekeeping, and as I recollect she always keeps a growl at the cold at home. Sir Guy behaves like an angel to her....

I hear they have a large party at Bowood, I suppose the usual routine. I heard of Truval at Longleat, not doing anything particular. That small Ealing address with all the little Truvals of the grove, babes and sucklings, amused me. He was bored at Longleat and deserves to be bored thro' life. I can only wish him a continuance of H. Montagu's friendship.

Lady Campbell to Miss Eden.
BUTE,
January 7, 1821.

Many thanks, my darling Emmy, for your delightful letter. Till you are shut up for six months in an old rambling house on the coast of the Isle of Bute in January, you cannot know the value, the intrinsic sterling, of such a letter as yours.... I am sorry poor Mary's Charing-Cross purgatory has begun again.

I think, if God grants us life, we are very likely to settle, when we do settle, somewhere near London. It is bad for the mind to live without society, and worse to live with mediocrity; therefore the environs of London will obviate these two evils. But I like the idea. I cannot bear Scotland in spite of every natural beauty, the people are so odious (don't tell Mrs. Colvile). Their hospitality takes one in, but that is kept up because it is their pride. Their piety seems to me mere love of argument and prejudice; it is the custom to make a saturnalia of New Year's Eve, and New Year's Day they drown themselves in whisky. Last New Year's Eve being Sunday, they would not break the Sabbath, but sat down after the preaching till 12 o'clock; the moment that witching hour arrived, they thought their duty fulfilled, seized the whisky, and burst out of their houses, and ran about drinking the entire night, and the whole of Monday and Monday night too. This is no exaggeration, you have no idea the state they are in—men lying about the streets, women as drunk as they,—in short, I never was more disgusted....

Lady Lansdowne did not send the Pelisse. She sent me ribbons, an Indian muslin gown, quantities of French-work to trim it, four yards of lace, a dozen pocket-handkerchiefs; and that touching Lord Lansdowne sent me a beautiful set of coral. She also sent me a white *gros de Naples* gown. In short, she has done it uncommon well, and I love her as much as I can, and who can do more?

Lady Campbell to Miss Eden.
January 21, 1821.

Many many thanks, my Dearest, for your kind letter. We certainly do understand one another *extraordinatr* well, as they say in Scotland. Your writing in London too is quite "from the depths I cried out." Emily, there is a sympathy of bores between us. Sir Guy and I have regularly been put out of humour every morning by the new *Times*, and it will come all the way to Bute, though he has written to agents and bankers and offices to stop it. Like old Time and pleasant Time and Time-serving, there is no arresting it, and its disgusting pages meet my eye and try my temper without cessation. Send me down a little genuine essence of Whig when you have time occasionally. Sir Guy is no politician at all, only I in a quiet way insinuate sound principles into his mind. Not but what I think a military man should be without party, so that the doses I give are very mild. I go no further than just liberality, and now and then drawing him into some remarks on the malversations of ministers.

I enter into your dinner and house bothers.

I don't find that variety in the beef of to-morrow and the mutton of to-day, which the *Anti-Jacobin* expatiates upon with such delight, and the joints diminish in sheep when we eat mutton. As for puddings, they are one and the same, and only one, and then when one has tortured one's brain and produced a dinner, and that it is eaten, my heart sinks at the prospect that to-morrow will again require its meal, *et les bras me tombent*....

Lord and Lady Bute are coming here. We don't know them at all, but I suppose we shall see them, which is bore, for nothing is so tiresome as to be near neighbours with people one scarce knows. One has one foot in intimacy, and the other in formality, and it makes but a limping acquaintance. I don't think Lady Lansdowne has quite got over my not marrying her way; she covers it up very well, but you know how soon you and I can see through all that, and I know also that Sir Guy is not likely to overcome that feeling in her. He is not a party man, he is not scientific, and unless he likes people he is very shy, and I see they will never make it up. But I always thought marriage must disarrange many acquaintances. I don't regret acquaintances; even to have had variety of acquaintances is an advantage, for the reason which makes a public school an advantage to a boy; it widens the mind. But to go on through life with them is heartless and thankless too. I mean to save my time, and keep it all for those I like and love.... We have lovely warm spring weather here, always breakfast with the window open and getting away from the fires. I must say the climate far exceeded my expectations. The garden is covered with thick white patches of snow-drops in full bloom. Don't this make your mouth water, and your eyes too, you poor misery in your cold smoke?

Good-bye, Dearest, have you been drawing and what? I don't mean just now in London, but in your lucid intervals, and are you well?

So far London is a place that cures or kills. Your own
PAMELA.

Lady Campbell to Miss Eden.

February 28, 1821.

Don't go out during this pestilential month of March, people may call it east wind and sharp, but it is neither more or less than a plague, that regularly blows thro' the Islands, and it is nonsense to brave it, just because it is not called pest, or yellow or scarlet, or pink fever, so don't go out.

I am spending a few days here at Mount Stuart, and you may see that I am writing with strange paper and ink, and have but a distant bowing acquaintance with this fine clarified pen.

You are quite right, one is a better human creature, when one has seen a mountain and it does one good. I only wish I could see a mountain with you.

Your Feilding fuss is so described, that I laughed over it for an hour; my Dear, I see it, and enter into your quiescent feelings on the occasion; things settle themselves so well I wonder other people always, and we sometimes, give ourselves any trouble about anything.

This is a good enough house, but somehow they go out of the room and leave one, and yet one has not the comfort of feeling alone and easy, and I caught myself whispering and Lucy too; I can't account for it, except by the great family pictures, that are listening all round in scarlet cloaks, and white shoes, and red heels and coronets. Kitty is to be married to-day—plenty of love but little prospect of anything else. Her future income is rather in the line of a midshipman's allowance, *Nothing a day and find yourself.*

I hope you will taste this saying, for I am partial to it, it gives one a comfortable idea, that in these days, when the Whigs complain of Ministerial extravagance, the Navy establishment will escape censure.

Lady Campbell to Miss Eden.

March 3, 1821.

Much to say I can't pretend, but something to say I can always find when I write to you. We left Mount Stuart to-day. Sir Guy, Lucy and I delighted to be at home. Aunt rather missing the cookery dishes, claret, champagne, and a sound house.

My mind is grown much more easy since I have clearly ascertained, weighed, and measured that I don't like Lord Bute, and of course I have a whole apparatus of reasonable reasons, to support my dislike *envers et contre tout*. He is proud not in that complimentary sense. Some people use the word implying a dislike of dirty deeds and a love of noble doings. He is not purse-proud nor personally proud of his looks; but the sheer genuine article pride which now-a-days one seldom meets with barefaced. He is proud of his ancestors, proud of the red puddle that runs in his veins, proud of being a Stuart, a Bute, and a Dumfries. He apes humility, and talks of the honour people do him in a way that sounds like "down on your knees." Talks of his loyalty as if Kings should kiss his hand for it. However though this is tiresome and contemptible, he has some of the merits that mitigate pride. He seems high principled and honourable, with sense enough for his own steerage, and I make allowances for his blindness which must make him center in self a good deal.

She is pleasant enough in a middling way, no particular colour in her ideas. She never moots or shocks, or pushes one back, but she don't go any further, content to dwell in decencies for ever. She likes a joke when it is published and printed for her, but I suppose a manuscript joke never occurred to her.

They never have anybody there, except now and then Mr. Moore, his man of business, who is in the *full* sense of the word corpulent, red-faced, with a short leg with a steel yard to it, and a false tuft; and he is Colonel of the Yeomanry. But I like him for a wonderful rare quality in any Baillie, but above all in a Scotch Baillie; he is independent and no toad-eater. He found fault with his patron's potatoes at the grand table, with a whole row of silver plates dazing his eyne; and he as often as occasion occurs quietly contradicts him....

General Way and his wife are to be at Mount Stuart next week. Sir Guy described General Way as an Adjutant-General, and a Methodist, which sounds such an odd mixture,—true Church Militant. They are great Jew converters. I have been reading a luminous treatise on Witchcraft, seriously refuting such belief. One rather odd circumstance is, that three-and-twenty books and tracts have been written since Charles II.'s reign in earnest support of the doctrine of Sorcery and Witchcraft....

I go on writing in case you are still shut up, it may amuse you tho' I have no event. An occasional mad dog spreads horror thro' the district; no wonder I enter into the poor dog's feelings, he belonged to the steam boat, and that was enough to send any Christian out of their senses, let alone a dog.

Lady Campbell to Miss Eden.

March 10.

What a delightful letter, and I feel perfectly agonised, not an idea, not a topic, not a word to send you in return. Sir Guy says I may do as I please, so I shall send the Highlands to the right about, and go south to you as soon as the weather is *travellable*, and that we have seen Sir Guy's old Scotch aunt at Edinburgh. I must see her because she is called "Aunt Christy." That name, you must acknowledge, is worth a visit.

I send you, my Darling, a small Heart with my hair in it. Put it on directly and wear it. I know it is a comfort to have a little something new when one is ill, as I learnt when I had the chicken-pox, and found great benefit in some gilt gingerbread Kings and Queens. Lucy used to bring me them twelve years ago; they were hideous, useless, and not eatable, but still they made a break in the day....

I wish I could instil in you a little of that respect and mystic reverence which I never could feel myself for Doctors, and Pestles and Mortars—that blind devotion which is so necessary to make the stuff efficacious, for by faith we are saved in these cases, as in cases of conscience.

I am sorry they have made you have hysterics, and won't let you have the Elliots, and conversation. That bluff Chilvers, with his Burgomaster appearance, as if he was magistrate of our vitals and poor bowels! I hate him ever since he offered me the insult of a blister, that first blister of hateful memory.

Write, or don't write, as it suits you. Lucy and Sir Guy are such friends, they quite doat on one another, and understand each other. Therefore wipe away all I said for nothing. That is my comfort with you, I can tell you and then scratch it out again as I please, and that is the only way to be constant in this changeable world, to be able to follow the changes of those we love, so as to be always the same with them.

Lady Campbell to Miss Eden.

March 15, 1821.

...We have been a day at Mount Stuart since I wrote, to meet a Sir Gregory and Lady Way—such bores! Oh! no, never. His brother is the great Jew-converter, and has now left his wife and house and estate and is gone a converting-tour into Poland. Some Israelites played him an ungrateful trick. He invited them to his house in Buckinghamshire to render thanks in his private Chapel for their redemption, but alas! they had not cast off their old man, for they stole all Mr. Way's plate, which he has found it impossible to redeem, they having most probably converted it into money and made off. These people are strictly pious characters, and on Lucy saying she had heard of Mr. Way, Sir Gregory replied: "An instrument, Madam, merely an instrument!"

Lady Way is too heavy, and so dressed out—all in a sort of *supprimé* way, and wears a necklace like a puppy's collar....

Did you see those pretty nice Feilding children when the Feildings were in London? I hope that nasty woman will not spoil them.

Have you had Mary Drummond in comfort since you have been shut up and ill?—like the indulgence of barley sugar with a cough; no remedy, but yet it is pleasant. Does Fanny still keep up "brother and sister" with Edward Drummond? I don't think even Fanny could do it. Sir Guy knows the one in the Guards (Arthur is not his name), and liked him better than Drummonds in general, for there is no denying that Drummonds are Drummonds to the greatest degree.... Send me your low letters, and your gay letters, and all you write, for I love it all.

Lady Campbell to Miss Eden.

March 22, 1821.

...Jane Paget's business shocked, but did not surprise me. I never saw any poor girl so devoured by Ennui, and I have so long found Bore account for all the unaccountable things that occur, that it solved Jane's marriage to me. She cannot exist without excitement, for she is completely *blasée* upon everything. Blasée is the genteel word; you would call it besotted or stupefied, if she had accomplished this vitiated destruction by dram-drinking or opium; but the effect, call it what you please, is exactly the same. I pity that poor Mr. Ball truly, for I don't suspect him of being equal to rule a wife and have a wife....

I forget to tell you a good idea of Lucy's, about Jane Paget's marriage. She said it was such a pity to see good articles selling off at half-price like ribbon in Oxford Street, to make room for a new spring assortment.

We are doing our Mount Stuart again. We have a Mr. and Mrs. Veetchie (a Commissioner of the Customs and has been in the army) and Lady Elizabeth and Mr. Hope. Mr. Hope can be pleasant now and then, but as dulness was paramount during our intercourse, I suspect the agreeableness to be a little gilding he has got from living with the wits of Edinburgh. There seems no source—mere cistern work. Your old Burgomaster Chilvers is clever, and I think as much of him as of any of them. But go on mentioning all he does, whether you are drenched in drugs.

Lady Campbell to Miss Eden.

April 1, 1821.

...Tho' I know they are all taking care of you with all their might, I feel I should do it better, because I want to be with you so very too much, that I feel cross with those who can be about you. Sir Guy thinks you are a lucky woman in being allowed only ten minutes of everybody's company; at least the chances are in your favour for escaping bores.

I hear of nothing but crash upon crash in London. Leinster and Mary Ross are obliged to join to help Lady Foley. Lord Foley is so completely ruined, it is supposed it will be impossible to save anything for his six unfortunate children, and Lord and Lady Foley cannot have the satisfaction of throwing the blame on one another. He has gambled, and she has had six guineas-apiece handkerchiefs. She has enjoyed the bliss of boasting she never tied a ribbon twice, or wore her sattin three times. I thought I had made a poor marriage, and was content, but I begin to believe that I am a rich individual.

I think you are right about William, I am sure he has taken a quirk about my marriage, because you see, my dear Emmy, it splits upon one of the very rocks of prejudice he has in his character. I would almost say the only one, but then it is a considerable stone, his *worldliness*. He would not have had me marry a regular established fool even he was rich, because again, the world might think the worse of me; but if I could, have met a rich quiet man without bells to his cap, made a good figure in London, and of whom some people might indulgently say—in consideration of his fortune, "Such a one I promise you has more sense than one would think, he is not such a fool as people give him credit for." If I had run the usual race of London misery with such a man, William would not have objected.

It is a crooked corner in him, I have often observed he has a childish respect to the opinion of London; and Paris has done him no good in giving him a notion that it don't signify what people do, so they keep it quiet, and make no open *scandale*. I have often wondered at this, because we mortals always try and trace a consistency in character, which is an ingredient never to be found in any composition, foreign to human nature altogether, which we still hunt after, and refer to and talk of, as if it was not as ideal as the philosopher's stone, a tortoise-shell Tom cat, or any other impossibility you like to think of.

Lady Campbell to Miss Eden.

April 10, 1821.

I have been again at Mount Stuart. Saw a civil Mr. Campbell of Stonefield, whom of course I ought to have called Stonefield *tout court*, but this seemed to me so improper and affectionate. I would not expose my conjugal felicity to such a slur, and I believe I affronted the Laird. He is a great man, having been at Oxford, of course the refined thing in education in Scotland; just as Lansdowne was sent to Scotland to give him a better coating of education. I suppose on the principle that the longest way about is the shortest road home. I see all those who are taken most pains with make the plainest figure. This man seems, however, to have preserved his whole row of Scotch prejudices unshaken, proud, and touchy.

Lady Campbell to Miss Eden.
THAMES DITTON,
July 16, 1821.

DEAREST EMMY, I have been so pestered and worried. I should only have worried you if I had written to you in the midst of my various bothers. I find I have about one half of my baby linen to get made, Aunt Charlotte having handsomely provided the caps and frocks and fineries, but turned me off with only half-a-dozen of everything needful, and not an inch of flannel. You are enough of a mother to enter into my feelings on the occasion.

I have had scene after scene to undergo with Aunt upon the unkindness of my not remaining to be confined here within the compass of a sixpence, and taking everybody's advice, sooner than hers, and, in short, not having her in the room with me. As I should have died of that, self-preservation gave me firmness to resist, and I declared I could not. All this was to be kept smooth to Sir Guy, for Aunt chose to be sulky with him. In short I have found the kindness of the house the cruellest thing on earth. I have not had a quiet moment, the neighbourhood have poured upon me.... Lucy is gone mad, for she is preparing to go to the Coronation. Your affectionate and own

PAM.

Lady Campbell to Miss Eden.
Tuesday, August 14, 1821.

...I am settled in Town since Saturday evening, and if Eastcombe has had reminiscences of me for you, Grosvenor Square has reminisced you to me, our evening walks, and Lady Petre, and Penniwinkle. Every valuable Bore I possess has by instinct discovered me in Town, and I have been surrounded with Clements, Cootes, and Strutts. However I had a visit from Bob as a palliative which supported me under the rest.

It is quite impossible to give an idea of the hurry and scurry of the people in every direction, and as if the rain only increased their ardour. Women with drooping black bonnets and draggled thin cotton gowns, and the men looking wet and *radical* to the skin. I catch myself twaddling and moralising to myself just as I went on about poor Buonaparte. They say fools are the only people who wonder, and I believe there is something in it, for I go on wondering till I feel quite imbecile.

However I own I am shocked (not surprised in this instance) that not a single public office or government concern should be shut. No churches at this end of the town either open, and no bells tolling.

Your small parcel delighted me and is the smartest I had. I have given every direction as to that being the first article worn, for I should not love my child unless it had your things on.

Miss Eden to Miss Villiers.
WOBURN, 1821.

MY DEAR THERESA, There never was a house in which writing flourished so little as it does here, partly that I have been drawing a great deal, and also because they dine at half-past six instead of the rational hour of seven, and in that lost half-hour I know I could do more than in the other twenty-three and a half. After all, I like this visit. It was clever of me to expect the Duchess would be cross, because of course, that insures her being more good-natured than anybody ever was. I am only oppressed at being made so much of. Such a magnificent room, because she was determined I should have the first of the new furniture and the advantage of her society in the mornings, though *in general* she makes it a rule to stay in her own room. In short, you may all be very, very good friends, but the only person who really values my merits is—the Duchess of Bedford, and once safe with her the house is pleasant enough.

We have had the Duncannons. I like her; she is so unlike Lady Jersey. Miss P. is something of a failure in every way, except in intrinsic goodness; but she was terrified here, and at all times dull, and as nearly ugly as is lawful. They have been the only ladies. Then, there are dear little Landseer, Mr. Shelley, so like his mama in look, and a great rattle; Lord Chichester, Lord Charles Russell, etc.; and a tribe of names unknown to fame, headed by a Mr. Garrett, who is a rich shooting clergyman with the most suave complacent manners!—one of those appurtenances to a great house I cannot abide.

Eliza is in the greatest beauty, and is a very nice person altogether. I think Lord Chichester succeeds here, and there is no denying that he is a creditable specimen of a young gentleman of the reign of George IV. We have been on the point of acting, but the Providence that guards *les fous et les ivrognes* evidently keeps an eye on Amateur actors and preserves them from actually treading the boards. Your most affectionate

E. E.

Lady Campbell to Miss Eden.
D'ARQUES, PRÈS DIEPPE,
Le 16 Juillet, 1822.

MY DEAREST EMILY, I have been robbed and pillaged and bored and worried, and hate France as much as ever I did, and so does Guy. Mama has made us a comfortable visit, but alas I cannot stay any longer, and conceive my joy! we let our house here, and return to England for my *Couche*. It almost makes up to me for the business. I shall be in London in August, there to remain six months. To show you how entirely and utterly false it is that you have not always and always had that very large den in my heart, let me beg and entreat that, if you can, you will be in or *near* Town, if you can manage it, during my confinement.

It would be existence to me. Oh Emmy, I have so much to unburthen and talk over with you—and you only. I am much pleased with what I have seen of Mama, and Guy likes her....

Conceive the fuss we have had! My Lansdowne recommended Bridget as my maid; Bridget turned out a thief and has robbed me to the amount of 70 Pounds, and acknowledged the fact before the Police, which is no consolation, her candour not replacing the articles. We declined the other consolation of pursuing her, whipping and branding, and five years detention; but only—mind you!—never trust Jane Kingston, Lady Bath's laundress, for Bridget declares upon oath having sent the things to her—my best lace among the rest.

On searching her things, a fine brodée handkerchief appeared, with Harriet embroidered in the corner, and as she lived with Lady H. Drummond perhaps the House of Drummond might wish to make reclamation.... Your own

PAMELA.

Lady Campbell to Miss Eden.

September 16, 1822.

MY OWN EMILY, Here have I been settling myself to my infinite satisfaction, after having endured the ordeal of France which I went through. Where are you? What are you doing? Remember I have bespoke you, October I expect to lay my egg. If you are within reach—oh, it will be such a comfort to me, I positively thirst to have a talk with you. I am so happy to be in England. Better to live on a crust or a crumb, which is not half so good in England, than upon penny rolls in France.

I understand Lord Worcester is already so bored with his bargain that he is to be pitied according to the good-nature of the world for anything that is passing wrong. It is sad that for the morality of the world, people will not be convinced that illegality and sin are not free from bore and ennui....

Tell me you are at hand or coming, for I downright long to see you, and in my *position* you should not let me long, though it would be no great punishment to have a child like you. Sir Guy sends his particular love to you. Your own affectionate

OLD PAM.

November 22, 1822.

Emily, these trembling lines, guided by a hand weakened by confinement, must speak daggers and penknives to you, for never having taken any written notice of me since you chucked me my child in at the window and went your way. As you come on Monday, I refer all to our meeting.

I want you shockingly.... Come to me soon, dear. Your affectionate

PAMELA.

Lord Auckland to his sister, Miss Eden.

NORMAN COURT,
October 29.

Thank you for your two letters which I would have answered sooner, but we shoot all day and are lazy all the evening.

I am not sure that you knew that Wall had been ill and near losing the sight from one of his eyes. He is considerably better, and shoots as usual, and has no doubt of perfectly recovering.

My trip to Fonthill was an amusing way of passing a spare day, and has left a strong impression of the immeasurable folly with which money may be spent. The house is too absurd, but the grounds are beautiful. Lansdowne has bought some pictures there which he was anxious for, as they belonged to his father. I have just heard from him. He is going for a few weeks to Paris, and like everybody else, is expecting you and me to pay him a good long visit at the end of the year. In his mild rational way he exceedingly regrets that the Cortes have not cut off the head of Ferdinand.

Lady Campbell to Miss Eden.

MY DARLING EM, Your letter has revived me, for I was smothered with Fog and so obfuscated I found myself growing callous of the density of the gloom, and my perception of my own dirt and my neighbour's grimness was diminishing. I was getting hardened, when your letter and a gleam of dingy yellow sun showed me the state of myself and the children, and I went up and washed myself and repented of my filth. The fog prevented Mrs. Colvile coming, which is provoking. I wanted to show her my boy; she has put so many of them together, she has an experienced eye on the subject....

The Ladies Fitz-Patrick, old Mrs. Smith, etc., are cooking up a match between Vernon Smith and Mary Wilson, old Lord Ossory's natural daughter with much money.

Emily does it strike you that vices are wonderfully prolific among the Whigs? There are such countless illegitimates among them, such a tribe of Children of the Mist.... Your own

PAM.

Lady Campbell to Miss Eden.

January 6, 1823.
Twelfth Night or what you will.

MY DARLING EMMY, Thank God you have written at last, I have worked myself into a fright this day or two that you were very ill. I have been very poorly, but am better. You are mistaken about that sucking lump being a favourite. I esteem him; he is a man of strict probity and integrity with steady principles, and he is a man would make any reasonable woman very happy in domestic life; but there is a refinement and charm in that Cain that makes a fool of me,—a great fool, for she don't much care for me, and is radically vicious.

We have got a house between Reading and Basingstoke, a mile from Strathfieldsaye, at a village called Strathfield Turgess:—delightful prospect, well furnished, roomy, with Cow and poultry included, garden meadow, for £84 per annum.

Lady Louisa Lennox had rather taken my fancy, and that negative mind of being Anti-Bathurst is a jewel in their favour. Emily, to have it gravely told me Lady Georgina Bathurst is a strong-headed woman, superior, with wonderful abilities, etc. *Cela m'irrite la bile*, when I know her to be prejudiced, worldly, entrenched by prejudices upon prejudice, till her very soul is straightened within the narrow limit of the Ministers, their wives, and her own family....

How is your Grantham? My Lansdowne is playing at *de petits jeux innocents*. I am of a guilty inclination and cannot taste those social innocences, besides, Emmy, we don't do such things well in England, it don't suit well, and to fail in a triviality is failure indeed, but the Wilt loves a caper. All this is very well, but I want to talk to you, Emmy. I have such quantities I cannot even tap in a letter, that I could talk out just in one ½ hour.

Louisa Napier is with Lady Londonderry, and the account I think very horrid. Every thing at Cray goes on the same, conversation, laughing, novels, light books, the attaches and habitués coming in, the very red boxes of office left in their places, not a shade of difference in her occupations, amusements or mode of life.

She seems as if determined there shall be no change. This may be fortitude, to me it is frightful. That habits should be so cherished and so rooted as to withstand such a shock as the disappearance of the only object she is ever supposed to have loved by Death, and such a death, is wonderful, and not to be understood if it is upon principles so erroneous....

I dined with the Wellesleys yesterday. Mr. Wellesley acknowledges having been distractedly in love with Sister, and was so pleased to see her at Hastings. He hopes you like the place. His son Arthur is such a cub, and thinks himself so very *every* thing, it made me quite low. Of the Wellesley girls, the top and bottom dish, or eldest and youngest, are of the specie Geese—the middle ones, Georgina and Mary, are quite delightful, and very uncommon in their way.

Lady Campbell to Miss Eden.

April 11, 1824.

Thank you for your last letter, thank you for Lord Lansdowne's after laugh, but thank you above all, for being still my own Emmy just the same as ever. I suppose you are going to Captain Parry's *fête* on board the *Hecla*, announced in the newspaper. I think he might have asked me, and then I could have got over his ordering all this snow from Gunter's. However I think he has rather overdone it. I understand there is to be a whole course of Walrus.

I had a letter from Sister, written at Lady Sarah's the day she left Strathfieldsaye. She is full of good, and agreeable; but yet, I never should be able to be quite friends with her. There is some gall about her which would always give me an afterthought, and keep me perhaps more on my guard with her than with many others who might betray me faster.

I wish you could have seen us all, we were so ill-sorted. As for poor Sister, among three Eton boys, one Oxford *merveilleux*, 2 silent girls, 1 military clergyman, 2 Colonels, some dancing country neighbours all wound up and going, I don't know how she survives. By the bye tell me what are a Mr. Adderley and a Miss Adderley to her? Something? Lord Buckinghamshire's legitimates by a former marriage, or Sister's illegitimates, or both their children, or no children at all? I was asked and could not tell. Don't racket yourself to death. I, who no longer sit at good men's feasts, certainly may magnify the fatigue, but I am sure you do too much.

May, 1824.—There is some saying, Chinese I believe, about not letting grass grow between friends, or words to that effect. Now, you must allow I have mowed it twice, but you will not keep it down, and if you will not, what's to be done?

Lucy is coming to me to-morrow in spite of her resolutions never to be with me during a groaning. Mrs. Napier, too, who is staying at Farm House with her husband and a few children, wishes much to be with me, and it will, I know, end in my running away into some Barn, like a Cat, to kitten in peace. No, my dear Emmy, you are the only person that can be agreeable to me even in a lying-in—*c'est tout dire*.

Lucy tells me she saw dear Robert, greatly to her satisfaction, one stray day she spent in London. So odd! for in general those are the particular days one can look out no face one ever saw before, unless one happens to be ill-dressed or in any disgraceful predicament of Hackney coach or bad company.... But strange to say, Lucy met Robert with decency and without distress. She says he is just the same, only sunburnt. How I wish I could see him, if he has any houses of low price and good dimensions, and furnished suited to a genteel but *indigent* or indignant Family? There is a talk of our leaving this, as the Landlord wishes to live here himself, and I should like to belong to Robert's flock, of being one of his *Ouailles*.

Lady Campbell to Miss Eden.

TURGESS,
May 14, 1824.

DEAREST EMMY, I was quite sorry I had sent my letter when the day after I found I was at liberty to talk about William de Roos's marriage. I am all delighted, and all that, and all I should be when I see him so happy. But tho' I have been going thro' all the palliating influence of confidant and in his secret, and within the mark of all hopes, and fears, and difficulties, yet I cannot shake off the idea that she is not good enough, he is *selon moi* such a dear creature, so much beyond the common run of man, of young men. Of course I rely on your keeping this alongside with your own ideas on the subject.

I believe she is improved, and I liked her once, when first she came out, and you know we certainly sober in this world unless we go mad; perhaps she may have taken that turn. In short there is much in her favour, but while he was marrying a beggar he might have had a pleasanter, but opportunity does all those things, there is no choice in the case. One negative advantage I have never lost sight of, she is not a Bathurst.

I do regret bitterly not seeing Robert. If I was not childing, I could have had a room for him, but somehow I shall be lying-in in every room and all over the place. Give my love to him and ask him seriously, if he knows of a family house that could suit us, as Sir Guy and I are very likely to find all the world before us next February, like Adam and Eve, only with better clothes and more children.

Is not it so like William de Roos to go to Ireland to avoid the wishing joy? He had business certainly, but still nobody but him could do such a thing. Many thanks for solving Sister's acidities for me. Your own

PAMELA.

Lady Campbell to Miss Eden.

Sunday, June 20, 1824.

DEAR EMMY, Yes, yes, you may still show pleasure, surprise, emotion, on seeing my handwriting again. Here, alas, my reign is over, my rôle of lying-in.... One month, one little month, was scarce allowed me; and I was again dragged into the vulgar tumult of common barren life. Provoking and vexatious events are no longer kept from my knowledge, the hush and tiptoe are forgotten, the terror of my agitation has ceased, the glory of Israel is departed! The truth is I am too well; there is no pathos, no dignity, no interest, in rude health, and consequently I meet with no respect. I have not even been allowed to read *Redgauntlet* in seclusion, and chickens and tit-bits have given way to mutton chops and the coarse nutrition adapted to an unimpaired constitution.

Emily! let me be a warning if you wish to preserve the regard of your friends, the respect of your acquaintance, consideration, attention, in short, all social benefits, don't get well—never know an hour's health.

I have got into a fit of nonsense, as you will perceive, a sort of letter-giggle; seriously now I want to hear from you, to know how you are.... Sir Guy is gone to Town to see his sister off to France. He is to sleep to-night in *Water Lane*, which sounds damp, but is convenient to the Steamboat by which Fanny Campbell sails or boils to Calais.... Your own

PAMELA.

Lady Campbell to Miss Eden.

STRATHFIELD TURGESS,
June 1824.

I wish I knew how you are, and where you are. William de Roos is the happiest of men, and Lady G. has won Uncle Henry's heart at Strangford by taking to gardening; I do hope it may turn out well and shame the Devil....

As I stood looking over a heap of weeds that were burning, they struck my own mind, as being somewhat like itself, you could see no flame, you could see no fire, and yet it was surely tho' slowly consuming to ashes. Now you see my indolence does just the same to my better qualities. There is no outraged sin, no crying vice, and yet this indolence eats into my life.

If you will but keep me in order, and pity my infirmities, when can you come to me?...

The great House is a bore, *selon moi*, but I will tell you all about it when you come. I have just read Hayley; considering I don't think him a Poet, nor his life eventful, I wonder why one reads it? The truth is, we are all, I believe, so fond of knowing other people's business, we would read anybody's life.

July 9, 1824.

Many thanks for your letter. It did indeed make my country eyes stare, and put me in such a bustle as if I had all you did—to do. I have had a great combat, but pride shall give way, and candour shall cement our friendship. The paragraph in your letter about Lord E. threw me into consternation, as well as those who might have known better, for, Emily, he has not written me a word about it, and would you believe it? I don't know who he is going to marry.... You rolled your pen in such a fine frenzy that I cannot read your version of his name no more than if it had been written with one of the lost legs of the spider tribe. I see it begins with a B., but the rest dissolves like the bad half of those prayers to Jupiter in Air.

I believe I should make your city hair friz again, if I were to detail my country week's work. However, I will be cautious. I won't speak too much of myself, which for want of extraneous matters, I might be led to do.... You keep very bad company with *them* Player-men, those Horticultural Cultivators of the Devil's hot-bed.

I suppose I shall hear you talk of the Sock and Buskin; it is all that Cassiobury connexion that makes you so lax.

Miss Eden to her Niece, Eleanor Colvile.

SPROTBOROUGH,
Sunday.

MY DEAR ELEANOR, Your Mamma seems to think you may like to have a letter, and I am vainly trying to persuade myself I like to write one.

The Miss Copleys have their Sunday School just the same as ours, with the Butcher's daughter and the Shop-woman for teachers; not quite so many children as we have; but in all other respects the two schools are as like as may be, and they are there all Sunday, which gives me time for writing.

Maria has just been telling a story of a Christening that makes me laugh. She and her sister stood Godmothers to two little twins in the village, and carried them to church. The children were only a fortnight old, and therefore were much wrapped up, and Miss Copley, who is not used to handling children, carried hers with the feet considerably higher than the head. She gave it carefully to the clergyman when he was to christen it, and together they undid its cloak in search of its face, and found two little red feet. They were so surprised at this that the clergyman looked up in her face and said: "Why, then, where is its head?" And she, being just as much frightened, answered: "I really cannot think." Maria at last suggested that in all probability the head would be at the opposite end of the bundle from the feet, and so it proved.

Good-bye, dear Eleanor, mind you get better. It is foolish to be ill; I found it so myself. Love to all. Your affectionate Aunt,

E. E.

Miss Eden to Miss Villiers.

, STONEY MIDDLETON,
August 1824.

MY DEAR MISS VILLIERS, George has gone to Scotland to kill the poor dumb grouse (or *grice*), as they ought to be in the plural, but I will transmit your direction to him, and if he can do what you wish I daresay he will, though I have an idea it is the sort of thing about which people chuse to look really important, and say they cannot interfere.

...Dear Lady Chichester! How lucky it is that people's letters are so like themselves. It is perhaps not unnatural but amusing too, I did not know till Lady Buckinghamshire mentioned it the other day when she was talking of this marriage that the Chichesters have the strongest possible feeling on the subject of connexion, and she said they would look on this marriage as a positive calamity. How very absurd it is, and it is a shame of Lady Chichester to exaggerate George Osborne's faults so much. He was not in fact very much to blame, in his disagreement with Lord Francis, and if it were not the way of the Osborne family to make their family politics the subject of their jokes to all the world, George would have been reckoned just as good as any boy of his age. I imagine that even Lord Chichester has found *his* son liked his own way as well as the rest of the world, but perhaps Lady Chichester and he do not impart to each other the little difficulties they find with those separate little families you mention....

We are so settled here that it seems as if we had never gone away, I believe one changes one's self as well as *Horses* at Barnet, I lose all my recollections of London, "that great city where the geese are all swans and the fools are all witty" and take up the character of the Minister's sister, as I hear myself called in the village. Robert's house is very comfortable, and I think this much the most beautiful country I have seen since I saw the Pyrenees. Some people might think it verging on the extreme of picturesque and call it wild, but I love a mountainous country. I go sketching about with the slightest success, the rocks are too large and obstinate and won't be drawn.

Mrs. Lamb came here Sunday, and we must return the visit some day, but by a great mercy I broke the spring of the pony carriage the other day. Your ever affectionate

E. E.

CHAPTER IV

1825-1827

Miss Eden to Miss Villiers.
Eyam,
Saturday.

MY DEAR MISS VILLIERS, What a shame it is that I should have been so long writing to you, particularly after Mrs. Villiers had made the discovery that my letters amused her. My sister Louisa and four of her children passed a fortnight here at the end of last month, and our whole time was spent in "exploring in the barouche landau," as Mrs. Elton observes.

By the time I have had nine or ten more of my sisters here, and thirty or forty of their children, I shall be tired of my own enthusiasm in the great picturesque cause; but at present all other employments are sacrificed to it. However, it may amuse you.

I shall continue to think a visit to Chatsworth a very great trouble. You are probably right in thinking the Duke takes pleasure in making people do what they don't like, and that accounts for his asking me so often. We have now made a rule to accept one invitation out of two. We go there with the best dispositions, wishing to be amused, liking the people we meet there, loyal and well affected to the King of the Peak himself, supported by the knowledge that in the eyes of the neighbourhood we are covering ourselves with glory by frequenting the *great house*; but with all these helps we have never been able to stay above two days there without finding change of air absolutely necessary,—never could turn the corner of the third day,—at the end of the second the great depths of *bore* were broken up and carried all before them: we were obliged to pretend that some christening, or a grand funeral, or some pressing case of wedding (in this country it is sometimes expedient to hurry the performance of the marriage ceremony) required Robert's immediate return home, and so we departed yawning. It is odd it should be so dull. The G. Lambs are both pleasant, and so is Mr. Foster and Mrs. Cavendish and a great many of the habitués of Chatsworth; and though I have not yet attained the real Derbyshire feeling which would bring tears of admiration into my eyes whenever the Duke observed that it was a fine day, yet I think him pleasant, and like him very much, and can make him hear without any difficulty, and he is very hospitable and wishes us to bring all our friends and relations there, if that would do us any good. But we happen to be *pleasanter* at home. However private vices may contribute to public benefit, I do not see how private bore can contribute to public happiness, do you?

Pray give my love to your mother, and believe me, your affectionate

E. E.

Miss Eden to her Sister, Lady Buckinghamshire.
LANGLEY,
July 15, 1825.

MY DEAREST SISTER, Do you recollect my asking you whether you would give us a dinner in the course of the year? Well, at one of our pleasant dinners the other day we were all so mortal agreeable that we settled we should go to Astley's on the 18th. The party consisted of Maria Copley, Lord Henry Thynne, Colonel Arden, Mr. Wall, Henry Eden, and our three selves. To that it was necessary to add for decency's sake Sir Joseph and Coppy. It occurred to me this afternoon whilst murmuring over the heat, which is extremely unpleasant, that Astley's would be the death of us all, and that if the weather continued in its present state, it would be better to change it for a water party.

It would be very pleasant if your carriage and two or three of those nice little poney-carriages you keep on the heather were to meet us at the water-side to bring us to your nice little place, and you receive us in your nice little way, and give us a nice little collation at about 6 o'clock, and let us walk about the place and then leave you, and talk you well over in the boat, as we go back again.

In the first place, these are all the people whom you have read about over and over again, and whom you are dying to see. Then, though they are ten now, yet by the end of the week they will not be above seven or eight.

Sir Joseph hates the water, so as I mean to make a vacancy for the present list I will ask your own Mr. G. Villiers to come with us, and he will be *such* a support to you. Well, what do you think?

My own interest in the question is this: that I am going to establish a coolness between myself and Lord Henry, who is exposing me to the remarks of the invidious public without any earthly purpose; and I had all the advantage at Burlington House on Thursday of being supposed to be honoured by a proposal from him in the face of many curious spectators, when he was imparting to me his intentions of admiring another person more than me. I do not know whether it was fun or spite, or a tryal of my feelings, or whether he is serious; but as I found that I did not care which it was, I do not mean to favour the world with the sight of any more such long conversations. It amuses them more than it does me, and henceforth I mean not to let him go *tagging* after me as he has done lately. The Astley party was made before this wise resolution, and I want to change it to a water-party, which will cut him out without offending him, as he never goes on fresh water, and we will ask Mr. Villiers in his place.

Don't let yourself be frightened, you will find us so pleasant.

Good-night. I can't help laughing when I see myself introducing the Colonel to you. Your most affectionate

E. E.

Miss Eden to Miss Villiers.
SPROTBRO',
Sunday, 1825.

You must have got hold of some other family in the same street. It is not *my* story you are telling me. I am Emily Eden, of No. 30, who has been marrying a brother in Derbyshire; then has been to Kent to visit a married sister; then found another sister setting off into Yorkshire, and took advantage of an offered place in her carriage and was deposited yesterday at Sprotbro'. I am really delighted that Mrs. Villiers is getting better. Is not Doctor Pidcock the man who cured Mr. H. Greville and whom Mrs. Villiers abused with unusual injustice, first because he was a doctor and no doctor could be of any use to anybody, and next because he was a quack and therefore no doctor. He is taking such a generous revenge! heaping such large coals of fire on her head! I hope he will go on, dear man!—skuttle-full after skuttle-full of fiery coals till she is quite well.

I saw your brother riding up the deep solitudes of Parliament Street the day I drove through London. It was an awful sight. The street so quiet you might have heard a pin drop.

Sister and I left Eastcombe last Monday and went to Gog Magog. I invited myself of course, but Charlotte bore it very well. I was there fifteen years ago in the capacity of a child: I therefore did not see much of her, or know anything of her, and except that, have not seen her but for two or three morning visits per annum; so it was a voyage of discovery, in the style of a North Pole expedition. The Frost intense— and a good deal of *hummocky* ice to sail through. However, I really liked it much better than I expected. Lord Francis is particularly pleasant in his own house, and young Charlotte very civil and good-natured. I found *nine* letters yesterday here and have had two more to-day, all requiring answers. I mean to put my death in the papers. It would be cheaper than if I really were to die from the over-exertion of writing eleven letters.

Robert's new relations write to me, which is kind, but hard, as I must answer them. Lord Bexley has given Robert the living of Hertingfordbury. I have written so much about it lately, that I have at last forgotten how to spell it, and I am, beside, related to it, and am in the habit of familiarly terming it Hert.

Robert leaves this place next week. At first we thought he was going to be immensely rich, but dear Lord Bexley in a fit of conscientiousness divided from Hertingfordbury the living of St. Andrews, which has been given with it for the last 150 years. He thinks it will be a good example to his successors if he divides them in a case where he has a nearer interest, as in a brother-in-law. I can't guess what his successor may think, and never shall know probably, as I never look to be Chancellor of the Duchy; but I can tell him that I think his relations think it extremely unpleasant, and it makes the benefit rather a doubtful one.

However, it is very good of him, only it is a pity where the principle is so good the result is not more agreeable. And he is so complacent and pleased with his decision! I have found out he is just what a sea-Captain said of one of Wesley's preachers: "a heavenly-minded little Devil." Your ever affectionate

E. E.

Monday.—I was prevented by a very long ride on Saturday from sending this. I am so grieved to see poor Captain Russell's death in the paper. It is not formally announced, but I see it in the Ship news mentioned by the captain of some other ship. Perhaps it may not be true, but yet I fear it is. I saw Eliza the other day in her way from Scotland, as I believe I told you, and she talked with such pleasure of her brother George's promotion. I had a letter from her a fortnight ago delighted that he had escaped the fever which his ship's company had all had. Poor thing! I am so sorry for her. She was so fond of him, and the unexpected loss of a dearly loved brother is a grief that must, like all others, be endured, but one that, God knows, time itself cannot heal, and hardly mitigate. I wonder where Eliza is now—whether they are gone to Paris. If you hear anything of her or of Captain Russell's death will you let me know? I suppose everybody feels most for the calamity under which they themselves have suffered, and from my very heart I pity Eliza, and it was impossible not to like Captain Russell for his own sake.

Good-bye, dear Theresa. Your ever affectionate

E. E.

Miss Eden to Miss Villiers.
HERTINGFORDBURY,
1825.

I say Theresa, I shall be in Grosvenor Street on Tuesday from twelve to four. Please, if you are in the land of the living, commonly called Knightsbridge, to come and see me and we will talk a few.

We (thereby meaning Robert, his wife, and me) arrived here from Derbyshire last night, and are quite delighted with this place. It is a real country place, not like a parsonage, with a little park something in the Irish class of parks, but with fine trees in it and a pretty garden, and everything very nice.

We are just come back from our first church here. There are a great many *nervous* points in a clergyman's life, and I think the first interview with his parishioners rather awful. I remember the time when I used to think a clergyman's life the most pitiable thing in the world. I am wiser now, and can see the numerous advantages a man has whose duties and pleasures must necessarily be one and the same thing.

Robert preached to-day a sermon I wrote, and to my horror I detected a disguised quotation from Shakespeare in an imposing part of it, which was not obvious till it was read aloud. However, it was probably not very apparent to anybody but myself. I was rather in hopes of seeing you in a corner of the Cowper pew, but it was quite empty. Well, I can't stay chattering here all day. Your ever affectionate

E. EDEN.

Miss Eden to her Sister, Fanny Eden.
LANGLEY FARM, BECKENHAM, KENT,
November 11, 1825.

MY DEAREST FANNY, Begin writing to me again forthwith. I have heard from the Copleys with fresh plans for my going there, so that I should not have been in want of a house.

Mary says Mr. H. Greville is so cross she does not know what to do with him. What if it is love for Isabella Forester. She is sorry he is so foolish, and if it is bile—she is sorry he does not take more pills.

Why, Foolish the 5th, don't you remember my white muslin gown with tucks and blue stars between them, and the body done with blue braiding, and I wore it the Chatham day, and it smelt of the tobacco old gentlemen were pleased to smoke in our faces, so I would not let it be washed for their dirty sakes till Wright showed it me by daylight and told me I was probably not aware I had worn it 30 times. And to be sure it was not the cleaner for it. Still, it grieved me to have it washed. I shall go and see our Caroline in town and shall come down with all my hair stroked up the wrong way by her remarks. Your most affectionate

E. E.

Lady Campbell to Miss Eden.

January 13, 1826.

MY DEAREST EMILY, I never was so provoked in my life at anything, and I cursed the aristocracy of the country, and I was told of it as coolly as if it was a distress in Ireland. Seriously, what provoked me was her never telling me till after it was all given up, and put an end to, for thank Heaven I have a small house, and therefore can always make room, and I could perfectly have put up Fanny, and you, and your maid.

I had the gratification of seeing the whole party swamped in Crambo, and water-logged in Charades, and a large party writhing in the agonies of English Xmas conviviality, without any young ladies, without any music to break the awful solemnity of the evening, and no Lord Auckland to make them gamesome.

Lord Dudley was their wit, and as there was nobody to play with him, I saw he tried to domesticate himself, as he could make nothing of his jokes, or, what was worse, saw them torn to pieces before his eyes by the avidity with which the hungry society seized on them, to support themselves thro' the day. But who could even domesticate in that drawing-room?

Sir Guy nearly died of Crambo, and was very near taking a Dictionary with him the next time. But as he is not at all of the go-along tribe he kicked, and would not cramb.

The event of the next time was Charades, and our enthusiasm knew no bounds when Lord Dudley joined the crew, and appeared with his coat turned inside out, and enacted a chimney-sweeper, and rattled a stick upon a bit of wood. Our rapture was indescribable, and it reminded me of the feelings of those who in ancient times beheld great men doing little things! Anecdotes which Historians always dwell on with that delight which human beings naturally feel on seeing a dry patch in a bog, or a green patch in a waste—the man who ploughed in Rome after heading the Yeomanry or Militia of the Republic; the man who picked up shells near the same place; that other who had the horticultural turn for sowing Lettuces—all these men were nothing in effect to Lord Dudley playing at sweep. I felt it deeply.

It was that day too he said when they offered him toasted cheese, "Ah! yes; to-day is Toasted-cheese day, and yesterday was Herring day!!"

How we all laughed!!!

How goodly is it to earn fair Fame! Once get your charter for a Wit, and you may sit down with all the comfort of being a fool for the rest of your life. One joke a year—not so much—even one *bad* joke now and then, is a better tenure than all those forms of carrying a Hawk, or the King's Pepper-box, at the Coronation, for an estate.

We had a ball at Bowood the night before Twelfth Night. It went off very well indeed. I had the pleasure of cramming my small Pam into a pink body and seeing it dance, and seeing everybody make a fuss with it because it was by many degrees the smallest thing in the room....

No; there never, never, never, was anything so cross as your not coming to Bowood this year, because I had looked to it just as you did, and had even distressed myself about how I should manage to see enough of you, and whether Lady Lansdowne would facilitate our intercourse, and I meant to show you all my new editions of children, and even make you superintend the new one, for certainly the one you picked up in Cadogan Place is the prettiest of the whole set. I cannot tell you how kind Lady Lansdowne is to me, and she need be so after putting you off; but she does really load me with kindnesses. However, we are not to stay in this house. It smokes and is too dear for us, so alas! I am again hunting a domicile. We get poorer and poorer, but as Guy bears it better and better, I don't mind.

I am glad you see William. He is so dear a creature! His Family cannot forgive him for having picked out a little happiness for himself his own way.... Your affectionate

Pamela C.

Miss Eden to Miss Villiers.

March 30.

MY DEAR THERESA, Robert and his wife are coming for a week to Grosvenor Street, and I must be there to order their dinner and sweep their room, so I shall go there on Saturday and stay in town ten days. I shall be very glad to see you again. Pray come as soon as you can—Saturday afternoon if possible. I want you to come in the light of something good, to take the taste of going back to London out of my mouth. It is an ugly place, is it not? Probably I shall forget my troubles to-morrow if I do not *fix* them by mentioning them to you to-day. I always find that when I have withstood a strong temptation to mention to my friend the worry of the moment, it ceases to be a worry much sooner than the grief which has gone through the process of discussion. But the struggle is unpleasant.

I liked Malachi particularly. I have not seen the answers, but hear they are very amusing, which is a pity. I have long vowed never to be amused by anything Mr. Croker should say or do, be it ever so entertaining, and "shall I lay perjury on my precious soul?" as Shylock says, for a mere pamphlet?

I have been trying to read *The Last of the Mohicans* and have come to a full stop at the end of the first volume. I am sure you will not like it. Those vulgar Mohicans only wear one long scalp-lock of hair—they don't *crêper*! Nasty savages! And so far from wearing full sleeves, it is painfully obvious that they wear no sleeves at all, and not much else in matter of cloathes.

Have you been uneasy about Sarah? Sister would have been if she could, but it came out unfortunately by the admission of those who saw her, that she had not been quite so ill as angry, and Sister weakly goes backwards and forwards to London on the chance of being admitted, and then hears Sarah is gone out airing. They say it is a fine sight to see the preparations for her airing. She "plays such fantastic tricks before high heaven" and the clerks of the Treasury; but whether she has succeeded in making any "angel weep" but dear Robin, I do not know. However, it is wrong to laugh, because I believe nervous complaints are great suffering, and at all events poor Mr. R. was frightened.

Good-bye, my love to your mother. Your most affectionate

E. E.

Miss Eden to Miss Villiers.

TUNBRIDGE WELLS, *Sunday, August 6.*

DEAREST THERESA, I had such a desire to write to you yesterday because it was not post day and I had no frank, and to-day it goes all against the grain, because I have plenty of time and George is come back to give me a frank and my letter can go. But you always make me write first; why, I never make out. Have you any good reason for it?

Our Tunbridge speculation is answering so well to us. I always knew I should like it, but George's content, indeed actual enjoyment of the place and way of life, surprises me. We have such a clean house, just finished, and we are its first inhabitants, so we run no hazard of being devoured by a flea hacknied in the arts of devouring and tormenting. I was just going to bother myself by inventing a description of our way of life, when George showed me his answer to a vain-glorious description of the joys of Worthing, which Mr. Wall, who is living there, has just sent, meaning to put us out of conceit with Tunbridge by the vulgar notion of the Agar-Ellis' man-cook and carriage and four, and so I shall copy part of George's answer.

It opens with a moral: "We are better off and happier than is properly compatible with a life of innocence and vegetation. Our house is delightfully clean and comfortable. The living very good. Fish caught at eight in the morning at Hastings is devoured here at three. The eggs, cream, and butter, are brought to us in an hourly succession of freshness. All the material of the kitchen excellent, and the appetite too pure to think that it is a female that cooks it. Then a few glasses of hock and some coffee, and an hour's repose, and we meet at Lady C. Greville's, Alvanley and his sisters, and the F. Levesons. We assort ourselves upon horses, into barouches, etc., and start for some of our inexhaustible lions; and we end our evening together with the feast of nonsense and the flow of tea." He ends his letter with a promise to be at Norman Court the 1st of September, and adds, "My guns are at home and the locks click sweetly. Water the turnips when it does not rain."

How much more foolish men are than women, particularly about their amusements. We none of us write to each other about our white sattin gowns that are hanging sweetly up at home.

George does not mention what is I think the most curious part of our life—that I am actually dressed and down at the Wells every morning before half-past eight, and he generally arrives only five minutes later. We dine at three and go to bed at eleven, and are in a ravenous state of hunger at all hours; and the consequence is that I can already walk three or four miles without being tired.

The Duchess of Kent arrived two days ago, and we live in a transport of loyalty. We insisted on illuminating for her and dragging her into the town, which naturally alarmed her, so she put off coming, meaning to step in unobserved. But that our loyalty could not suffer; and I never stepped out without 50 yards of rope in one pocket, and a Roman candle in the other, for fear of accidents. However, I believe she was allowed to drive up to her own door, but there were some fine illuminations afterwards.

Lord Alvanley is an amusing incident at this sort of place, and it is a pity he is not more likeable, because there is certainly nobody more amusing. He goes away Tuesday, but he liked it so much he means to come back again. We all parted yesterday evening, quite worn out with laughing, and yet I cannot recollect what he said. But it was very delightful. Except these tea-drinkings we could not be quieter or more independent in a country home of our own. Nobody visits of a morning, and in the evenings they are all in their coloured morning dresses.

You will be happy to hear that our three-shilling coarse straw bonnets are only a shade too good for the style of dress here.

I wish you were here. The man who built this house might have guessed we should like to have you. The upholsterer knew it, for there are more beds than enough, two in each room, but there are only three good bedrooms, and neither Fanny nor I could sleep except in a room by ourselves. But you must let me know your plans, because George will be obliged to go away in a fortnight more, and unless any of my sisters mean to take his place, which I do not suppose they will do, I think you might give us a visit. It is the sort of life you would like. I have not done so much drawing for years as during the last week. I have copied those six Prints on six cards for that tiresome Hertford fair, and they looked so pretty in that small shape I was quite sorry to send them to Robert.

What nice weather you have for your Gravesend expedition. Is the great review of Tide-waiters taking place to-day? I have not the least idea what they are, what are the origin, manners, and customs of the nation of Tide-waiters? If they are people who wait till the tide serves they will flourish for ever. The poor dear tide never serves anybody, and if they gain their bread by tide-waiting, what floods of tears they must shed at Othello's description of the Pontic Sea, which knows no retiring ebb....

I am decidedly in what Swift calls "a high vein of silliness" this afternoon; but it is the fault of the weather and of being in the country, which, after all, is the only thing that makes actual happiness. Your affectionate

E. E.

Miss Eden to Miss Villiers.

THE GRANGE,
Sunday, 1826.

MY DEAREST THERESA, I should have written sooner to tell you where to write to me, but I was rather in hopes George would let me stay another month at Tunbridge. Everybody was going away, so we might have had a very small house for half the price we gave for ours, and as the servants will eat whether they are there or in Grosvenor Street, I thought we might have lived more economically than in posting all over England. However, after much correspondence, George, who terrifies me by the way in which he spends his own money, settled that the expenses were nearly equal, and that being the case that he would rather have us with him. "I never met with such an instance of politeness all my life," as the immortal Collins observes,—not the Professor Collins, but the far greater "Pride and Prejudice" Collins. And so we packed up and came here, and I expect George and Mr. Wall to arrive every minute.

In shooting season they only travel on Sundays, I observe. We lived at Tunbridge almost entirely with the F. Levesons. I had a great idea that I should dislike her, which was a mistake, and if I were given to *engouements*, I should suppose I were suffering under one now for her, only it came very gradually, which is not the case with that complaint, I believe. First a decrease of dislike, and then not caring whether she were in the room or not, and then a willingness to walk towards her house, and then an impossibility to walk in any other direction.

The last fortnight we had the de Roos's, who dined with the F. Levesons's as often as we did, or else we all dined with the Peels; and if we dined early, we rode after dinner and met again for tea. I can ride four hours at a time now without the least fatigue and walk in proportion. I like the Peels too, only I wish Lady Jane would bind him apprentice to a tinker, or a shoemaker, or to anybody who would make him work, as he seems to have an objection to the liberal professions. From mere want of employment, he has fancied himself into bad health, and does nothing but hold a smelling-bottle to his nose all day, even at dinner. How it would annoy me if I were his wife!—because he has talents enough, and can be pleasant when he is roused. I cannot think how any clever man who has not estate enough to find his property an occupation, can consent to be thrown by his own choice out of all professions. I should be a lawyer to-morrow if I were Lawrence Peel, or a lawyer's wife if I were Lady Jane. She might persuade him into it I am sure, if she would try, and it would be so much better economy than consulting Doctor Mayo three times a day, which he does sometimes.

There is nobody here but Lord Carnarvon and his daughter, and Mr. Newton the painter, and one of the sons of the house. This is such a delicious house now it is finished, and heaps of new books and good pictures.

I intend to make much of a friendship with Newton. Mr. Baring tells me he has seen a great deal of you, which is an additional reason why I should make his acquaintance. He seems to me clever and paradoxical and a little Yankeeish and perhaps conceited, but that picture of Macheath is a great *set off* against any faults he may have. It is impossible, too, that I can know anything about him, as I only saw him for five minutes at the other end of the breakfast-table; but I like to state my first impressions. They are invariably wrong, and now I know that, they are just as good as if they were right, I may believe with much assurance the contrary of what I think.

Is your brother George in town? And did I fancy, or could he have told me that I might enclose to him at the Custom House a parcel above the usual weight. I want to send to my sister-in-law some interesting little caps I have been making which will not be much above weight. Your most affectionate

E. E.

Miss Eden to Miss Villiers.

HERTINGFORDBURY,
Monday, September, 1826.

MY DEAREST THERESA, Your account of yourself pleases me, partly because it is evident the proper remedy for your illness has been found out, and also because you write so much more legibly, which is a good sign....

I do not know what state of appetite you are in or how much you eat, but could not you live lower, and so require fewer leeches? Give up that egg you mix so neatly with your tea and put on the leeches less.

You ask if I care about the present state of politics? Why, dear child, I never cared for anything half so much in my life,—almost to the pass of being sorry I am out of town this week. I am trying to *subside*, simply because I do not think any of our people will get anything in the scramble; but still it is amusing to see such a mess as all the other side is in, and any change must be for the better, you know we think....

I doubt if the Chancellor is safely out yet. He writes such characteristic letters to an old sister-in-law of his who lives in this village, talking of his release from fatigues that were too much for him, and rest for his few remaining days, etc.

We dined at Panshanger yesterday. Lady Cowper is miserable at being out of all the ferment of London. She is a Whig only by marriage, I suspect, and a regular courtier at heart, but talks bravely just now, with only occasional regrets that the Duke of Wellington should have been so *ill-advised*....

I saw Lady Ouseley yesterday and she is quite aware how ill you have been, and that you could not write to her. I never can give my mind to her conversation, but she looked very melancholy, and yet I cannot recollect that she mentioned any misfortune except that Sir Gore had the rheumatism. Janie looked to me like a standing misfortune. She is so very plain, and she does not pay the slightest attention to her poor melancholy mother.

I am glad you are reading those books. To be sure, you are reading Boswell's *Life of Johnson* only now. I knew that, the *Memoires de Retz*, Shakespeare, and a great part of the Bible, almost by heart before I was eleven years old; so then there was not a thought left for me to think upon manners, men, imagination, or morals. Everything is in those books. On scientific subjects I never could understand other people's thoughts, and am guiltless of having had one of my own even on the simplest question. My sentiment, later in life, I took by the lump, in absolute cwts. out of *Corinne* and Lord Byron's Poems, and so, as I said before, I have never had a thought of my own and I do not believe any of us can, in the way we are all educated; and I suppose it is lucky, as they would be foolish thoughts probably if they came.

God bless you, dear, and go on getting better. Your ever affectionate

E. E.

Miss Eden to Miss Villiers.

BOWOOD,
September 24, 1826.

MY DEAR THERESA, I am in such a bad mood for writing, that I could not set about it with a worse grace, only you will not write to me if I do not write to you.

I am devoted to the arts just now, and to the improvement of my small mind, which I have brought to a high state of cultivation by studying fifteen books at a time, some of them amazingly abstruse, such as the *Life of James Mackoul the Housebreaker*—very improving. Also I have finished my Denham's *Travels*, and the *Life of Professor Clarke* and *Les Barricades*, a diluted sort of history, partly history and partly dialogue, which Lord Lansdowne likes because it is the fashion at Paris, but it is uncommonly stupid. And I have been dipping into Pothier's *Histoire de l'Eglise*,—and in short, if we stay here a week there is no saying how much I shall read, or how little I shall remember.

Think of the agonies of coming here last Monday doubtful if we were expected or not! *Il Fanatico per la Musica* (by which form of words I opine that the Italians translate: Lord Lansdowne) passed last week at the Gloucester music meeting, so he did not receive George's letter in proper time, and of course there was some mistake about his answer, as there always is about any letter that signifies, and so we did not know if this week suited them. A warm reception from her is in the best of times doubtful, and arriving against her wish would have been horribly degrading. George never will enter into those sort of feelings, but that only makes them worse. However, he promised, if he found we had not been expected, to go on to Bath, and then we had a beautiful wild scheme, if I could have made my mind up to twelve hours' steam-boat, of going from Bristol to see Elizabeth Cawdor. But unfortunately we found our rooms here all ready, so we shall not see Wales this year. The Lansdownes were quite alone, expecting us, and she in the most cordial affectionate state; the place, which I have never seen but at Christmas, quite beautiful, and in short, I never liked Bowood half so much before. That was sure to be the consequence of expecting to dislike it.

Our Newton we have overtaken here again. He left the Grange rather in a huff some days ago, affronted somehow about his singing (at least so I heard, for I was not in the room to hear it); but he went away suddenly and ungraciously. I certainly don't like him, he is so argumentative, and talks so much of himself. His opinion of your brother George amused me particularly. He raves about you, but sensibly and properly, and calls you Miss Villiers. I have not a notion what line you take when you praise me, but he will distrust your judgment in future whatever you said, for he is one of the people to whom I must be odious. I go and look at his picture of "Macheath," which is in the drawing-room here, and which I think one of the best modern pictures I know, and collect a large mass of esteem and admiration for the painter, and rush into the library and address myself to him while it is all smoking hot; and before I have been five minutes there, all my good opinion turns sour and bitter and tough and cold, and he might just as well never have painted the picture at all.

Moore has been here the last three days, singing like a little angel. He has some new songs that make one perfectly and comfortably miserable, particularly one, set to a very very simple air, and with a constant return of the words, "They are gone," etc. He was singing it here on Friday, and there was a huge party of neighbours, amongst others a very vulgar bride who is partly a Portuguese, but chiefly a thorough vulgar Englishwoman, calls Lord Lansdowne "Marquis" when she speaks to him, and turns to Lady Lansdowne all of a sudden with "Law, how 'andsome you look." Just as Moore had finished this, and we were most of us in tears, she put her great fat hand on his arm and said, "And pray, Mr. Moore, can you sing Cherry Ripe?" George and I, who were sitting the other side of him, burst out laughing, and so Moore was obliged to make a good story out of it afterwards; else he owns he was so angry he meant to have sunk it altogether. Your ever affectionate

E. EDEN.

Miss Eden to Miss Villiers.

EASTCOMBE,
October 1826.

MY DEAR THERESA, I must be come to my second childishness and mere oblivion, for I cannot recollect whether I have answered the letter you wrote to me at Shottesbrook, and which followed me here, or not. If I have written, you had better put this in the fire, because it must be the same thing over again. One thing I know: That I have written above *twenty* letters since I came here. My family are all dispersed, and I have unwisely enlarged my list of friends, and my acquaintances have been uncommonly troublesome; and in short, I have been ill-used in the article of letter writing.

I have such miserable letters from my poor dear Pamela. It breaks one's heart to read them, and yet she is very good. She wrote to tell me of Lucy's death *immediately* after it occurred, and wrote in the greatest agony, but even then resigned, at least trying to be so, and thinking much of the life of trouble which poor Lucy would have had before her. Pamela said, "Think of her Aunt, think of her poor husband, think of all but *her*, for she was miserable and it was in mercy that God took her." And I believe her death to have been in fact occasioned by the state of excitement and anxiety in which she had lived since her marriage; and she had little chance, with her strong feelings and the peculiar circumstances of her situation, of anything but an increase of anxiety. Pamela writes me word to-day that her four servants—all she keeps—are in the scarlet fever, and her eldest little girl had just begun with it, and she has had, ever since Lucy's death, a sort of nervous pain in her throat that prevents her swallowing anything but liquids, and is grown very weak. I am telling you a long story, but I think you are interested about her, and it is such a melancholy situation that I can think of nothing else. To be sure, I have, as it is, a great many more blessings than I deserve; but it is hard that the want of a little foolish money should keep me from the best friend I have in the world at the only time in which I could be of use to her. However, if it had been possible, George would have taken me to her, and there is no use in murmuring at impossibilities. God knows I can enter into her feelings as a sister; and now that she has so much sickness in her home, it is cruel to leave her with a half-broken heart to struggle through it by herself. And yet I do not see how it is to be managed. Pamela writes but little of the scenes she has been through. She says she cannot endure to express her feelings in writing, though she thinks she would be better if she could talk it over.

Captain Lyon was coming home in January, but perhaps this will prevent him. Poor creature! What an arrival it will be if he has set off before this news reaches him.

You are quite right. I followed you in Berkshire, and next week I am going to Robert. It is doubtful whether his child will live, and Mrs. Eden has hardly been allowed to see it; but she wrote yesterday in the greatest spirits saying there had been a great change for the better, and the baby was then in her room; so I trust now it must be thought out of danger. What a horrid piece of work a lying-in is! I am more and more confirmed in the idea that a life of single blessedness is the wisest, even accompanied, as Shakespeare mentions, by the necessity of chanting faint hymns to the cold lifeless moon, which, as I have no voice, rather discomposes me. I shall astonish the moon, poor fellow, when I set off, but as for going through all my sister-in-law has done this fortnight, I could not, and would not, for all the Roberts in creation.

I cannot come to Knightsbridge just now, I am sorry to say. It is highly flattering, my sisters are all fighting for me, and with a very superior cool air I allow them to divide me.

I will not say anything about Sarah; she is too bad, if she knows what she is about. Poor Mr. Robinson was summoned back from Wrest yesterday, where he had been amusing himself three days. She sent him word she was dying, and when he arrived in the greatest haste yesterday, she was gone out airing. He was very cross, but too late. It relieves Sister from a very fatiguing attendance, and that is all the good I know.

I shall probably have to unsay all I have said of Newton, for George has discovered he thinks him pleasant, which is an unexpected blow. Do not twit me with inconstancy if I say so too. Your most affectionate

E. EDEN.

Miss Eden to Miss Villiers.
EASTCOMBE,
Sunday, 1 o'clock, October 30, 1826.

DEAR THERESA, I am sorry you had the trouble of sending for me yesterday, for Mary Drummond settled when I arrived that my remaining here would allow her to go home to her children, so she went home after dinner last night and I sent up to London for my things and all here was in such confusion, and there was so much to write that I could not write to you. The poor child is still alive, and yesterday afternoon we had all talked ourselves into spirits about her, though Warren and West continue to repeat that they cannot allow the slightest *expectation* of her recovery to be entertained. Since that, my sister's maid writes me word this morning that she has had a most wretched night, constantly screaming and groaning without one moment's quiet, and that the attendants all thought her very much worse, but that Warren did not think her materially so, as they did.

Think what it must be to witness. Sister has not been out of the room since seven yesterday morning, and with the exception of Tuesday night has sat up seven nights. She sees no one, but I had a composed letter from her last night. Sarah sat up on Friday, and from fatigue and anxiety gave way yesterday morning entirely, and had several fainting fits. Nobody can tell what he goes through, and he is, I think, as nearly angelic in his feelings and conduct as it is possible for man to be. The doctors speak of him with tears in their eyes. Fanny and I are going to walk there now and may perhaps see him, but at all events some of the doctors. You have no idea what it is the waiting here, expecting every hour to have directions to have this house prepared to receive them. They will all come here as soon as it is over. Yours affectionately

E. E.

Lord Auckland to Miss Eden.

LONDON,
October 30, 1826.

I have not been able to hear anything about you to-day, and am almost fearful I shall go out of town without doing so. At all events direct to me at Pixton, Dulverton. Your last note was far more cheerful, but yet it is a frightful and wretched state of things. I saw Mrs. Villiers yesterday, and Newton to-day; he is putting Theresa's monkey into one of his pictures, and goes to Knightsbridge to draw him. She seems to be ill.

November 21, 1826.

I saw your de Roos yesterday, and he begged me to tell you that Sir Guy Campbell has an appointment in Ireland which will put him and Pam more at their ease—£600 a year. It is very satisfactory.

Little Macdonald is going to be married to an Irish widow, an old acquaintance and attachment with a very small jointure. He is going over to be married, and returns to attend the January Sessions. John Murray, too (you may remember him at Edinbro'), is going to be married. He was on his way to Bowood, and passed a week at Sydney Smith's on his road, who had to meet him a fat Yorkshire lady of forty, with £60,000, and rather blue. Just the thing for him, and it was all arranged, and Sydney Smith is delighted, and expects visits from Scotchmen without end.

Lansdowne is in town, but she is not, and the Lambs are here, and the Duke of Devonshire, who says he is too poor after Russia to go to Chatsworth. But he has a cloak of black Fox worth £500 and is happy.

Miss Eden to Miss Villiers.

EASTCOMBE,
Tuesday night, November 1826.

DEAREST THERESA, You will have heard before this that all is over. I could not write sooner, and I knew you would hear. To the last the poor dear child's sufferings were dreadful, and she never had one moment's consciousness....

Lord Grantham arrived at the moment she expired. I wrote to him on Saturday to say he had better come, or rather to ask him if he did not think so, and he came off instantly, and I am so glad now, for you have no idea of the good effect it had on Mr. R.

Poor Sarah surprised me more than anybody. She cried a great deal, but was perfectly reasonable in her grief, and has fortunately taken the turn of feeling that it is only by her exertions her poor husband can be supported at all, and she kept repeating all the morning how much worse her calamity might have been, that at all events she had him left and ought not to repine. She thanked Sister, and, in short, nothing could be better than her conduct.

All hours come to an end at last; all griefs find, or make, a place for themselves. Don't you know what I mean,—how they work themselves into the mind, and so, by degrees, the surface of life closes over and looks smooth again, and I always think what a blessing it is in these cases there are so many little things that must necessarily be talked over and done. It fills up the time.

Sarah and Mr. R. come here to-morrow, and then go to Nocton for the funeral.

I think this day has lasted a year, and I cannot see to read, and my eyes are sore, and Sister cannot bear the light. In short, you must bear with me to-night. I am tired to death in my mind, and it rests me writing to somebody.

It was such a house of misery—the poor little French girl and the governess crying in one room; Warren with his cold sarcastic manner talking to West, who was crying like a child. And yet he need not. He was right from the first, and perhaps that is a painful feeling, to think that all the misery he saw, might have been spared if he had not been thwarted....

There is nothing I would not have given to escape the journey to Nocton. I had a sort of cowardly wish that George would not let me go (though I would have gone too, at all events), and I was almost sorry when his letter began, "You are quite right, and so go." And yet I have been often pretending to wish that I had more positive duties to do. We are such horrid hypocrites to ourselves. I am going to Nocton, I suppose, from the same feelings that lead Catholics to go up the Scala Sancta on their knees—a sort of superstition. It must be right, it is so unnatural and disagreeable; and yet I am very fond of Sister, and Sarah was once very kind to me, and is now again. It is very wrong; when you praised me in your letter it smote my conscience. Almost everybody but me has a pleasure in doing right. I have often thought how much you must have to learn on the subject of calamity for the loss of friends, but do not learn it before you must.

Lord Grantham has been such a comfort to them all. Your most affectionate
E. E.

Miss Eden to Miss Villiers.

Nocton, Lincolnshire,
Monday evening, December 13, 1826.

Bless your foolish heart! No, child, there is nothing the matter—never *was* anything worth mentioning. We have ruralized some time in this rustic Bedlam, and some of us got loose on Wednesday; but we are all caught and shut up again, and there is no harm done except 250 guineas gone and spent in post-horses, and we are all thin and exhausted with anxiety and shame, some for themselves, and some for others. I believe I sent you, at the time of Clarke's last visit, my farce of the new "Mayor of Garratt," with the plot made out into scenes, and specimens of the dialogue; but a good five-act comedy has written itself since Wednesday. Sarah is willing to laugh at it all herself now, and does so, I hear;—and after all, poor thing, it is no wonder she is nervous about health just now. All her fears I can excuse, with the death of her child from mismanagement constantly weighing on her mind; and the folly she is betrayed into, her fear is responsible for; but as she knows that her mind is beyond her own control, the provoking thing is that from the moment she begins to be ungovernable, she refuses to see anybody except servants who cannot contradict her.

As long as Mr. Robinson is forthcoming that does not signify, as to a certain degree he prevents her doing anything outrageously foolish; but he was *took* with a bad headache on Wednesday, such as he often has, a regular case of Calomel and black dose which the Lincoln doctors prescribed, and said he would be better the next day. But in the meanwhile Sarah worked herself into such a state that she sent off at eight in the morning two expresses, one for Clarke who lives in Norfolk, and another for Henry Ellis, Doctor Warren, West, and I fancy any others of the profession who chose to come. She would not see Sister, or rather speak to her; for Sister once went into her room and found her (who has not had her feet to the ground since I was here) walking about like anybody else, and actually *running* into the library to write her letters.

Poor dear Mr. Robinson got quite well as the day went on and the dose went off, and then Sarah began to be frightened at what she had done; and then she saw Sister and was content to be advised, and a third messenger was sent off to stop all the doctors he could find on the road. He turned back Warren in his chaise and four at Biggleswade; and West in his chaise and four, a few miles beyond. Before the express came back, we were living in the pleasing expectation of going in to dinner,—Sister, Anne, Mary, and I—each arm in arm with a doctor—Clarke, Warren, West, and Swan—the Lincoln man. I wanted to make a pleasant evening of it, as there was not much sickness about, and after dancing a quadrille with them that we should take a little senna tea, and then have a good jolly game at Snap-dragon with some real Epsom Salts.

I forgot to mention that Sarah, with fatigue and worry, had made herself so ill that a fourth express went on Thursday to fetch Clarke again. She makes all these people travel in chaises and four *par parenthèse*; Clarke came on Saturday night, and then it was to be broke to that dear good gull Mr. Robinson that any doctor whatever had been sent for. I had no idea before that she could have been enough afraid of him to have kept anything from him; but he even read that paragraph in the paper about himself and wondered what the mistake could be.

However, Sister, as usual, was persuaded to take a great deal of the scrape on her shoulders, and Clarke, who seems clever enough, undertook to announce and explain the rest. Mr. R. was, I heard, horribly annoyed at first, but is resigned now, and it is all smothered up in her dressing-room where she has shut him up, and I do not know when he will be allowed to call himself well again.

I hear she is very low now the excitement is over, but wisely declares she shall do just the same next time, and he begs he may go as his own express. Poor man! he has a bad prospect before him, but I do not think that he minds it.

She professes the degree of religious feeling that is seldom met with, and which appears to me inconsistent with any worldly feelings whatever, above all with her feelings for *self*. The *quantity* of her religion it is impossible to deny, but I doubt its *quality* being right; and when I see that her high-flown mystical ideas end in making everybody round her perfectly miserable, I go back to the suspicions I have entertained for some time that the old simple religion we were taught at four years old out of Watt's catechism is the real right thing after all. "If you are good, you will go to Heaven, and if you are naughty, etc., etc." You ought to know your Watt's catechism. I shall learn mine over again, and begin quite fresh in the most practical manner.

Oh, by the bye, and another thing I have found out and meant to tell you is, that Virtue is *not* its own reward. It may be anybody's else, but it is not its own. I take the liberty of asserting that my conduct here has been perfectly exemplary. I never behaved well before in my life, and I can safely add I never passed so unpleasant a month.

Well, my dear, good old George arrived to-night, which is payment for everything, and he has not blown his head off to signify. There are no marks visible by candle-light, though he looks ill from starving. I have been very poorly myself with a cold caught by the open windows, and what it appears is called swelled glands. I never knew anything but a horse had that complaint or something like it, and that then they were shot; and as far as humanity goes that is a good cure. I went stamping and screeching about one day like an owl with the pain. If I get better we are going to Woburn, George says; but if I continue poorly I shall leave him there, and go home on Saturday. It is astonishing how kindly I feel towards Grosvenor Street. I am almost wishing to be settled there, for the first time in my life.

I am sorry to give up Sprotbro', but if we had gone there, we must have done Erswick first where the Copleys will be, and where there is a great charity bazaar meeting and a ball, and all sorts of County troubles, and George prefers Woburn.

I am sorry not to see Maria Copley; Anne and Mary are still here, and I quite agree to all you say of Anne. I am so fond of her, and so is Sister. Mary is very dull, but seems amiable. I cannot tell you whether Sarah is kind to them. You must see her to understand the state she is in; but she is not unkind to anybody, and never now finds fault with anybody she speaks of. She very seldom speaks at all, unless she is excited to defend some religious point.

She sometimes smiles when Mr. Robinson and I have been talking nonsense, but does not say anything. Your most affectionate

E. E.

Miss Eden to Miss Villiers.
NOCTON,
December 15, 1826.

MY DEAR THERESA, I wish to apprise you not to go in search of me in Grosvenor Street, because I am not there. "I am very bad with the ague," as people must be in the habit of saying in these fenny districts. I 'ticed my poor dear George out of town into this horrid place, and here he is with nobody to play with and nothing to do, and missing his Woburn shooting.... Still the idea of another's bore is a heavy weight on my mind.

You will be happy to hear that Mr. Robinson is very well. George says he never saw him better, and he makes a point of telling him so three times a day at least. The poor man is starving, as Sarah will not allow him to dine except in her dressing-room at two o'clock, because, as she does not dine down with the family, she says she cannot trust to his promises not to eat more than is right, as she is not there. He happens to have an immensely good appetite since his headache, and frets like a child about this; but has not courage to dine like a man on the most unwholesome things he can find. I would live on mushrooms and walnuts and fried plum-pudding if I were him.

This conversation passed verbatim yesterday, but do not for your life mention it again. He wanted to go to the stables when he was out walking, but said Sarah had told him not. However, he went boldly to her window and knocked at it. "Sarah, I wish I might go to the stables?"—"No, dearest, I told you before not to go."—"Yes; but I want to see my horses. Mayn't I go?"—"No, darling, you said you would not ask it if I let you go out."—"Yes; but one of my horses is sick, and I want to see it."—"Well, then, if Mama will go with you, you may." So Sister actually had to go with him to take care of him. She told me this, and did not know whether he was ashamed of it; but I saw him in the evening and he repeated it, evidently rather pleased that he was made so much of. He is a poor creature after all, Theresa, though you are so fond of him. Your most affectionate

E.E.

Anne and Mary went on Wednesday. I did not see them the last two days, but Mr. Auckland still does not admire them. I wish Anne would be as pleasant in society as she is alone with one. I think she is nervous.

Miss Eden to Miss Villiers.
NOCTON,
December 1826.

DEAREST THERESA, There is a shameful substitution of the donkey for the poney who ought to take these letters to post, so allowing for the difference of speed, the letters go an hour and a half sooner than usual! and Mr. Robinson has just sent up the frank for you, he says the letter must go in ten minutes, so it is no use my trying to make a letter. I have mentioned your and Mrs. Villiers's enquiries constantly to Sarah, and read her aloud bits of your letter yesterday. I think she likes enquiries.

It is more than I do; I pass my life answering them still, because people whom I never saw or wish to see, know dear Miss Eden will excuse them if they trouble her again, etc. I don't excuse them at all, but I am obliged to answer their letters just as if I did.

It is difficult to know what to say.... When first we came down I thought her really low for two days, though it struck me as odd that she was so little attentive to him. However, I believe she thought him too cheerful, though God knows it was the falsest cheerfulness ever was acted.

Since Saturday she has been exactly in the state in which she was before poor Elinor's death. She talks and thinks of nothing but her health, and I really believe (and I do not think it is want of charity that makes me so, for I pity her still) that a thought of her child does not cross her mind twice in the day.

She is absorbed in herself, and has been more animated since she has been—or called herself—ill, for she talks of her complaint without ceasing and without reserve. It will be said more than ever she is in the family way, for they have sent an express for Clarke, and we are expecting him to-night, and nobody knows what to say to him when he comes.

I think she is a little ashamed about Clarke, and I grudge the hundred guineas, which would be better bestowed on weavers, or the people in the village here.

Sister tried to be candid about it last night, and said that Clarke would probably stay a day or two when he came, and he would amuse Sarah; I suggested that for half the money I could have persuaded several pleasant men to come from London to stay double the time, so it must not be defended on the plea of economy.. She could not help laughing, because in fact she is less taken in than anybody. The cold of this place surpasses anything I have ever felt. Yours

E.E.

CHAPTER V

1827-1828

Lady Campbell to Miss Eden.
CORK,
May 21, 1827.

SAILED at two, Saturday; landed at passage within the Cove of Cork last night at six. All sick, but the children so good and patient. I was quite proud of my brood, even the Baby showed an *esprit de conduite* that edified me. Six boats came out and fought for our bodies under the ship till I thought we should be torn to pieces in the skrimmage. They, however, landed us whole, when another battle was *livrée* for us among the jingle-boys who were to whisk us to Cork. We were stowed in three of these said carrioles called jingles, driven by half-naked barefoot boys who began *whirrrring, harrrrowing*, cutting jokes, talking Irish, and galloping in these skeleton carts till the children caught the infection, laughed and roared and kicked with delight. A violent shower came on. Who cares? thinks I, they must have Irish blood in their veins, for this is very like English misery, but they naturally think it *Fun*. We arrived in tearing spirits, very wet, and were cheated of a considerable sum in shillings. We are in an excellent Hotel and set off early for Limerick. Nobody dare travel late in this poor country. Oh, Emily, it is melancholy to see the misery and cunning and degradation of these poor people. I could cry, and I sit looking about, having heard so much of them all, that it appears to me I am recollecting all I see!... Such beggars! they show me such legs! and one was driven up in a barrow, legless!

LIMERICK,
May 29, 1827.

Here I am settled *dans mes foyers* in a roomy, comfortable, homely mansion, with dark black mahogany unwieldy furniture and needlework chairs ranged round the room in regiments, and a glowing embery turf fire.

We have a field before the house with a walk round it; we look upon the broad Shannon and the Clare Mountains.... We have a complete *leper*, a Lazarus, outside our door, which gives me a sort of Dives feel, very unpleasant to my conscience, and sumptuous fare every day, and purple and fine linen, keep running in my head, that this very day I mean to go and make a treaty of peace between this lame beggar and my conscience that I may rest. I have also a stiff straight-cut schoolmaster who opens the gate. He is of the established Church, teaches boys, makes shoes, and was a soldier.

We have fine Artillery Barracks; we have a Lunatick Asylum not so large as the Gaol, and serves three counties; which shows the country abounds more in Knaves than Fools. But oh, the misery, the desolate look of the whole country, the beggary—I shall never get used to it. And the whole country looking as if it was capable of being the richest in the world. This large river flowing on without a boat upon it, crowds of people talking and sauntering about in rags, complaining of having no work.... The whole country looks sacked. However it is reckoned very quiet just now.

This part is reckoned very rich and prosperous. Our living is excellent, meat, milk, eggs, and poultry, and fish so cheap, I feel as if it was quite a pity I cannot eat more at once.

July 6, 1827.

...We are getting a little outrageous in this county, and very much so in T'p'rary, for we lack potatoes there, and hunger sharpens the wits, so we just *lift* the flour and potatoes cast for our use. Is it possible that Lord Anglesey is to be our Lord-Lieutenant? Am I really to pray for him, and for the sword the King puts in his hand, every Sunday in church? Oh dear, dear! What a wretched country this is—it wearies the spirit to see it.

Miss Eden to Miss Villiers.

BIGODS, ESSEX,
Sunday, July 1827.

I have been longing for a letter from you.

I have not seen an individual out of this house since I entered it three weeks ago, except one day when we dined at Lord Maynard's,—the most melancholy ceremony, barring a funeral, I ever assisted at. Conversation is one of the social duties not practised in Essex. Mary and I talked our level best, and they must all have thought us either the most delightful people in the world, or the most impudent.

The very names of the neighbours are as monosyllabic (a very puzzling word to spell) as their conversation. Mr. Brown and Mr. Wish and Mr. Rush and so on, so contrived, I am certain, to avoid prolixity. The work of education goes on from morning to night. Six small Intellects constantly on the march, and Mary, of course, is hatching a seventh child. I own I am glad I am not married, it is such a tiresome fatiguing life; and though as a visitor I delight in the children, yet I would not be so worn and worried as their mother is on any consideration. I think she fidgets too much about them, but a large family is a great standing fidget of itself, and I suppose one would be the same under the same circumstances.

I like this undisturbed sort of life, only the days go so fast when they are all alike. There is a good, hard, reading library in the house, and I am quite glad to find that when I cannot have novels I can read other books just as well.

George seems to have found London very amusing to the last. He wrote to me the other day after he had been supping at Lord Alvanley's, who was in great delight at some Paris pantaloons he had heard of,—*Peau de Pendu*; and if the Pendu was the right size the Pantaloons fitted without a wrinkle and without a seam of course. George is by way now of being settled at Eastcombe. He has had a great many parties down there to dinner, some that must have been hard trials to Sister,—Sir J. Copley amongst others.

The B. Barings were to dine there Friday. I do not think Lady Harriet will suit Sister. Do not let it go any further, I tell it you in the greatest confidence,—but in fact you are beginning to find out that the Barings are rather failures—I mean as to agreeableness. It will be some time before Mr. Baring fails in the moneyed sense of the word; but I see you, in fact, think, of the Grange just as I do:—charming place and family, but a dull visit, and to my last hour I shall go on saying, as you do, and as *I* always have said, that Harriet is a very superior person. But nobody will ever guess how dull I think her. I like Baring père the best....

I am glad you are more just to little Mr. Wall. I tried to be so unjust to him myself that I do not like to find anybody else so. After all, he makes one laugh, which is a merit, and he is a warm friend, and if he is a little ridiculous, it is no business of ours. Heaven help Mrs. Wall—if there ever should be such a person. But there never will....

I hope we shall go to Ireland; but it seems to be in a troublesome state and I should hate to be *piked*. If we do go, I shall be so pleased to see your George again. You need never be the least jealous about Lady F. I like her character very much, and her society very well; but I never should think of having for her the real warm affection I have for you, or expect the return from her I expect from you. It is quite a different thing,—what is called great esteem, I suppose. She does not care a straw for me. Our Irish journey is fixed for the 29th, next Monday week, the day we fixed when you were in Grosvenor Street, but Mary ain't brought to bed a bit more than she was then, and I have some doubts whether I shall be able to go as soon as that. The doctor here thinks my lungs are in fault, but there never was a Doctor who saw me for the first time that did not think the same, and afterwards found out his mistake, and I always confute them by recovering so quickly.

I cannot say half I had to say: all my moralities about poor Mr. Canning, and then I have had such an amusing letter from Pam, and Sarah is worse than ever. Your most affectionate

E. E.

Miss Eden to Miss Villiers.

BIGODS, ESSEX.

This is to be a simple line, because I am in what Mary Palk used to call a religious bustle, occasioned by the difficulty of being in time for church if I write my letters. And the post-time and church-time clash cruelly, and I have made this such a week of rest as to writing that I am horribly in debt. I cannot help thinking George's cold contempt for anybody who leaves London at all, which broke out into words the day before I left town, relieved his indignant heart, and I think he will perhaps let me stay. I cannot understand your not liking the country; it is an inconsistency in your character, and if I did not spurn an argument, I might almost deign to point out to you unanswerable reasons for hating London—as a place I mean, not as a means of seeing one's friends. Its effect on one's *liver* you will not dispute.

We sit out of doors all day. I should not like to paint myself, but I have done some sketches of the children in that chalk style, that certainly betray unequivocal marks of genius; inasmuch as their nurse, who was mine in former days, declares she had no idea Miss Emily could take them off so well, and she would not mind having them pictures for herself—which is wonderful for her to own.

Mary is very well, all things considered. I wish you could hear her play; I always think it the prettiest music in the world. She plays a great deal now. I heard from Pam to-day; very well, and resigned to Limerick. I wish you could manage through your Mr. Jones, or any better way, that she might have her mother's letters from Paris without paying 2/10 for them, which she says is the whole of her income. Can you manage it?

Miss Eden to Miss Villiers.

BIGODS,
July 12, 1827.

Well, I had nearly seized my pen yesterday, and leaving all decorum and propriety, throwing aside all the prudent and guarded forms and usages of society, was on the point of writing to your brother, merely from complete distrust of his being up to the tricks of the Goderichs. I was going as his friend-in-law, the friend of his sister, to implore him for once not to be a simple gentleman-like fool, not an honourable-minded generous idiot—in short, to stand up for his rights, and not to take the offer of 7/6 or 7/4 which Lord Goderich would in all probability make to him for the use of the house for a week and a compensation of the loss of the rent for the ensuing three months. He might not have offered so much; but I merely state the case in the grand Liberal manner.

Some obscure passages in Sister's letter yesterday, and a very accurate observation for many years of the manners and customs of the Goderich tribe, led me to imagine they were trying to throw the house back on your hands; and I wish to exhort you all not to catch it if they throw it at you ten times a day. Charles Drummond desired me to add that as far as £10 would go to assist in any prosecution against Sarah for breach of contract, he should be most happy to subscribe it. However, I waited for your letter, and am happy to see that for *once* I was mistaken about the Goderichs as you do not mention that any shabby offer was ever made. Accepted, of course, it could not be. You know the usual answer is, that everything is in the hands of the agent, and you have nothing to do with it, and that Mrs. Villiers would of course say. *I* still mistrust them, and cannot quite understand some of Sister's expressions. Her story otherwise tallies wonderfully with yours, except, that though you were in the next house, you cannot know how very much Sarah contrived to outdo her usual self in this instance. Sister is fully aware how tiresome she herself was. I should like to send you her letter, only it is so long; for it is very amusing, though it is a shame to let anybody see the abject slavery in which she and Mr. Robinson live.

It is quite a Fowell Buxton case. They are always so kind as to call Sarah's horrid bad temper—excitement; and Sister says that none of them have ever seen Sarah in such a state of excitement (such an overwhelming rage, evidently) as she was in this time. She would not hear of the slightest contradiction, and Sister said she had been obliged to write every half-hour to poor Mrs. Villiers without being able to make Sarah even listen to her representations. She was quieted at last by a quantity of Laudanum, besides her own way to satisfy her. The last would be a pleasant sedative to most of us.

Miss Eden to Lady Campbell.

BIGODS, ESSEX,
July 1827.

DEAREST PAM, This may be excellent weather for the hay and corn, but it is not good for writing, does not bring out letters in any good quantity. I cannot write when I am hot, and besides, I have been taking a good week of repose down here with Mary, and have carefully abstained from any exertion greater than sitting in the shade, with a book (turned topsy-turvy for fear I should read it) in my hand. I had so much to say to you, too, about that breakfast at Boyle Farm and your brother—rather old news now; but as your old butter seems very fresh by the time you have sent it over to us, it may be the same with our news sent to you.

In the first place, your brother has made himself extremely popular with all Lord Ellenborough's enemies, which comprise the whole of what is usually called London society. Lord Ellenborough went to Astley's about ten days ago, and his own box was overstocked; so he went to another belonging to Mr. Anson, Lord Forbes and a party of gentlemen, your brother amongst others, but Mr. FitzGerald did not come in till after Lord E. had settled himself there. When he *did* come, Lord Ellenborough chose to consider *him* as the intruder into his own box, and threw him several of those looks which he considers irresistible, whether in contempt or supplication. Probably also he shook those horrid grey locks at Mr. FitzGerald. However, early next morning he received a note from Mr. FitzGerald that he had observed the *insolence* of his looks and could not submit to it, and Lord Ellenborough must either meet him, or make him the most ample apology, not only in words to Lord Forbes, but by letter to himself. So Lord Ellenborough *did* make the most ample apology in words to Lord Forbes, and then wrote a letter of five pages to Mr. FitzGerald, four of them apologetical and the fifth, they say, a very high eulogium of your brother's character, courage, morals, and all. Mr. FitzGerald observed that was all very well, but he "should keep an eye on Lord E. to the end of the season!" They say it was delightful to see Lord E. walking about at Boyle Farm looking so bland and benevolent, and so well-mannered. That is the way the story is told, and, I really believe, as little exaggerated as may be, and you have no idea of the delight it excited. Lord E. has the advantage of being entirely friendless, and the insolence of his look is just the very thing that wanted correction.

I suppose you heard the general outline of the Boyle Farm breakfast, if not, I could send you our card. Lord Alvanley, Lord Chesterfield, Lord Castlereagh, Mr. Grosvenor, and the Sarpent were the five givers; but in fact they each subscribed £300, and the Sarpent had the management of the whole. Mr. Grosvenor asked humbly to be allowed to ask two friends, which was refused, tho' he said it was really an object to him; and upon investigation it turned out that the two friends were his father and mother. The conversations about the invitation must have been like those between the Triumvirate,—Lepidus Alvanley giving up an ugly aunt in exchange for two ugly cousins of Augustus Chesterfield's, and these the *bassesse* of London. It never came out in a finer manner. You and I remember about four years ago when the Sarpent came gliding into Almack's—and no woman spoke to him, and he—even the Sarpent's own self, looked daunted; and now he sent out his cards naming on them the pretty sister of the family, asking Lady Caroline Murray, and leaving out the eldest and youngest sister (tho' Lady Mansfield was the first reputable person who took him up at all); desiring 22 of the prettiest girls in London to come in costume—patterns and directions sent with the card—and I actually heard people of good character, who have stooped to ask him constantly to dinner, lamenting that now he would not look at them for fear of being obliged to ask them. He called to ask the Barings—at nine o'clock the night before the breakfast, apologised for not having been able to spare an invitation for them before, and added, "the only condition I make is a new gown; I believe there is still time for that." They went! In new gowns! I believe there never was a more beautiful breakfast when all was done—those sort of men *will* succeed! Everybody seemed pleased with it. What stories may have risen from it have not yet transpired. And Mr. de Roos said to Lady Jersey, he trusted the whole thing had been done most correctly—he should be miserable if there could be even a surmise of the slightest impropriety...! Fanny and I sent our excuse—partly from not wishing to go, and then it would have been necessary to spend immensely on dress, which I hate. There is such a story about the Miss Strutts asking for an invitation, too long to write, but so amusing. Your own affectionate

E. E.

Miss Eden to Miss Villiers.
BIGODS, ESSEX,
Wednesday, July 1827.

MY DEAREST THERESA, If you are still in town, which I expect and hope, call in Grosvenor Street late on Friday (after your Aunt) and you will have the felicity of finding me, and perhaps of taking me home to dinner.

George writes me word to-day that there never was such a mistake as my being out of London (which I cannot understand, as by his own account it is a desert), and that he finds it quite impossible to make up his summer plans without seeing me, and if I cannot come up alone, he must come and fetch me. Then Mary says she shall go demented if I am not here again by the 1st of August; so to save them both all further trouble I shall go up Friday for a few days, hear what George has to say, see you, take leave of the Copleys, finish up the House Accounts, claim my allowance, pay my bills, lock up the tea and sugar, look over the House Linen, go to the Play, call on Lady Grantham, and then come back to stay, if George leaves me time enough, till Mary is confined. She insists on my being with her (I mean in the house), and, of course, I had rather too be with her if she likes it; but if an equally near relation should happen about the same time to require my attendance on the drop at Newgate, I should prefer that employment of the two. Shorter and pleasanter, I guess. I am so disgusted with our foolish laws which could not hang, could not even punish, that William Sheen who cut off his baby's head. It appears we may all kill any child, so as we call it by a wrong name; and as nursing disagrees with Mary, I have some thoughts of calling her baby Peter Simkins, and cutting off his head as soon as it is born. But I must say that our laws never are of any use when there is a real crime to be punished.

I wonder whether you are still in town. I hope you are. If George makes any engagement for me Friday, I might dine with you, perhaps Saturday. George says he gives a grand entertainment at home that day, and as he was not aware I was to be at home then, I shall probably be *de trop*, though he does not specify whether he has asked the Professors of the London University, or the Keepers of the wild beasts, or all his mistresses, saving your presence. But I should like to dine with you. I do not know what has given George this sudden fit of indecision as to his summer. He had invented such a good plan, that he and I should take Fanny to Knowsley, deposit her there, cross over to Ireland, make a little tour there, see Pamela, come back by Stackpole, see Elizabeth, and then go to Norman Court and the Grange for our shooting. It was a pretty idea of his, but then he is naturally a great dear. However this strikes me as rather an expensive journey, so I do not press it, and if he has thought better of it, I shall encourage his more economical thoughts. If not, I shall be very glad.

Sister has offered us Eastcombe and the use of all her servants for the summer, if we want it.—So good-bye for the present. Your most affectionate

E. E.

Miss Eden to Miss Villiers.
BIGODS,
Saturday, August 11, 1827.

MY DEAREST THERESA, I do not consider that *hash* of Mrs. Villiers' and yours a fair answer to my letter. You said actually nothing, and she left off just as she was coming to the pith of her discourse. But I must write to somebody to-day, else I shall die of a reflection of astonishment and indignation. I shall blow up, I shall go off, I shall break down, I shall boil over, all about Lord Goderich; and yet it is twelve hours since I have had George's letter, and I dare not write to him for fear I should differ entirely in my view of the subject from him. He states facts only (cunning dog!) and not his opinion; but only to think of Lord Goderich being Prime Minister, and Lord Lansdowne under him; and if he is Prime Minister, what is Sarah? Queen of England at least. I still think the arrangement will all fail when it comes to particulars; but still the mere idea is so odd. Even at the beginning of the session, Robin was considered highly presumptuous to aspire to being Leader in the House of Lords, and at the end of it there was not a doubt anywhere, I thought, of his total want of Talent. And yet he is to be Prime Minister! All the poor little children who read History 100 years hence will come to the Goderich administration, and as they will never have dined in Downing Street, or lived at Nocton, they will not have an idea what a thorough poor creature he is.

Thank Goodness, I have never been taken in by history. But our poor King! I have pitied him all the week, and now I pity him still more, because as he lays his old head on his pillow he must feel that he has outlived the talent of England—that, in fact, he has not a decent subject to produce. Hateful as those Tories are, I declare I think it would have looked better to Foreign Powers to have produced Mr. Peel and the Duke of Wellington again. I wonder if the King knows anything of Sarah, and what a poor wretch Robin is? But it is so like her luck! She has always all her life had what she wished, even to a child. Not but what her confinement is now put off again till the middle of November, by authority; and in the meanwhile she sees nobody.

Lady Campbell to Miss Eden.
LIMERICK,
August 28, 1827.

Glad to see you, my own Emmy?—I think I shall be glad indeed.... The past four months of my life I would not wish to my Enemy's dog, but I am better now, and can jog on a little. Emily, it will be too much delight seeing you here, particularly if I can have you in the house.

My only fear is that you and Lord Auckland will not be comfortable. So many children, not a very good cook, an uncertain climate, and a Life Guardsman who cannot wait, and to whom I dare not speak, as my remonstrances agitate him so much. I actually hear him perspire behind my chair.

I will not press my reflections on Mr. Canning's death upon you, as they probably would not be very fresh, but will you tell me why I was sorry? Poor Lady de Roos, who has a pretty extensive system of what I call *individual politics*, was in hopes of seeing Lord Bathurst and Lord Melville return to the places whence they came. These two being the very ravellings of the fag end. All idea of racketting us to Liverpool is over, and I rather think we shall have our choice of going to Dublin, but I do not wish to move till Spring at all events....

I know nobody here that I like or ever wish to see again, except a Miss Ouseley, and she is gone to Dublin; so only imagine what a delight it will be to see you, putting our original stroke of friendship out of the question.

Miss Eden to Miss Villiers.
LONDON,
Saturday, September 1, 1827.

MY DEAREST THERESA, I ought to have written sooner, but I have been so languid and sick. Mary's lying-in was the most charming amusement in the world. I believe that is one of the points on which we have argued with all the extra-pertinacity that our complete ignorance naturally gave us, and for once I think you were right. It is *not* the awful business I thought it had been. She was ill a very short time, had no nurse (because hers did not hurry herself to arrive so much as the child did), has recovered without a check, and I left her on Wednesday nursing Mary the 2nd with great satisfaction to herself and child.

George has been as usual all kindness—willing to give up all his shooting, and go with me to the sea, or even *to* sea, which did me good when I was formerly declining; and to-day is the 1st of September, and he is sitting here with me nursing and coaxing me up, and the partridges are all flying about the world, and he not shooting them. I think I shall be able to go on Wednesday, and the worst come to the worst, we can but come back again, and I shall not feel so *guilty* towards him and Fanny.

As usual there are plenty of people in London, and I had as many visitors yesterday as in the middle of June. Lady Lansdowne was here most part of the morning, Mrs. G. Lamb, Mr. Foster, Mr. C. Greville, who heard I was sick, and came to ask if his carriage could not take me out airing every day at any time. There is nothing like those wicked *roués* at heart; they are so good-natured! But what touched me yesterday was poor Lady Grantham's coming here for an hour and being just as much interested about my foolish ailments as if she had not her favourite child dying at home. Amabel was as ill as possible on Thursday but a shade better yesterday, I never saw a more touching sight than Lady Grantham, I have thought of nothing else since. She is so calm and quiet and so perfectly miserable; she looked like a statue yesterday, there was such an immovability in her countenance and such a wan white look about her, even her lips looked quite white and still; she still has a little hope but seems to give herself as much as possible to preparing Amabel for *her* great change and herself departing with her. What would one give to save that child for her!

Sarah is, you will be happy to hear, behaving with the most perfect consistency. She fancied she was in labour three days ago, and had all the workmen sent off from the buildings in Downing Street—just as if they could not all be in labour together. If it is true (and of course it is as Shakespeare says it) that the fantastic tricks of men dressed in a little brief authority (and the Goderich authority seems likely to be brief enough) do make the Angels weep, what a deplorable time the Angels have had of it lately with Sarah! They must nearly have cried their eyes out. She has adopted a new form of tyranny with Sister; would not let her be at Eastcombe, but makes her stay in Downing Street; and then will not see her, but desires she may never leave the house....

I cannot tell you the stories of his *ineptie* and which those who do not know him thoroughly might well take for unfair dealing; but that he is not capable of. I fancy there never was a more wretched man—so worried he cannot eat. Sister said she should hardly know him at home. He rattles in company. Your most affect.

E. E.

Miss Eden to Miss Villiers.
September, 1827.

I was at Knightsbridge yesterday, and trust that poor Mabby's suffering will not be prolonged now above two or three days. Anne said the change even in the last twelve hours was marvellous; she looked like a different child, so drawn and deathlike. She was quite placid and seemed sinking very quietly, except when that horrid cough came on. Her voice was no longer audible. All the details of Lady Grantham's conduct are beautiful. I never loved her so well as I do now, and the adoration Anne and Mary have for her exceed what I have ever seen, astonishing too that they dwell constantly on the idea that they are *nothing* to her compared to Amabel. What is to become of her when all is over? It will make a complete change in her whole system of life. Anne and Mary seem to look forward to everything that can be arranged after all is over, to alleviate their mother's misery; they are excellent girls. Lord Grantham was here three days ago. Unfortunately I was not well that day and could not see him. They say he passes almost the whole day in tears.

I always forget to tell you that Sarah sent to say that if I liked to stay at *her* house at Knightsbridge, instead of London which disagrees with me, I was quite welcome. I had a great mind to go, merely to pull your things about a little. They are very civil just now. Lord Goderich sends me game every day, and I write him facetious notes in return. Your most affectionate,

E. E.

Miss Eden to Miss Villiers.
DUBLIN,
Monday, September 17, 1827.

MY DEAREST THERESA, I am as sleepy as a horse, or whatever is the right comparison, but time is so scarce you must take me as you can have me. Actually in Dublin, Miss Villiers.—Landed yesterday morning at ten; embarked at six the evening before; cabin to ourselves; favourable wind; silent captain; no fleas; sea smooth as glass; and I sick as a dog.

There was not the least excuse for it, but I cannot help it. I kept up beautifully the first three hours, and then George would make me go and look at the beautiful cabin, and taste the excellent coffee; and of course the motion of the beautiful cabin disagreed with the excellent coffee—and there was an end of me. We all went regularly to bed, but that did not profit much, as there were above a hundred Irish haymakers in the other part of the vessel, and by a singular hazard they were all musical, and all hundred sang all night. However, George dragged me on deck again early in the morning, and then I got better, and it was a beautiful morning, and the bay of Dublin is (as you have probably heard) a beautiful sight, and altogether I never made a voyage of less suffering.

We are in a very comfortable hotel, the master of which is notorious for a passion for old plate, and everything we touch is silver, and such beautiful embossed articles. But it is actually tiresome, everything is so heavy and metallic. George says he never was so tired of silver since all his early reading about Peru; but it is an odd expensive taste for an hotelkeeper, and he has indulged it many years.

George dined at Mr. Lamb's yesterday, and seems to have met a very amusing Irish party. I sent my excuse and went to bed, as I do not think my health is up both to sights and society, and I like the first best. We have had such a nice day to-day. Went early to visit Mr. Lamb and see the Phoenix Park, and then down to Woodlands, a beautiful villa with a famous glen, etc., then to the Liffey waterfall, which was so very pretty, and I sat there for two hours and drew it, while George rambled about and read, and at last found such an amusing Irishman to talk to us, so like old Thady, or any other of Miss Edgeworth's people. I cannot help laughing all the time they speak (merely at the look and brogue, not at what they say). Then we went to a cottage for some eggs and bacon, and came back by another road to Dublin.

To-morrow we dine at Mr. Lamb's, and the next day go for a three days' tour to the County of Wicklow, etc.; come back here for a night, and then go to Pamela. I do so enjoy it all. I am afraid after we have done Pamela, and fallen into the hospitalities of Lady Glengall, Lord Kingston, etc., who all seem most dreadfully well disposed to us, I shall like it less....

I never saw such a jaunting-car nation. The middle ranks seem to live in those vehicles, and the common people pass their days apparently sitting smoking at the doors of their cabins, the children with hardly as much cloathes on as a decent savage wears. Such groups we saw to-day! I feel much more in a foreign country than I should at Calais, and am only preserved from that illusion by the whistling of "Cherry-Ripe" which all the little naked Lazzaroni keep up.

Knowsley was full of people, we were generally thirty-four at breakfast, and I suppose more at dinner, but Lady Derby would not let me dine down above once. We had the greatest difficulty in getting away, and she kindly invited me if I felt worse to come back and die respectably at Knowsley. Poor Fanny was horribly low when we came away at being left; but I have no doubt is as happy as the day is long by this time. There is going to be a Fancy Ball, and a musical festival, and all sorts of things, and there is no denying that our friend Lady Derby is a most agreeable person.

I enclose a letter I have had from Sister to-day, not because you will not have heard all about poor dear Amabel, but it contains an atrocity of Sarah's about the funeral, hardly credible when one thinks of Lord Goderich this time twelve months. My four *writing* sisters are all in different parts of England and all expecting letters, the more because I am travelling about and have less time to write. Your most affectionate

E. E.

Miss Eden to Lady Campbell.

BESSBOROUGH,
Tuesday, October 30, 1827.

MY DEAREST PAM, We shall actually sail to-night, and perhaps it will be economical in the long run; for I have been very sick the last three days hearing the wind blow, and the packet talked of. But it is like leaving you all over again. You know we never shall meet again, I know we shan't—I am grown quite desperate about it, and, as I cannot get at you and cannot do without you, I am rather puzzled as to what will be the result. I must take up the thread of my discourse where we left off.

I was so horribly low after you went, stayed an hour in my own room which, as that pinafore'd housemaid had forgotten to *do it out*, is I suppose the strongest proof of friendship I could have given. Then the day cleared up, and my headache cleared up, and Lady Glengall took me to see the platting school. I am quite vexed you did not see that; it is such a gratifying sight, and curious besides. While we were there, a policeman came up to Lady Glengall: "Me lady, where will we put Connell?" "Who's Connell?" "Why, *the stiff*, me lady. Where will we put him convenient for the coroner?" So she went off to make poor Connell convenient, and I to sketch the castle, and while I was there Connell's procession came over the bridge. Such a howling!

Lord Arthur Hill and Mr. Carnegie dined there that day. The next day we went to the review, after sundry demurs on the part of her Ladyship; but I think she has at last made up her mind to make up her quarrel with the regiment, and in proof thereof, Carnegie and Ford again graced the festive board at Cahir with their presence. The sight of all those grey horses and red men at full gallop, and that beautiful band which played to us afterwards, increased my military ardour into perfect heroism. Sir Charles was more Sir Charlesey than ever! I quite agree with old Lord Donoughmore, who is a Penruddock jewel of a man, a sort of *bourreau bienfaisant*, and who observed, when we told him Sir Charles could not come to Knocklofty till the following day, "Well then, you must do without a Tom-fool for one day—eh?" Make Lord Arthur show you Lord Donoughmore—I mean *act* him. Before we went to Knocklofty on Wednesday, Lady Glengall drove me to Ardfinan, and there did we discuss Brooke and his intentions, and she declares he is desperately in love with Miss Acton, and is only by way of moping at Cahir. Think of being Brooke's moping house!

You do not know me, Pam, you do not value me. Lady Glengall knows me better—she is after all the friend of my heart. I never was so praised alive as I was that day. I may have "Richard" only for the asking. In fact there is nothing wanting but just his consent and mine—absolute trifles. I observe those ladies who have been addicted to flirting never believe that any woman under 60 can be without some little interest of that sort; and I cannot help thinking that I am suspected at Cahir of being engaged to Lord Henry Thynne. It was that Brooke's innuendos led me to the suspicion, and something Lady Glengall said might have meant it. However, I do not know. Only, if you hear me accused of that crime—and she means to see a great deal of you—will you have the kindness to mention that I am neither engaged nor attracted to poor dear Lord Henry, or any other individual? I do not mind their saying so, if it amuses them, but only Brooke must not go trumpeting about fancying I am pining, or ought to be pining, for dear Lord Henry, who is an excellent child, and if he came in my way I think his education might be finished about the time your Pam would be coming out, but in the meantime I have never aspired to any other post than being his confidante. Perhaps I mistook Lady Glengall's hints, for the fact is she seems to know so much more about me than I do about myself, that I am quite puzzled and diffident about my own historical facts. But I think this is a point on which I am best informed of the two. If I am engaged to anybody it would be fair to tell me, that I might act the character better. However, I must say I like Lady Glengall much better than is convenient, and the girls are perfect, and I liked our Cahir visit—and she appreciates you properly.

Oh, Pam! how horrid it is to think that we parted there, because you are such a treasure to me, and we are going to lead the rest of our lives apart. I feel exactly as if this were my last Will and Testament. Mind you consider it as such!

I am as low as a cat this morning. I wonder whether we shall come over again either next year or the year after. Knocklofty was pleasant enough; old Donoughmore is such a duck, and there were two pretty nieces and a sub-nephew, and Tom-fool and Lord Arthur . We stayed two nights instead of one, as there were no post horses to be had. Lady Duncannon got home quite safe and is looking very well again—more like Mary than ever amongst her nine present children, and talking of her three absent ones, and nursing up her thirteenth. I have quite recovered my intimacy with her, and tell her as usual of all things. She says she was so ill at Cahir she hardly knew how to sit up.

I must go and see after that eternal packing. George says that even if it is the *Meteor*, a packet which, as far as I understand, is in every respect unsafe and uncomfortable, we must sail to-night. So I look upon myself as food for fishes, and as he must be lost with me, I shall not have the fun of gliding about as a grisly ghost and standing at his feet.... Your own affectionate

E. EDEN.

God bless you, my darling! My love to Sir Guy—his picture has travelled hitherto with the greatest success.

Miss Eden to Miss Villiers.

Stackpole, Pembrokeshire,
Saturday, November 3, 1827.

MY DEAREST THERESA, I never should wonder if you had thought me idle about writing. It would have been a terrible proof of the fallibility of your judgment if you had. I might as well have attempted to build a house as to keep up a correspondence during the active life I have been leading. I was once in hopes of tiring you out, and that you would write again without waiting for me, but we know each other too well. I was thinking the other day that it is unpleasant to reflect how well you know me, and how thoroughly I know you. No means of taking each other in, no little scenes, no explanations, no nothings.

My dear, such a happy six weeks as I have passed! I am so fond of Ireland. I have made 44 sketches and an equal number of new friends, am grown quite strong and well, and I have had nearly three weeks of dear old Pam's society. Besides paying her a visit, she went with us to Mount Shannon, and met us again at Cahir, thereby taking out the sting of my visit to Lady Glengall, who, *par parenthèse*, I must mention is now the friend of my heart. You all of you do very well for the common friendships of life, but in Ireland only has the whole extent of my merit been discovered. Seriously, Lady Glengall continued to make her house very pleasant. There was nothing she did not do to make Pamela and me comfortable there; arranged all sorts of picturesque expeditions. Lord Glengall gave us quite a pretty little fête at a cottage they have on their estate; we were out every day from breakfast-time to eight o'clock dinner, and then we had very good society in the evening—and Lord Glengall is very civil in his own house. It seemed hardly worth while coming to Tipperary, or County 'Prary, as the natives call it, when half of us belonged to Grosvenor Street and might have met at the expense of calling a coach.

Mr. B. Greville had been at Cahir ten weeks, all the county supposing he meant to marry Lady Charlotte, but the Glengalls all declare he is only by way of pining after Miss Acton. I could not make it out, nor could Pamela; only it was obvious that Lady Charlotte would not have had him if he had asked her. She and Lady Emily are two of the nicest girls I ever saw, and a melancholy proof of the uselessness of education—I mean melancholy for my dear sisters, who are slaving their lives away at education. They cannot wish for nicer daughters than the Butlers.

Altogether I liked Cahir. Killarney was one of the most satisfactory visits we paid; the lakes far surpassed even the extravagant expectation I had formed, and then the Kenmares are such charming people. However I will not write to you any more of my raptures; you will be bored to death. Perhaps you had rather hear that I had three days of extreme bore at Mitchell's—in the midst of all this enjoyment,—Lord Kingston's. Last Tuesday we crossed from Waterford to Milford. Oh, Theresa, such a passage! "If ever I do a good-natured thing again," as Liston says. Pamela may stay in Ireland to all eternity, and she need not ask me to come and see her. At all events, she must not mention it for a month; I shall be at least that time forgetting my sufferings. Even George owns to having passed a miserable night, and he has always despised my sea terrors, and the captain called it a very rough passage, so a very simple arithmetical process will enable you to calculate the sufferings of the passengers. Take the sum of the captain's assertions, multiply by 500, etc., etc.

The Cawdors had sent out the Custom House cutter to take the chance of meeting us, and that landed us within four miles of their house; so we were here at half-past-two. Our carriage did not arrive till ten at night. It was very attentive of them to send out the cutter, but if ever I willingly go again into cutter, steamboat, barge, wherry——. Well, I'm alive, and that is wonderful. The Duncannons fortunately made us stay an extra day with them, for the packet in which we were to have crossed originally, after beating about Milford for twelve hours, was obliged to put back again. "What a narrow escape I have had," George says, "of never seeing my native country again. I suppose if we had been in that packet you would have insisted on settling in Ireland, and I must have done so too!"

This is a very fine place and a comfortable house. It seems odd to be restored to a quiet English country-house life. I have lost the habit of going to sit in my own room, and cannot conceive why we do not breakfast early and go off after some distant lake or ruin. However, Elizabeth and I were out sketching most part of yesterday, and are going again to-day, and George has at last had two days' shooting. Think of his not having had a day's shooting till the 1st of November! And he actually looks over my sketch-book every evening and comments upon it with the greatest interest. In another month I should have taught him to sketch himself.

We stay here a week, and then go to Mr. Wall's. Direct to Grosvenor Street as the safest plan. What do you say about Sarah? We have all a great deal of unbelief to repent of. She was really in great danger for some hours, but is now as well as possible, Sister tells me in her letter to-day. Only—Sarah does not believe it. Fanny is at Knowsley, and they have been very gay there. No more time. I wonder where you are, but suppose Knightsbridge to be a safe direction. What a deal we shall have to talk about! I kept a journal, thinking as I could not write to all my friends I would let them see my Irish ideas in that form; but it degenerated after the first week into personalities, and is unshowable. Ever your most affectionate

E. E.

Miss Eden to Miss Villiers.

Langley Farm,
Sunday, 1827.

MY DEAREST THERESA, How d'ye do? I hope you have had your health better, Ma'am. I took to fretting about your having returns of pain in your head, but if ever I tried to say you had not been *quite* so well, everybody screamed out, "Oh yes, I am happy to tell you that Miss Villiers is *quite* well, never was so well. She has danced at a ball, and written an opera, and is perfectly well indeed." So I give it up. But are you really quite well, and where are you? I shall send this to your brother George, who is in town, as with infinite promptitude I conjectured, from seeing him at the Play with such a regular London party, such pomp and circumstance of hats and feathers, and Clanwilliams and Jerseys. I did not like the looks of them after the simple unadorned uncloathed Irish, but I did not see any of them to speak to.

Since I wrote to you, I have been to Norman Court for ten days. Such luxuries! such riches! It is too disgusting that that little Wall should have it all. We had a very pleasant party of gentlemen there—Mr. Luttrell amongst others, to whom I am devotedly attached. And he was in the highest good humour all the time, thanks to the goodness of the cook, and the comforts of his own room. No ladies, but old Mrs. Wall, who is worth ten of her son. She drives me to desperation by being so much better, in real goodness, than any of us will ever be, and yet very pleasant withal. I do not see that we have the least chance of meeting her hereafter. We shall be in a very inferior class.

Then I went to Laleham where I passed a very comfortable fortnight with the F. Levesons, and on Friday I came to town for a night and yesterday came here. I stayed in town chiefly to see Lady Bath, heard she was very cross about me, did not mind, went in with my most jaunty *débonnaire* manner, stood the brunt of one little sentimental reproach, and then we were as dear friends as ever. She is looking very well—certainly younger than when she went away. Char is decidedly plain; rather a Montagu cut about her. Lady Bath brought me such beautiful ear-rings—and my ears are not bored! So I was obliged to avow with as much shame as if I had lost my ears in the pillory that I could not have the pleasure of wearing them.

Then I went to Downing Street. Such a mess! She is crosser than ever, now she has all her wishes gratified. In short, all the stories that we have all known of her are nothing compared to what we might know now. Sister will not hear of her being crazy, though I have proved to her how advantageous it would be to Sarah's character; but at all events it is impossible that poor weak man can be our Minister much longer. I was rather in the Opposition Society at Laleham, and it is extraordinary the number of good stories the Opposition letters bring of Lord and Lady Goderich. However, all those of her meddling in Politics are perfectly unfounded. Her attention to her own self is never disturbed for a moment, and she does not ever ask for any public information. Gooch is appointed her third physician in ordinary, and she was unusually cross on Friday because he had not called before two. She had had Clarke and Pennington, but as she observed with the sweetest resignation, "Physicians, I believe, always neglect their dying patients."

I have two sisters here, and about eighteen small children. I mean *their* children, not mine. Love to Mrs. Villiers. Ever your affectionate

E. E.

Miss Eden to Miss Villiers.

GROSVENOR STREET,
Wednesday, December 2, 1827.

MY DEAREST THERESA, Your last note was entirely dateless, and as it has been disporting itself about the country in search of George, it must have been written a considerable time, I guess.

I went to see Sister yesterday. She is expecting Sarah at Eastcombe on Saturday, and I really believe likes to have her there! It is lucky there is a difference in tastes! Sarah now has *four* physicians in ordinary. They all met to consult a few days ago, and Pennington stood by the fire soliloquizing and was heard to say: "Well, this is the first time, I suppose, that we four ever met to consult when there was no complaint to consult about." She is too much absorbed in herself to care even about the baby, and does not bring it to Eastcombe with her. Sister asked me to come at the same time, which of course I declined, and I took the opportunity of speaking my mind to her, for I think she is nearly as much to blame as Sarah. She was not affronted or convinced, so it all went for nothing. Your ever affectionate

E. E.

CHAPTER VI

1828-1829

January 7, 1828.

Stayed at Grosvenor Place on our way home to dinner, and saw Mary with the three children dressed to go to the Duke of Atholl's for twelfth cake. Came home at 9, I suppose, to settle in town. How I hate it! But then I have had a very excellent absence of six months from it, and enjoyed my Irish tour, and my summer altogether as much as I expected. Found an invitation to Cobham, to Lady Darnley, and invitations to Madame de Lieven's and Mademoiselle de Palmella's parties to meet Dom Miguel. Such a horrid look about these invitations.

January 9, 1828.

Theresa Villiers came here, and Mary at five, and said that Lord Goderich had resigned the day before, and that the King had sent to the Duke of Wellington to desire him to make a new Government.

It was hardly possible to regret the last, it was so weak, and Lord Goderich so inefficient and ridiculous, chiefly owing to Sarah, but the triumph of one's enemies is always an ugly business.

January 12, 1828.

Lord Lansdowne dined alone with us. I never saw him in such good spirits or more agreeable. So extremely communicative, and so delighted to have done with office. He says the whole thing is an intrigue between Mr. Herries and Sir William Knighton. The instances he gave of Sir W. Knighton's influence over the King are quite wonderful. Lord Lansdowne does not believe, as all the rest of the Whigs do, that Lord Goderich has betrayed them. He says that at present they are all Ministers still, and that the King had signified to them his wishes that they might still continue so—which, as he puts it all into the hand of the Duke of Wellington, means nothing; and that they are to wait till the Duke makes them some proposition they cannot accede to, and then to go out.

He said Lord Goderich was very nervous when he first saw him yesterday. Lord Melville is talked of as Prime Minister.

January 18, 1828.

Mary lent me her carriage. Saw Sarah dressed and walking about her room, not looking particularly ill, quite forgetting her plaintive manner. She told me Mr. Huskisson had consented to take office under the Duke, for which she abused him in her old eager manner. Saw Lord Goderich, looking like the poor wretch he is.

January 30, 1828.

Dined at Lady Charlotte Greville's. Met the F. Levesons, the Duke of Devonshire, Lord Morpeth, Lord Ashley and Mr. Talbot. A pleasant dinner. The Duke told me he had been very sorry to resign and he was furious with Lord Goderich, that the King told him that the day Lord Goderich resigned one of the gentlemen of the bedchamber, knowing nothing of what had passed, asked Lord Goderich to give him a lift to town; that the King had the curiosity to ask him on his return what he thought of Lord Goderich, and that the gentleman said he thought him very pleasant: he had joked and laughed till they came to Hounslow, and then fell asleep, and this immediately after having resigned—not only for himself, but for all his colleagues without their consent.

February 14, 1828.

Got two places at the House of Commons, asked Theresa to go with me. Mr. Hobhouse moved a vote of thanks to Sir E. Codrington, and made a good speech, Mr. B. a very tiresome one, Sir J. Mackintosh rather a learned one; and Mr. Peel not a bad one, during which we came away, almost starved to death. Dined at 11.

February 15, 1828.

Had a place at the House of Commons again. Borrowed Lady Bath's carriage and went to see her first. Found Lady Francis Leveson at the House. We were both very anxious for the explanation that was expected from Mr. Huskisson. Mr. Peel made a good speech on Finance, and proposed the Finance Committee. Mr. Baring proposed that Mr. Huskisson's name should be added to it. Mr. Brougham said a few words in the same sense; then there came a silence, every one expecting Mr. Huskisson would speak, and that somebody would ask him to explain. But nobody got up, and Mr. Goulburn moved an Adjournment which was received with a shout of laughter, and they all rushed out. We were all horribly disappointed, nobody found their carriages ready. Mrs. Horton's carriage took seven of us, and left me in Grosvenor Place.

March 11, 1828.

Went out with Lady Harriet Baring upon trial to see if I liked her. Do not know now. Bought a bonnet at Madame Carsan's (not paid for).

March 12, 1828.

Dined at Mrs. A. Baring's,—what she calls my dinner, one she gives every year to which I am supposed to ask the company. The B. Barings, H. Mildmays, Theresa, H. Villiers, Mr. Labouchere, Mr. Luttrell, Mr. A. Greville, Mr. Ponsonby and F. Baring. Went on to Devonshire House, where George and Fanny had dined.

Miss Eden to Miss Villiers.

LANGLEY,
Saturday, January 5, 1828.

DEAREST THERESA, I have been trying by the help of the newspaper to form the slightest guess of your movements, but I cannot make them out.

Sarah's reform lasted nearly three days, and she is now herself again, in the most finished perfection. Her hatred to Blackheath and her violent love of Downing Street prove to me that she sees the time is near when they must leave the latter abode, and the only thing makes me doubt that he is going out, is her avowed wish that he should leave office. Her indifference about her baby, after all the fuss she made, is so in harmony with the rest of her cross-grained character, that I contemplate it with the fondest admiration.

I know no news to tell you. The laundry here was robbed on Tuesday, which seems to afford the children great amusement. I have experienced the pleasure of a robbed laundry before, and it does not amuse me now—much. I asked Wright if I had lost anything. "Only your best cap, and your two best frills, and your best worked habit-shirt, and your best lace,"—none of them having been better than their fellows till they were stolen. Ever your affectionate

E. E.

Lady Campbell to Miss Eden.

ARMAGH, 1828.

Here I am *translated* to Armagh. I got through the journey and all the bother wonderfully by Georgina St. Quintin's help. I parted with her in Dublin, where I spent five days, and where I found Lady Glengall, Mr. Villiers, Lord Forbes, Lady Erroll. But I was glad to leave Dublin; even in those few days I saw so much *tracasserie* and fuss about nothing, that I would not live there on any account if I could help it. Emmy, I find that I am totally unfit for what is called the world, or anything like it. I have forgotten its ways and its language,—in short, I have seen too much sorrow to be up to it. I thought Dublin itself beautiful, and Lady Glengall was most good-natured,—crammed me into one of her own Hats and sent me to a ball at the Castle which was beautiful. I dined with all the military people, and came away nothing loth. The tyranny of the Few over the Many does not strike the eye so much here, although I believe this to be the very heart of it—the positive *pips* of the orange.

I have seen my new General. They say he is very gentlemanlike and good-natured. He seems to me stupid and vulgar, but pray *double-lock* this, for we cannot afford to quarrel with another General. We are nearly ruined by this last move, that is one of the things that makes me low. I am not at all sure that we shall not be obliged to *sell out* now, from money difficulties. So much sickness, and a move has thrown us back horribly, so you must bear with me now and then, my own Emmy. When I do not write it is because I am fretted and full of care. I keep up my spirits wonderfully, and am quite well as to health, and Sir Guy, too, fights on manfully. He means to try all he can before he sells, but if he cannot manage, we *must* sell and say no more about the matter; but only think how much better off we are than others in the world. Write to me, my dear Emmy, for your letters do me good and cheer me. I was quite glad to talk about you to Mr. Villiers.\ He seemed to think it was *extraordinary* how much you loved me, and I began to think it oddish myself, for certainly *je ne vaux pas grand chose*, when I come to consider.

May 27, 1828.

Will you make another attempt to find Abby, he resorts much to that Mulligatawny fount frequented by Turtle, and on the banks of which curry grows spontaneous,—the Oriental Club?

I do not much like this place, but we have many negative blessings—a quiet peaceable General, an Adjutant-General full of abstruse erudition. Talking of this man, by the bye, I want to know whether the Committee of useful knowledge know that there are gangs of half-informed science-mongers, who are going about quoting the information they plunder out of the library, and bringing it out as their own topics, without giving notice of where they have taken them. This said Colonel Moore (nephew to Sir Graham) is a nefarious pilferer, and tried to cram the information of the Duke's Bill down my throat as his own discovery.

Emily, the day is at hand when we shall sigh for a plain fool and the sight of a natural will be good for sore eyes. We shall, it is hardly doubted, have a row here, for our Orangemen are frantic, and *will* walk and *will* play their horrid tunes. We had a man killed in a fray a week ago about a drum.

Lady Campbell to Miss Eden.

June 2, 1828.

MY DEAR EMMY, You are right, there is nothing like answering directly, but my dear child, I have nothing to tell you. Here one day certifieth the other, and I see no one, nothing happens—lessons and walks and eating—and now and then a bore drops in by way of a change. And the people speak so as to be tolerably understood, and their rags are sufficient to cover them, and there is not that variety of dislocation among the limbs of the beggars, which now and then accorded us a topic in the south. You might as well expect a letter from a silkworm out of the very heart of its cocoon....

I like my house although it has only its snugness and a cheerful view to recommend it; but the people as yet rather bore me. In short, my dear Emmy, I return to the old song:—I don't care *that*—for acquaintances. I had rather have my hedge of life with its gaps and rents, than patch it up with rubbish; and if the goodly cedars are laid low, the place that knew them shall at least remain void, and show that such things were. I really feel this more and more every day. I love my friends better than ever, but making an acquaintance is positively disagreeable. Your letters are such gleams to me. That alliance of Car and her pretty little hands with Moloch Mostyn did enchant me.

Do you know, Mrs. Vansittart's consent ought to be more known. It is the longest step emancipation has made this age. You see, Emmy, she was quite right about the girl's beauty, and you quite wrong.

I wish you could see my shaved head. I look like a Greek pipe-bearer, or Haggai himself, or something very much out of the way. But all my hair was really coming out. They say I shall have a good crop in six months, and be able to turn it up in a year.

We are in doubts still about our finances. I do not well know what is to become of us, but I try not to fret. I wish you would make a friendship with the Downshires, that would conduce to your coming to the North country.

Do you think Lord Auckland is to be moved this way? What people do you see most of? Which of my deputies is filling up my place? Is it your Bath or Maria Copley? What is become of Miss Villiers, and how is poor Lady Grantham?... How are you yourself? Good-bye, Dearest. Ever your own

PAMELA CAMPBELL.

Miss Eden to Miss Villiers.

EASTCOMBE,
August 31, 1828.

I suppose my genius is to be cramped into this single sheet, which is very unpleasant.

I was very glad to get your letter, as well to hear something about you, so as to know where to write. It is an excellent plan your writing a few times at different places. Your letter amused me particularly. You have done adventures enough now for some time, and may pursue your way safely without any danger of shocking me with the want of incident.

No, I am not fastidious, because I *dis*like very few people (those might be called enemies); and I like a great many for their good qualities without liking their society (those are my acquaintances); and then I like a great many more for good qualities, or agreeableness, or their affection for me (those are my friends); and amongst those are a chosen few particularly *perfect*, combining the three advantages, and those are my intimate friends. And unless I can be with either of the two last classes, I have not a sufficient love of society not to prefer being alone. But I do not at all despise or dislike those I do not wish to be with,—quite the contrary. I respect them to the greatest degree, only I do not care about them, and I cannot praise them as I do the others. Your system of general praise would bring you by degrees to think it equally pleasant to meet Sir Gore Ouseley and Mr. Luttrell, Mr. Lushington and Lord Alvanley, and you would like me to say Harriet Baring is as pleasant an incident at a dinner as yourself. No thank you; I prefer my distinctions. The dark shadows of *bore* bring out the lights of agreeableness, and I like to *perceive* a difference, even if I do not act upon it. However, do not let us argue by letter; there is no room for it.

My dear, my Irish journey is defunct, dead, deceased, annihilated, and I shall follow its example if things go on so. You may, if your English papers follow you, have seen that a man of the name of Austin has *defaulted* from Greenwich Hospital, after having cheated it to a great amount. It is not worth telling you the story, besides, I have thought of nothing else till I am sick of it; but it has worried and annoyed George, who is Auditor of the Accounts, to a degree that I cannot express. Austin has been taken at Limerick, but that does very little good, and only gives the additional trouble of arranging the manner of prosecuting him, which will be a difficult business, as our laws, according to the accurate observations I have made on them for many years, are calculated chiefly for the protection and encouragement of crime; and besides encouraging husbands to kill their wives, and masters their apprentices, have had an eye to the safety of Austin, and all the thousands of pounds that were found in his trunk cannot be touched. I do not precisely see the justice of his taking our Irish journey, and leaving us to settle his accounts, but I suppose it is all right. The investigation of the whole business has been put into George's hands, and there is so much that is disagreeable in it, besides confining him to the neighbourhood of Greenwich, that he has been very low, poor fellow! But like a sensible man, he sent for me to keep up his spirits; and we have been here the last three weeks, and shall be here a fortnight longer, and then I fear we shall have to go to London.

Well, I hold it wrong to grumble, but I do not love London at any time, and above all, not in September; and I grudge the loss of his shooting, and I hate to see him so bothered.

I went to town last Tuesday, as I heard of a large covey of friends that might be shot flying, and I saw Maria just come from Tunbridge, looking better but not well. Lady Grantham, looking ill, from Tunbridge also; Coppy, freshly imported from Dieppe in great spirits; Lady C. Greville passing on to Dublin; and various other acquaintances.

This is a stupid letter, but if you knew how much I have been worried the last three weeks you would think it bright of me not to be stupid. I will write again soon. Your most affectionate

E. E.

Mind you sketch all day.

Miss Eden to Miss Villiers.
EASTCOMBE,
Sunday, September 21.

MY DEAREST THERESA, If I had the remotest idea what to say to you I should like writing better, I think; but I never can write to anybody abroad. I can't fancy them. What are you like? Do I know you? Have I ever seen you? Have we a thought in common? You are skipping about an Alp, and I remain here like a post, and I give you my honour things have entirely done happening.

I told you about our Greenwich troubles. They have not improved, and you will have a high opinion of my fortitude and also of the extremity of *bother* that has obliged me to mount my mind up to the heights of actual resignation, when I tell you that George and I are going to town the 1st of October to settle, (October being my favourite month of the year, and when I should naturally be disporting myself on the Giant's Causeway). And yet I am as meek as a mouse, and have not grumbled about it at all, and flatter myself that George finds me as *cheery* as possible. It will put you in a rage, but who cares when you are 1000 miles off! But besides the motive of not plaguing him, I am kept up by a fond hope, which indeed almost amounts to certainty, that I shall not be in London at all next year, at least not in February. We shall let our house and live in his apartments at Greenwich for some time—within reach if you have anything to say.

I do not often think I do right, but I really have behaved very well the last two months. I am glad they are over, for it has been a worrying time and I hate to see George plagued. We have never stirred from here except for two days to see Robert.

Panshanger was full to the brim of vice and agreeableness, foreigners and roués. It sounded awful, and I declined paying a morning visit, which is at the best an awkward business, to twenty people all accustomed to each other's jokes. But Lady Cowper sent her carriage for me the last day, so that I could not help myself. Most of the party was dispersed, except Lord Melbourne, Sir F. Lamb, and Lord Alvanley, who was more amusing than ever. Lady Emily looked very pretty, and Lady Cowper was as usual very agreeable.

F. Robinson's history has come to an end I think. Lady Cowper seemed very cool about him and they have not met since in London. Considering that those brothers and sisters are in all probability as little related to each other as possible, they are the most attached family I ever saw. Ever your most affectionate

E. E.

Miss Eden to Miss Villiers.
GROSVENOR STREET,
November 2, 1828.

MY DEAREST THERESA, I have been rather of the longest about this letter. To be sure you set me a bright example. I thought you must have tumbled off an Alp and hurt yourself, or have been run over by an Avalanche which drove on without stopping to ask. That would have been accidental death, with a Dividend of one shilling on the Avalanche.

I was very glad to get your letter with such a good account of yourself. What a nice summer you will have passed. I rather hope, whether your house is let or not, that you will squeeze out every half-penny and see as much as you can,—which, to be sure, is highly disinterested of me, because the convenience it would be to me to have you at home just now is incalculable. But you are better abroad, and then, if you come home now, there is no saying when you will be allowed to go again. It ought to have been one of the rules of the game that one might be allowed not to begin the *expenses* of travelling again till the point where they ceased before. I mean, that as you have once paid your way to Florence, you ought to go gratis there next time, and then begin buying your freedom to Rome.

We came to London last Monday, George and I having passed our whole summer at Eastcombe. He still has a great deal of business at Greenwich, but is beginning to see his way through it and is, at all events, in better health and spirits. We shall probably live only part of the year at Greenwich, and there is a very nice house *in* the park belonging to George's office, with a little greenhouse next to it, and it may by courtesy be called a *small* villa. For my part I shall like it extremely, but George hates the idea of it so much that I say nothing. He is sure to do at last what he ought, and though he declares he can never go there, we go on very quietly buying furniture, arranging with servants, etc. You see (this is between ourselves) that rather than be bored with this business which he has taken in utter aversion, he would almost prefer giving up his office, thereby making himself uncomfortably poor. I think that's great nonsense, and that he would repent when he had done it.

Because he has met with dishonesty once, he is not more likely to meet with it again, and as he is always making business for himself, at the London University or Zoological Gardens or somewhere, he cannot want to be idle, and had better do what he is paid for, than what he is not paid for—both if he likes it. But at all events the first is the best, so I go on taking no notice, and he is recovering fast his usual activity.

I daresay London will be pleasant enough in a week or so. I see plenty of stray people about it. Ladies with very *considerable* figures, and attentive bored husbands attending them in the short walks they are able to take, not to be out of sight of the monthly nurse.

Lady H. Baring being one of the most considerable, and Bingham one of the most attentive, I went with them to the Adelphi on Wednesday and was in agonies all the time. The house was so full there would not have been room for even the smallest baby in addition.

It is very odd that the Duke of Wellington will not say one word as to the intentions of the Government, because as it is, nothing can be more terrific than the state of things. I begin to believe what some people say—that he has no plan and does not know what to do. In short another Goderich come to judgement.

The Copleys have been at Chatsworth—an immense party, private theatricals, dancing, etc., and they were all enchanted.

It amused me that Coppy should act Antonio in the "Merchant of Venice," she must have been such a good figure, and somehow the idea tickled my fancy particularly. I think she must have done it well. Antonio is an excellent over-friendly bore, and though it is wrong of us, you know that is the light in which Coppy strikes us.

The Duke of Portland, as usual, does not take joy in Lady Lucy's marriage, and gives her no money. His is a good plan: he holds out his daughters as fortunes till somebody proposes for them, and then he gives them nothing because they accept the proposal. And then in a rage his sons-in-law threaten to carry off their wives to some horrid climate. Lord Howard is going to try the West Indies.

The London University has opened with most unexpected success. They have nearly 250 students entered already, and several of the Professors have distinguished themselves much in their introductory lectures, and there have been crowds sent away who were anxious to hear them. George got your brother Charles a place to hear a lecture the other day among the council. He never can make out the names of your brothers, except George, but goes boldly on calling them all "Villiers" and then comes to me to class them. Ever your affectionate

E. E.

Miss Eden to Miss Villiers.
GROSVENOR STREET,
November 19, 1828.

MY DEAREST THERESA, George and I went to Norman Court about a month ago, met a very pleasant party there, and had enjoyed ourselves nearly a week, charmed to be out of town, delighted to be killing the poor dear dumb pheasants, and recovering a great deal of lost health, and nursing up an equable flow of spirits, when a letter arrived to say my sister, Mrs. Vansittart, was taken dangerously ill. We had to set off directly, travelled all day—such a horrid journey, particularly the last stage, for we expected to find all was over. However, thank God! that was not the case, though she was in the greatest danger.

You will see the Mostyns at Rome. I do not know what they will have settled to do. There was no use in telling Car how ill her mother was. Caroline's recovery must be extremely slow, in fact she has not only to recover intellect for herself, but for her husband and 13 children. She has thought and acted for them till they cannot think or act for themselves, and anxiety for them makes her recovery more hazardous.

It has been an unpleasant month! I saw the Lansdownes on Wednesday—just arrived, enchanted with their tour. Only they complained bitterly of the cold all through France and at Paris, and are astonished to find us all so hot. There never was such a season. Very favourable weather for the young pines. I suppose we shall grow them in the open air.

Mademoiselle Taglioni is the greatest heroine in Paris—the finest dancer ever seen. "Toutes les autres danseuses *tombent*," Vestris says; "Mademoiselle Taglioni redescend." Full gowns and full sleeves are arrived at a degree of fullness Lady Lansdowne says, which makes it necessary for all the poor husbands to sit backwards in the carriages.

They say Fred Robinson's marriage with Lady Emily Cowper is settled. I heard it accidentally a fortnight ago and did not believe it, and now I do. Robert says Fred is staying at Panshanger quite alone with the Cowpers and he never saw anything like the love-making, rather absurd, and a bore altogether for the Cowpers. Did I tell you how I had been reading General Miller's "South America," and had been taken by it? The man himself is in London, on his way back to Peru, and George brought him home to dinner one day. It is pleasant to hear the adventures of an adventurer, and he is remarkably unassuming. He has one fault, in being horribly wounded, and I am particularly weak on that point. A common cut finger disagrees with me, and he does not seem to have a single *whole* finger left. However he is a hero, and I bore it wonderfully,—kept thinking of American independence, and the cause of liberty all over the world, and was only squeamish, not sick. We are busy furnishing our Greenwich House, and tending fast towards the King's Bench. I wish you would come home; you will come just as we go. I have not answered your last letter,—no room, but go on writing, I like it.

Love to Mrs. V. Ever your most affectionate

E.E.

Lady Campbell to Miss Eden.

ARMAGH,
November 26, 1828.

Emmy, are you with child? Or have you had a husband and four children in the hooping-cough? Or have you been driven mad by Orange factions? If none of these evils have befallen you, you might have written me a line more. I know yours was the last letter, but think of me and all my sufferings! And above all, the standing disappointment of not seeing you, when I was literally airing the sheets and killing the fowls for you. And there I was without encumbrance, a free woman, ready to go all over the Causeway—and as I fear I am now beginning a child, I do not know when I shall be my own woman again.

Sir Guy has literally had the whooping-cough and is not well yet, and you who know what Lord Auckland is with a swelled face, may imagine what Sir Guy is with a whoop rending his lungs. The children have all had it rather lightly, but are still rather disagreeable and like a rookery. My dear, I had a glimpse of Lady Wallscourt at the Inn. I spent half an hour with her; she is afraid of the whooping-cough and would not come to me. I think I ought to *bénir la providence* that bricks and mortar stood my friends, and that she could not find a house; for truly I think you anticipated justly that she would not exactly be the person I should wish to spin my days with. However, I will work up a little good feeling and liking towards her next Spring, when she may want it,—and, my dear, I must confess to you that the slang of good society, even, is now grown irksome to me, I suppose from want of habit, particularly when it is not supported by any ideas.

However, my Dearest, don't think I am bitter. Indeed I love to think of all the good there is in the world,—not for your sake, though you are my great link. But then I consider you as my world in itself.

I hope it will not be in the power of any swindler to keep you from me next year, for I really cannot do so long without a clearance of ideas. There will be such old stores to dispose of. Emily, I am ashamed to confess to you how I have suffered from the Orange spirit of this horrid black North. I am ashamed to tell you how wickedly irritated I was, I am getting better now. The fearful evil I feel of this party spirit is, it is so catching. It kindles all the combustibles of contradiction and retaliation within one, till, though it was *injustice* that irritated me, yet I fear I should not have dealt justly towards them. I am not sanguine, I think nothing will be done; and I wish I thought better of the Association. I am constantly told *indirectly* that the friends of the Catholics should fear their ascendancy, for if they begin a *massacre* they will cut down *friend* and foe. Pleasant little images!... It is such a comfort to me that by leaving the world one can get rid of its taint to a certain degree; for I do not think I could bear to hear one half of the things I used to think nothing of at all some years ago.

I cannot tell you how kind to us Lord Gosford has been. We spent a few days with him in his remnant of a house. I never would cut up my old gown till I had another to my back, which has been his case. He pulled down three-quarters of a liveable house and began a large granite Castle, and inhabits the gore of the house. However, we were very merry in the Lambeau. I think he does seem the most good-humoured person I ever saw....

I am quite glad Lord Gosford liked me, because when I am very long away from you I am afraid you will find me so rusty and grown shabby. He is very pleasant. It was quite refreshing to be in a green liberal atmosphere at Caledon. I like him too; he is such a plain matter-of-fact man, and I think there is a good deal of steady ballast of that sort wanted on the Liberal side, because it gives twice as much confidence as talent. Lady Caledon knew something of you but not right. I was obliged to teach her a good deal, she thought you so devoted to the world. You see—you know what I mean. Now I was dying to tell her that it was the world loved you. The children behaved well, which was a relief to me. It is the first time they have been let loose in company. Fanny is really a very nice girl, and has very good manners, and I am quite pleased that seven years' toil should really be rewarded so well, so much beyond my hopes.

Lady Campbell to Miss Eden.

December 6, 1828.

I believe in this world it is always *surest* and safest to write to those we love best, when life weighs heavy on our spirits; we have many more chances of hitting the right string. Alas, how often I delayed writing to you when I felt low and anxious, and had fears and fits of depression because I would not darken your page; and when I felt lighter I wrote a letter which, after all must have jarred upon you Dearest, when you were still in the *slough*! ... I like your Greenwich plan much. I think it will suit you and do you good. I know I shall live to see you a real saint. Then where we are to put Lord Auckland I cannot well make out, unless he ripens into a sort of Wilberforce, but my imagination does not yet carry me so far.

I have been reading Jebb's *Sacred Literature*. I like it although one is obliged to hop over a good deal of Greek etymology.

Oh, how I want you to talk to, for it is such an age since we really cleared our minds, and you know, Emmy, we do belong to one another upon some Geometrical System of fitness that we cannot well describe. But my idea is that by finding out what E.E. is to P.C., you ascertain what P.C. is to E.E.

CHAPTER VII

1829-1830

Miss Eden to Miss Villiers.
GROSVENOR STREET,
Wednesday, April 30, 1829.

MY DEAREST THERESA, How attentive we become! frightened to death at the idea of our near meeting, *unwritten* to. I had your Genoa letter three days ago in the leisure of Hertingfordbury, where I have been Eastering, and could have *drawn* my pen on the spot to answer you, but I thought some account of the Hatfield theatricals would be more diverting than pure unadulterated daffy-down-dillies and cowslips.

Robert and I went over to Hatfield on Monday, which was the second repetition of the plays. The 1st piece was "A Short Reign and a Merry One." Mr. Phipps the chief performer; Major Keppel very good; Mr. Egerton clever; Lady Salisbury herself I thought the only failure, but some people thought her good, so perhaps I was wrong. Her dress disfigured her cruelly. The second piece was Lady Dacre's translation of the *Demoiselle à Marier*—Lady F. Leveson, Mr. J. Wortley, and Lord Morpeth the chief performers; and it was impossible anything could be better. In short, the whole evening has lowered my opinion of the merits of professional people. I went expecting to find the *gentlefolk* all tolerable sticks on the stage, awkward, affected, and only helped through by an indulgent public, and I found I never had laughed more heartily, never had seen a play really well acted in all its parts before, and Lady S., whom I thought the least good, was only objectionable because she was like an actress on the real stage.

The singing was very pretty. Mr. Ashley, Mr. Wortley, Lady F. Leveson, all distinguished themselves. At the end of the first piece, each of the performers sung a little Vaudeville couplet, and Jim Wortley sang one to the Duke of Wellington, who was in the front row, that was applauded and *encored* and applauded again, and chorussed with great noise. It turned, of course, upon the hero, and the double crown, and Waterloo, and Catholics—you know how these little ideas are dished up—and there was an allusion to the same effect in the Prologue, also received with acclamations.

The Duke seemed very much pleased, and told George to-day the Hatfield theatricals were very good fun. I meant to make this only a half sheet, but I see a long stream of untouched topics before me, so here goes for a whole sheet and rather wider lines.... The Duke of Norfolk, Lord Clifford, etc., took their seats yesterday under the auspices of Julia, Lady Petre, and the two Miss Petres, and several Catholic ladies grouped under our Protestant throne, and now there only remains to come the introduction of that wily dangerous Edward Petre into the House of Commons, and England must fall, and then, I suppose, will get up and begin again.

Poor Lady Derby died on Friday after great sufferings and a very long illness. I think it ought to be made a rule of the odd game we all play here that those old attached couples should die together Baucis and Philemon fashion. The survivor's is a hard place.

Fanny has been, of course, very anxious and unhappy, and has certainly lost a very kind friend in Lady Derby, who expressed the greatest affection for her to the last.

We shall not be the least settled at Greenwich, or near it, when you come back. A fortnight ago when we went there the workmen said they thought they would be out of the house in ten days. George went there yesterday, and they said they thought in about a *fortnight* more they should have done! A month hence, perhaps, they will ask six weeks more—that is the way painters generally go on. However, our wonderful weather excuses them. It is colder than Christmas and rains eternally. As far as we are concerned it has done its worst. We could not let this house till we find another to go into, and we shall not easily find a tenant after this week, so you will find us here, and here we shall probably stay till the 1st of June.

I only came to town yesterday, so I know little London news. People are dying rather than otherwise. I do not know whether there is much else going on. There is the Drawing-room to-morrow. Malibran has been rather a disappointment to the musical world, I hear, but I have not seen her. F. Robinson pays unremitting court to Lady Emily Cowper. I cannot conceive anything so tiresome, particularly at her age, when, as I remember, the pride of one's life was to be distinguished by older people than oneself. Moreover, that dear good-looking bore, G. Cole, holds it to be his duty to stick by Frederick and flirt *en tiers* as well as he can. We have grown to be a very depraved set of incendiaries, and it makes me perfectly miserable to think of the peril of our beautiful cathedrals. York Minster gone, and two days ago an attempt was made to set Westminster Abbey on fire. The fire was put out without much harm being done, but no clue has been found to the man. The country is too full; a great deal of distress; great national debt; a redundancy of Spitalfields weavers; and in the course of a good hanging they might hit on these incendiaries, and no sacrifice would be too great for Westminster Abbey.

You know I let your house for three weeks, and the Vansittarts liked it. It seemed odd and unpleasant visiting anybody but you there. Come home soon. God bless you. Love to Mrs. V. Your ever affectionate

E. E.

Miss Eden to Miss Villiers.
PARK LODGE, GREENWICH,
Monday evening, July 8, 1829.

MY DEAREST THERESA, There never was such provocation, such a combination of untoward events. I was in town to-day, went up to return Maria Copley to her home, could have brought you back with me; and Lady Buckinghamshire's carriage which goes up to town to-morrow morning would have taken you home again. I just ask you, "Did you ever?" *Songez-y un peu!* Such a plain path so entirely missed. I like you to know the worst, because there is no use in my ranting and raving about as I have this evening, if you do not do your share. I wonder when you wrote to me. If only last night, the thing could not have been helped. You never could have had an answer in time, but if you wrote on Saturday, which I should think was more probable, I just ask you if it is not a little provoking? Now we shall have no talk at all, ever again, our minds must be so over-loaded that writing will be of no earthly use, and you will not see our home while it is new and pretty—in short, there never was such a misfortuneable occurrence. I went on hoping till eight you would come. If it had happened yesterday I should not have wondered. Till that unfortunate day we had all been happier here than we ever had been in our lives, but yesterday was "a day of misfortunes," like Rosamond's day in Miss Edgeworth's book. The footman was suddenly laid up by a violent attack of gout; one of the maid-servants was taken dangerously ill; one of the horses took to kicking *itself*, of all the things in the world! and hurt itself very much, which it deserves, but it is very inconvenient to us; the cream was sour at breakfast; we got quite wet through going to church, and again coming back; the puppy and kitten fought; there was no mint sauce to the lamb at dinner;—in short, "it was a sight worthy of the gods to see a great man (or, as in my case, a great woman) struggling with such calamities."

We preserved our cheerfulness wonderfully. I wish you had seen our house; we are all so fond of it. My friends have exhausted themselves in presents *with* their names, and have now begun again anonymously. I brought from Grosvenor Street a box to-day directed to me, containing a lamp for the drawing-room, and now it is hung up I should be glad to know who sent it.

I went to wish Lady Bath joy a week ago. I never was so pleased with any marriage as that. Is Lord Henry settled or not? I understood he went down to the Grange meaning to propose, and on Wednesday I heard a long account of his visit, of Mrs. Baring's agonies of fidget because he did not speak out, and of Harriet's confidence in his intentions, and how they both grew hourly more shy and more silent. But he had let all the rest of the party disperse, and was staying on alone at the Grange, and was expected to have stayed with the purpose of proposing without so many witnesses. Poor fellow! He seems to have been shyer than ever. I know you will again think it odd of me, and I am sure I cannot explain it, but by dint of hearing so much of their anxieties, and knowing what his must have been, I grow fidgetty as one does reading a story, that the catastrophe should be happy.

It will be a shame if he makes her unhappy. Otherwise, I do not know that they will suit very well. Lady Bath asked me about it, and did not seem very anxious for it,—said he required animation. I hardly knew what to say when she said she was afraid by what she heard of Miss Baring that was not the line, etc. I rode off on her amiability, good sense, £50,000, etc. I hope Lady Bath may take a fancy to her; she will want something to replace Char, but I rather doubt it.

Where am I to direct to you? I could be at home all the week in case any of your other engagements should fail, only come in time to prevent my dining at Eastcombe or elsewhere. Your ever affectionate

E. E.

Miss Eden to Miss Villiers.

August 1829.

I took a solemn oath that if the post brought me any letter this morning I would, on the first sight of Bidgood with the silver waiter *orné de lettres*, tear myself from my drawing and give up the rest of the morning to this detestable writing employment; and, you brute, there *is* a letter from you, and a good letter too, and I must answer it. And yet if you were to see my drawing! I got up at half-past eight this morning that I might have a long enjoyment of it, and of course have been interrupted every five minutes, though I was drapering a red velvet cloak with all sorts of beautiful catching lights and carmine and ultra marine and all the lovely colours in the world mixed up in it. My black heads are framed and hung up in George's room. I do not like to say how *they* look, but the room is evidently improved within the last week. I have been at Putney from a Saturday to a Wednesday, my dear—"a *procédé*," as Mr. de Roos would call it, a friendly attention, but extremely inconvenient, and moreover I think it bored me ever so little—not much—but it did not amuse me. I like the girls, of all things, and wish for nothing better than a talk with Anne, but there is a want of sense about Lady Grantham which becomes wearisome in a very long *tête-à-tête*, and we had several. Lord Henry stayed a whole week at the Grange, but nothing came of it. Let us fondly hope the discouragement came from her side. I do not fancy the woman ever being made the victim; and perhaps she found him duller than she expected, and Mr. Baring probably found him poorer. Anyhow, it might not have answered, and I daresay it will all do very well as it is; or he may, in a thoroughly *manly* spirit (by which I mean the usual conduct of a man) have settled that though he could propose any day, he could go out grouse shooting only on the 12th of August, and that the grouse might grow wild, while she would remain tame (I have only put that in for the love of antithesis, not from pique or attraction), and so that he had better attend to the grouse first, and come back to the Grange afterwards. Lady Bath said he met her and the Buccleughs at Longleat and was in great spirits, and she believed did not care a straw for Miss Baring, but she *knew* nothing from him of it....

I passed all Wednesday afternoon with Lady Bath, who was in the highest good-humour, and the whole family resplendent with happiness, except dear old Bath, who handsomely avows his joy was a mistake, and he has not the least idea what is to become of him. I saw Char, and the Duke too; and after they all went out riding Lady Bath and I went poking all over the house, looking for the presents he had given her. Such quantities of pretty things! And these were only his little daily gifts, for the jewels were not finished. "The diamonds and emeralds will both be superb," Lady Bath said; "but I think the pearls the handsomest set I ever saw."

Think of that little Char with all those things! And she looks as simple and unaffected as ever,—very shy and very happy.

Miss Eden to Miss Villiers.

October 19, 1829.

MY DEAREST THERESA, Lady Harriet says she wrote to you yesterday to announce that we were going to talk you over. I think it my duty to write to-day to announce that we have talked you over,—done our *devoirs* bravely. The substance of our comments you would not of course be curious to hear. Having thus obviously made you thoroughly uncomfortable, and this being Sunday evening and consequently to be devoted to works of charity, I add from pure benevolence that Lady Harriet has said nothing that is not in your praise, confirms the remarkable fact that the heads of the Baring Clan are all turned by you, and if it were not for that circumstance, which, as she says, must be provoking to her, it appears to me she is as fond of you and Mrs. Villiers as it is possible to be. She is very charitable and very pleasant to-day.

I was not the least taken in by all your paltry evasions about not writing to me. You never care a straw for me when you can have Louisa Baring. I am constrained to avow that Harriet Baring and the Red Rover have always been my successful rivals with you and everybody else. Please the Fates, I will set up some new friends for myself, and occupy myself so exclusively with them that you shall not be able to get a word from me for a month.

Well, I have no doubt Harriet Baring has every merit under the sun, only you never will persuade me she is amusing. There is no merit in being amusing, so that is not against her. I am glad she is in good spirits; and it seems that neither she, nor her family, nor Lord Henry Thynne, nor his family, wished for the marriage. It is rather lucky than otherwise that they did not marry, though as the Barings want connection, and he wants money, it was a natural marriage for all the world to insist upon,—a clever idea, though it did not work well.

I passed such a nice morning yesterday, though my ulterior object was to go to town to try on some gowns. But George and I began the day early, and went to visit Chantrey, who showed us quantities of beautiful things, amongst others a monument to Bishop Heber that is quite beautiful, is not it? I tried to sketch it for you and failed, but he is blessing two kneeling Hindus who, to the best of my recollections, have not a stitch of clothes on (the climate is warm, you know), but the dearest bald head you ever saw, with one long lock from the top. They are so graceful—I mean seriously. Then we saw the Colossal statue of Mr. Pitt, he has just cast in Bronze, and he gave up a whole hour, in which he could have chipped a bit of covering to those poor Hindus, to explaining to me, who am fussy and dull if anybody begins an *entirely* new subject, how a bronze statue is cast, and how the weight of the least moisture in the cast is ascertained even to the 1000th part of a grain, and how the original cast is made. In short, I was quite learned about it yesterday, and as his clay models disgusted me with mine, I had some thoughts of turning the library into a foundery, and of melting down all the saucepans, and casting a statue of George in his shooting jacket, 14 feet high; but I have forgotten to-day how to do it. Chantrey was so good-natured, and gave me excellent advice about modelling, and is having some tools made for me, and I am always to have as much clay from him as I like, which will be a vast advantage, for his clay must have a habit of twisting itself into good shapes, and probably the raw material I obtain from him will be more like a human figure than anything I shall ever build myself.

I had some luncheon with Lady Harriet, met a considerable quantity of acquaintances all prowling about the quiet streets, finished up my wardrobe, bought some *company* work, paid a few bills,—in short, bored myself as much as was good for me. Miss Kemble's reputation goes on increasing, which delights me. I have not seen anybody that does not think her very superior to anything we have had for years, and if they will leave her alone, and all the Magnates of the land will not insist upon marrying her instantly, she will be a great treasure. C. Kemble was giving a very touching account of her the other day to some cousins of mine. Her resolution to go on the stage was taken only a month before, at the time of his great difficulties, and he had never seen her rehearse but twice. He says there never was such a daughter, and he thinks her very clever.

I wish you had not done your Longleat. I had always meant you to be there with us—quite reckoned on it. Can you insinuate to Lady Bath that it is possible we may come two or three days sooner than I said at first, if she lets us. The Lansdownes are going to Brighton for a month, and want us to make Bowood on our return, instead of the time we mentioned. I shall be very glad to see Lady Bath, but if I might be excused the trouble of moving from home, I should not fret much. I gave Mr. Hibbert Lady Bath's invitation, but he fears he must now stick to his business, though as it cost him ten shillings a day in hackney-coaches to transport his lame self to the city, I have proved to him that it would be an economy to the firm of Hibbert, if he went by the stage to Longleat. I always wonder what those West Indians do up in Leadenhall street. What is the use of their going from the west to the east of London to write about a plantation in Jamaica. If you were to go from Longleat to Newcastle to write directions about your garden at Knightsbridge it would be as sensible. I have often tried to make Mr. Colvile tell me what he does in Leadenhall Street. I believe they eat tamarinds and *cashew* nuts (I do not know how they are spelt) and ginger all day there. Good-bye. Your ever affectionate

E. E.

Miss Eden to Miss Villiers.

(*Friday*). I began this two days ago, and you see how far I went. I have a passion at the moment for modelling in clay, an accomplishment I am trying to acquire from an old German who lives on Blackheath. The interest of the pursuit it is impossible to describe. I cannot imagine why I ever did anything else; it is the worst *engouement* I ever had, and so entirely past all regulating, that I think the best way now is to tire it out, so I model from morning to night. I wish I were not obliged to write to you, you uninteresting, unfinished lump of clay. George interests himself in the art, and with his usual amiability stepped up to town and brought me some tools. Think of our going to sit down to dinner the other day, in our accustomed domestic manner, soup and a mutton-pie; and Lord and Lady Jersey, F. Villiers, and Lord Castlereagh arrived *at* seven for dinner. No entrées, no fish, no nothing, and the cook ill. However, it turned out very pleasant.

I believe Lady E. Cowper will end by marrying Lord Ashley. She says she never has felt a preference for anybody, and will do just what her mother wishes. Lady Cowper is sorely puzzled, and he is in a regular high-flown Ashley state, wishing he had never proposed, that he might have watched over and adored her in silence.

Miss Eden to Miss Villiers.

NORMAN COURT,
Monday.

MY DEAREST THERESA, I do not find this visiting system good for the growth of letters. I have less to say when I see fresh people and fresh houses constantly, than at home, where I see the same every day. Your last letter, too, gave me an inspiration to answer it on the spot, but I had not time then, and so it subsided. You poor dear! Are you still liable to be haunted by recollections and tormented by the ghosts of past pleasures—youthful but weak? I have *had* so many feelings of the sort you mean, that your letter interested me particularly; but then it must be at least five years since the last ghost of the last pleasure visited me, so imagine the date of the pleasure by the date of the ghost—and the remains of *youthful* interests do not disturb me any longer. It is always *childhood* I return to, and exclusively the sight of Eden Farm and aught connected therewith that swells my heart to bursting, and *that* I never see now. Everything else is mended up again, and for the life of me I cannot understand how I ever could have been so sentimental and foolish as it appears I must have been. I say no more; but my old extract book has thrown me into fits of laughter. Calculate from that fact the horrid and complete extinction of sentiment that has taken place. You will come to it, and be surprised to see what a happy invention life is. I am afraid I like it too much. We have been at Shottesbrook. Caroline Vansittart is so uncommonly well; there are hardly any traces of her illness. The dear children will be children till they die of old age.

Then we went to Ewehurst which the Drummonds have rented from the Duke of Wellington. It is a very fine place, but an old house, and so cold. All the children had colds, and all the Aunts caught them, of course; only, instead of catching one cold I caught six, and have done nothing but sneeze ever since.

We stayed there a week and came here this day sen'night, found the house more luxurious and comfortable than ever after the cold of Ewehurst, and Mr. Wall in great felicity. Old Mrs. Wall I think much the most delightful old lady I ever knew. Lady Harriet we found here, and the Sturts, and the Poodles, and Mr. Pierpont, and latterly we have had a Doctor Daltrey, a very clever man who has thrown a pinch of sense into the very frivolous giggling conversation we have sunk into.

It has been rather amusing. Lady C. Sturt and Lady Harriet are rather in the same style of repartee. We all meant to dislike the former, but found her, on the contrary, very pleasant. She amused George very much, and Mr. Sturt was an old friend of ours. We should have gone on to Crichel, but our time and theirs could not be brought together. Lady Harriet is in her very best mood, and I always think it is a very pleasant incident, such excessive buoyancy of spirits. She is full as fidgety about Bingham as any wife would be, even any of my own sisters, who have a system of fidgeting about their husbands. I think he will arrive to-day. In fact he could hardly have come sooner if he set off even the very day he meant to. She insists upon it he is naturalized in Russia and has taken the name of Potemkin, and she is teaching the child to call him so:—"Come, dear; say Potemkin. Come, out with it like a man! Potty, Potty, Potty—come Baby!"

To-day we are to have a dinner of neighbours, chiefly clergy; two Chancellors of different dioceses and various attendant clergy, besides dear little Arundell who dines here every day. We flatter ourselves there will be great difficulties of precedence when we go into dinner, and have at last settled that the two Chancellors go in hand in hand like the Kings of Brentford, and that we must divide the inferior clergy amongst us—take two apiece.

Mr. Wall sometimes gets frightened at our levities and fancies we shall really say to his guests all that we propose for them.

George still gets into hysterical fits of laughter when I mention your idea of his being in love with Lady Harriet, which was unlucky at that time, for it did so happen that he could not endure her then, and he went up to town the day she came to stay at Greenwich, because he thought her so ill-natured. She happened to abuse, in her ignorance, *the* lady of the hour. But even he likes her here, thinks her very amusing, and much better-hearted than he expected, and he, like you, no longer wonders why I like her. Altogether this visit has answered.

Sister has been to Wrest, where the old stories are going on:—doctors sent for the middle of the night. In her last letter she said she believed that the Goderichs were going off at an hour's notice, and that she should be left alone at Wrest, till she could alter all her plans. In the meantime there is nothing really the matter with the child.

You never tell me where to direct. I shall try Saltram. Love to Mrs. Villiers. Ever your most affectionate
E. E.

Miss Eden to Lady Charlotte Greville.
Melbury, 1829.

I am sorry to write to you on paper that has evidently been in bad health for some time, but I cannot find any without this bilious tinge. Lady Bath told me that you were the giver of that pretty lamp in the drawing-room at Greenwich Park. I am so glad to know who it is I am to thank, and very glad that "who" is "you." I tried a little of gratitude on two other friends who seemed obtuse about it. The pride of my life is the quantity of pretty things that my friends gave me when we settled. I like your name to be found in the list.

I suppose you are still in Ireland, and I direct my letter on that supposition. I have not written to any of your family for a long time. I cannot write while I am travelling about, as I hold it "stuff of the conscience" to comment on the owners of the houses I am in, and it would not be the least amusing to hear they were all charming people.

However, I must say that about Lord Ilchester, as I believe you do not know him, so it is news to you; and he certainly is the most amiable being I ever beheld. He has given up his own happiness as a lost case since the death of his wife, and his whole life is spent in trying to make other people happy. I never saw so *gentle* a character, and am no longer surprised at George's attachment to him. It has lasted ever since they were at school together; and as I had never seen much of Lord Ilchester at home, and he was nothing shining in society, I used to wonder why George was so very fond of him. But I see how it is now.

To be sure, an inch of amiability is worth yards of cleverness for the real wear and tear of life. Lord Ilchester's spirits have been thoroughly bent down once by the loss of his wife, and though he has mended himself up again to a certain degree, yet he is all over chinks and cracks, that shake on the slightest touch. I could not bear to allude before him to the possibility of any husband liking his wife, or any mother educating her children. The quantity of *célibataires* that I bring forward in conversation is incredible. I hope he is quite convinced that there is not such a thing as a married man left in creation.

Mr. Corry, who is here, does not intend that the race shall be extinct. He is desperately in love with Lady H. Ashley, so desperately that he can think of nothing else, and I believe talks of little else; but between his brogue and the confusion of his ideas I am not always sure what he is talking about. He never sleeps, but writes half the night—whether sonnets to her, or pamphlets on the state of Ireland, he will not tell me. But he is in a constant state of composition, writing notes all the evening to be arranged into sense at night. From the dark romantic hints he throws out for our information, I imagine he has hopes of marrying her in the course of next year. I hope he will not be disappointed. I like anybody who is so really in earnest as he is.

We paid a long visit at Longleat—very successful, inasmuch as Lady Bath was in the highest of good humour, and Tom Bath is dearer to my heart than ever. Lord Edward was at Longleat the latter part of our visit, and a great addition. He is totally unlike all the Thynnes I ever saw—full of fun and dashes out everything that comes into his head, astonishes them all, but governs the whole house. They all laugh the instant he opens his lips.

CHAPTER VIII

1830-1831

Miss Eden to Miss Villiers.
Saturday, January 1830.

MY DEAREST THERESA, I *did* write the day I had your first letter. To be sure you were not bound to know it, for I put my letter by so carefully, that at post time it was entirely missing. Then I was *took* with a cold, and took to my bed, and by the time I was well enough to institute a successful search for my lost letter, it had grown so dull and dry by keeping that it was not worth sending.

So you are snowed up at an inn. Odd! Your weather must be worse than ours, though that has been bad enough, but no great depths of snow. I think you sound comfortable. I have the oddest love of an Inn; I can't tell why, except that I love all that belongs to travelling; and then one is so well treated. I have nothing to tell you, as I wrote a very disgustingly gossipy letter to Lady Harriet which was to serve you too, and I have seen nobody since, except the Granthams. I suppose there are live people in the provinces; there are none in town—no carriages—no watchmen—no noise at all.

We had four London University professors to dinner on Thursday (and Mr. Brougham was to have come, but was, of course, detained), proving that madmen were sane or some clever men mad—I forget which. However, our Professors were *very* pretty company. I did not understand a word they said, but thought them very pleasant.

Have you read Moore? So beyond measure amusing! It is abused and praised with a violence that shows how much party feeling there is about it. The vanity both of the writer and the writee is very remarkable, but it does not prevent the book from being very amusing, and I think it altogether a very *fair* piece of biography. Moore was not bound to make Lord Byron's faults stand out; there are plenty of them and striking enough without amplification, and he mentions them with such excuses as he can find.

George goes to Woburn to-morrow for the last week of shooting. Lord Edward Thynne's marriage went off—because the butcher would not be *conformable* about settlements. I am sorry, for I liked Edward very much when we were at Longleat. He is quite unlike the others, so lively and easy. I wish he had not equally bad luck in the line of fortune-hunting. Dublin must be going into deep black for your brother, to judge by the papers. I wonder whether Popular mourning is like Court mourning—the gentlemen to wear black swords and fringe, and the ladies chamois shoes—two great mysteries to me. I am so glad he has been so liked. Your most affectionate

E. E.

Miss Eden to Miss Villiers.
GROSVENOR STREET,
Thursday, April 1830.

MY DEAREST THERESA, Observe how we write! Not a moment lost, and I shall have the last word, but I meant to write to you yesterday, because the very morning after my last letter, I found by a confidential advice from Longleat that I had forwarded to you a regular London lie about Edward Thynne, and that his marriage, so far from being off, was negotiating with great success. However, it was a secret then; but Lord Henry came yesterday to tell me it was declared, and to-day I have a letter from Lady Bath, apparently in ecstacies: "Write and wish me great joy. You are the first, the *very first*, to whom I have written my dear Edward's marriage, and I know you will be pleased. Write to me directly."

I am not at all pleased, and have not an idea what to write. I think if Edward had been thirty-three instead of twenty-three, had *wearied* of the world, as the Scotch say, and been disappointed in love several times, as all people are by that time, it would not have been unnatural that he should have married for an establishment; but a boy of that age has no right to be so calculating. I cannot quite make out the story. I heard from a great friend of the family who had been employed in the negotiation that it is the sick plain sister Lord E. marries; that he did not pretend to care about her; supposed if he saw her once before their marriage it would be enough—and so on, which was disgusting.

Lord Henry yesterday carried it off better—said she was rather pretty, well educated, well mannered, and that Edward was in love, and all the right things. Perhaps he is right. I did not know what to tell you about Longleat, it was so long ago. I do not think *your* Barings will like Lord Henry's present pursuit. The same name and the other family; but do not for your life say a word of it to them, as I vowed the deepest vows to him yesterday that I would not do him any mischief. Not that I know how I could, and I would not if I could, but I presume he dreads family communications which, as the A. Barings and H. Barings do not speak, I laboured to convince him yesterday were not to be dreaded.

I am quite alone here, George went to Woburn Monday, and Fanny to Eastcombe. I have just cold enough left to excuse myself from dining out with my attached friends and family, so that I see a few morning visitors and have the evenings all to myself. The pleasure of it no words can express. I never can explain what is the fun of being alone in the room with the certainty of not being disturbed; but that there is something very attractive and pleasing in the situation it is impossible to deny. I feel so happy, and sit up so late, and am so busy about nothing.

I had a remarkably pleasant set of visitors yesterday. Your brother George, amongst others, followed Lord Henry, and as usual I was enchanted to see him.

Good-bye dearest. I wish you were come. Your most affectionate

E. E.

Miss Eden to Miss Villiers.

Thursday evening, May 1830.

DEAREST THERESA, Thank you for writing to me. Your letter told me many particulars I had wanted to know, though the one melancholy fact of her deplorable condition Lady F. Leveson wrote to me yesterday. I never was more shocked or grieved. I wrote to Lady Cawdor last night, but begged her not to write, as nothing is so trying as writing in real anxiety. Poor Lady Bath! It is melancholy to think we are not to see her again. After all, we all thought about her and cared about her opinion more than for most people's; and she was more of an object to us than anybody out of our own families. She was a very kind friend to me when first I came out and when I knew nobody and nobody cared about me, and I cannot name anybody from whom I have received so much gratuitous kindness, particularly at times of trial, and we all of us, you as well as I, never could bear being in a scrape with her. We fretted and were affronted and so on, but there was no *bassesse* I did not condescend to, to make it up again. I liked her society, and altogether loved her very dearly, and the idea of her present situation poor thing, is very, very painful. I hardly wish her recovery, because it seems doubtful if it would be complete, and the recovery of bodily health alone is not to be wished.

Poor Lord Bath; it will be a dreadful loss to him. I shall really be very glad if you will write again, whatever happens. Once more thank you. Ever your affectionate

E. E.

Miss Eden to Lady Campbell.

GREENWICH PARK,
Wednesday, August 1830.

I know I did not answer your last letter. I wrung it from you, and it enchanted me, and at first I would not answer it for fear of plaguing you, and after a time I would not answer it for fear of plaguing me—and so on—and latterly I have done nothing but work in the garden—and how can you expect a day labourer, a plodding operative, to write? Shaky hands, aching back, etc.; but on the other side, hedges of sweet peas, lovely yellow carnations, brilliant potentillas, to balance the fatigue. George and I have quarrelled so about the watering-pot, which is mine by rights, that for fear of an entire quarrel he has been obliged to buy. I wish you could see our house and garden, "a poor thing, but mine own." I am so fond of it, and we are so comfortable.

I wonder whether you really will go to the Ionian Isles. I have just as good a chance of seeing you there as in Ireland, so if you need it I should. We shall never move again, or if we ever did, I should have a better claim to go after you to the Ionian Isles, where we have never been, than again to Ireland.

Mrs. Heber, the Bishop's widow, has just published two more Vols. of her first husband's life, and finding it lucrative, has taken a second husband, a Greek, who calls himself *Sir* Demetrie Valsomachi, and he has carried her off to the Ionian Islands, where you will find her collecting materials for the biography of Sir Demetrie.

We think and talk of nothing but Kings and Queens. It adds to the oppression of the oppressive weather even to think of all the King does. I wish he would take a chair and sit down. We have only been up once to see him, at that full-dress ball at Apsley House, where he brought brother Würtemburg, and the whole thing struck me as so tiresome. I could not treat it as a pageant—only as a joke.

However, tho' our adored Sovereign is either rather mad or very foolish, he is an immense improvement on the last unforgiving animal, who died growling sulkily in his den at Windsor. This man at least *wishes* to make everybody happy, and everything he has done has been benevolent; but the Court is going to swallow up all other society. It is rather funny to see all the great people who intrigued for court places, meaning to enjoy their pensions and do no work, kept hard at it from nine in the morning till two the following morning—reviews, breakfasts, great dinners, and parties all following each other, and the whole suite kept in requisition.

Miss Eden to Miss Villiers.

BROADSTAIRS,
Wednesday, September 1830.

MY DEAREST THERESA, How idle I have been about writing, have not I? But then Hyde told me about the daily packets that he forwarded from Staffordshire and from Devonshire, and so I thought in the bustle I should not be missed, and the real truth is I have been very unsettled the last ten days. George and I went to Hertfordshire to see Mary Eden before her confinement, and from the bore of moving, put it off so long that we came in at last for the beginning of her catastrophe. She was in the greatest danger, poor thing, at last, but thank God is quite safe now, and her boy too.

We went to pass a morning with Lady F. Lamb at Brocket, and saw a great deal of the Panshanger tribe. The Ashleys are as happy as I suppose the Listers mean to be, only I think you must be a shade less demonstrative. Lord Ashley seems to do amazingly well with all the uncles and brothers, and Lady Cowper dotes (or doats, which is it?) on him.

We came back to Greenwich for one day, and then with the utmost courage, the greatest magnanimity, Fanny and I stepped into a Margate steamboat and set off on a visit to Mrs. Vansittart at Broadstairs. George stood on the steps of Greenwich Hospital, left, like Lord Ullin, "lamenting." We were so late we could with difficulty persuade the steamer to take us in; but at last we boarded her and took her. To my utter surprise I was not the least sick.

This is a nice little place. We know nobody here but Lady G. de Roos, and she is in the same predicament, so we see a great deal of each other.

Caroline ought I believe to account for 14 children, but she has somehow contrived to disperse and get rid of all of them but two very small things of five and six. I ask no questions. I hope the others are all safe somewhere, and in the meantime she is remarkably well and happy. We have a room apiece, and one for our maid, and she must have been terribly afraid we should be bored by the quantity of excursions she has planned for us. We have been to Margate and Ramsgate, and are to go to Dover, and if George comes, perhaps to Calais. But that I think foolhardy. To-day she and Fanny are gone sailing off to some famous shell place. I prefer dry land, if it is the same thing to everybody, so I stayed at home, and I have a fit of sketching on me that amounts to a fever. The day is too short. I am so glad we like being here so much, which sounds like a foolish sentence, but Caroline really has been so kind and active in arranging everything and was so bent on making us come, and is so hospitable now we are here, that I should have been doubly sorry if it had turned out a failure. I was only sorry to leave George, but perhaps he will come and fetch us.

The day we went through London to Hertfordshire your George went to the play with us, and I was afraid we should have to carry him out. He went into strong hysterics at the *Bottle Imp*, which is certainly one of the most amusing things I ever saw.

Maria wrote so kindly and affectionately to me about your marriage. You would have been pleased with her letter. And old Lansdowne wrote also in such terms about both of you and his delight at the marriage of two people he liked so much, that I do not see why we should not always meet you at Bowood, except the fear that Mr. L.'s domestic peace may be endangered. People were talking of the possibility of a revolution in England the other day, and what they should do for their livelihoods, and Lord Alvanley said, "If it comes to that I know what I shall do; keep a disorderly house and make Glengall my head waiter." That is a bad story to end with, but I have no time for a better.

Two more letters to write; and a lovely day and fine autumnal weather makes me so happy I cannot bear to lose a moment of it. Ever your most affectionate

E. E.

Miss Eden to Lady Charlotte Greville.

Thursday, October 1830.

MY dear Lady Charlotte, Your note reached me only yesterday, as it made a little detour to Middleton in search of George; but with all that delay it was the first intelligence I had of Lady F.'s safety. The *Morning Herald* never mentions anything pleasant, and Charles Drummond, whom I had charged to make due enquiries of Mr. H. Greville, of course forgot it. How glad I am she has a girl at last! I think we all deserve some credit for it, for all her friends have gone on day by day so duly wishing for a young lady for her, that I cannot but think we may have great pride in the result. It is unknown the trouble Lady G. de Roos and I gave ourselves about it all the time we were at Broadstairs. My sisters, who are learned in those matters, assured me Lady F. would have a girl this time, she was so long about it. Did you know that girls, with that tact and penetration we all have, shew a greater reluctance to coming into this bad world than boys do, who are always ready for any mischief? Girls put off coming into this world as long as they possibly can, knowing what a difficult life it is. Just mind, as you are on the spot, that this little concern is like its Mama. I should like her to be exactly the same, should not you?

We enjoyed our Broadstairs so very much, and all the more, because it was not Ramsgate. I took the look of Ramsgate in great aversion. We knew nobody at Broadstairs but Lady G. de Roos, who was without her husband, and therefore very glad to be a great deal with us. The quiet and *dowdiness* of Broadstairs is a great charm. We were out all day, sketching or poking about for shells. I wonder whether you went to Shellness, a little creek whose shores are covered with shells—not a stone or a bit of sand—all shells. I never saw such a curious place. We made one long expedition to Dover, and if ever I went to the sea on my own account, I mean not on a visit to anybody, I should pitch my tent at Dover. It is so very beautiful and so cheerful looking. We stayed a fortnight at Broadstairs.

George seems to have a very diplomatic party at Middleton: Esterhazy, Talleyrand, Madame de Dino, the expectation of the Duke of Wellington, etc., etc. Colonel Anson, I suppose you know, has ascertained that he has £15,000 less than nothing, which would be an uncomfortable property to settle on, and Lord Anson says he can do nothing for him but give him a living. If he ends by taking orders, I think Thorpe will find his congregation fall off considerably; there will be such a press to hear that popular preacher Anson.

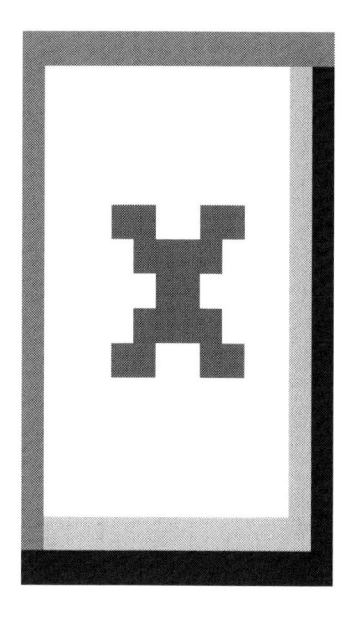

Lady Cowper has written to ask us to Panshanger next week, but I believe George will not be able to go; he has a shooting-engagement in another direction. However, till he comes back from Middleton, I do not know. I am not ambitious to move again, as we must so soon go to that vile London for that foolish Parliament, and our little garden is so full of flowers, and gives so much occupation in collecting seeds and making cuttings, that I grudge leaving it, even for a day. In all the reproaches that are lavished on these Ministers, I wonder nobody has ever written a biting pamphlet on their only real fault, which is bringing us all to London the end of October—a sort of tyranny for which a Minister would have been impeached in better days. I am dreadfully at a loss for some political feelings. I cannot find anybody to wish for, and, upon the whole, am in the miserably dull predicament of *rather* hoping things may remain as they are. I suppose that mean Huskisson set are coming in, which is unpleasant, but as they were sure to *fourrer* themselves in somehow or anyhow, I am prepared for it. I never hear from Maria. I suspect they are bored at Sprotbro', as she is always silent when she is bored.

My best love to Lady F. with my entire approbation of her conduct about this little girl. Ever your affectionate

E. E.

Miss Eden to Mrs. Lister.

GREENWICH PARK,
Thursday evening, November 1830.

MY DEAREST THERESA, It is particularly clever of me to write to you to-night, because it does so happen that there is not a pen in the house and the shops are all shut. There was *one* pen this morning, but I suppose dear Chiswick has ate it. That comes of having stationery for nothing; as long as we had to pay for it, I had heaps of pens and paper. George has found a quill in one of the drawers, and I, who never could mend a real ready-made pen, have cut this raw material, this duck's feather, into an odd-shaped thing. But it marks pretty well, only it is great fatigue to drive it along, because I could not make a slit in it.

I want to know if you and Mr. Lister cannot come and dine with us while we are here. I never should have thought of asking anybody in such weather, but I had *offers* from three friends this morning to come here next week, so that it is quite allowable to ask all my other friends. I daresay you did not think I had above three in the world, but I have.

When will you come? I know you can't the beginning of next week, because I have just had a note from Lady Salisbury asking us to meet you at Hatfield, but after that perhaps you can come. We cannot go to Hatfield. The Chancellor has offered to take me to the Lord Mayor's dinner on Monday, and I think it will be amusing and mean to accept.

Sarah Sophia says she proposes to take her food here on Tuesday. She never allows us an option. I wonder when it will be time to quarrel with her about politics or something else? Is not it *due to ourselves* to have some explanations with her? I do not know what about, but a note or two ought to pass, first dignified and then pathetic, and then end with a dinner. I have no idea of the dinner without the explanation first. She has treated everybody but us with one.

My garden is very flourishing and I have had the delight of sowing seeds to a great amount since Monday. I wish gardening were not so fatiguing. I like it so very much, but I am dead tired every night, and moreover there has been a *reform* in our Society for visiting the Poor, and they have changed our plan of visiting, and given me a district at the farthest end of the town. A mile off at the least. Such a bore, and I have quite a new set of people to make acquaintance with. However, the acquaintance is soon made. I visited eight poor women this morning, and they had each had ten children, and had "buried the last, thank God, last year," and they had all had beds to sleep on once, but had pledged them for rent, and they all could get nothing from the parish, and they generally ended with, "and if it would please God to take my poor old man, I could go home comfortably to my own parish." "But *is* your husband ill?" I asked. "No, Ma'am, not particular ill, but it may please God to take him and then I can go home." I can see how extreme distress must destroy all affection, and how those very poor people must think that their children who die young, have made a great escape. You cannot imagine the misery of these pensioners' wives. The husbands are well taken care of in every respect, but the wives have actually nothing. We seldom find above one in three with bedding or any furniture whatever. We are shamefully well off, Theresa. I always think of that frightful parable, "Remember that thou in thy lifetime receivedst thy good things," etc. It is an ugly thought, is it not? And we have so many good things. I am always so happy here that it frightens me. So good-night, I am sleepy and will not think about it. Your most affectionate

E. E.

Miss Eden to Mrs. Lister.

PARK LODGE, GREENWICH,
Wednesday.

DEAREST THERESA, I shall take it as a great compliment being asked to dinner anywhere by anybody, but as a matter of choice I should prefer dining with the Lord Mayor habitually—not from any gourmandise, I beg to mention, for in my days I never saw such uneatable food. The soup had been saved, I imagine, from the day that the King did *not* dine at the Guildhall, and consequently a little salt had been thrown in every day just to preserve it. The preservation had been effected, but how many pounds of salt had been used it is difficult to guess. Nobody offered me anything else but a slice of half-cold peacock, whose tail feathers were still spread and growing. However, though as mere dinner it was a failure, the flow of soul was prodigious. We were so unanimous, so fond of each other. Dear Don Key himself in such spirits, and Mrs. Key and all the small bunch of Keys so polite and attentive. "What curious creatures we are," as that old *Machy* in *Destiny* (have you read it?) keeps observing; and all the forms of civic life are more curious than the rest. The Lady Mayoress receives all her guests without stirring from her chair, though it is obvious from her old habit of attending to her shop that she is dying to get up to *serve* them all. The Lord Mayor walks in to dinner before all his visitors, leaving the Duke of Sussex, etc., to take care of themselves, and then he and his wife sit by each other without the relief of a third person. Their domestic felicity has, I fear, received a check for life, because every time Key got up to speak his sword hitched in his wife's blonde, which, of course, was very unpleasant. It made the blonde all fuzzy. However, he is a good Lord Mayor, and so polite to His Majesty's Ministers that they were some of them in agonies of fright he was going to propose all their healths individually, and it was only prevented by Lord Grey's getting up from dinner before one-third of the toasts had been given. That sort of audience is very alarming, I believe. Lord Grey said he never felt so frightened in his life, and Lord Lansdowne, whom I sat next to, told me that if his health came next, he had not an idea what was to be done. He felt sure he could not say a word. I quite understood it. An audience of ladies whom they all knew well, and who were all likely to laugh, besides 500 other people all staring at them as a show, must be rather trying.

It was great fun to see the Chancellor looking demure and shy while he was *loué vif* by the Lord Mayor. He is very amusing with his popularity. Of course we were rather late at the Mansion House. The Chancellor always is five minutes too late everywhere. However, we arrived in solitary grandeur after all the other carriages had gone away, and were received with unbounded applause by the mob. I wonder which of us they meant to approve of. I am disappointed in the magnificence of the city. The whole set-out is *mesquin* to the greatest degree. Nothing but common blue plates and only one silver fork apiece, which those who were learned in public dinners carefully preserved. I lost mine in the first five minutes. The city ladies are so ill-dressed too; such old gowns with black shoes, etc. I went back to Grosvenor Street at eleven, moulted my feathers and changed my gown, and got home at twelve.

George had a holiday yesterday, and worked in the garden from breakfast till dinner. You have no idea what a good collection of plants we are making. We quarrel very much about the places in which they are to be put, and pass the evenings in tart innuendoes about my Eccremocarpus which you liked, and my Ipomaea seed which you sowed, and which has never come up. But the general result is great amusement.

I do not think four horses will be able to drag me back to town; I like this so much better. Your brother George wrote me word he had the gout. Ever your affectionate

E. E.

Miss Eden to Mrs. Lister.

GROSVENOR STREET,
Monday.

MY DEAREST THERESA, I was not at all in the mood to write, and was almost glad you did not write to me because of that dreadful bore of an answer which you would expect; and I have been so *very* ill! Besides that, I have been a fortnight at Eastcombe *tête-à-tête* with

Sister, and forbidden to speak on account of my dear little lungs which had been coughed to atoms, so conversation did not give me much help to a letter. Moreover, they gave me all sorts of lowering medicines—hemlock and henbane, or words to that effect (I never can remember the names of drugs)—and made me so languid that the weight of a pen was a great deal too much for my delicate frame. However, I believe they have nearly cured me, and it does not signify now it is over, though I still think that if there were an inflammation on the chest to be done, it would have been more for the general good that O'Connell should have it instead of me. Anything to silence that dreadful tongue of his, which is frightening the Isle from its propriety most rapidly. They say that he said to Lord Anglesey at one of his levées, "I shall give you some trouble yet, My Lord," to which Lord A. answered, "Yes, I know you will, but I shall hang you at last." It is a neat dialogue, and the story is a good one, and certainly would have been true if O'Connell had been at a levée. As he has not, there is of course no foundation for it, but we can believe it all the same.

Barring Ireland, which I do not fret about, because we have been in the habit of conquering it once in every thirty years and it is time now for a fight, things are looking more prosperous. Our revenue they say is good, and our manufactories are flourishing to the highest possible degree. George saw some of the silk people on Saturday, who told him that several of the great silk houses had refused to take any more orders, having as much to do as they can this year. Birmingham is very busy; the wool trade is in the greatest prosperity; in short, if Parliament were never to meet again, if that were to be *the* reform Lord Grey would propose, we should do very well.

It is very unlucky that we never can have what we want all at once. If corn is plentiful, there is not a morsel of loyalty to be had for love or money, and when the market for wool is good, morals are at their lowest pitch.

I was rather sorry to come home again, for when I am out of town I forget all my party feelings; but I was obliged to come back as soon as I was strong enough, for George has not a chance of getting out of town even for a day.

Have you seen the 2nd Volume of *Lord Byron*? It is a wicked book, and having made that avowal it is unlucky that I feel myself obliged to own that it is much the most interesting book I ever read in my life—much. I never was so amused, and the more wickeder he is in his actions, the more cleverer he is in his writings. I am afraid I like him very much—that is I cannot bear him really, only I am glad he lived, else we should not have had his *Life* to read, to say nothing of his poetry. He had some good points; such extreme gratitude to anybody who ever showed him kindness; and if he had lived I still think that he would have been converted, and that once a Christian, there is nothing great or good he would not have been equal to. He had such magnificent talents—an archangel ruined—and I think he regretted the height from which he had fallen. Still the book is a bad book. I was obliged to stop yesterday and recall *mes grands principes* before I could remember that it was not wrong or ill-natured of Guiccioli to insist on his wife's separation from Lord Byron. Moore talks about it as an unprincipled disturbance of Lord Byron's domestic felicity, and with such earnestness, that he very nearly took me in.

I wish I had seen you act. Lord Castlereagh's epilogue was in the papers, with a few lines added, *not* with a view of pleasing him. Your affectionate

E. E.

CHAPTER IX

1831-1835

Miss Eden to Mrs. Lister.
GREENWICH PARK,
1831.

MY DEAREST THERESA, I would take a larger sheet of paper, but it does so happen that ever since we have nominally had stationery for nothing, I have never been able to find anything in the nature of paper, pen, or sealing-wax; indeed, for some time one pen served the whole house. It never came to my turn to have it, as you perceived, and I scorned to buy one. The country may yet afford a quarter of a hundred of pens, at least I suppose so.

You were quite right, I really did look at the end of your letter for your signature. The date, and your beginning, "You must have forgotten who I am," and your writing such a simple hand, put me out, and I said to George, "This must be some Carnegie or Elliot cousin, by the token of Edinbro', whom I ought to remember." I was so pleased when I found it was you; though your expecting an answer is odd, not to say troublesome. However, anything to please you.

What a delicious tour you have had. I cannot imagine anything much pleasanter. The two articles in your letter that disappoint me are, that it does not appear you are intensely bored by the Scotch, considered as members of society; nor that you are sufficiently mad about the beauty of Edinbro'. I think the old town so much the most picturesque thing I ever saw, and the scenery all about it so beautiful. In short, such a slow drawly people have no right to such a romantic capital. They are very tiresome, poor dears! but I suppose they cannot help it; else, if they would speak a thought quicker, and even catch even the glimmer of a joke, and give up all that old nonsense about Chiefs and plaids and pretenders and so on, I should grudge them that town less.

I have been living here very quietly nearly three months, I think—that is as quietly as is compatible with the times; but it has been an eventful summer. What with the opening of bridges, crowning Kings and Queens, and launching ships, I have seen more sights and greater masses of human creatures than usual; and then there has been some talk of a Reform in Parliament, a mere playful idea, which may not have reached you, but which has occasionally been alluded to in conversation here. What a business they all made of it last week. They speak amazingly well, those dear Lords, but they are not so happy at voting....

I could quite understand those Tories if I could find one who would say the Bill is thrown out for good, but I have not seen one who does not say it must pass in three months, so why refuse to consider it now? London has been an ugly-looking sight. We drove up to it most days to see George, and to take him down to the House, because I like to see him safe thro' the crowd.

Women in London have made themselves so extremely ridiculous and conspicuous, by their party violence, and I have no reason for thinking I should have been wiser than others, if I had been in the same state of excitement. Besides, it is such a bore to be very eager, it tires me to death, and yet one catches it, if other people have the same complaint.

The gardener has taken up all the geraniums. That is not a light grievance, it portends frost and spoils the garden. I wish you had seen it this year, I am certain there never were so many flowers in so small a space.

Anne Robinson came here for three days, and took a fancy for gardening, but I am afraid it did not last. She paid us such a nice visit I asked Lord Morpeth to meet her, thinking that a proper *procèdé*. Then somebody who had been dining at Putney told me I was quite wrong, and that Mr. Villiers was the person to ask. So I *driv* up to town like mad and caught him before dinner-time. I thought as he had a Dawkins-Pennant to look to, it was rather hard to interfere with Lord Morpeth's chance, but I need not have had that delicacy about a fair division of fortune.

Lord Morpeth came here for a longer visit the following week, and I do not think he has the remotest intention of making up to Anne, or any other person. He is absorbed in politics, and says it would bore him to change his situation. Your ever affect.

E. E.

Miss Eden to Mrs. Lister.
30 GROSVENOR STREET,
Thursday .

MY DEAREST THERESA, Not the least affronted. It never crosses my mind to invent any other cause for anybody's silence, but the simple fact that the bore of writing a letter is almost intolerable, and I never fancy anything, either that they are affronted or ill, or *hurt* (don't you know how many people are delighted to feel hurt), or dead; but I simply suppose they are not in a writing humour....

I am glad you liked Bowood. I saw her on Monday on her way through town, quite enchanted with Paris and with the fuss that had been made with them. She likes your brother Edward very much, and seemed to have seen a great deal of him. I have not seen Lord Lansdowne yet, but he is to stay on in town some days longer. I wish there were any chance of our meeting you at Bowood, but I fear it is not very likely. In the summer they said they hoped we would come in the winter, but I never go there without a renewed invitation for some special time, because it is always a doubt, I think, whether she likes all the visitors he asks, and I hate to go in uncertainty.

I have been passing a fortnight at Panshanger—went with George for three days, and then Lady Cowper made me stay on. It is a most difficult house to get away from, partly because it is so pleasant, and then that her dawdling way of saying, "Oh no, you can't go, I always understood you were to stay till we go to Brighton," is more unanswerable than all the cordiality of half the boisterous friends, who beg and pray, and say all the kind thoughts that they can think of.

We had heaps of people the first part of my visit: Lievens, Talleyrand, Madame de Dino, Lady Stanhope, Palmerston and Mahon, George, Lionel Ashley, Fordwich, and William Cowper (who is a great dear), and heaps of people who acted and danced, and it was all very pleasant.

People are wonderfully clever, I think, and as for Talleyrand I doat upon him. I have been dining with him since at his own house, and elsewhere, and could listen to him for any number of hours. There *are* weak moments in which I think him handsome, just as it used to cross my mind sometimes whether the Chancellor was not good-looking—decidedly pleasanter to look at than that young Bagot, who walks up Regent Street quite miserable that it is not wide enough for the crowds that he thinks are looking at him.

My last week at Panshanger I was alone with the family, which is always pleasant. I do like Lady Cowper's society so particularly; in short, I like *her*. She may have a great many faults, but I do not see them, and it is no business of mine anyhow; and so everybody may reproach me for it if they please, but I am very fond of her.

As for your plan for me—kind of you, but it won't do at all. He was there all the time, and I left him there, and he always honours me with great attention, but by the blessing of Providence I do not take to him at all. I am too old to marry, and that is the truth. Lady Cowper remained convinced of that fact, and told me one day that if I were younger I should be less quick-sighted to Lord M.'s faults, which is true enough. I do not think him half so pleasant as Sir Frederick, whom I met the time before, and probably just as wicked, and he frightens me and bewilders me, and he swears too much. However, we ended by being very good friends, which is creditable under the circumstances, and though I am sure it is very kind of my friends to wish me married, and particularly kind that anybody should wish to marry me, yet I think now they may give it up, and give me credit for knowing my own happiness. "We know what we are, but not what we may be," as somebody says, *Ophelia* I believe; and I know that I am very happy now, and have been so for some years, and that I had rather not change. If I change my mind I shall say so without shame, but at present I am quite contented with my position in life and only wish it may last. If I were younger, or less spoiled than I have been at home, I daresay I could put up with the difficulties of a new place; but not now. I cannot be blind to the faults of the few men I know well, and though I know many more faults in myself, yet I am used to those, you know, and George is used to them, and it all does beautifully. But in a new scene it might fail.

I can derive but little vanity from Lord Melbourne's admiration. I stand very low in the list of his loves, and as for his thinking well of my principles, it would be rather hard if he did not, considering the society he lives in. And he has found out that I am not clever. I like him for that, and for saying so.

Lord Alvanley is utterly ruined again, has given up everything, and his creditors allow him £1200 a year. Poor Colonel Russell leaves £35,000 of debt. What horrid lives of difficulty those men must lead.

We settled in town a week ago, as the drives from Greenwich were becoming cold and dark for George. There are several people in town I know. Maria is looking very well and seems pleased and contented—neither in great spirits, nor otherwise.

We have seen Colonel Arden very often lately; he and Mr. Warrender having been kept in town for the hopeless purpose of arranging Lord Alvanley's affairs. I suspect dear Alvanley is after all little better than a swindler. He writes beautiful letters to Lord Skelmersdale, one of his trustees, and says he feels he deserves all the misery he is suffering, which misery consists in sitting in an arm-chair from breakfast till dinner-time cracking his jokes without ceasing. He has taught his servant to come into the room and ask what time his Lordship would like the carriage, and what orders he has for his groom, because he thinks it sounds cheerful, though he has neither carriage nor horses. But it looks better. When Brooke Greville was describing to him the beautiful gilding of his house in Hill Street, which is a wonderful concern, Lord Alvanley said, "My dear Brooke, if you would carve a little more, and gild a little less, it would be a more hospitable way of going on." Yours ever

E. E.

Miss Eden to Mrs. Lister.
GREENWICH PARK,
Thursday evening, April 18, 1832.

MY DEAREST THERESA, I should not much wonder if you *were* coming to the crisis; that feeling so well is suspicious. Never mind; "all things must have their end," as *Isabella* says in the Tragedy, and "all things must have their beginnings," as your child will probably say if you will give it an opportunity. I quite forgot to mention to you to let it be a girl, I like girls best. I see Mrs. Keppel, to save all disputes, has brought both a boy and girl into the world; but that is such an expensive amusement, you would not like that. If it is a boy, you ought to call it Arlington as a delicate attention to Mr. Lister. I mention these little elegant flatteries out of regard to your domestic peace, as from various observations I have lately been driven to make amongst my acquaintances, I do not think wives pay half enough attention to their husbands, though this does not apply to you.

Yes, as you say, that division is satisfactory to Lord Grey, but still if there were a shadow of an excuse for making a dozen Peers without affronting two dozen who *are* made, I should be glad.

The division was a pleasing surprise to me. I had been awake since four that night, and at last had settled that George must have come home and gone to bed, and that nobody had voted for us but just the Cabinet Ministers, and then I heard the house-door bang, and knew by the way in which he rushed up stairs how it was. Now it is over, and that our enemies have not triumphed, I am left with a sort of wish—that is, not a wish, but an idea—that it might have ended (just for fun) the other way. I should so like to know what would have come next. It is all so like a game at chess, and I was anxious to know how Lord Grey would get out of check. However, I am delighted with the game as it is; only it *would* have been a curious speculation, wouldn't it? I see we are to have longer holidays, which makes me dote upon them all, both Greys and Salisburys, for so arranging it, and George is enchanted with it. He comes to-morrow, which is good for my gardening tastes and bad for my church-going habits.

There are lectures at the church every evening by an excellent preacher, and when George is in town, Fanny and I dine early and go to them. But I behaved so ill last night. I was shown into a large pew, a *voiture à huit places*, where there were seven old ladies, highly respectable and attentive, and four of us sat opposite to the other four. The clergyman, the curate of the parish, made a slight allusion to his superior *officer*, the rector, who happens to be ill, and made a commonplace remark on his own inferiority, etc., whereupon one of the old ladies began to cry. The next, seeing that, began to cry too, and so it went all round the pew, but so slowly that the last did not begin to cry till a quarter of an hour *at least* after she had heard of the rector's illness, and till the sermon was fairly directed against some of the difficulties of St. Paul. Their crying set me off laughing, and you know what a horrid convulsion that sort of suppressed laughter, which one feels to be wrong, turns into. I hope they thought I was crying.

Our hyacinths are too lovely; quite distressing to see how large and double they are, because they will die soon. If they were only single, poor little wretches, it would not signify their lasting so short a time. I think the great fault of the garden is the constant flurry the flowers are in. Perhaps you have not found that out, but fancied they were quiet amusements; but that is an error. They either won't come up at all, or they come at the wrong time, and the frost and the sun and the rain and the drought all bother them. And then, the instant they look beautiful, they die. I observe that a genuine fancier, like George, does not care a straw for the flower itself, but merely for the cutting, or the root, or the seed. However, I must say he contrives always to have quantities of beautiful flowers, hurrying on one after the other.

God bless you, dearest. I have not much to say, but my sisters all tell me to write just before they lie-in—that anything does for an amusement then; so I suppose it is right. Shall I have "Arlington" to-morrow, do you think? Your most affectionate

E. E.

Miss Eden to Mrs. Lister.
GREENWICH,
Friday evening, 1832.

DEAREST THERESA, I shall be charmed to see you any day you like, the sooner the better. Two or three stray people have suggested themselves for various days next week, but I am not sure who are the people, or what days they mean to come. I do not mean anything *pert* to George, but if he has a fault, it happens to be a total disregard of all notes and messages confided to him. However, I do not know of anybody coming that you would think objectionable. I should have suggested Monday because, as Caroline Montagu (Lord Rokeby's sister) is coming to pass the day with Fanny, she might have brought you, and returned you, which you would probably prefer; but then what is to become of Mr. Lister? George cannot be here, and though you and I going one way, and Fanny and her Caroline the other, and all meeting for dinner would do very nicely, Mr. Lister would be bored out of his life. But any day you please will suit me, so as you can let me know in time to cook a bit of vittals for you.

I went to town yesterday to see Maria and do my congratulations, and I passed a long time with her, and am quite satisfied that she is unfeignedly happy and that she really likes him. Sir Joseph cannot control his joy at all, and was very amusing with his account of his own manner to Lord Grey and of Lord Grey's to him. That angel of a man Charles Greville (quite a new light to see him in) gave himself a degree of trouble that astounded me to procure places for us to see Taglioni last night, and he succeeded in fixing us in Devon's box with the Harrowbys and found us a carriage—in short, there never was anything so good-natured. So we stayed and saw her, and drove down here after it was over.

What a wonderful invention she is. I am satisfied now that she is not a mere live woman; but probably she is, as she insinuated in the ballet *La Sylphide*. Monsieur de Voisins sat next to us, and his ecstacies and Bravos, and the rapturous soliloquies he indulged in, have left me with a strong impression of his domestic felicity. To be sure, it is a miracle in our favour, that there should be a man in the world, who is enchanted to see his wife flying about a theatre with no cloathes on, and that that individual should have married Taglioni! Your ever affect.

E. E.

Miss Eden to Mrs. Lister.
GREENWICH PARK,
Thursday evening, July 2, 1832.

DEAREST THERESA, I found your note when we came home late last night from Richmond, where we had been to pass the day and dine with the G. Lamb's; consequently your party was dispersed and you were in a sweet sleep before I knew you had been "at home," and I was in a sweet sleep too, five minutes after I got home, and shall be so again, I hope, as soon as I have sealed this note. These days in the country are wholesome in that respect. We came here very early this morning, did our Churches like good Christians, and have given a dinner like Ditto, for we have a highly conservative party down here, at least what would have been conservative if, as my housekeeper justly observed about the gooseberries, the season for conserving was not gone by.

We have had the Jerseys, Lord Villiers, Lord Carnarvon, and dear C. Baring-Wall, besides the smart tassel of young Jersey children. George was as happy as a King with all his old friends, so I am delighted they came, and after all Lady Jersey is very good-humoured.

Lord Carnarvon has a pouting-pigeon way of talking, which is rather amusing, but upon the whole I find Tories rather less lively, or perhaps a shade more dull, than Whigs. They growl more, and do not snap in that lively way I should have expected. However, I am no judge: "man delights not me nor woman either," as dear Hamlet had the candour to observe. He had seen something of society. I daresay he longed to be left to his flowers and his Chiswick, and a comfortable chair under the portico. To be sure his father made a bad business of sleeping in the garden, but then it could not have been so sweet or so full of flowers as ours.

We go back to town to-morrow afternoon, but I begin to see the time coming when we shall settle here. I wish you would take to treat yourself entirely as a sick person for a fortnight. But you won't, so there is no use saying anything about it. Your ever affectionate

E. E.

Viscount Melbourne to Miss Eden.
WHITEHALL,
August 13, 1832.

MY DEAR MISS EDEN, Many thanks for your kind enquiries. I have been laid up for a day or two, but am much better, and in tearing spirits, which is always the consequence of being laid up. Abstinence from wine and regularity of diet does me much more good than the malady does me harm.

I hope I shall get into the country soon, for I quite pine for it. Robert, I am told, is the only man in Hertingfordbury who has registered. Has Lady Francis written to him for theological arguments? I understand that she has been simply defeated in religious dispute by an Atheist of the neighbourhood—a shoemaker, or something of that sort—and has been seeking everywhere for assistance. The man argued for Natural Philosophy for so long, that she was not prepared to controvert.

Do not the Malignants pour somewhat less malignance, or are they more irritated than ever? Adieu. Yours faithfully,

MELBOURNE.

Miss Eden to Mrs. Lister.
Wednesday .

DEAREST THERESA, I had meant to have written you a long letter, but have been interrupted in a thousand ways till it is too late; but perhaps a line will be better than nothing. I was so much obliged to you for writing me that long letter. It told me exactly all I wanted to know about you—your health, your feelings, and also the little particulars I have no means of ascertaining. I never had courage to ask Mr. Villiers even how you are. Don't you know the difficulty there is of approaching even in the slightest degree *the* subject that one is most anxious about, and as the *surface* with him is quite calm, I am always careful not to venture even on a word that might disturb it. He and Mr. Edward Villiers dined here yesterday. George is very anxious to have your George here as much as possible, and thought they had better come for their Christmas dinner as their own family is away, so he asked them both, and I was very glad to renew my acquaintance with Edward, though in some respects, from likeness of voice and manner, which probably you would not be aware of, it was painful to see those two come into the room together.

However, they must be a great comfort to each other. I never saw *my* brother George so occupied with another person's grief as he is in this instance. He is asking and thinking every day what can be done for Mr. Villiers. God knows there is nothing; but still I always recollect that in those horrid times of trial, affection from anybody is soothing, if it is nothing more, so I am glad when it is shown.

I was at Oatlands when your letter came, and Lady Charlotte , who is a kind-hearted person I always think, was most anxious to know all about you and Mrs. Villiers. I thought her very well, all things considered. Lady F. seemed to me particularly out of spirits, and all her letters have been so since her father's death. I imagine, that in addition to any other trials, they are in some trouble about their affairs, or that Lord F. thinks so, and makes himself unhappy, which troubles her.

The Gowers have taken Bridgewater House off their hands. Maria Howick is come back from the North. Everybody talks of her low spirits and constrained manner. Though I do not think her in high spirits, I do not think *I* see much difference in her. She is probably timid with her new family and her new position, but whenever I see her alone I am quite convinced she does not think herself unhappy, and when she is quite at her ease again I think other people will think so too.

God bless you, my darling Theresa, I will write again in a few days. Your ever affectionate

E. E.

Miss Eden to Mrs. Lister.
GROSVENOR STREET,
Thursday, December 1832.

MY DEAREST THERESA, I fear that Lord Ribblesdale's death must be to you and Mr. Lister an additional grief, as I recollect you were fond of her, and she seems to have had not the slightest warning of this calamity. It was very kind of Mr. Lister to write to me, for I was in a state of great anxiety about your health and with no near means of hearing anything about you. What can I say to you, dearest? My love for you and my deep, deep pity for your bereavement you cannot doubt, and as for any attempt at consolation, who can be sure that even with the kindest intentions, they may not aggravate the grief they wish to soothe. I always felt in calamity that though I seemed to want kindness from everybody, yet that all they did was like the work of surgeons, the most skilful made the pain of the wound more evident; and I think I may hurt you if I dwell on your loss, or seem neglectful if I do not, and yet I know so well all you must be feeling.

I was reading yesterday a book of extracts, etc., that I wrote when I lost my own darling brother. As there were several things in it that I thought you might like, and though I did not want anything to remind me of feelings that seem as *true* on that subject as they were years ago, yet it made me better able to follow you in your present hours of trial and to know what you are going through. With a mother, husband, and child with you, and all the rest of your family, whom you love so dearly, assembled about you, you have more earthly support than many can have to look to; and the consolations of religion none are more likely to find than yourself. Indeed, that is a subject on which I think a stranger intermeddleth not, for God alone can comfort the heart He has cast down, and He, I trust, forgives the repinings which He alone knows.

I wish you would make the exertion of writing one line to me. I love you very dearly, and never feel it more than when you are in grief. Your affectionate

E. E.

Miss Eden to Lady Charlotte Greville.
(At Oatlands, Weybridge),
December 24, 1832.

MY DEAR LADY CHARLOTTE, ...London is so particularly thick and sloppy that it would not surprise me if I slipped out of it again soon.

I have got that invitation to Panshanger I wanted, but as I would rather not go into Hertfordshire till the ball season is over, that will do later, and Eastcombe is open again now.

I am broken-hearted about the Essex election, and the only gleam of cheerfulness I have had has been occasioned by half a sheet of notepaper which I filled with the beginning of my new novel. I wrote nearly a sentence and a half which I composed in two days. Mr. Sale, the singer, called here this morning, which he often does, and used to give me lessons gratis, which was kind but tiresome. To-day he could not, because there is no pianoforte in the house, so we talked about Mrs. Arkwright's songs, which he says he teaches to numbers of his scholars (there is no end to his pupils). But there are great faults in the scientific parts of her compositions, which he could correct in five minutes—in short, he talks of a mistake in counterpoint as we do of breaking one of the Commandments, and when I said she was a great friend of mine, he said he should be quite delighted to correct anything she sent to the Press, and always without touching the "air," and he was very polite about it. Do you think it would affront Mrs. Arkwright if I asked her, or that she would not take it as it was meant, as a kindness, from such a lump of science as Sale is? Shall I ask her? Yours affectionately,

E. E.

Hon. Mrs. Norton to Lord Auckland.

DEAR LORD AUCKLAND, As you are the only person in your family who have not "cut" me, perhaps you will allow me to apologise *through* you, to your Sister, for my rudeness last night.

Say that, as far as concerns her, I consider my conduct on that occasion vulgar and unjustifiable, and that I beg her pardon. Yesterday was a day of great vexation and fatigue—which of course is no excuse in the eyes of strangers (whatever it may be in my own), for rudeness and want of temper. I am very sorry. My apology may be of no value to her; but it is a satisfaction to *me* to make it. Yours truly,

C. NORTON.

Lady Campbell to Miss Eden.
October 25, 1833.

DEAREST EMMY, Eleven years ago we were together. To-day is Edward's birthday, and I still see that house in Cadogan Place, and the window at which I sat watching for you, my own dear Friend. I like to think how long we've loved each other without a shade of alteration between us; *du reste*, I need dwell on such things to smooth my mind after other rugged bits of life. Your godchild is a good, peaceable, fat lump, with black eyelashes and a pretty mouth, which is all I can make out of her yet.

I recovered tolerably well the first fortnight, since that I have been but poorly. Anxiety and worry keep me back. However, it is all over now, for our matters are pretty nearly arranged. Sir Guy sells out; it is our only resource; it is the only way of paying what we owe, getting rid of debt....

I conclude you are now sitting with your own goldfish under your fig-tree, you who live under the shadow of your own old Men. By the bye, with your blue pensioners, I am sure you will feel for us in the dispersion of our red pensioners. There was a great cry heard in the Hospital, Kilmainham weeping for her old men, because they are no longer to be! However, they are respited, for my enemy Ellice put his pen through their existence, and Mr. Littleton too, and ordered even the fashion of their dispersion, but forgot to enquire particulars, and they have stumbled upon an Act of Parliament, and so must wait till another Act breaks through it. Ellice dropped his pen, and was obliged to pick it up again. Your affectionate

PAMELA CAMPBELL.

Miss Eden to Mrs. Lister.

GREENWICH PARK,
Sunday, December 15, 1833.

DEAREST THERESA, I have just had a letter from your brother George, and though probably you heard from him by the same opportunity, yet it is always a pleasure to know that one's brothers are heard of by others as well as oneself. It makes assurance doubly sure, which that clever creature Shakespeare knew was not once more than enough, in this unsure world.

Mr. V. seems very happy and very well, and will probably be more personally comfortable when he is the owner of a few tables and chairs. It was such a relief *off* my mind (as a friend of mine says when anything is a relief *to* her mind) to find that he had received an enormous letter I wrote to him some time ago, a thing like the double sheet of the *Times* in private life, and which had been so long unacknowledged, that I felt sure that it had been captured, and that I should see a horrible garbled translation of it copied from a Carlist paper, and headed "Intercepted Correspondence," whereupon I must simply have changed my religion, gone into a convent, and taken the veil. The *propriety* of my letters surpasses all belief, so I should not have been ashamed in that sense; but when I write to your brother, or to Lord Minto, or to that class of correspondents, I always rake together every possible anecdote and fact—or what is called a fact—and write them all down just like a string of paragraphs in a newspaper. I always suppose nonsense would bore them, so the horrid letters are made up of proper names, and if there is an unsafe thing in the world to meddle with it is a proper name, and that is the bother of a letter that goes abroad, particularly to such a country as Spain. I saw George was just as fussy about a letter he had written to your brother; but now we know our little manuscripts have found their way safely, we mean to write again—at least I do, the first time I find anything to say. At present I am out of that article.

We have been living here rather quietly, not very though,—at least I dined in town at several great dinners, at the Lievens, etc., that fortnight the Ministers were all in London, and we went up several times to the play with the Stanleys, and several of them came and dined here, and so on during November. Then, George has been frisking about the country at Woburn, Brocket, etc., shooting; and on Saturday he and I are going to run down to Bowood for a week. It is an expensive amusement and not worth the trouble, barring that it is worth while acknowledging the kindness of the Lansdownes. He rode down here from London to ask us, but I never go on his invitations. But, however, he wrote again as soon as he got back, and then Lady Lansdowne wrote to insist on our fixing a day. So, though I know she never wishes her invitations to be accepted, yet if she will write, she must take the consequences, and so we are going. I hear the Nortons are to be there, which will be funny. I do not fancy her, but still she will be amusing to meet for once.

We settle in town after that, at least Fanny and I do. George is going to a great meeting of Ministers at Goodwood. I think it such a good thing, the Ministers have all taken to go shooting about in a body. It prevents their doing any other mischief. That is the way an enemy might state it. I, who am a friend, merely presume they must have brought the country to a flourishing state, since they seem to have so much leisure for amusing themselves.

We have two of Robert's boys staying with us while Mrs. Eden is recovering from her sixth lying-in. The eldest of the five younger children is just five years old. Pleasant!

I send this to the Council Office as you desire, and have a vague idea that C. Greville will read it, and throw it into the fire—officially of course, I mean. Ever, dearest Theresa, your affect.

E. E.

Miss Eden to Lady Campbell.

GROSVENOR STREET,
Tuesday, .

DEAREST PAM, Thank you just for giving me a push off—not that of all the days in the year I could have chosen *this* for answering you. I am in long correspondence with Louisa (Mrs. Colvile) about that flirtation, that little interesting love story I imparted to you, and, as usual, the young people are to be very miserable, because that £100 a year which has been left out of everybody's income, when incomes were created, is not forthcoming; and as usual again, I take the grand line of "all for love and my niece well lost." Moreover, I think a small income in these days is as good as a large one twenty years ago; and that anything is to be preferred to a disappointment. But all this—together with due attention to dignity one side and love the other, and no two people ever understanding each other—keeps me writing at the rate of twelve pages a day. I am quite tired of the manual labour, and as I feel convinced that three months hence they will be married, I grudge these *protocols*.

What fun your visit was to me, and I shall always think that last sin of your drive to Greenwich and back was the best spent wickedest two hours we ever passed. I have been twice for a few days to Eastcombe. Saturday and Sunday we pass at Greenwich. George gardens for about fourteen hours on Sunday, which I suppose is wrong, only that is his way of resting himself. Your most affectionate

E. E.

Lady Campbell to Miss Eden.
March 26, 1834.

DEAREST EMMY, I daresay the very sight of a letter from me frights you. I was very sorry after I had written the nasty bitter letter. When I wrote that, I was ill-tempered too! and one always writes harder than one feels. However, my own Emmy, I had rather have written it to you than to any other, tho' you may not thank me for *la préférence*, if any one can bear with me it is you, however. You mistook me if you thought that I thought that either dear Lord Auckland or the Lansdownes had not done their utmost for us! God knows I feel far more sure of Lord Auckland's kindness to me than of my own Brother's. But there is much danger in our sort of distress of getting embittered, my Darling. I pray against this temptation, and strive against this most fervently, and I do trust my cheerfulness has never flagged, and that I blame no one. We have done all we can, and I will not fret....

Your little Godchild is a dear child, with immense eyes and four teeth. She is wise, clever and quiet, and all your Godchild ought to be, but not so pretty as some of her sisters. As they say the commodities are always in proportion to the demand for them, I expect a great cry for girls in a few years.

I have been to our Court but twice. I was told it was imposing, and I did think there was a good deal of imposition. He is sharp and clever and does work like a horse, but I do think one man about him very dangerous, and that is Blake the Remembrancer. I cannot help thinking that man very double, nay, triple. There are no bounds to the gossip of our little Court; the master likes it and is fed with it. I do not think he is very popular, but that does not signify; here, the way of flesh and all parties seems to be discontent, and murmur and grumble. Think of the Wilt being married,—*Ciel*!... Your own

PAMMY.

Lady Campbell to Miss Eden.

1834.

I am over head and ears in your affairs. I have so much the bump of speculation and lottery in my soul that I am decidedly of your opinion, and would at once keep Greenwich and the Thames, than put my head under that very excellent and comfortable extinguisher of the Exchequer, particularly if my head were as *bien meublée* and well arranged as your George's small crop-eared shaven little crown. We always dressed our heads alike *outside*, no curls. I would most certainly take my chance and not dowager myself into the Exchequer....

I suppose Government, to hold together, must go upon the principle of each Minister bringing a certain quantity of sense and an alloy of folly. Now, surely, some of your colleagues bring a peck of dirt and very few grains of reason. Are you obliged to eat it all?... My dearest, tempt me not with the sound of pleasant books, I am all day at Latin and Greek with the boys, I very nearly wrote your name in Greek letters.

Write to me; it cheers me, and I want cheering often, dear Emmy. I grieve at your account of Lady Lansdowne. She has not the constitution for the illness of being cured by the London physicians, I am very sure. Solomon, after he had taken all the physic in the world, exclaimed: "Vanity of vanities."

Your Godchild has a mouthful of teeth. Tell me something of your Sisters, of William Osborne, of that marriage of your niece, and particularly of the fate of those *orchises* we took down that day we ran to Greenwich, did they ever come up?

Miss Eden to Lady Campbell.

GROSVENOR STREET.

...I do not really care about my position in this short life, but I like to be actually *posished*, don't you? I believe we shall end by remaining at Greenwich, influenced chiefly by the enormous price of villas.

I am sorry Lady Lansdowne writes in bad spirits, for barring the melancholy circumstances attending Kerry's marriage, I should not have thought this a troublesome year to her. The Wilt himself seems full of attention to her, and if she hates London society, this is a charming year, as such an article does not exist. You have no idea how odd it is. Except herself, no person ever thinks of giving either ball or party. I own I think it quite delightful; no hot rooms, no trouble of any sort, and a great economy of gowns and bores.

We thought much of the Unions for ten days, but they are going by. There never was such luck as the Tailors starting by such ridiculous demands. The middle classes, even down to servants, took against them, and there seems to be very little doubt that, in a very few weeks, they will be totally beat and the whole Union fund exhausted.

It is rather amusing to see them wandering about the Parks, quite astonished at the green leaves and blackbirds. There were about fifty of them playing at leap-frog the other morning. Only conceive the luxury of going home after that unusual exercise, and after beating their wives for making such good waistcoats, sitting down cross-legged to rest themselves. They cost the Union £10,000 the first week, and £8,000 the second, and as the whole amount of the Union fund is £60,000, it is easy to guess how long it may last. It will end in frightful distress. The great tailors are getting foreigners over, and employing women with great success.

I have been in a state of agitation with a touch of bother added to it, which would have made my letters very *hummocky*. That giving up Greenwich was nearly the death of me, and our glorious promotion was inflicted on us on a particular Thursday, Epsom race day, which George and I had set apart for a holiday, and a *tête-à-tête* dinner, and a whole afternoon in that good little garden. We went all the same; but, as for gardening, what was the good of cultivating flowers for other people's nosegays! So there I sat under the verandah crying. What else could be done, with the roses all out, and the sweetpeas, and our orange-trees, and the whole garden looking perfectly lovely; and George was nearly as low as I was.

And then we had two or three days of bother for our future lives, because, though I now never mean to talk politics, and to hear as little of them as may be, yet I suppose there is no harm in imagining just the bare possibility that the Government *may* not last for ever. However, he is assured now of a retiring pension. If he chooses to play at the game of politics, he must take his chance of winning or losing; and moreover, this would not have been a time for separating from poor Lansdowne, who has behaved beautifully all through these troubles. So now we are fairly in for it, and after the first troubles are over, I daresay it will do very well. It is the kind of office he likes, and he is, of course, flattered with the offer of it, and Lord Grey has been uncommonly kind to him.

We went on Tuesday to see the Admiralty, and I believe we shall be moving into it the end of next week. It is a vast undertaking. The kitchen is about the size of Grosvenor Square, and takes a cook and three kitchen-maids to keep it going, but the rest of the establishment is in proportion, which is distressing, as I look on every additional servant as an added calamity. I will trouble you with the idea of *this* house—your old acquaintance—with a bill stuck in its window, "To be sold,"—rather shocking! Looks ungrateful after we have passed our best days in it; but still I cannot fancy being much attached to *any* London house, so I do not mind about this. Our idea is to get a villa sufficiently small to be adapted to our income, whenever the day of dignified retirement comes; to move our plants and books to it, and gradually to furnish it, and then to make it our only home for the rest of our lives. I should like that better than any other life. Ever your affectionate

E. E.

Lady Campbell to Miss Eden.

Tuesday, June 10, 1834.

How do you do, and how do you feel? How does one feel when one becomes sister to the Admiralty?... Stanley seems a terrible loss, but at this distance I cannot judge, of course. You will think me, of course, a Radical, but I think he is wrong, for the Irish Church always did strike me like a Hot-bed for raising Horse-Beans,—some would tell you for raising thistles, but I don't go quite so far. I saw Mrs. Ellice, she is in such a Grey fermentation, it might be dangerous, but she foams it away in such long talk that it is very safe.

I saw Mrs. Foggy as she is called; pleasant, merry, and going on very well; people begin to get accustomed to her ways, and, I think, like her on the whole! Darling dear Foggy is in good humour, and all seems right. She is amusing, certainly, but certainly *elle parle gras*, as the French say, when people speak improprieties. I always think part of her education must have been carried on in the Canal boat, like *Vert Vert*, when he got away from the nuns.

The Protestants are bristling all over this unfortunate country since the Reform. I have seen nothing like the excitement among them. The Catholics do not appear so excited. This is plain enough. The loss to 200,000 is immense, whereas the gain to 8,000,000 is comparatively small.

Miss Eden to Lady Campbell.
HAM COMMON,
Tuesday, July 23, 1834.

Yes, it is very odd—absolutely curious. But tho' you and I live in two different islands—two different worlds—yet your letters always are just what I think, and know, and say, and they fit into my mood of mind, and you carry on the story I am telling—and you know all I did not tell you, and say all I did not know—and the whole thing amalgamates. That Littleton creature! Is not there an unity in that story of him with all I know? Let's write his life. Did not I meet him at dinner the very week after the stramash, when everybody crossed the street if they saw him coming, they were so ashamed *for* him? It was at a dinner at the Chancellor's, the first given after Lord Melbourne's appointment, and he was there, and Lord Lansdowne, and several others, and Charles Grey as sulky as possible. And next to him sat Mr. Littleton—and the first thing he chose to begin talking about across the table was something about "one of the *tustles that O'Connell and I have had*." It set all our teeth on edge, everybody being naturally with a predisposition to *edge*-ism, and none of the ferment of the change having had time to subside—and he the guilty author of it all! I really would not have alluded for his sake to the letter O. I said to Lord Lansdowne: "Well, I am surprised at him, for I have refrained from talking about him, from really expecting his mind must give way, and that there will be some horrid tragedy to make us all repent having abused him." And he said, "That is exactly my feeling. I look at him with astonishment; I can hardly believe he is what he seems to be." I suppose it really was true, and that he did not mind. We tried, for two or three days, I remember, to declare he looked very ill, but now you say he had not lost a night's rest, I give up that point. It never was very tenable.

The young Greys have all been pre-eminently absurd, Lord Howick more than all the rest. He told me he had been to all the clubs, and calling at all the houses he knew, to spread every report against the Chancellor he could think of, and coming from him, of course, it was set down as coming from his father, who is as unlike his sons as he well can be. I do not wish to entrench on Mrs. E.'s province—how tiresome she must be!—but she can say nothing of Lord Grey I don't think. He is the only great man I ever had the good luck to see—consistent and magnanimous—two qualities that I never met with in any other politician. I have closed my political accounts with him.... I am sure I cannot tell you generally anything about the Government. Politics have answered so ill to me in my private capacity that I gave them quite up, and can only tell you these private gossipries of the time. I have not read a debate since last Easter, and can only wonder how I could be so foolish three years ago as to think politics and office the least amusing. I suppose to the end of our days we shall all wonder at ourselves three years ago. But I have had such a horrid uncomfortable year this year; I never was so tired, so out of breath, so bored. You may well ask where we lodge. At a little cottage on Ham Common, hired by the week, without a scrap of garden, but where by dint of hard labour, a doctor, and quantities of steel draughts, I have recovered a little of the health I lost entirely by being kept eight months in London, frying over the coals.

I declare I believe I have lived ten whole lives in the last ten months; we have been so unsettled, which is the only state I cannot abide. First George was to have that Exchequer place with Greenwich, and we made up our plans for that, and were to part with Grosvenor Street; then Greenwich was cut off from the Exchequer, and we prepared to give that up; then the Government found it convenient to make him keep the Board of Trade, and we went back to be as we were.

Then came the Stanley secession and we thought we were all to be out, and reverted to the Exchequer, and looked at every villa round London. Then came the Admiralty, and George sent me to Greenwich to pack up and sell and give up everything, (the only spot of ground I care about in the world).

Well! That was done, and as the goods were on their road, just turning into the Admiralty gate, and just after we had paid Sir James Graham for *his* goods, and stuck up a bill in Grosvenor St. "To Be Sold"—out went dear Grey.

Then for two or three weeks we did not know what to do. And then in all that hot weather, at last we settled to move, and the arrangement of that great Admiralty was enough to murder an elephant. Then, when George set off on his Tour of the Ports, we came here, and just as we got settled, a Mr. Brogden bought Grosvenor Street, so that I had to go up and pack that up, and rout out the accumulated rubbish of sixteen years, and move all the books, etc.

However they have done their worst now, we have parted with both our houses, and all our goods, and when we are turned out, must live in a tent under a hedge.

I have got a little black King Charles's spaniel of my own, that I mean to boil down, and make into a comfortable "sup of broth" when we come to that particular hedge "where my tired mind may rest and call it home."

I somehow feel as if I were sitting by watching George's mad career, and wondering where it will end.

I never set eyes on him—you have no idea what the labour of the Admiralty is—he never writes less than 35 letters every day in his own hand, besides what the Secretary and all the others do.

Every Levée is a crowd of discontented men who would make an excellent crew for *one* ship, he says, but as they each want one, he is obliged to refuse 99 out of every 100. However he is as happy as a king, I believe, only he has not had time to mention it. He likes his office of all things.

The Admiralty is a splendid home to live in, but requires quantities of servants, and the more there are the more discontented they are. Everybody says what fortunate people we are, and I daresay George is, but my personal luck consists in having entirely lost his society and Greenwich, the two charms of my life; in being kept ten months of every year in London, which I loathe; and in being told to have people to dinner—without the means of dressing myself so as to be always in society. I wish Government would consider that, tho' a man be raised high in office, yet that the unfortunate women remain just as poor as ever.

Louisa (Mrs. Colvile) has just had her seventeenth child; Mary (Mrs. Drummond) her ninth; and Mrs. Eden is going to have her seventh.

Lord Melbourne made a good start in the House of Lords as far as speaking went. I do not know what ladies have hopes of him, but the "Fornarina," as he calls her himself, has him in greater thraldom than ever. I see him very often and confidentially, but both of us without any sinister designs.

Miss Eden to Lady Charlotte Greville.

HAM COMMON,
Friday.

MY DEAR LADY CHARLOTTE, I sent a note to thank you for my beautiful purse down to Mr. Spring-Rice to frank, not knowing he was away from home, and now that is come back to me I may thank you also for your account of Lady F. I am so glad the business is over at last; it was very hard upon her to have it hanging over her so long, and I congratulate you on being at ease about her. As for another grandchild—your *grand quiver* is so full of them already, that I suppose you hardly have room for any more. I think it would be such a good plan, if after people have as many children as they like, they were allowed to lie-in of any other article they fancied better; with the same pain and trouble, of course (if that is necessary), but the result to be more agreeable. A set of Walter Scott's novels, or some fine china, or in the case of poor people, fire-irons and a coal skuttle, or two pieces of Irish linen. It would certainly be more amusing and more profitable, and then there would be such anxiety to know *what* was born. Now it can be only a boy or a girl.

I expect and hope that Lady F. in about ten days will be walking about looking younger and stronger than ever.

My purse is quite perfection, and I cannot thank you enough for it. I am only afraid it is still more attractive than the last you gave me, which so took the fancy of one of those men who sell oranges in the street, that he snatched it off the seat of the carriage in which I was sitting and ran away with it. Your ever affectionate

E. EDEN.

Lady Campbell to Miss Eden.

Tell me any old news you have by you, for I never see a newspaper by any chance, and live in the wilds,—woods I would have said, only we are scarce of trees. I hear news once a month from Mrs. Ellice. I think she seems Lord Wellesley's Madame de Pompadour, and so happy! She is quick and lively, but *furieusement intrigante* I should imagine, from what I hear of her; and her vanity has such a maw that she swallows the rawest compliments. She was recommended to me by Mrs. Sullivan,—not merely introduced to my acquaintance, but fairly confided to my heart. Well, my dearest, I went with my friendship in my hand, ready to swear it before the first magistrate, expecting to find a warm-hearted *étourdie* full of talent and genius. Well, we met, and I knocked my head against the hardest bit of worldly Board you ever met with. Full of business, with a great deal of the grey claw and *accaparage*. So I buttoned up my heart to my chin, and we talked good harsh worldly gab, and we are charming persons together.

Miss Eden to Mrs. Lister.

HAM COMMON,
Monday evening, October 28, 1834.

DEAREST THERESA, I am kind to write to-night, for Fanny and I poked out an old backgammon board of the General's and began to play, and I beat her two single games and a gammon, so that in coming to my letter I am probably leaving "fortune at the flood, and all my after life will be bound in flats and shallows." All your fault.

Our cottage is a real little cottage, belonging to an old General Eden who, on the score of relationship, let us have it for almost nothing. It is very clean and old bachelorish, and he lets with it an old housemaid who scolds for half-an-hour if a grain of seed drops from the bird's cage, or if Chance whisks a hair out of his tail; we are grown so tidy and as she is otherwise an obliging old body, she has been an advantage to us. We took the house only by the week, and as my health has entirely recovered the complete break-up it came to, from our long detention in London, and as his Lordship is living alone at that Admiralty, we depart on Wednesday to settle ourselves there till the

Government changes, or I am ill again. However, I do not mind London so much in cold weather. I have been very busy this last week *setting up* house, as the Ministers will be most of them in town next month without their families, and George has announced an intention to make the Admiralty pleasant to his colleagues. I have but one idea of the manner in which that is to be achieved, and hope the cook may turn out as well as Mr. Orby Hunter's recommendation promises. Oh dear! I dread the sight of their dear old faces again, and of that "full of business" manner which they get into when they meet in any number.

I wish I could write like Mrs. Hannah More, and have money enough to build myself a Barley Wood, and resolution to go and live there. I am so taken by that book and amazingly encouraged by it, for she was as dissipated and as wicked as any of us for the first half of our life, so there is no saying whether we may not turn out good for something at last.

We have been here eleven weeks, quite alone, but walking and driving eternally, and very few interruptions except an occasional visit from, or to, the F. Egertons and W. de Roos's, and a royal dinner, luncheon, and party at the Studhouse, which always turns out amusing. The King is so good-natured that it does not signify his being a little ridiculous or so; it is impossible not to love him. The Albemarles do the thing in the handsomest manner as far as the dinner, establishment, etc., goes, and I think the Studhouse a charming possession. She always gets all the King's Ministers that she can find to meet him, and it charms me to hear her *judgments* of people:—How unlucky that the Spring-Rices should *look* less well at a dinner than the Stanleys; and what luck she was in in having such a showy person as Lady Bingham last year in the neighbourhood; not adverting to the possibility that one person may be pleasanter than the others, and admitting that, their position being changed, they do not amount to being *persons* at all.

I suppose that things are going on well, for I never saw people in greater glee than the Ministers are. Lord Melbourne is in the highest state of spirits, which seems to me odd for the Prime Minister of the country. They all went off from the last luncheon at the Studhouse early, leaving only the W. de Roos's, Fanny and me and Lord Hill to go round Hampton Court Palace with the King,—a long and curious process, as he shows it just like a housekeeper with a story for each picture. It was pitch dark, so it does not much matter if the pictures were as improper as the stories, for I saw none of them, but it lasted two hours, and in the meantime the Ministers, having had their dinner so early, had set fire to the two Houses of Parliament just for a *ploy* for the evening. That is the sort of view the Tories take of it, and it sounds plausible, you see; and from Lord Hill's staying to see the Palace it is clear he had not been let into that plot.

No, I did not see the fire,—wish I had—will trouble them to do it all over again when there are more people in town. Is Lord Fordwich the new Under Secretary? I asked George and he said he did not know, and I asked Lord Melbourne and he said he could not tell me—both very good answers in their way and such as I am used to, but it leaves the fact of Fordwich's appointment doubtful, and I heard from Lady Cowper three days ago and she said nothing about it.

There was a great *sough* of India for about a fortnight, but I always said it was too bad to be true, which is a dangerous assertion to make in most cases, it only hastens the catastrophe. But this was such an extreme case, such a horrible supposition, that there was nothing for it but to bully it; and the danger is over now. Botany Bay would be a joke to it. There is a decent climate to begin with, and the fun of a little felony first. But to be sent to Calcutta for no cause at all!! At all events, I should hardly have got there before George got home again, for I should have walked across the country to join him, if I had gone at all. I think I see myself going into a ship for five months! I would not do it for £1000 per day.

Good-night, dearest Theresa. I see *Ann Grey* is out, and rather expect that will turn out to be yours too. Is it? Your ever affectionat
E. E.

Miss Eden to Mrs. Lister.
ADMIRALTY,
Monday, November 23, 1834.

MY DEAREST THERESA, Yes,—you see it all just in the right light; but what will come of it nobody can say.... The truth is, till Sir Robert or his answer comes, they have not the least idea themselves what they are to do, or to say, or to think, and I should not be the least surprised if he were to refuse to come, and many people think that from the ridicule of the Duke's position and conduct now, the whole thing may crumble away before Sir Robert can arrive.

The King is said to be very cross about it, and at the unconstitutional state of affairs. It has been the oddest want of courtesy on the Duke's part insulting the Ministers for his own *in*convenience. Mr. Spring-Rice's *keys*, besides his seals, were sent for two hours after the Duke kissed hands on Monday, so that he could not remove his private letters even, and has never been able to get them since. He is naturally the *gentlest* man I ever saw, but is in that state of exasperation that he would do anything to show his resentment.

On Friday the Duke sent to Lord Conyngham to say he begged he would dispose of no more patronage, to which Lord Conyngham answered very properly that he had resigned, and was keeping the office solely for the Duke's convenience (it is a patent office), and that he would leave it with pleasure the next minute, but as long as he remained there he should certainly do what he thought best with his patronage. The Chancellor was to have given up the seals on Saturday, when he would have cleared off all arrears and closed the courts, etc., and this was understood at the beginning of the week; but on Thursday the Duke wrote to him that he must give up the Great Seal on Friday morning. It appears that nobody but the King has a right to ask for the Great Seal, so the Chancellor wrote to tell the Duke what was the proper *étiquette*, and at the same time wrote to Lord Lyndhurst, with whom he is on the most amicable terms, saying that the Duke, besides being three Secretaries of State, President of the Council, etc., was now going to be Lord Chancellor, so he should give notice to the Bar that the Duke would give judgment on Friday afternoon, and sit to hear Motions on Saturday morning. He came here quite enchanted with the serious answer from Lord Lyndhurst, saying the Duke had no such notion, etc.

I suppose anything equal to the ill-treatment of Lord Melbourne never was known.

The Tories go on asserting, in the teeth of his *advertised contradiction* (for he was driven to that), that he dissolved the Government, and advised the Duke, etc. There is not a *shadow* of foundation for that. He went down to Brighton to propose the new Chancellor of the Exchequer, not anticipating any difficulty. His colleagues were all dining here that day, and were expecting him back perhaps in the evening, as he had so little to do! He found everything he said met by objection, and at last the King asked for a night's consideration, and on Friday put a letter into Lord Melbourne's hand, very civil personally to him, but saying he meant to send for the Duke.

Lord Melbourne never expressed any difficulty about carrying on the government; never complained of difficulties in the Cabinet, which do not exist; never advised a successor,—in short, it was as great a surprise to him as to the rest of the world, and as the Court Party go on saying the contrary, I mention this.

The truth is that that party—Lady T. Sydney, Miss D'Este, the Howes, Brownlows, etc., have all been working on his, the King's, fears, and exacted a promise that when Lord Spencer died the King should try the Tories, which he has quite a right to do; but he should not have forced Lord Melbourne to take that office of great responsibility and then have dismissed him without any reason, or without Lord Melbourne's making any difficulties, and he made *none*. I could convince you of this by several notes from him, besides the fact being now generally known. He says in one note: "I do not like to tell my story; I cannot. Besides, I hate to be considered ill-used; I have always thought complaints of ill-usage contemptible, whether from a seduced disappointed girl, or a turned out Prime Minister." So like him! Our people have all been very cheerful this time, and it has been *privately* an amusing week.

Ours is the only official home left open, and as the poor things were all turned adrift, with nothing to do, and nowhere to go, they have dined here most days (I have found *such* a cook!), and several others have come in, in the evening.

Our plans are beautifully vague. We have no home, and no place, and no nothing; but as we have a right to a month's residence after our successor is gazetted, and as he cannot be appointed for a fortnight, there is time enough to look about us. George leans to a place in the country large enough to give *him* some amusement, and that is cheaper than a small villa which I should rather prefer, but either would do very well. In short, I do not much care so as he pleases himself. We have *esquivéd* India, a constant source of pleasure to me, though I keep it snug, as he is rather disappointed at having missed it, so I must not seem so thankful as I am. I should like to go abroad for a few months, but the session will probably be an interesting one and he would not like to be out of the way. Your ever affectionate

E. E.

CHAPTER X

1835-1837

Lady Campbell to Miss Eden.
July, 1835.

I HAVE really escaped with my life—*I ain't dead yet*, but such a big monster of a girl!—a regular Megalonia of a female, that if you happened to find a loose joint of hers you would think it must belong to an antediluvian Ox. Je vous demande un peu what am I to do with a seventh girl of such dimensions?

Well, my own darling, your letter came just as I was allowed to read, and it cheered me and delighted me, because you know we cannot help thinking just the same, and my weak sides shook with laughter, and then I cried because I do love you so much that I take a pining to see you, and I am sure you do long to have me within reach of your Ship Hotel or Ship Inn, for you are too wise to look upon it as more than your Hostelrie!...

Do you remember how we always liked a maxim? I like a maxim, and I like a good stout axiom, and a good compact system laid out straight without any exception in any rule, a good due North and South argument, and without any of your dippings of needle and variation of the compass. All this we had in the Tories—but, alas, where are they now? *Ils ne sont plus ces jours*, and I believe *we are* the Tories. I think that Lord Winchester, *e tutti quanti*, must feel like the old woman after her *réveil* when she found her petticoat cut off above the knee by that most clever pedlar Peel.

Do you ever see him now? What a fight Peel made of it, and as Plunkett said to me, "Alone he did it," and I forgive him two or three sins, because, that tho' he is a bad Chancellor, he loves the Immortal.

My dear, I grieve to say what a *desperately good* Chancellor Sugden made. Couldn't we hire him? All parties liked him except the ultra-radical dreg of the canaille. He is vain and pompous; but he amused me because his vanity is of such a communicative nature that he would talk his character out to me by the hour, and I like any confession, even a fool's. But a clever man's is very amusing, and I pick out a bit of human nature and human character as attentively as I see botanists pick petals and pistils.

It is very good of Lord Auckland to stand for my girl. I really believe she is harmless, for she could knock me down, but she is merciful! What shall we call her? I had some thoughts of Rhinocera. She was born the day the Rhinoceros landed, or Cuvier, because I was reading his life and works just before she was born, and took a passion for him.

Might she not be called Eden?—Her other name is to be Madeline—her Godmother's name....

My baby was christened Caroline Frances Eden, and I constantly call her Eden. I think it sounds very feminine and *Eve*-ish.

Miss Eden to Lady Campbell.
ADMIRALITY,
July 1835.

MY OWN DEAREST PAM, George wrote to tell you of the awful change in our destination, and I have been so worried, and have had so much to do with seeing and hearing the representations of friends, and taking leave of many who are gone out of town and whom I shall never see again, that I could not write.

Besides, what is there to say, except, "God's will be done." It all comes to that. I certainly look at the climate with dread, and to the voyage with utter aversion. Then, we leave a very happy existence here, and then, worst of all, we leave my sisters and a great many friends. But still, there is always another side to the question, and I suppose we shall find it in time. One thing is quite certain, I could not have lived here without George, so I may be very thankful that my health has been so good this year that I have no difficulty on that account, as to going with him. And as other people have liked India and have come back to say so, perhaps we shall do the same.

What I would give for a talk with you—that you might put it all in a cheerful light. It makes no difference in our affection or *communion* that has stood the test of such long absence that 14,000 miles more will not break it down.

I am going to-morrow for ten days to Mary ; she is in a desperate way about our plans....

By all means stick an "Eden" into your child's name. Your most affectionate

E. E.

Miss Eden to Lady Campbell.

ADMIRALTY,
1835.

My dearest Pam, Our letters crossed, and yours was just what I wanted, and you are as great a dear as ever, only I am never to be allowed to see you....

A week ago we began our preparations. You do not and cannot guess what that is—and I have despaired of writing you even a line—I never knew before *really* what it was to have no time. And besides the deep-seated real Indian calamity, you cannot think what a whirl and entanglement buying and measuring and trying on makes in one's brain; and poor Goliath himself would have been obliged to lie down and rest if he had tried on six pairs of stays consecutively. We sometimes are three hours at a time shopping, and I could fling myself down and scratch the floor like a dog that is trying to make a feather bed of the boards when I come home.

It is so irritating to want so many things and such cold articles. A cargo of *large fans*; a *silver busk*, because all steel busks become rusty and spoil the stays; nightdresses with short sleeves, and net nightcaps, because muslin is too hot. Then such anomalies—quantities of flannel which I never wear at all in this cool climate, but which we are to wear at night there, because the creatures who are pulling all night at the Punkahs sometimes fall asleep. Then you wake from the extreme heat and call to them, then they wake and begin pulling away with such fresh vigour that you catch your death with a sudden chill. What a life! However, it is no use thinking about it.

My present aim in writing is to ask whether there is not anybody in or near Dublin who can make a sketch of you, something in the Edridge or Slater line, not very extravagant in price, and if you do not mind, sitting for it for me. I will send its price by Lord Morpeth, when he goes, and you must send it me either by a private hand, or if not, we can have it sent under cover to George, if it is carefully packed. Will you?

What do you think of the Lords? It is hardly possible to conceive such hopeless folly, and it is clear that they are the only living animals that cannot learn experience.

We shall be off in less than a month I believe, not that I believe anything somehow,—I feel too dreamy and bewildered. Your ever affect.

E. E.

Miss Eden to her Sister, Mrs. Drummond.

ADMIRALTY,
Saturday .

My very dear Mary, Your note was a sad blow to me; but perhaps it is best that we should so have parted, and I am very thankful that we should have had this week together. I am thankful for many things—that we love each other so entirely; that you have a husband who has been so invariably kind to all of us, and whom I can love in return; and then, that your girls seem to me like real friends, and almost like my own children. All these are great goods and absence cannot touch them. God bless you, my darling Sister. Your ever affectionate

E. EDEN.

Lady Campbell to Miss Eden.

CARTON,
September 1, 1835.

I fear there is no good sketcher in Dublin, but there is a man who does paint something like a miniature, and does catch a likeness, and it shall be done for you next week, my darling. I never have you out of my mind a minute, and I always thought I should not be sorry if a change sent a Tory out instead of you.... I feel cheerful about you because you are doing what is right, and only think what you would have been suffering now if you were seeing him prepared to go without you.... Shall we take good in this world and not take the evil, *our old compensations*? You might have lived years without either you or George knowing how much you loved each other, and is there not an utter delight in this feeling of devotion twice blessed?

Let me know how I am to write to you, and how to send my letters. How little did I imagine when I read of India, and looked on those hot, misty, gorgeous Indian views, that I should ever garner up part of my heart there. I am staying here. I always like them, but there is a want of colour and life and impulse. There are many positive virtues present, and an absence of all vice and evil, but yet something is wanted. There is the dreaminess of Sleepy Hollow upon them.

Send me a bit of your hair, my darling, and always bear me in your "heart of hearts, as I do thee, Horatio." I cannot believe it yet, nor do you, dearest, in spite of the preparations, and it is best you should not believe it till it is over....

It must be done, and so it had best be well done! and I will not hang to your skirts and make it harder for you to go forward and do right, only I felt all the love I have borne you for all these years choking me till I sobbed it well out, you whom I loved as my own sister.... I was not surprised at it; I felt it would be, it was so like life—such a horrid piece of good fortune, such a painful bit of right to be done.

How right the Wise Men were to come *from* the East! Only, I should not have been particular about going back again; I had rather have stayed and sat in Herod's back-parlour for the rest of my life.

When once it is over you will be very busy and very amused. Emmy, I mean to open an account with you. I mean to keep a letter always going to you, and so tell you every week what I am thinking about, because, you know, in India, without any vanity, I may be very sure my letters will be valuable. It will cool you to read anything coming from the damp West.... I have been so eager about the Corporations, for Corporation in this Country means abomination! And when I heard them all spitting and scratching about the Tithe Bill, I thought what will they say to the Corporation Bill that sweeps so much farther.

There is a great deal of rage and fury fermenting here, but I think there will be no explosion. I own I am sorry to see that the fury of the Orangemen, tho' it may not drive the lower orders of Protestants to fight, will, by making him fancy himself ill-used, persuade him to emigrate. Thousands are preparing to emigrate.

I do not hope to see Ireland better in my time, and it often makes me so sad, for I do love it with the love one feels towards the child that is most weak, most sick.

Miss Eden to Mrs. Lister.
ADMIRALTY,
Thursday, September 1835.

MY DEAREST THERESA, I was very near you yesterday, and at the time I had appointed, but my heart failed me about taking leave for so long a time, and as I took one of those fits of lowness which sometimes come over me now (partly from real bodily fatigue), I saw I should do nothing but cry if I went to you, and that would be hard upon you and tiresome withal. Besides, taking leave is at the best of times a hateful process, so I would not go to you. And now, God bless you and yours, my very dear friend. I daresay when I come back I shall find *you* just what you are now, and *yours* very much increased in number and size.

Be sure to write to me a fortnight at the very latest after you see our departure announced, and put your letter under cover to Lord Auckland, Government House, Calcutta, and put it in the common post, if that is more convenient to you. Otherwise, if you can find anybody to frank it to Captain Grindlay, 16 Cornhill, he is our agent, and will at all times take charge of letters and parcels for us. Pray give my best love and wishes to Mrs. Villiers. Ever your affectionate

E. E.

Miss Eden to Mrs. Lister.
ADMIRALTY,
September 1835.

MY DEAREST THERESA, I have received your pretty bracelet with tears, which is a foolish way of accepting what is very dear to me, but every day my heart grows more sore, and I look with greater despondency to an utter separation from such kind friends as mine have proved themselves. I did not need anything, dearest, to remind me of you. Our friendship has happily, as far as I remember, been entirely free from even those little coolnesses and irritations which will mix sometimes with the closest intimacies. I cannot recollect the slightest *tiff* between us, and therefore I have no fears of the *effect* of absence, but still the absence itself is most painful. And your bracelet will then be an actual comfort to me, and besides thinking it so particularly pretty in itself, I am glad that it is one that I may wear constantly without fear of injuring it. I have put it on my arm, and there it will stay, I hope, till we meet again.

I am just setting off to Eastcombe to fetch home Fanny, who will be delighted with your recollection of her. To-morrow we are to go to the *Jupiter* to settle the arrangements of our cabins, but Wednesday, late in the day, we will go to Knightsbridge.

God bless you, my very dear friend. Many thanks for this and all the many kindnesses you have shown me. Your ever affectionate

E. E.

Lord Melbourne to Miss Eden.
SOUTH STREET,
September 24, 1835.

My Mother always used to say that I was very selfish, both Boy and Man, and I believe she was right—at least I know that I am always anxious to escape from anything of a painful nature, and find every excuse for doing so. Very few events could be more painful to me than your going, and therefore I am not unwilling to avoid wishing you good-bye. Then God bless you—as to health, let us hope for the best. The climate of the East Indies very often re-establishes it.

I send you a *Milton*, which I have had a long time, and often read in. I shall be most anxious to hear from you and promise to write. Adieu. Yours,

MELBOURNE.

King William IV. to Miss Eden.
WINDSOR CASTLE,
September 26, 1835.

The King cannot suffer Miss Eden to quit this country without thanking her for the letter she wrote to Him on the 24th inst., and assuring her of the satisfaction with which He received it.

His Majesty has long been aware of the sincere attachment which exists between Lord Auckland and his amiable Sisters, and of his anxiety for their Welfare and happiness, and he gives him credit for this exemplary feature of his character, not less than He does for the ability and correct zeal with which he has discharged his Public Duties.

Lord Auckland's conduct at the Admiralty has indeed been so satisfactory to the King, that it is impossible He should not regret his Removal from that Department, though His Majesty trusts that the Interests of the Country have been consulted in his nomination to the high and important Situation of Governor-General of India, and sincerely hopes that it may conduce to his own advantage and satisfaction.

His Majesty is not surprised that Miss Eden and her Sister should have determined to accompany so affectionate a Brother even to so remote a destination, and He is sensible how much their Society must contribute to his comfort, for the uninterrupted continuance of which, and of their welfare, He assures them of His best Wishes.

WILLIAM R.

Miss Eden to Lady Campbell.
N. Lat. 17, Long. 21,
February 18, 1836.

MY DEAREST PAM, I got William to write to you from the Cape, as we were in a flurry of writing, visiting, and surveying Africa, and he had more time, having been there before. We have had a very smooth sea, and I can read and draw and write, and as we all are perfectly well, there is not much to complain of, except of the actual disease—a long voyage, which is a very bad illness in itself, but we have had it in the mildest form and with every possible mitigation. At the same time I cannot spare you the detail of all our hardships, and I know you will shudder to hear that last Saturday, the fifth day of a dead calm, not a cloud visible, and the Master threatening three weeks more of the same weather, the thermometer at 86 in the cabin,—tempers on the go and meals more than ever the important points of life,—at this awful crisis the Steward announced that the coffee and orange-marmalade were both come to an end.

No wonder the ship is so light, we have actually ate it a foot out of the water since we left the Cape. "Nasty Beasts," as Liston says. Your lively imagination will immediately guess how bad the butter is, and I mention the gratifying fact that two small pots of Guava Jelly and the N.E. Monsoon sprung up on Monday, and we hope their united forces may carry us to the Sandheads.

I never could like a sea life, nor do I believe that anybody does, but with all our grumbling about ours, we could not have been 19 weeks at sea, with so few inconveniences. Captain Grey is an excellent seaman, and does more of the work of his ship than is usual. The officers and midshipmen have acted several times for our diversion, and remarkably well.

The serious drama, *Ella Rosenberg,* was enough to kill one. Ella's petticoats were so short, and her cap with her plaits of oakum always would fall off when she fainted away, and a tall Quartermaster, who acted the confidant, would call her Hella, and never caught her in time!

Some of the sailors were heard talking over the officers' acting, and saying, "They do low comedy pretty well, but they do not understand how to act the gentleman at all."

How little we thought in old Grosvenor Street days, when we sat at the little window listening to the organ-man playing "Portrait charmant" while the carriage was adjusting itself at the door, that we should be parted in such an out-*sea*-ish sort of way. That in the middle of February, when we ought to be shivering in a thick yellow fog, George and I should be established on a pile of cushions in the stern window of his cabin, he without his coat, waistcoat, and shoes, learning Hindoostanee by the sweat of his brow. I, with only one petticoat and a thin dressing-gown on, a large fan in one hand and a pen in the other, and neither of us able to attend to our occupations because my little black spaniel will yap at us, to make us look at the shark which is playing "Portrait charmant" to two little pilot-fish close under the window.

I should like to go back to those Grosvenor St. days again. I have had so much time for thinking over old times lately, that I never knew my own life thoroughly before. I can quite fancy sometimes that if we could think in our graves (and who knows), my thoughts would be just what they are now—the same vivid recollections of former friends and scenes, and the same yearning to be with them again. There is hardly anything you and I have talked over, that has not come to life in my mind again, and I could wring my hands, and tear my hair out, to go back and do it all over again.

The cottage at Boyle Farm, W. de Roos's troubles, Henry Montagu, the Sarpent, even that old Danford with the wen, Mrs. Shepherd and the Hossy Jossies. Dear me! Did I ever have jollier days with anybody or love anybody better?

Do write and tell me all about yourself now, and your children—I don't half know them. There is a tassel of small ones, like the tassel at the end of a kite's tail, that I know nothing about—not even their names. Tell me all their histories. There is an Emily, I know. What shall I send her from Calcutta if we ever arrive there? It is now five months since we have been travelling away from letters, and I feel such hot tears come into my eyes when I think of....

Monday, February 29, 1836.—I thought we should have been coming home with our fortunes made by this time, but we are still within a hundred miles of the Sandheads. At this precise moment we are at anchor in *green* water, so different to the deep blue sea, near some shoals, which is advantageous, because we can pick up our petticoats and pick our way to land.

Thursday. In the Hooghly.—At last, by dint of very great patience and very little wind, we have arrived, got the pilot on board early yesterday morning, saw Saugur, which looks as if it had been gnawed to the bone by the tigers that live on it. We are surrounded by boats manned by black people, who, by some strange inadvertance, have utterly forgotten to put on any cloaks whatever. We have a steamer towing us, a civil welcome from Sir C. Metcalfe; a Prince of Oudh, who has been deposed by an undutiful nephew, and deprived of several lacs of rupees, asking for his Excellency, well knowing that the first word even in Hindoostanee is valuable, which is so much his Excellency's opinion, that he wisely refuses to hear it, and, above all, we have received a profusion of letters from home, ten fat ones for my own share. Nothing unpleasant in them, which, considering some are dated five weeks after we left England, is something to be thankful for.

Cecilia de Roos's marriage; and poor old Lady Salisbury, it somehow seems as if nothing but fire could destroy her. I am going down to look over the box that contains the dresses in which we are to appear at our first Drawing-room to-morrow, and my blonde gown may, and in all probability will, come out quite yellow and fresh-patterned by the cockroaches. Your most affectionate

E. EDEN.

Miss Eden to Mrs. Lister.

BARRACKPORE,
March 24, 1836.

MY DEAREST THERESA, In the utter bewilderment in which I live, from having more to do in the oven than I could get through comfortably in a nice bracing frost, I quite forget whether I wrote to you on my first arrival. I sent off so many letters, necessarily precisely like one another, that I have forgotten all about them, except that they announced our arrival after a five months' voyage, and that we were in all the nervousness of a first arrival in a hot land of strangers.

We have been here three weeks to-day, and are so accustomed to our way of life that I cannot help thinking we have been here much longer, and that it is nearly time to go home again. It is an odd dreamy existence in many respects, but horribly fatiguing realities breaking into it. It is more like a constant theatrical representation going on; everything is so picturesque and so utterly un-English. Wherever there is any state at all it is on the grandest scale. Every servant at Government House is a picture by himself, in his loose muslin robes, with scarlet and gold ropes round his waist, and his scarlet and gold turban over masses of black hair; and on the esplanade I hardly ever pass a native that I do not long to stop and sketch—some in satin and gold, and then perhaps the next thing you meet is a nice English Britschka with good horses driven by a turbaned coachman, and a tribe of running footmen by its side, and in it is one of the native Princes, dressed just as he was when he first came into the world, sitting cross-legged on the front seat very composedly smoking his hookah.

Then, after passing a house that is much more like a palace than anything we see in England, we come to a row of mud-thatched huts with wild, black-looking savages squatting in front of them, little black native children running up and down the cocoa-trees above the huts, and no one appearance of civilization that would lead one to guess any European had ever set foot on the land before. The next minute we may come to a palace again, or to a regiment of Sepoys in the highest state of discipline, or to a body burning on the river-shore, or another body floating down the river with vultures working away at it. Then, if George is with us, we may meet a crowd of white-muslined men who begin by knocking their heads against the ground, and then give their long petitions (asking for some impossibility) in the Hindustani language, or else an English petition, which is apparently a set of words copied from some dictionary. No sense whatever—otherwise an excellent petition.

I have described our Calcutta house and household so often that I cannot do it again. It is all very magnificent, but I cannot endure our life there. We go there on Monday morning before breakfast. We have great dinners of 50 people, "fathers and mothers unknown," to say nothing of themselves. Every Monday and Wednesday evening Fanny and I are at home to anybody who is on what is called the Government House List. What that is I cannot say; the Aides-de-Camp settle it between them, and if they are the clever young men I hope they are, they naturally place on it the ladies most agreeable to themselves.

On Thursday morning we also receive any people who chance to notify themselves the day before. The visiting-time is from ten to one in the mornings, and we found it so fatiguing to have 100 or 120 people at that time of day that we have now chosen Tuesday evenings and Thursday mornings, and do not mean to be at home the rest of the week. There are schools to visit, and ceremonies half the week. Yesterday we had an examination at Government House of the Hindu College, and the great banqueting-hall was completely filled with natives of the higher class. Some of the boys in their gorgeous dresses looked very well, reciting and acting scenes from Shakespeare. It is one of the prettiest sights I have seen in Calcutta. On Thursday afternoon we always come here, and a prodigious pleasure it is. It feels something like home. It is sixteen miles from Calcutta, on the river-side. A beautiful fresh green park, a lovely flower-garden, a menagerie that has been neglected; but there is a foundation of a tiger and a leopard and two rhinoceros', and we can without trouble throw in a few light monkeys and birds to these heavy articles. It is much cooler here, and we can step out in the evening and walk a few hundred yards undisturbed.

Then, though we ask a few of the magnates of the land, and a wife or a daughter or so each time, they are lodged in separate bungalows in the park, and never appear but at luncheon and dinner, and are no trouble. We are so many in the family naturally, that seven or eight more or less make no difference at those times, and I take a drive or a ride on the elephant alone with George very regularly.

I never see him at Calcutta except in a crowd. In short, Barrackpore is, I see, to save me from India. I believe the Aides-de-Camp and secretaries all detest it, but there is no necessity to know that. George has made William Osborne Military Secretary, which gives him a very good income, and plenty to do. He has talent enough for anything, luckily likes occupation, and is very happy. Captain Grey is living with us, but the *Jupiter* sails the end of next week. I am afraid he will have a tiresome journey home; he takes back many more soldiers than the ship can conveniently hold, and not only that, but such quantities of wives and children.

I hope you have written to me; you would if you knew the ravenous craving for letters that possesses the wretches who are sent here. They are the only things to care for; you cannot mention a name that will not interest me, whereas I can never find one that you have ever heard before. Fanny desires me to say she wears your brooch constantly. I need not mention that of my dear bracelet. I hope in a few weeks we shall find something to send home, but hitherto we have found nothing but very dear French goods. Please write.

Give my love to your brother George when you see him or write to him. Now that I am dead and buried I sit in my hot grave and think over all the people I liked in the other world, and I find nobody that I knew had more community of interests and amusements with their kind. I often long for a laugh and talk with him, but it would be too pleasant for the climate.

Tell me an immense deal about yourself, and do write, there's a duck. Your most affectionate

E. E.

Miss Eden to Lady Campbell.

Government House, Calcutta,
August 16, 1836.

MY DEAREST PAM, Your long, dear letter has actually found its way here—came in last week quite by itself, having travelled 15,000 miles with nobody to take care of it, and it arrived feeling quite well and not a bit altered since it left you. I cannot sufficiently explain the value of a letter here; rupees in any number could not express the sum which a letter is worth, and I do not know how to make you understand it. But, you see, the scene in India is so well got up to show off a letter.

I was suddenly picked up out of a large collection of brothers, sisters, and intimate friends, with heaps of daily interests and habits of long standing, devoted to the last night's debate and this morning's paper, detesting the heat of even an English summer, worshipping autumn, and rather rejoicing in a sharp East wind, with a passion for sketching in the country, and enjoying an easy life in town—with all this we are sent off out of the reach of even *letters* from home, to an entirely new society of a most second-rate description,—to a life of forms and Aides-de-Camp half the day, and darkness and solitude the other half—and to a climate!!

Topics of interest we have none indigenous to the soil. There is a great deal of gossip, I believe, but in the first place, I do not know the people sufficiently by name or by sight to attach the right history to the right face, even if I wanted to hear it, and we could not get into any intimacies even if we wished it, for in our *despotic* Government, where the whole patronage of this immense country is in the hands of the Governor-General, the intimacy of any one person here would put the rest of the society into a fume, and it is too hot for any super-induced fuming....

The real *calamity* of the life is the separation from home and friends. It feels like death, and all the poor mothers here who have to part from their children from five years old to seventeen are more to be pitied than it is possible to say. And the *annoyance* of the life is the climate. It is so very HOT, I do not know how to spell it large enough.

Now I have stated our grievances, I must put all the per *contras* lest you should think me discontented. First, George is as happy as a King; then our healths, as I said before, are very good, though we look like people playing at Snap-dragon—everybody does. And though it is not a life that admits of one doing much active good, some is always possible in this position, and then it is a life of great solitude, which is wholesome.

Then, as a set-off to discomforts peculiar to the climate, we have every luxury that the wit of man can devise, and are gradually acquiring the Indian habit of denying ourselves nothing, which will be awkward. I get up at eight, and with the assistance of Wright and my two black maids—picturesque creatures as far as white muslin and scriptural-looking dresses can make ugly women—contrive to have a bath and to be dressed, and to order dinner by nine, when we meet in the great hall for breakfast.

When I describe my life, you must take for granted the others are all much the same, except that His Excellency's tail is four times longer than ours at least. Well, I have all my rooms shut up and made dark before I leave them, and go out into my passage, where I find my two tailors sitting cross-legged, making my gowns; the two Dacca embroiderers whom I have taken into my private pay working at a frame of flowers that look like paintings; Chance, my little dog, under his own servant's arm; a *meter* with his broom to sweep the rooms, two bearers who pull the punkahs; a sentry to mind that none of these steal anything; and a Jemadar and four Hurkarus, who are my particular attendants and follow me about wherever I go—my tail. These people are all dressed in white muslin, with red and gold turbans and sashes, and are so picturesque that when I can find no other employment for them I make them sit for their pictures.

They all make their salaam and we proceed to breakfast which is in an immense marble hall, and is generally attended by the two Aides-de-Camp in waiting, the doctor, the private Secretary, and anybody who may be transacting business at the time.... At six the whole house is opened, windows, shutters, etc., and carriages, horses, gigs, phaetons, guards, all come to the door, and we ride or drive just as we like, come home in time to dress for an eight o'clock dinner, during which the band plays. We sit out in the verandah and play at chess or *écarté* for an hour, and at ten everybody goes to bed.

The week is diversified by a great dinner of fifty people on Monday; on Tuesday we are *at home*, which was originally meant for a sort of evening visiting, but it is turned into a regular dance, as the hotter it is the more they like dancing. Thursday mornings, Fanny and I are also at home from ten to twelve for introductions, people landing or coming from up the country, and for any others of society who wish to see us.

It is very formal and very tiresome. They look very smart, come in immense numbers, sit down for five minutes, and, if there are forty in the room at once, never speak to each other. But it is a cheap way of getting through all the visiting duties of life at one fell swoop. On Thursday evenings we used to go to Barrackpore to stay till the following Monday, but now we only go once a fortnight. We are an immense body to move if it happens to be a pouring day—about four hundred altogether.

Barrackpore is a really pretty place. I am making such a garden there, my own private one, for there is a lovely garden there already, but a quarter of a mile from the house, and nobody can walk half a quarter of a mile in this country.

It seems so odd to have everything one wants, doesn't it, Pam? I wanted a vase for fish in my garden; a civil engineer put up two.

The other day we ordered the carriage at an undue hour, and there were no guards, and there was such a fuss about it—the Military Secretary writing to the Captain of the Body Guards, and he blaming the Aide-de-Camp in waiting; and I thought of the time when the hackney coach *adjusted* itself to the Grosvenor Street door, and of William de Roos's sending Danford away from the play that the hack might seem an accident, as if the carriage had not come.

Those were the really jolly days. I wish we could go back to them. You cannot imagine how I enjoyed your history of your children, those are the letters to send to India. Other people or papers tell public news. What a pleasure it is to have a letter!

I am so glad you like Lord Morpeth, I always did love him; I wish you would tell him to write to me in that odd cramped hand. Poor Mrs. Beresford, she goes on Wednesday next; I shall be glad when she is safely off. She takes a box for you, with a gown George gives you which I thought would be useful for your Castle drawing-rooms, and some handkerchiefs William sends you, which I have had worked for him by an old native, with a long white beard, who works like an angel. I mean to send my godchild a present the next opportunity. Yours,

E. E.

Miss Eden to Mrs. Lister.
GOVERNMENT HOUSE,
August 24, 1836.

MY DEAREST THERESA. After I wrote you that long letter of upbraiding for never having written to me, your Edinburgh letter, which had reached the respectable age of ten months, was forwarded to me, it having been mislaid with a large packet of other letters, and remained four months in the Custom House! So pleasant when one is almost stamping with impatience for letters—or rather, would be so, if the climate did not prevent those active expressions of feeling.

I think I told you how the American edition of *Dacre* had been one of my first purchases here, and I read it over with considerable pleasure. I do not know exactly what I mean, but I do not think you and your book are like each other. I do not mean any disparagement to either; there may be a very pretty fair mother with a very pretty dark child, both good in their way, but not like, and I cannot put your voice to any of the sentences in your book, or say to any part of it, "So like Theresa!" I am glad of that. I hate those *banale* likenesses of books to their author. Why did you not tell me the name of your new book? I daresay everybody has read it and discussed it in England, and *I* don't know its name. And to think of you writing about it in that vague way to me, 15,000 miles off!

The English editions of novels are to be had here for about three guineas apiece. They charge rupees for shillings, and a rupee is about two shillings and a penny. I have bought quantities of American editions of English books; but then it is a bore waiting till a work is two years old before one reads it. The Americans are valuable creatures at this distance. They send us novels, ice, and apples—three things that, as you may guess, are not indigenous to the soil. I own, I think the apples horrid, they taste of hay and the ship, but the poor dear yellow creatures who have been here twenty years, and who left their homes at an age when munching an unripe apple was a real pleasure, and who have never seen one since, fly at this mucky fruit and fancy themselves young and their livers the natural size, as they eat it. The first freight of apples the Americans sent covered the whole expense of the ship's passage out.

We are all so grieved to-day for poor Mrs. Beresford, whom you may remember as a Miss Sewell, going out with Mrs. Hope. Colonel Beresford is the Military Secretary to Sir H. Fane, and came here just a year ago. She has always declared the climate disagreed with her, and as she hated this place and its inhabitants, they did not like her, and said her ailments were all fancy. I never thought so; and she has proved the climate really disagreed with her, by having a violent fever that has lasted two months. The doctors said there was nothing for it but a return to England. Colonel Beresford came out with Sir H. Fane by way of bettering his fortunes, but as they have been here only a year, they have not yet got over the expense of coming out, so there was nothing for it but her going alone. She is one of those people entirely dependent on her husband's care. I hardly know such another attentive *servant* as he is to her—weighed her medicines, carried her about, etc.—in short, been what she could not find here for millions—an excellent English nurse.

On Tuesday she was to have gone on board, and I wrote to offer her carriage, assistance, etc., and got back a wretched note from him saying a sudden and rapid change had come on, and she was not expected to live an hour. However, she has lived on, and the doctors still say that, though they do not think she can live, the only chance for it will be going to sea; so she is to be carried on board this afternoon with her little girl, who is a dear little thing, but wants a cool climate too. I cannot imagine a more painful time for Colonel Beresford than the next few months, for as he is obliged to go up the country with the Commander-in-Chief, and *The Perfect*, her ship, may not speak another till they get to the Cape, it may be six months before he hears if she survives the first week of change. If she does, I think she will recover. I am so sorry for them; and here, where we are a limited set who know each other at all, one thinks more of these stories.

I never could take to the Calcutta society, even if there were any, but there is not. Almost everybody who was here when we landed five months ago are gone either home or up the country. They come to Calcutta because they are on their way out to make their fortunes, or on their way home because they have made them, or because their healths require change of station, and they come here to ask for it.

To-day was our *receiving* day. We receive visits from eleven to one every Thursday morning, and out of seventy or eighty people there were few who were not new introductions. "Have you been here long?" "Only just landed from the *Marianne Webb*—a tiresome voyage." "Did you suffer much at sea?" And so on. "Did you come in the same ship?" "No, we are just come from Lucknow." And then there comes all the story about the hot winds up the country, and whether it is worse or better than Bengal. So tiresome! I rather like to see the new arrivals, if they do not put off calling for more than a week, as they arrive with a little pink colour in their cheeks which lasts nearly ten days, but I heard one of our visitors to-day, who has been in India twenty years, declare seriously that he hated that colour; he thought it looked unnatural and like a disease. I begin to see what he means.

God bless you, dearest Theresa. I want to send this by *The Perfect*, and am so tired with our visits I cannot write any more. I hope you have written again and sent yours. I hoped to send you something pretty by this ship, but (it is not a mere *façon de parler*) in this rainy season there is not an item of any description to be bought in Calcutta. Nobody opens even the packages that arrive by mistake, as twenty-four hours spoils everything, but when the cold weather begins, they say that the merchants will have plenty of scarfs, silks, etc., from China and up the country. I want something Indian. We have written to China for any or everything, in the meantime. Your most affectionate

E. E.

Miss Eden to——.

GOVERNMENT HOUSE,
November 3, 1836.

Your last letter came to me by a Liverpool ship, so I think it right to write by the same conveyance, and the more so because our stock of London ships is low. Only one in the river, and she came only two days ago, and I suppose it will be six weeks before she will be well stocked with mosquitoes and cockroaches, and quite comfortable for passengers again.

It is what is by courtesy called the "cold weather" now, and it is charming to see some of the old Indians wrapped up in rough white great-coats, rubbing their withered hands, and trying to look *blue*, not being aware that their orange skins turn brown when there is the least check of circulation. You have no idea what sallow figures we all are, and I mention it now because in another year I suppose the real Indian blindness will have come over me, and I shall believe we are all our natural colour.

The new arrivals sometimes stagger us, but we simply say, "How coarse!" and wait with confidence for the effects that three weeks' baking will have, and a delicate tender yellow is the sure result.

With all the fine cold weather they talk of, I have not been able yet to live five minutes, night or day, without the punkah, and we keep our blinds all closed as long as there is a ray of sun. I do not mean to deny that the weather is not improved, but when the chilly creatures who have passed forty years here say triumphantly, "This must remind you of an English November," they really do great injustice to my powers of recollection. I should like to show them a good Guy Fawkes, with the boys purple with cold, beating their sides, and the squibs and crackers going fizzing along on the frosty ground.

This is our gay season. The Tuesday balls at Government House have become the fashion and are popular with the young ladies, and there is going to be a fancy ball given by the bachelors of Calcutta, which we not only condescend to go to our noble selves, but Fanny and I have organised two quadrilles, dressed them in remarkably unbecoming dresses, assured them that they are quite the right thing, and have made the whole scheme delightful by agreeing to their wish to meet at Government House without their chaperons, and go with us.

My quadrille consists of eight young ladies, and if the care with which I have selected their partners does not settle at least six of them happily, I shall think it a great waste of trouble, red velvet, and blue satin.

Miss Eden to Mrs. Lister.
CALCUTTA,
December 29, 1836.

MY DEAREST THERESA, Doctor Bramley is sending a little delicate offering in the way of Chinese wood-carving to Lady Morley, so I take that opportunity of sending you a scarf of Dacca muslin, worked at Dacca, and which is considered the best specimen of the kind of thing here; but then we have lost all knowledge of what is really pretty, I believe. I am almost certain we are very nearly savages—not the least ferocious, not cannibals, not even mischievous—but simply good-natured, unsophisticated savages, fond of finery, precious stones and tobacco, quite uninformed, very indolent, and rather stupid.

I wish the holes in my ears were larger, that is all, for I have lately seen in my drives some Burmese with large wedges of amber, or a great bunch of flowers, stuck through the holes of their ears, and I think it has a handsomer effect than our paltry European ear-rings. Besides this silver scarf, I see that I must write to you about Mr. Lister's appointment which I *lit* upon accidentally in a heap of English papers, and which will, I hope, be a great and permanent addition to your comfort. I cannot say how glad I was to read it; a patent place sounds comfortable, and as all you wanted in life was a little more income, you may guess that I am very really happy one of my best friends should have just what she wanted.

We have no letter of so late a date as the papers, so I must wait for particulars till another ship vouchsafes to sail in.

How odd it will be if we all end our lives comfortable *rich* old folks and near Knightsbridge neighbours. If we live to come home, we shall be very much better off than we could ever have expected to be, for there is no doubt that the Governor General's place is well paid. It may well be, for it is a hard-working situation and a cruel climate. But still, it is all very handsomely done on the part of the Company, and it is so new to us to be in a situation in which it is possible to save money, that the result of the month's House Accounts is a constant surprise to me. Not more surprising than that our House Accounts should be of that extensive nature that it requires a Baboo, an aide-de-camp, and myself, to keep them correctly.

I wonder whether you have seen our Knightsbridge house. I hear it is very pretty and I often think what fun it will be settling there.

I should like to know what you think of Mrs. Bramley supposing you know her, because I cannot make out why she does not come out to join her husband. He is a very delightful person, I should say almost without comparison the pleasantest man here, more accomplished and more willing to talk, and with very creditable remains of good spirits. She has a sharp little sister, a Mrs. Cockerell, here, almost pretty and very ill-natured, at least so they say, but we have not found her so the little we have seen of her. She and her husband are going tiger-shooting to the Rajmahal hills, for, impossible as it seems in this endless-looking plain, there *are* hills, 150 miles off. "Cock Robin" and "Jenny Wren," as the little Cockerell couple are familiarly termed, make one of these excursions every year, and Fanny and William mean to join the party, with two or three others. It will be a very good change of scene for her, and something out of the common course of life. Travelling in the marching fashion, which is the way they mean to go, is slow but amusing for a little while. Two sets of tents, one to live in on Monday, while the other is carried on twelve miles, so as to be ready on Tuesday. Everybody in India has their own set of servants, who are no more trouble travelling than living at home. They find their own way from station to station, cook for themselves, sleep on the ground, and, in short, are quite unlike the fussy lady's maid and valet who dispute every inch of the imperial and expect tea, beer, feather beds, etc., at every bad inn on the road. But then, to be sure, it takes about fourteen natives to do the work of one English servant. I suppose William and Fanny could not march without thirty servants of their own, besides guards, elephants, etc. All these, they say, make excellent sketching, which is one of the amusements I look to, when we set off on our great march next year.

I keep up my drawing, but entirely in the *figure* line, as there is no landscape in Bengal, and also the glare is so great that nobody could draw it if there were; but every servant in the house is a good study, and I shall very soon be sending home some sketches. I wish your book would come out. I want a new novel very much. My best love to Mrs. V. Ever, dearest Theresa, your most affectionate

E. E.

CHAPTER XI

1837-1840

Miss Eden to her Sister, Mrs. Drummond.

GOVERNMENT HOUSE,
January 16, 1837.

THERE is a Lady Henry Gordon here, on her way home with two of the loveliest children I ever beheld. One of them puts me in mind of her aunt, poor Lady M. Seymour, but it is still more beautiful. They are older than most children here, and have come from a cold part of the country with fresh rosy cheeks. George and I had met them twice on the plain when we were out riding, and had bored everybody to death to find out who they were. William knew Lady Henry when she was a sort of companion to Lady Sarah Amherst, and a victim to old Lord Amherst's crossness, so he went to call on her and discovered our beautiful children. They have dined here since, and I want her to let us have them at Barrackpore, as she is too busy preparing for her voyage to come herself, but I am afraid she will not. Her husband is a very particular goose, and a pay-master in some particular department, and she does all his work for him. Nobody knows at all how he is to go on while she is away.

Miss Eden to Mrs. Lister.

GOVERNMENT HOUSE,
January 25, 1837.

MY DEAREST THERESA, I will take your plan of sitting down forthwith and answering your letter (of August 18th, received January 23rd) on the spot, before the pleasure of reading it wears off. It means I am going to answer your letter directly, and I am so obliged to you for asking me questions—just what I like. Intellect and memory both are impaired, and imagination utterly baked hard, but I can answer questions when they are not very difficult, and if they are put to me slowly and distinctly; and besides, I am shy of writing and boring people with Indian topics. I used to hate them so myself. But if they ask about an Indian life, as you do, and about the things I see every day, why, then, I can write quite fluently, and may heaven have mercy upon your precious soul! So here goes:

"Do you find amongst your European acquaintances any pleasing or accomplished women?" Not one—not the sixth part of one; there is not anybody I can prefer to any other body, if I think of sending to ask one to come and pay me a visit, or to go out in the carriage; and when we have had any of them for two or three days at Barrackpore, there is a *morne* feeling at the end of their visit that it will be tiresome when it comes round to their turn of coming again. I really believe the climate is to blame.

"They read no new books, they take not the slightest interest in home politics, and everything is melted down into being purely local." There is your second question turned into an answer, which shows what a clever question it was.

Thirdly. It *is* a gossiping society, of the smallest macadamised gossips I believe, for we are treated with too much respect to know much about it; but they sneer at each other's dress and looks, and pick out small stories against each other by means of the Ayahs, and it is clearly a downright offence to tell one woman that another looks well. It is not often easy to commit the crime with any regard to truth, but still there are degrees of yellow, and the deep orange woman who has had many fevers does not like the pale primrose creature with the constitution of a horse who has not had more than a couple of agues.

The new arrivals we all agree are coarse and vulgar—not fresh and cheerful, as in my secret soul I think them. But that, you see, is the style of gossipry.

Fourthly. It *is* a very moral society, I mean that people are very domestic in their habits, and there are no idle men. Every man without exception is employed in his office all day, and in the evening drives. Husbands and wives are always in the same carriage. It is too hot for him to ride or walk, and at evening parties it is not considered possible for one to come without the other; it is quite out of the question. If Mr. Jones is ill everybody knows that Mrs. Jones cannot go out, so she is not expected.

Fifthly. I believe in former days it was a profligate society, as far as young men were concerned, the consequence of which is that the old men of this day are still kept here by the debts they contracted in their youth. But the present class of young men are very prudent and quiet, run into debt very little, and generally marry as soon as they are out of college.

Then as to the Hindu College. The boys are educated, as you say, by the Government, at least under its active patronage, and they are "British subjects," inasmuch as Britain has taken India, and in many respects they may be called well-educated young men; but still I cannot tell you what the wide difference is between a European and a Native. An elephant and Chance, St. Paul's and a Baby-Home, the Jerseys and Pembrokes, a diamond and a bad flint, Queen Adelaide and O'Connell, London and Calcutta, are not further apart, and more antipathetic than those two classes. I do not see how the prejudices ever can wear out, nor do I see that it is very desirable. I do not see that any degree of education, or any length of time, could bring natives to the pitch of allowing any liberty to their wives. Their Mussulman creed makes it impossible, and as girls are married at 7 or 8 years old, and after that are never seen by any human being but their husbands, there is no possibility of educating them, and in fact education could only make them miserable. Even our lowest servants of any respectability would not let their wives be seen on any account. They live in mud huts, something like Irish cabins, and in half of that hut these women pass their lives.

Wright has tried hard to persuade my Jemadar (a sort of groom of the chambers), who is a superior man of his class, speaks and reads English, and is intelligent, to let her see his wife, but he will not hear of it. The Ayahs who wait on us are not at all considered, though I have never made out to my satisfaction how bad they are.

There is an excellent Mrs. Wilson here, who for 20 years has been trying to educate the lower orders of native females, but she told me the other day, that she has never been able to keep a day-scholar after she was 6 or 7 years old, and she has now removed her whole establishment 7 miles from Calcutta. She has collected 160 orphans, who were left utterly destitute after a great inundation in 1833. They were picked up on the banks of rivers, some even taken from the Pariah dogs! Mrs. Wilson took any that were sent to her, a great many died out of whole cargoes that were sent down. It is the prettiest thing possible to see her amongst her black children, she looks so pleased and happy; she is in her widow's dress without another European near her, and as she told me the other day, with no more *certainty* of funds than would supply her for her next six weeks. In short, in a position which would justify a weaker person in sitting down and taking a good cry, but she was as cheerful and as happy as if she had not a care on her mind.

Sixthly. I do not speak a word of Hindustani, and never shall, because I have three servants who all *understand*, though only one speaks it, and the aides-de-camp are at hand for interpretation. I wish I had learnt it. But there is nothing to read in it, it is difficult to learn accurately, and as I said before, I am not driven to it by the servants. In all this immense establishment there are not more than six who speak English, and if my Jemadar dies, I must. The only time I miss the language is out riding. When more than one of us ride, there is an aide-de-camp with us, but as Fanny constantly goes out with William, I found a *tête-à-tête* with George was much to be preferred to that bit of state, so he and I ride out alone, and of course he is met by a petition at every odd turning, and sometimes we both long to enquire into the case or to tell the man what to do, and it seems so stupid not to be able to do so.

The guards do not understand a word of English, and the Syces who run by the side of the horses are remarkably cute at understanding our signs if they have reference to the horses, but have no idea on any other subject.

Seventhly. The Ménagerie is almost full. An old tiger, and a young one who is just beginning to turn his playful pats into good hard scratches and is now shut up in a cage grown up and come out, as we should say on arriving at that dignity; a leopard, two cheetahs, two porcupines, two small black bears, sloths, monkeys of sorts that are caught about 100 miles off and shut up, and parrots, and heaps of beautiful Chinese pheasants. *Zoological Garden beasts* do not walk about wild, but there are a great many parroquets wild in Barrackpore, and alligators in the rivers; and we have met, much to my discomfiture, some huge snakes. There are vultures without end, and the great adjutant birds who live on the top of Government House and walk about the compound all day, would have surprised one in England; but I take it that when we commence our march up the country we shall see many more strange animals. As it is, I am quite satisfied still with the natives. I never see one that would not make the fortune of an artist, particularly at this time of the year. There are so many Arabs come down for the races, and the Burmese or Mugg men, are come with fruit and fish, and yesterday when we went out there were a crowd of Nepaulese, with such beautiful swords and daggers, at the gate. We sent to ask what they wanted, and they said, "Nothing, but to see the Lord Sahib go by." I am going to send for one to add to my drawings of costumes.

There! Now I have done it thoroughly. I think you are cured of asking questions, but it has amused me writing all this.

I wrote to you December 29th, and sent you a silk scarf in a parcel that poor Doctor Bramley was sending home to his wife. He was with us at Barrackpore three weeks ago, was taken with fever last Monday fortnight, and died in seven days. There never was such a loss both publicly and privately, but the former especially. There is nobody here who *can* take his place at the Hindu College. He was a very delightful person in his way and the man we saw most of, as George had a great deal of business always to do with him, and he was very sociable with us. It is a horrid part of India, those sudden deaths. Your most affectionate

E. E.

Miss Eden to Mr. C. Greville.

BARRACKPORE,
April 17, 1837.

MY DEAR MR. GREVILLE, they say that a letter written to-day will still be in time for the overland packet, and for all the adventures to which the *Hugh Lindsay*, the *Dromedary Dawdle*, the *Desert*, etc., may entitle it. Waghorn I see is not at Cairo—another calamity! I am in opposition to George's government on the great Waghorn question. I cannot see why they do not pay him anything he asks, and give him an East Indian peerage, or anything else. All the letters that come quickly to us are invariably stamped "to the care of Mr. Waghorn, Cairo," and if I thought he were there now, I should, in defiance of the authorities here, address this "to the care of dear Mr. Waghorn"! I suspect you would then have it in less than two months; now, if you receive it in 1838 my fondest expectations will be gratified.

I cannot go back in our life more than 36 hours. It is all the same thing, so I will suppose you called on Thursday morning, and after your visit we came up to Barrackpore in the evening. You know what a horrid bad road it is this side of the half-way home, and therefore will not be surprised to hear that one of the leaders, the horse that you always say is the handsomest of the new set, stepped on a loose stone and came down like a shot. The postillion, who weighs about 1½ lbs., as a small native should, was pitched out of sight into a neighbouring presidency; I believe the leaders ran over the fallen horse, who kicked at them, and they of course kicked him. The spring of the carriage was broken, and the four Syces and the postillion and the guards, being all good Mohammedans, of course looked on contentedly, knowing that what must be—must be. Luckily W. Osborne for once had no other conveyance but our carriage, so he jumped out at the side, and we all tumbled out at opposite doors, and he *Hindustani'd* the Syces and cut the traces, and we were all put to rights (barring that one horse), and not the worse, thank you. Only it is so much too hot in this country to have adventures.

We were all assiduously fanning ourselves when the accident happened, but no fan would have helped us after that. Think of jumping out of a carriage in a hurry with the thermometer at 95. I will give you a journal of yesterday, to show the vividness and endless variety of our amusements.

Breakfast at nine—an operation which lasts seven minutes, because nobody has any appetite, and George has no time. Then we discussed the papers.... In the afternoon, a neighbour sent a note requesting admission to a new native school George has built in a park, for a Brahmin boy of good caste. I gave the father Brahmin a note to the schoolmaster, and with the proper craft of a native, he went and fetched two more of his children and said the note was intended to admit them all three. But the schoolmaster, as all schoolmasters should, knew how to read, and refused them, so when George and I drove to the school in the evening, we found them and about twenty others all clasping their hands and knocking their heads against the ground, because they were prevented learning English, and all saying "Good morning, Sir," to show how much they had acquired. They say that at all times and to everybody, since the school has been opened.

Then we drove to the Garden, when Chance and his suite met us, and he swam about the tank for half an hour, and the tame otter came for its fish, and the young lynxes came to be looked at, and we fed the gold pheasants and ascertained that that rare exotic the heartsease was in flower, but the daisy, the real English white daisy, has turned out a more common Oenothera, and it proves that neither daisies nor cowslips can be nationalized here. I myself think the buttercup might be brought to perfection, but I know I see those matters in too sanguine a point of view.

We came home hotter than we went out. William and Fanny had been on the river, which was still worse. Dinner was not refreshing.

Then we all went out in the verandah, where there are great pans of water used for wetting the mats put over the windows, and the Aides-de-Camp found a new diversion in putting Chance in one pan, while three of them lifted the other and poured the water over him. He growled, as he used to do at you, to show he did not think those liberties allowable, but immediately jumped into the empty pan to have the bath repeated, whereat we all laughed, for that amounts to a good joke in India. But we never laugh more than two minutes at a time; it is too fatiguing. So then we went, like Lydia Bennet, to a good game at Lottery tickets. Our intellects fell last year from whist pitch, and now they have fallen below *écarté*, but the whole household can understand Lottery, and except that it is too much trouble to hand a rupee from one card to another, we all like it very much.

At ten o'clock, Fanny and William and I went to a little sailing-boat he has here, and we should have sailed, and it would have been cooler if there had been any air. But there was a lovely moon, and the Hoogly is a handsome bit of river, and we floated about for an hour, and then went to bed. And so ends that eventful day.

We are all very well, though I have been rather ailing for ten days, but in a general way you are quite right; I *have* very much better health here than I had at home. So all my abuse of the climate is gratuitous; I do not owe it any spite, except for being so very disagreeable. I trust there is a letter from you somewhere on the sea. George has sent for this, so God bless you. I have not time to read it over. Yours ever,

E. EDEN.

Miss Eden to Mr. C. Greville.
GOVERNMENT HOUSE,
Sept. 11, 1837.

MY DEAR MR. GREVILLE, George says he thinks I ought to write to you, which is rather an impertinent thought of his, because he does not know that I have not been writing to you every day, and he does not know that I have nothing to say, and that out of that nothing I have already furnished him with eight letters for this overland post. But he says there is ¾ of an hour yet before the last Bombay dawdle goes. Three-quarters of an hour for the preparation of a letter that is to travel 15,000 miles!

I am not going to comment on the dear young Queen; that I have done in the other letters. But I never think of anything else, and we are all dying of fevers brought on by court mourning, and curiosity coming on the rainy season. Our own approaching journey is one other great interest, and we all declare we are packing up. It is almost as fatiguing lying on the sofa and wondering what is to become of all one's property as actually packing up, and may perhaps by perseverance produce some result. But hitherto I have not done more than that personally. The faithful Byrne, and the rest of his staff, have gradually removed many of the comforts, and in two days the band and the horses and most of the servants depart, and, as William Osborne observes with real consternation, we shall not have above eight servants apiece left to wait on us.

Certainly some of the arrangements are amusing. I asked Byrne just now what our Ayahs (or black Lady's Maids) were allowed to put their travelling-gear in. "Half a camel!" he said, with an air of reproach at such desperate ignorance. "Oh, half a camel *apiece*," I said, looking intelligent, and laying an emphasis on *apiece* as if that had been my doubt, and you know one hears such strange stories of camels carrying a supply of water for their own private drinking, quite honestly, though they have drunk it already, that I was ready to believe the Ayah, veils and bangles, travelled the same way. But Byrne obligingly added that each camel carried two trunks, one of which each Abigail might claim.

The steamer to Benares will be the most tiresome part of our journey, there is so little to see on the banks; but once in camp I mean to commence an interminable course of sketching. I hope my sister Mary will show you some of the sketches I sent home about two months ago. I think they would amuse you.

Our great anxiety now is for the arrival of the *Seringapatam*, a new ship, quite untried, *A1*—a mark the papers put here to a ship that is making its first voyage, but what it means I can't guess. Still, to this untried article is confided the trousseau of myself, of Fanny, and two other interesting females belonging to the camp who will, if the *Seringapatam* does not come very soon, be starved to death in camp, reduced as we are to white muslins and chilly constitutions. The *Coromandel* I am also anxious for, as I have a nephew on board; but still you know I have 48 nephews, and only one box of gowns, so if there is to be a little adverse weather, etc.

We are going to give a dinner on Monday to the party that will go with us in the steamer, and to rehearse our hardships. The punkahs are to be stopped, as the heat on the river is always stifling; cockroaches to be turned out in profusion on the floor; extra mosquitoes hired for the night; the lamps to be set swinging; the Colvins and Torrens' children to be set crying; Mrs. MacNaghten, on whom we depend for our *tracasseries*, to repeat all that any of the company have ever said of the others; Mrs. Hawkins, who is very pretty, to show Hawkins how well she can flirt with all the aides-de-camp. Altogether I think it will be amusing.

There! I have no time for more. This ought to bring me two answers at least. I am more ravenous than ever for letters. We are all well, more or less. Yours very truly and heartily,

E. EDEN.

Miss Eden to Mrs. Lister.
GOVERNMENT HOUSE,
October 2, 1837.

MY DEAREST THERESA, A sort of a nominal, no—cousin of yours, Mr. Talbot, is going home in the *Reliance*, and it gives me a good opportunity of sending you a Bird of Paradise feather, as he can put it into his portmanteau, and it will be no trouble to you, nor to him, nor to anybody. Of course I shot it myself, and found the nest, and am bringing up the young Paradises by hand, and they promise to have handsome tails which I will send you in due course—that is the sort of thing I mean to assert at home.

In little more than a fortnight we shall be off on our great journey to the Himalayas. Everything we have in the shape of comfort is gone—servants, horses, band, guards, and everything embarked a month before us, as we shall go by steamer to Benares, and though that is slow work, it is necessary to give the country boats a considerable advance. The Ganges, you see, is not an easy river to navigate.

Miss Eden's Letters

Sixty-five elephants and 150 camels will carry our little daily personal comforts, assisted by 400 coolies, and bullock-carts innumerable. They say that everybody contrives in the *mêlée* to receive their own camel-trunks and pittarhs safe every night; but I own I bid a long farewell to every treasured gown and bonnet that I see Wright bury in the depths of a camel-trunk.

We are all enjoying the thoughts of this journey—not that I shall ever believe till I have tried that it is really true a tent can be as comfortable as Government House, with its thick walls and deep verandah and closed shutters. Still, we shall be travelling to a better climate, and that is everything. Then there will be eligible sketching, both buildings and figures, and we shall have occasional days of quiet and solitude. And once up in the mountains I expect to be quite strong again, and there is actual happiness in mountain air, independent of all other comfort.

What became of that book you said we should have to read some time ago? I have been vainly watching for it.

This must go. It has been sent for twice, and if you knew the impossibility of doing anything in a hurry you would appreciate particularly this semblance of a letter.

We are going what is called "in state" to the play to-night "by particular desire"—not of ours, but of the Amateurs who have got up a play for us before our departure. The thermometer is at 90, the new theatre is without punkahs, the small evening breeze that sometimes blows ceases entirely in September and October, and we are in black for our King. Rather a melancholy combination of circumstances. *Priez pour nous!* God bless you, dearest. Your most affectionate

E. EDEN.

Miss Eden to Mrs. Lister.

ALLAHABAD,
December 1, 1837.

MY DEAREST THERESA, I have never had but two letters from you since I came to India. No wonder! I daresay the letters contrive to turn off the instant they are out of your hands, and go to some better and nearer climate. The odd thing is that my letters, which ought to know better, do not seem to rush home with that impetus which would be natural under the circumstances. At least, my sisters, whom I write to morning noon and night, write nothing but complaints of the want of letters. If I felt the least guilty I should feel provoked, but as it is I receive all their murmurs with the gentle resignation of injured innocence.

I am at Allahabad, Theresa—"More fool I; when I was at home I was in a better place": as dear Shakespeare, who knew all about Allahabad, as well as everything else, observed with his accustomed readiness. I do not know more about it, seeing we only arrived this morning. Our tents are pitched on the Glacis of the Fort, an encampment sacred to the Governor-General, and this Glacis, as you in your little pleasing way would observe, is not Glacé, seeing that I have just desired an amiable individual clothed in much scarlet and gold to pull the Punkah, which, by the *prévoyance* of the Deputy Quarter Master General, has been wisely hung in my tent. You see, what is called the cold weather is really cold and remarkably pleasant in the mornings, and our march, which we generally commence in the dusk at half-past five, and conclude before eight, is very bracing and delightful. But then that horrid old wretch the sun comes ranting up; the tents get baked through; and all through the camp there is a general moulting of fur shoes and merino and shawls, then an outcry for muslin, and then for a Punkah to give us breath. We cannot go out till it is nearly dark; and then about dinner-time, when we cross over from our private tents to the great dining-room, we want cloaks and boas and all sorts of comforts again. Those cold hours of the day are very English and pleasant.

I hate my tent and so does George. We incline to a house with passages, doors, windows, walls that may be leaned against, and much furniture. Fanny luckily takes to a tent kindly, but the majority of our camp, consisting of various exemplary mothers and children, are of the house faction.

Our chaplain and his Scotch wife, who speaks the broadest Scotch I have ever heard, have been *eating* with us all to-day, for, as Mrs. Wimberley observed, "It's just reemarkable: the cawmels kicked all our crockery off their bocks yeesterday, and to-day our cooking-tent is left on the other side of the Jumna, so we've just nothing to eat."

We crossed the river at the confluence of the Ganges and Jumna this morning.

Last night we went down on our elephants to see the advanced guard of the camp pass over. It was a red Eastern sky, the beach of the river was deep sand, and the river was covered with low flat boats. Along the bank were tents, camel-trunks, fires by which the natives were cooking, and in the boats and waiting for them were 850 Camels, 140 Elephants, several hundred horses, the Body Guard, the regiment that escorts us, and the camp-followers. They are about 12,000 in all.

I wish it was possible to make more sketches, but the glaring light is very much against it, and the twilight is very short. There are robbers in camp every night. That is part of the fun. We met an officer yesterday riding for his life in the cold hours of the morning with only a white jacket and trousers on. He looked shivery, and it appeared that the Dacoits had entered his tent in the night, taken all they could turn to account, and as European cloaks are of no value to a native, they had cut the buttons and lace off his uniform and minced up into small pieces all his linen. There is no end to the stories of the cleverness of Dacoits, and that is one of the things I hate in camp. The instant it grows dusk, the servants come in and carry off every little atom of comfort in the way of furniture that one may have scraped together, and put it outside the tent under the charge of a sentry. It is the only chance, but it makes a gloomy-looking abode at night.

We are cut off from a great part of our tour by the dreadful scarcity in the Upper Provinces. There is no fodder whatever to be had, and a great camp like this makes in the best of times a great run on the price of provisions.

We shall lose the sight of Agra, which I regret; otherwise I am not sorry to miss the great stations. We are so plied with balls and festivities, and have to give so many great dinners, that the dull road is perhaps the most amusing after all.

I wish you would write. I always excuse you because I presume you are hatching both a child and a novel; but if I do not soon hear of one or the other, I cannot tell what excuse to make. I wrote to your brother George. George and I were agreeing the other day that he is the only friend who has utterly and entirely failed us; and yet somehow we cannot believe it of him. But he was the only person we knew well who took no notice of us even when we were coming away.

Now it is lawful to forget us, but it was rather shocking of him, was not it? Pray give my love to your mother and Mr. Lister. Ever, dearest Theresa, your most affectionate

E. E.

Miss Eden to Mrs. Lister.

SIMLA,
April 28, 1838.

MY DEAREST THERESA, I had meant to have answered your letter by the last overland post, but I was poorly just as it started, and it is rather a doubt whether it will be a safe conveyance this time. Something wrong about the steamer, or the Arabs, or the dromedaries, or some of those little items that go to make up an overland post. However, I can but try.

Your account of poor Lady Henry interested me very much. Indeed, everybody must be interested in her, but the melancholy fact is that it is totally *impossible* to help them. We saw a great deal of Lord Henry at Meerut, and took pains to show him great attention as he was in a shy state after the results of that investigation. There was not the slightest shadow of distrust as to his intentions, poor man! but his utter incapacity made it rather surprising that Lord Amherst ever should have given him an office of such trust, and not the least surprising that he should have been robbed and cheated in every way, by the number of crafty natives under him. I was thinking of any pendant to him in London for your information, but I hardly know anybody with such a *silly* manner—something like Petre, but more vacant and unconnected. He seemed thoroughly good-hearted, and very anxious about his children, who, he told me, were to go either to Boulogne or Bordeaux, he did not know which, but a great way from London! He was living with Captain Champneys, his successor in the paymastership, and seems quite contented to sit in a large arm-chair and look at Champneys in a fuss, which he has been in ever since he got the appointment. Indeed, he wrote me word yesterday that he found it so difficult to guard against the knavery of the Baboos attached to the office, that he never could enough regret having left his Aide-de-Camp with us.

George told me to say both to you and to Lady Morley that there is nothing he wishes so much as to help Lord Henry, but that in the present state of India there are no situations that are not responsible and hard-working, and even if it were possible (which it is not) to give one of these to a man who is a great debtor to the Government, Lord Henry is really not capable of one.

I did not know till I came up the country how really hard-worked Europeans are. It is lucky for them, for it is only the necessity of being in these *Cutcherries* or offices all day, that prevents their sinking altogether under the solitude of their lives and the climate. In most stations there are not above two or three Europeans, and in many only one.

There were two young men here yesterday who talked quite unceasingly; it was impossible to put in a word, and at last one of them said that he had been eight years, and his brother four, in stations where they never saw a European. They were both in horrid health, of course (everybody is in India), and so they had got six months' leave to see what the hills could do for them, and they said they were so delighted to find themselves again with people who understood English, that they were afraid they had talked too much. It was impossible to dispute the fact, but still I was glad to hear their prattle; it evidently did them good. Our band was their great delight; they had not heard any European music for so long.

We tried to get up a dance two nights ago—a total failure I thought. Most of the people here are invalids, and as there are no carriages, and no carriage-roads, they can only come out in Jhanpamas (a sort of open Sedan), and the nights are cold. The whole company only amounted to forty, and I thought I never saw a heavier dance, but some of them thought it quite delightful, and I am afraid will wish for another.

It is even more delightful than I expected to be in these hills; the climate is perfection, and the pleasure of sitting out of doors looking at those lovely snowy mountains, and breathing real cool air, is more than I can say.

The change from those broiling plains was so sudden. At Bareilly the thermometer was at 90 in our tents at night, and the next day at Sabāthu it was at 55 in the middle of the day. Such a long breath as I drew!

These mountains are very beautiful, but not so picturesque, I think, as the Pyrenees—in fact they are too gigantic to be sketchable, and there are no waterfalls, no bridges, no old corners, that make the Pyrenees so picturesque, independent of their ragged shapes. But I love these Himalayas, good old things, all the same, and mean to enjoy these seven months as much as possible to make up for the horrors of the two last years, and as for looking forward, it is no use just now.

I think George will find Calcutta so extravagantly hot that perhaps he will consent to go home sooner. That would be very satisfactory. The deaths there have been very numerous this year. Almost all the few people we knew intimately in the two years we were there, are dead—and almost all of them young people.

Do you remember my writing to you about poor Mrs. Beresford's death? He is here now with a second wife, twenty years younger than himself, to whom he engaged himself three months after the first wife's death; never told anybody, so we all took the trouble of going on pitying him with the very best pity we had to spare! Such a waste!

What became of your second book? I cannot even see it amongst the advertisements. I am disconsolate that we have had the last number of *Pickwick*, the only bit of fun in India. It is one of the few books of which there has been a Calcutta reprint, lithographs and all. I have not read it through in numbers more than ten times, but now it is complete I think of studying it more correctly.

Mention much about your children when you write. I find the letters in which my friends tell me about themselves and their children are much pleasanter than mere gossip. They really interest me—there is the difference between biography and history. My best love to your mother, and remember me to Mr. L. It is very odd how easily I can bring your face to mind when I think of you. Some faces I cannot put together at all cleverly, but I see you quite correctly and easily. Don't alter, there's a dear. Your most affectionate

E. E.

Miss Eden to Mr. C. Greville.

SIMLA,
June 10, 1838.

A letter from you of November (this being the 10th of June) has just come dropping in quite *promiscuous*. Though I have had one of a later date, yet this has made me laugh and has put me in the mood to write to you forthwith.

Your remarkably immoral views as to the mischief that religion does in a country were wrong in the abstract, but they unfortunately just chimed in with some views his Lordship had been worried into taking, and he is quite delighted to have a quotation from your letter to act as motto to one of his chapters. Here we have such a medley of faiths. The Hindus convey a pig carefully cut up into a Muhammedan Mosque, whereupon the Mussulmanns cut up the Hindus. Then again the Mussulmanns kill a cow during a Hindu festival, and the Hindus go raving mad. Then an *un*sensible man like Sir P. Maitland refuses to give the national festivals the usual honours of guns, drums, etc., which they have had ever since the English set foot in India. In short, there is an irritation kept up on the plea of conscience, where the soothing system would be much more commendable and much easier.

I must say that, except in the Upper Provinces, where once or twice we have met with some violent petitioners, the Hindus and Mussulmans live most peaceably; so that they have separate cooking-places, and that the Hindu's livery Tunic is made to button on the right shoulder and the Mussulman's on the left, they ask no other differences. We have about an equal number of each in our household, and in Bengal they are all very friendly together.

We are very much interested in our foreign politics just now. It is all very well your bothering on about Canada, and giving us majorities of 29 in favour of Lord Glenelg (your last letter of February had mentioned that the Tories never would vote with the Radicals on such a party question: Peel was above it!! How he always takes you in!). Those little, trivial, obscure questions are all very well in their way, but my whole heart is fixed on intelligence from Herat, and I live in a state of painful wonder as to what Dost Mahomed's real relations with Persia and Russia may be.

One serious grievance is that the steamer which was to have taken our letters home this month was ordered off to Persia to bring away Mr. MacNiel, if he wished to come, and our letters are "left lamenting," like Lord Ullin, on the beach at Bombay. That is the sort of thing George does in the plenitude of his power, and which you know shocks us free-born Britons; and then we think of Trial by Jury, and annual Parliaments, and no Poor Laws, and Ballot, and "Britannia rules the waves," and all the old story.

We have had a picturesque and pleasant deputation of Sikhs from Runjeet Singh, which we have returned by a Mission composed of Mr. MacNaghten, *our* Lord Palmerston, a dry sensible man, who wears an enormous pair of blue spectacles, and speaks Persian, Arabic, and Hindustani rather more fluently than English; of William Osborne, who goes in exchange for a nephew of Runjeet's who came here; of Captain MacGregor, another Aide-de-Camp; and of Doctor Drummond, who has left our little sparks of life to go out by themselves, because Runjeet was particularly anxious to be attended by the Governor-General's own physician. They are all under the conduct of Captain Wade, the Political Agent at Lahore, who has lived so much with natives that he has acquired their dawdling, soft manners and their way of letting things take care of themselves.

They are all at Adeenanuggur, a summer palace of Runjeet's, where, by way of being cool, their houses are furnished with Tatties and Thermantidotes, a sort of winnowing-machine that keeps up a constant draft, and with that the thermometer ranges from 102 to 105. Poor things! In the meanwhile they are perfectly delighted with Runjeet, as everybody is who comes within his influence. He contrives every sort of diversion for them. I hardly know how to state to you delicately that the Mission was met at the frontier by troops of Cashmerian young ladies, great dancers and singers, and that this is an extract from W. Osborne's letter to-day, which I ought not to copy, only it will amuse you: "Runjeet's curiosity is insatiable—the young Queen, Louis Philippe, how much wine we drink, what George drinks, etc. His questions never end. He saw me out riding to-day, and sent for me and asked all sorts of impertinent questions. Did we like the Cashmerian girls he had sent? Did all of us like them? I said I could not answer for the others; I could only speak for myself." But Runjeet's curiosity is really unbounded, as William states it. He requested George to send him samples of all the wines he had, which he did, but took the precaution of adding some whiskey and cherry brandy, knowing what Runjeet Singh's habits are. The whiskey he highly approved of, and he told MacNaghten that he could not understand why the Governor-General gives himself the trouble of drinking seven or eight glasses of wine when one glass of whiskey would do the same quantity of work. He had asked one gentleman to a regular drinking-party, which they were dreading (as the stuff he drinks is a sort of liquid fire), and his great amusement is to watch that it is fairly drunk.

George says that your letter costs you nothing, so I enclose an account of Runjeet's Court, which young MacGregor wrote me. If you have had enough of him you can burn the letter unread, but I have a faint recollection that the only Indian subject that was interesting at home was "The Lion of the Punjâb." It is a matter of great importance just now that he should be our faithful ally, so we make much of him, and I rather look to our interview with him next November. "If this meets encouragement," as Swift says, I will give you an account of it.

Whenever we want to frighten any of our neighbours into good conduct, we have one sure resource. We have always a large assortment of Pretenders, black Chevaliers de St. George, in store. They have had their eyes put out, or their children are in hostage, or the Usurper is their own brother, or they labour under sundry disadvantages of that sort. But still there they are, to the good. We have a Shah Shujá all ready to *lâcher* at Dost Muhammed if he does not behave himself, and Runjeet is ready to join us in any enterprise of that sort.

Still, all these *tendencies* towards war are always rather nervous work. You should employ yourself more assiduously in plucking Russia by the skirts and not allow him to come poking his face towards our little possessions. Whenever there is any important public measure to be taken, I always think George must feel his responsibility—no Ministers, no Parliament, and his Council, such as it is, down at Calcutta. To be sure, as you were going to observe, *if* he ever felt himself in any doubt, he *might* feel that he has my superior sense and remarkable abilities to refer to, but as it is, he has a great deal to answer for by himself.

I daresay he does it very well, for my notion is that in a multitude of counsellors there is folly—"wisdom" was a misprint. And then again, if the Directors happen to take anything amiss, they could hardly do less than recall us. I certainly do long to be at home, not but what I am thankful for Simla, and am as happy there as it is possible to be in India, but still there is nothing I would not give to be with friends and in good society again, with people who know my people, and can talk my talk. Here, society is not much trouble, nor much anything else. We give sundry dinners and occasional balls, and have hit upon one popular device. Our band plays twice a week on one of the hills here, and we send ices and refreshments to the listeners, and it makes a nice little réunion, with very little trouble. I am so glad to see Boz is off on another book. I do not take to *Oliver Twist*; it is too full of disasters.

I must nearly have bored you to death, so good-bye. Please write again. Yours most truly,

E. EDEN.

Miss Eden to Mr. C. Greville.

SIMLA,
November 1, 1838.

There is a small parcel going to you per Miss Fane (not a ship, but the General's daughter, Miss Fane), which you are to take care of, and eventually it will be a pleasing little occupation for you. It is a journal of William Osborne's, kept while he was at Runjeet Singh's Court, and illustrated with some drawings Fanny has made from nature designs, and from some sketches made by one of our Aides-de-Camp, and altogether it may eventually make rather a nice little publication, and we think you will be just the man to edit it, and to cram it down the throat of an unwilling bookseller, extracting from him the last penny of its value—and a great deal more. It is not to be published till George gives his consent, and as it gives an account of the Mission which formed the alliance, which is to end in the war—which may end we don't know how—and as William will indulge in levities respecting the Company highly unbecoming the Governor-General's Military Secretary, who is in the receipt of £1500 a year from the said Company, and as for many other "as's," it is not to be printed till further advice. It is trusted to you with implicit confidence. Lord Stanley, Fanny says, is to be allowed to read it, but I have not heard of any other confidant, so you are not to go rushing about with treble raps, and then saying: "Here are a few pages about Runjeet, a man in the East, King of the Punjab, or Shah of Barrackpore, or something of that sort, which I think would amuse you. You may run them over, and lend them to anybody else who will take the trouble of reading them." That is not the line you are to take—not by any means. On the contrary, after a long silence, and with an air of expressive thought, you are to observe: "I have been reading this Memorandum—in fact, I wish I could send it to you; but there are reasons. However, never mind; there is no harm in my saying that I have been reading a journal. I almost wish it might be published; but yet, I do not know. However, if it is, I am sure you *for one* (a great emphasis on 'for one') would be amused to the last degree. A friend of mine in India, a young man, odd but clever, passed some time with Runjeet Singh, and kept a sort of diary. Curious and odd. You may have heard of Runjeet Singh,—Victor Jacquemont's friend, you know; only one eye and quantities of paint. I wish I could show you the little work, etc." And so, eventually, you know, it might come out with great *éclat*. I think William may write a second part of the Interview at Ferozepore, which might be very gorgeous, taking our army into account, as well as the meeting of the two great people.

ROOPUR,
November 13, 1838.

I wrote the above before we left Simla, when we had a good house over our heads and lived in a good climate, and conducted ourselves like respectable people, and people who knew what was what. Now we have returned to the tramping line of life, and have been six days in one wretched camp, the first few so hot and dusty, I thought with added regret of the Simla frost. And now to-day it is pouring as it pours only in India, and I am thinking of the Simla fires. It is impossible to describe the squalid misery of a real wet day in camp—the servants looking soaked and wretched, their cooking-pots not come from the last camp, and their tents leaking in all directions; and a native without a fire and without the means of cooking his own meal is a deplorable sight. The camels are slipping down and dying in all directions, the hackeries sticking in the rivers. And one's personal comfort! Little ditches running round each tent, with a *slosh* of mud that one invariably steps into; the pitarrah with the thin muslin gown that was carefully selected because the thermometer was at 90 yesterday, being the only one come to hand; and the fur pelisse, that in a wet rag-house slipping from a mud foundation would be pleasant and seasonable wear, is gone on to the advanced camp. I go under an umbrella from my tent to George's, because wherever there is a seam there is a stream; and we are carried in palanquins to the dining-tent on one side, while the dinner arrives in a palanquin on the other. How people who might by economy and taking in washing and plain work have a comfortable back attic in the neighbourhood of Manchester Square, with a fire-place and a boarded floor, can come and march about India, I cannot guess.

There were some slight palliations to the first day in camp: some English boxes, with new books and little English souvenirs from sisters, nieces, etc. And then I have a new horse, which met us at the foot of the hills, and which has turned out a treasure, and is such a beauty, a grey Arab. He is as quiet as a lamb, and as far as I can see, perfect—and a horse must be very perfect indeed that I get upon before daylight, when I am half-asleep and wholly uncomfortable, and which is to canter over no particular road, and to go round elephants, and under camels, and over palanquins, and through a regiment, without making itself disagreeable.

The army will be at Ferozepore two days before we shall. The news from Persia is so satisfactory, that probably only half the force will have to cross the Indus, and it is very likely that Sir H. Fane will go home, and Sir W. Cotton later.

Miss Eden to Mrs. Lister.

Simla, 1839.

MY DEAREST THERESA, Your letter, which I received three weeks ago, was most welcome, though it was "the mingled yarn, of which we spin our lives." Your happy bit of life with your brother, and your prospering children, and your journey, which always (so as you stop short of India) gives a fresh fit of spirits, and then your return, and that melancholy catastrophe.

I cannot say how grieved I was for that. Such a happy young life, and one that was of importance to so many others! I hope Lord John will be allowed to keep those children, and I suppose she will have left them under his guardianship. I suppose he would hardly object to all the children being together. I see by the papers that you have been at Cassiobury with poor Lord John.

Everybody writes what you say of Sir G. Villiers—that he is not the least altered, which I own surprises me, because as far as I am concerned he has been decidedly "changed at nurse," and just simply because he would not answer the two long letters I wrote him, I settled that he was not the original G. Villiers, with whom one could talk and laugh any number of hours, and whose visits were a bright spot in the day, but that he was a mixture of a Spanish Grandee in a reserved black cloak, with a mysterious hat and plume, etc., or a Diplomat in a French comedy who speaks blank verse. But "it is the greatest of comforts," as Mrs. Bennett said about long sleeves, to know that he is unaltered. I should be sorry if those horrid Spaniards had gone and spoilt one of our pleasantest men, and I still think that a system of sending out bores to foreign courts would be an improvement.

Foreigners would never know how it was. A bore would be softened by being translated into another language, or he might simply pass as an original—*un Anglais enfin*; and then we might keep all the amusing people to ourselves. I should like to have seen your brother; and how I should like to see your children! I have no doubt they are as pretty as you say; the little boy always had a turn that way. I cannot make out whether there are any more coming, but I suppose you would have mentioned it if there were, and I think you are apt to increase your family in a dawdling way, not in that rapid manner with which my sister used to produce ten or twelve children all of a sudden, and before one was prepared for the shock.

We came back to these dear good hills about a fortnight ago, and I love them more dearly than ever. The thermometer was at 91 in our tents, and after two days' toiling up the hills, we found snow in our garden here. That is all gone, and the flowers are beginning to spring up. The snowy range is so clean and bright, it looks as if one might walk to it, and the red rhododendrons are looking like gigantic scarlet geraniums in the foreground. I cannot sketch hills at all: they are too large here, and there is no beginning nor end to them—no waterfalls, or convents, or old buildings to finish them off.

We were about four months and a half in camp this year, so the blessing of being in a house again is not to be described. I never am well in the plains, and this year it would have been perverse not to have had constant fever. We had rain every week, which kept the tents constantly dripping, and we were very often apparently pitched in a lake, and had to be carried through the water to dress. I was hardly a month the whole time free from ague, and how George and Fanny are so constantly well is a matter of astonishment to our doctor and every one else.

The Punjab was an interesting bit of our tour, and I am very glad we have seen Runjeet Singh and all his Indians in their savage grandeur. He very nearly died just before we came away, which would have been a dreadful blow in the political way, but he has happily rallied again.

I should like to show you some of my Sikh sketches, though I have horrible misgivings that, except to those who have run up Sikh intimacies, and who prefer Shere Singh to Kurruck Singh, or *vice versa*, they may be tiresome performances. I have, in the meanwhile, had several of my sketches copied by the miniature painters at Delhi, and they have made some very soft likenesses from them. Do you ever draw now? Or have you no time?

There are 96 ladies here whose husbands are gone to the wars, and about 26 gentlemen—at least there will, with good luck, be about that number. We have a very dancing set of Aides-de-Camp just now, and they are utterly desperate at the notion of our having no balls. I suppose we must begin on one in a fortnight, but it will be difficult, and there are several young ladies here with whom some of our gentlemen are much smitten. As they will have no rivals here, I am horribly afraid the flirtations may become serious, and then we shall lose some active Aides-de-Camp, and they will find themselves on Ensign's pay with a wife to keep. However, they *will* have these balls, so it is not my fault. Your ever affectionate

E. EDEN.

Miss Eden to Lady Theresa Lister.

SIMLA,
June 17, 1839.

MY DEAREST THERESA, I have had a letter of yours to answer more than a month, but this is a bad time of year for writing home. We try all sorts of plans; but, first, the monsoon cripples one steamer, and the next comes back with all the letters still on board that we fondly thought were in England. Then we try an Arab sailing vessel; but I always feel convinced that an Arab ship sails wildly about drinking coffee and robbing other ships. This is to go to the Persian Gulf, and if you are living at your nice little villa, Hafiz Lodge, on the banks of the Gulf, I think it just possible this letter may find you. Otherwise, I do not see why it should.

And now for your letter. First: I see you are now Lady Theresa. Ought I to make any difference in my little familiarities? Secondly: as touching Lord Clarendon's marriage, which had been mentioned so often as decidedly settled that I began to fear there could be no foundation for it—I never have faith in a report that lasts three months without becoming a fact. However, I am very glad it is all right now. I remember he always liked her, and she has had rather a trying life of it, which will fit her all the more for the enjoyment of happiness.

You talk of your uncle's will as if it had been unsatisfactory. I was in hopes Lord Clarendon was rolling in riches—I do not know why. You should never write as if I knew anything. If you mention a will, you should state it, beginning with "sound health of mind and body," and ending with the witnesses' names; otherwise we never know anything in India, and what little we do know we forget, for want of people to talk it over with.

We cannot remember if that poor Lady H. Villiers died; but I think she did, and if so, I do not see who the late Lord C. could leave his money to, except to the present one. However, he will be well off now, at all events. Lady Verulam, I own, I think a sad and very large objection, but only at first; and as I rather hope to hear by the next mail that your brother is in office, politics and business will prevent any very wearisome intercourse.

Thirdly: as to those unfortunate H. Gordons. His memorial for leave to retire is gone home to the Court of Directors, and George has no more to say to it than you or I have. It rests entirely with the Court, but George thinks they will give him leave to go home, as the idea of his paying that large debt out of his wretched income is absurd, and he is, in fact, a mere expense to them. But about the pension—there again no authority, not even the Court, can help him. I see constantly in the Calcutta papers that when anything the least unusual, or even doubtful, with regard to the Pension Fund is contemplated, then it is put to the vote of the whole Army, and always carried economically. Still, if the Court give him leave to go home, I am sure it would not be worth his while to live here in misery for the sake of the small addition to his pension. I suppose it cannot be more than £100 a year altogether, and I should really think it could not hurt Lady C.

Cavendish to make that up out of her own allowance. You will have had my letter explaining the absolute impossibility of George's doing anything here for him. There is no such thing, Heaven knows, as a sinecure in India. For military men there are Staff appointments, which are, of course, in the gift of the Commander-in-Chief.

We have been uncommonly gay at Simla this year, and have had some beautiful tableaux with music, and one or two very well acted farces, which are a happy change from the everlasting quadrilles, and everybody has been pleased and amused, except the two clergymen who are here, and who have begun a course of sermons against what they call a destructive torrent of worldly gaiety. They had much better preach against the destructive torrent of rain which has now set in for the next three months, and not only washes away all gaiety, but all the paths, in the literal sense, which lead to it. At least I know the last storm has washed away the paths to Government House.

The whole amount of gaiety has been nine evening parties in three months—six here, and three at other houses. Our parties begin at half-past eight, and at twelve o'clock we always get up and make our courtesies and everybody goes at once. Instead of dancing every time, we have had alternations of tableaux and charades, and the result has been three Aides-de-Camp engaged to three very nice English girls, and the dismissal of various native Mrs. Aides-de-Camp. Moreover, instead of the low spirits and constant *tracasseries*, which are the foundation of an Indian station, everybody this year has been in good humour, and they all delight in Simla, and none of them look ill.

Our public affairs are prospering much, but I will not bore you with details. We really are within sight of going home, dearest Theresa, but it makes me shiver to think of it. I am so afraid something will happen to prevent it.

I do not count Simla as any grievance—nice climate, beautiful place, constant fresh air, active clergymen, plenty of fleas, not much society, everything that is desirable; and when we leave it, we shall only have a year and a half of India. The march is a bad bit; I am always ill marching, and our hot season in Calcutta makes me simmer to think of it. Then, the last five months will be cool, and we shall be packing. And then, the 4th of March 1841, we embark, and in July of the same you will be "my neighbour Lister," and we shall be calling and talking and making much of each other. I should like to see your children. No, I do not approve of Alice for your girl. There is an unconscious prejudice in favour of the name "Alice" which has risen to an alarming height, and I think it my duty to oppose it. It gives me an idea of a slammerkin milk-and-water girl. However, do as you like, only don't blame me if Alice never looks tidy. Love to Mrs. Villiers. Ever your affectionate

E. E.

Miss Eden to Lady Theresa Lister.
SIMLA,
June 29, 1839.

MY DEAREST THERESA, To-day an old sea letter of yours (January 23) has come to hand, containing all that I wanted to know, so as there is an odd opportunity of writing (a Chinese clipper going from Calcutta to Aden, and the letters to find their own way from thence—such a post office arrangement!) I take advantage of it....

This letter is six months old, but still very acceptable, and it shows that I still have some right original English feelings,—that I have been brought up in good Knightsbridge principles.

That old Lord Clarendon was a brute; I always thought so. But what can be the use of carrying on a farce of that sort to the end? He cannot pop his head up even for a minute to say, "How I have tricked you!"—supposing he was proud of it. My only hope is that Lady Clarendon, who will find it difficult amongst her own nieces to hit upon a worthy heir, will do what Lord Clarendon ought to have done. This must go forthwith. Ever, dearest Theresa, your most affectionate

E. E.

Miss Eden to her Brother, Robert Eden.
PINJORE,
November 2, 1839.

MY DEAREST ROBERT, Here we are again fairly in the plains, and to be sure the plains are not the hills—an axiom the profound wisdom of which you cannot appreciate, unless you had been yesterday luncheoning with us at the Fir Tree Bungalow, with the snow in sight, the cool air rushing about, and everything as it ought to be in October, the cones tumbling off the fir trees, and the fern red and autumnal, and then you should have been snapped up by your *Jhanpannies* and run away with down-hill, till in two hours you found yourself at Barr, the thermometer at 90 in the tents, a man pulling the punkah for a little artificial air, and nothing but dust and camels to be seen for miles round.

We came on eight miles to this place this morning, and stay two days to allow time for our goods to arrive; but it is almost hotter than Barr. Poor dear Simla! I had a great mind to cry when I saw the last glimpse of it yesterday; but still I look upon this march as one step towards home.

The army is on its way back from Cabul, but as Dost Mahomed is supposed to be not far from the frontier, a larger force remains behind than was at first intended. However, nothing can be known till the spring, for the boundary between here and Cabul is impassable from snow, even for a messenger during the winter. However well the expedition has succeeded with reference to Russia and Persia, and to the safety of this country from foreign enemies, I really think it is more important in the effect it has had in India itself. Natives are totally unlike anything we know at home; and they have had for some years an idea that their fate, or what they call the good-luck of England, was to change, and the Nepalese have been fomenting this notion with great care, so that there were many petty states quite ready for an outbreak.

Every post now brings letters from Residents all over India, saying that the success in Afghanistan has not only astounded the natives, but given them faith again in English luck in general, and in their Lord Sahib in particular. The further the news spreads, the more effect it seems to make. There has been one very odd proof at Kurnaul in the Madras Presidency of the *thinness* of the crust over the volcano on which we all sit in this country. The only wonder is it does not explode oftener. The Nawáb of Kurnaul has been often accused of disaffection, and lately of having concealed stores. He was uncommonly angry, as people are when they are accused of anything true or false, and desired three commissioners should be sent to examine his jaghir. They found nothing and were coming away, but some of the military authorities got information from the Nawáb's own people, summoned more forces, and asked for another search. He said they were quite welcome to go into his fort, and his prime Minister should go with them. Nothing was visible; but his workmen betrayed him. They pointed out dead walls which were covered up, concealed pits that were opened, etc., and everywhere arms were discovered. More guns than belong to the whole army of ; rooms full of double-barrelled guns, and bags of shot attached to each; and shells, which the natives were supposed not to know how to make. His Zenána was turned into a Foundry, etc. There never was a thing done more handsomely. As he has an income of only £100,000 a year, of course he must be in league with richer and greater potentates, and his own 1500 followers could not have made much use of all this artillery. He made a little fight for it, but he is in prison and his territories are seized by the Company—one of the cases in which Lord Brougham would probably like to talk about native wrong and British encroachments. George says the Directors occasionally write a fine sentence about not attending exclusively to British interests, just as if the British were here for any other purpose, or as if everybody's interest were not to keep the country at peace.

Lord Elphinstone has done this Kurnaul business very sensibly and well.

Shah-i-Bad,
November 8, 1839.

I have kept this open in hopes of the overland post. It won't come. We are progressing slowly and painfully. George and I think we have been a year in camp; but other people say only a week. The heat is quite dreadful, and I think I feel my brain simmering up in small bubbles, just as water does before it begins to boil. We are in Mr. Clerk's district, and he has let Henry Vansittart come with the camp, which delights him, and he learns a little bit of camp business, regulates the price of flour at the bazaar, talks big about the roads, and by way of showing how good they are, overturned his buggy and himself last night. But he is pleasanter on his own ground than at Simla. My best love to Mary. Ever yours most aff.

E. E.

Miss Eden to Lady Theresa Lister.
CAMP UMBALLA,
November 5, 1839.

MY DEAREST THERESA, I have not heard from you for a long time, but one of the last overland letters mentioned that you had been ill, so it is tempting to write and hope that you are well again.

The wife of the Private Secretary came with me from Simla, because in compliment to my weaker health I made shorter marches to the foot of the hills with the last fat baby, Auckland Colvin refusing to sit anywhere but in her lap, and the baby before that refusing to go to sleep unless she slept in the same tent with him, in which there were the three children, two Portuguese Ayahs, and the children's favourite bearers. No light, because the candles had been sent on by mistake to the next ground; no carpets, because ditto; so that the servants kicked up a dust even in their sleep. Several Pariah dogs were playfully avoiding the Jackals, and about thirty bearers sleeping or smoking on the kynants, or the space between the lining and the outside of the tent. "*That I saw*," as Sydney Smith used to say in his charity sermons when he was stating a particular case of distress which he not only never had seen, but never heard of.

This was in our encampment in the hills, when the climate was still delicious. Now the thermometer stands at 90 in the tents, and these unfortunate ladies begin to march at four in the evening. I do not know that the horn signifies, as I defy anybody to sleep in camp more than two hours, and it is being uncommonly acute to snatch at that the first week, till the sentries have learnt to stop the tent-pitchers and camel-drivers from knocking down and packing up all night at unlawful hours. I got Captain Codrington, our Quarter-master, to stay behind last night instead of going on to pitch the advanced camp, that he might see and hear what a quantity of illicit pitching and packing went on, and the result was that he imprisoned 160 tent-pitchers, 56 camels, and removed out of hearing the neighing horses of half the clerks in the public offices, and we all went to sleep for at least half-an-hour, which was very grand. Moreover, it is a rule that nothing should leave the ground till the Governor-General's carriage goes by, and a gun is fired to announce that highly important event; so to-day this rule was enforced, and in a country of hot dust, which this is, a very good rule it is. But it was funny to see the crowds of old men and beasts the advance guard had stopped, camels and elephants innumerable, our own band, several hundreds of grass-cutters' ponies laden with grass for sale, palanquins full of small half-caste babies, everybody's pet dog with their bearers, sofas and arm-chairs. My own tame pheasants in their wooden house I saw in the *mêlée*.

Marching disagrees so much with me, that by the doctor's advice, and George's desire, I leave the camp at Agra, and go straight down to Calcutta, where I hope to be the middle of February. George does not expect to be there before the 1st of April, but I rather hope he will, driven by the heat, cut off some of his tour as the time draws nearer. We have been joined on the march by several officers returning from Cabul, and very flourishing they look, and they cannot make out that their sufferings have been what the papers tried to make out. Captain Dawkins, of Lord Auckland's Bodyguard, who has been through the campaign with a regiment to which he lawfully belongs, has come back looking fatter than most Falstaffs, and he brought back three of the sheep which he left with us at Ferozepore last year, so that danger of starving was not great.

God bless you, dearest Theresa. This is a very stupid letter, but then it is better than none, which is what I have had from you. And you cannot imagine how hot it is. Your most affectionate

E. EDEN.

CHAPTER XII

1840-1842

Miss Eden to Mr. C. Greville.
BARRACKPORE,
March 13, 1840.

MY DEAR MR. GREVILLE, I give it up; I succumb; I see clearly I was all wrong; generally am, quite mistaken, very sorry, very stupid, etc. But you and every friend I have will do me the justice to say that since the first year we passed here I have mentioned openly that I was regularly twaddling, that I hardly remembered a proper name, and *never* knew what was meant for jest or earnest. I have written it home twenty times, and it is not a complaint peculiar to me, but common to everybody who has passed a hot season or two in India. Their brains are fairly stewed down into a harmless jelly; and it is a merciful dispensation that, as they have not bodily strength to laugh at a joke, they have not wit left to understand one. I still think that your irony was too fine even for England—I mean, I might have been puzzled there; here, of course, I took it all *au pied de la lettre*. I should not have minded it so much, if just at the moment when George had hazarded himself in a line that must have ended in success or in impeachment, he had not been turned upon by almost all the Indian authorities, and every paper without exception. I did not care for their opinions, wretched little buzzings of Indian mosquitoes, but when an imposing English hornet came down upon me with the same small Toryisms, as I thought, I could not stand it. However, I see it all clearly now, so let us make it up. "Hostess, I forgive thee: look to thy servants. Wash thy face. Come, thou must not be in this humour with me."

I rather expect the next overland may bring out a copy of William's book; it is just the sort of thing which will make a great sensation here. Everybody makes a point of fainting away if their names are mentioned in the public prints; they have simple hysterics if they are merely mentioned in a list of passengers by a steamer, etc.; but if their names are coupled with a comment on their conduct or promotion, they fall into a dream. Therefore a book upon a subject that may be connected with politics, by a Military Secretary to the Governor-General, will be too much for their nerves. I depend upon your Preface for annihilating them. We are really looking to it with great anxiety, and considerable prospect of amusement. The papers will wrangle for a month if you have made any mistake as to the various members of the Singh family, of which they know nothing themselves. Then *the* Prinsep, who wrote a book about Runjeet, which you have probably made use of, is now a Member of Council, the greatest bore Providence ever created, and so contradictory that he will not let anybody agree or differ with him. If you have made any use of his book, I mean solemnly to assert that I *know* from the best authority you have never heard of it or him, that it was a great pity you had not, etc.

Your friendship with Mary is certainly rather funny, but once begun, I think it will go on progressing. Please to let me know if you see the slightest inkling of a flirtation for either of the girls. They are the greatest dears I know, and though I had rather they should not marry till next year, that I may be by to approve, still I should like to hear of it too.

We came up here this week to see if it were cooler than Calcutta (vain idea!), and to receive the visits of the station, which, as there are eight regiments at Barrackpore, were numerous and dull. We had two hours of fat generals and yellow brigadiers clanking in and out of the room yesterday; but one visit was rather amusing. The lady was like Caroline Elliot in her young days; married to come out here; landed a month ago; is in perfect horror at India; and evidently the poor husband has lost any charm he ever might have had by his guilt in inveigling her out here. I asked if she had got into her own house yet. "I have not seen a house at Barrackpore. Tweddell has taken a barn for me, but I am not in my own barn yet." "Have you found a good Ayah? She would help you." "I have got some black things Tweddell calls servants. I do not understand a word they say." She said she went to bed immediately after dinner, and I asked if she dined late. "How can I tell? There is no difference in the hours. Always shut up in a prison to be stung by mosquitoes. And then Tweddell told me I should be a little Eastern Queen. Oh, if I could go back this last year." She was dressed up to the last pitch of the last number of the *Journal de Modes*, which, poor girl, will not be of much use at Barrackpore, where the officers are too poor even to dine with each other; and I own, I think Tweddell has a great deal to answer for, and *is* answering for his sins in a wearisome life. But to the by-standers who have not seen a fresh English girl nor a hearty English aversion for some years, she was an amusing incident.

Did you know much of Lord Jocelyn at home? He has seen his Agra and Delhi since he left us, is now doing a bit of tiger-shooting, and then is coming down as fast as he can to join this Chinese expedition. His regiment does not go, but George has got Captain Bethune to take him as a guest. I think I should like to go marauding to Canton. We found at Calcutta a box of bronze curiosities, etc., that we had ordered before this little painful misunderstanding with Lin, etc., and they give a great idea of what might be picked up by an experienced plunderer. Yours ever,

E. EDEN.

Miss Eden to Mr. C. Greville.
BARRACKPORE,
Sunday, April 19, 1840.

MY DEAR MR. GREVILLE, The March overland is just come in, and they say that if we send an express to Calcutta, to overtake the *other* express which was going off with George's despatches this afternoon, everything will come straight at Bombay. In my own mind I see nothing but a long train of innocent Bengalese running after each other, each with a letter in his hand, the thermometer at 150, and the head man of the train waving the small quantity of muslin he deigns to wear to a distant puff of smoke in the Bay of Bengal.

However, as our friendship has had such a frightful *secousse* and wants steadying, I pay you every possible little attention, so I write this hurried line to say that the few letters which have yet arrived, and two stray papers, all speak in the highest tones of The Book, and of its success, and how well it is got up, and we are longing for a copy of it, and George is politically at ease from its being spoken of as a *personal* narrative, and altogether it seems like an amusing incident. William is full of gratitude for all the trouble you have taken about it.

We have subsided from the interests of Afghan politics into the daily difficulties of keeping ourselves from being baked alive. I may say we have *risen* to this higher pursuit, for it is much the more important of the two, and of much more difficult achievement. China promises to be amusing; they are arming themselves and fitting up little innocent American ships, and collecting war junks; and my own belief is that they are so conceited and so astucious that they will contrive some odd way of blowing up all our 74's with blue and red fireworks, take all our sailors and soldiers prisoners, and teach them to cut out ivory hollow balls.

Lord Jocelyn is staying with us, but will sail in about ten days in the *Conway*. He goes merely as a volunteer with representatives of the Dragoons, and George has arranged that he is to be passed into any ship that is likely to see most service. He has great merit in the ardour with which he looks about for information and for service, and I hope the Chinese will not take him prisoner.

So the dear little Queen is now Mrs. A. C. I hope she will be happy; and they may say what they like of her, but she certainly contrives to conduct herself wonderfully, through a great many trying ceremonies,—never awkward, and yet just shy enough, and I like her so for being so affectionate to Aunt Adelaide.

Pray tell Mrs. Drummond I have had her letter and Theresa's journal, much to my heart's content, and I would have written her another line, but I am horrified at the price of letters. Not but what I guessed my journal would cost a great deal too much—but £2. 8. 0! I am horrified in the English sense. Here that would be dog cheap—24 rupees. I never speak to anybody for less.

The long hand of my watch caught in the other, and the watchmaker charged 20 rupees for bending it up a hair's breadth. But still, £2. 8. 0 for a letter! I flatter myself your office pays for this. Good-bye. Ever yours,

E. EDEN.

Miss E. Eden to Mr. C. Greville.

CALCUTTA,
July 6, 1840.

My dear Mr. Greville, At last a copy of *The Court and Camp* has reached Calcutta, and was picked up by an alert Aide-de-Camp, who was in the shop when it arrived. It is immensely well got up, and altogether, I think, a pretty little book, and more of a book than I expected. It is a pity more copies did not come by one ship, for there are quantities bespoken. But in the meanwhile everybody is borrowing this, and they all delight in the introductory chapter, because, of course, not one of them has the least idea of the *history* of the Sikhs as connected with India, nor of India as connected with anything else, so they are all delighted at learning it so cheaply, and they look upon you as a prodigy of Eastern learning. There are one or two misprints in the book, which do very well for England, but is the sort of thing they will take up here, where their intellects are below mistake par, but just up to a misprint; and I should imagine that the Agra Akbar will wonder at the ignorance of the aristocracy who can call a thermantidote a phermantidote, and that the *Delhi Gazette*, which is courtly, will say it ought to be phermantidote, and that they could give the Greek derivation, only they have no Greek type.

I think you ought to feel a sort of paternal interest in the Sikh dynasty, and would like to know that Kharak Singh still retains the name of King, and Mr. Clerk (the Governor-General's agent) says that Noormahal's attentions to his father in public increase in proportion as he deprives him of all power. He says Noormahal all through the Durbar is occupied in wiping the dust from Kharak's band, when not a particle has settled, or with a Chowry in driving away flies from his father's hand, which they never approach, and that Kharak, though a fool, is wise enough not to like these demonstrations of tenderness.

The fleet left Singapore for Macao on the 30th May; the fear of bad weather prevented their waiting any longer for Admiral Elliot. William Osborne and Lord Jocelyn seemed very well satisfied with their accommodation in the *Conway*, and were gone on in her. William asked some of the Chinese at Singapore whether their way of making war was like ours, and they said, "Much the same, only more guns and less drum." He asked what they thought of the steamers, which were, in fact, quite new to them, and they said, "Oh, plenty at Pekin; only little smaller." I am in a horrid mood of mind at all these requisitions from home that are to keep us here another year; and have turned rank Tory on the spot, and can think of nothing but the quickest means of turning the Ministry out, and then of rushing down to the river-side and beckoning to the first ship. But surely we never shall be kept here. I don't think the people at home have an idea what a place it is, but they *will* know hereafter, if they go on behaving so in this life. And as for the idea that any Governor-General is to stay till everything is quite quiet and peaceable in this great continent, you might as well ask the fish to stay in the frying-pan till they have put out the fire.

There always must be some great piece of work in hand here. In the meantime, life is passing and friends are dying, and we are becoming so old that it will be impossible to take up the thread of existence again with the young things like the Drummonds, etc., whom I had looked upon as the supports of my old age. It will never do to stay.

We are to have at dinner to-day a son of Theodore Hook's, just arrived. He does not look as if he could improvise, or do much better if he *provised*; but I never saw the father, so he may look stupid, too, without being so. I see there are two of T. Hook's novels published lately, and trust the son may have partially brought them out.

I have become a great whist player upon the one-eyed monarch principle. Nobody else can play at all, and when the Governor-General and the Commander-in-Chief dine together, it is obvious that they must have their rubber, and so I and the Aide-de-Camp or the Doctor play with them. Can't you see the sort of thing? Shocking whist, but it helps the evening through. I play much better than Sir Jasper, but worse, George says, than anybody else he ever saw. Ever yours,

E. EDEN.

Miss Eden to Lady Campbell.

CALCUTTA,
July 17, 1840.

MY DEAREST PAM, Your friend Mr. Taylor arrived this week with the letter you gave him ten months ago—perhaps not bad travelling for a letter of introduction, though not exactly rapid as a means of receiving intelligence. However, a letter's a letter, and I am the last person in the world to complain.

George has seen your Taylor, and says he is very promising, and I have asked him to Barrackpore for love of you and in the strongest reliance on your Edward's judgment. Otherwise, there *is* a brother of his in this country now (thank goodness up the country) that used to drive me demented—just the opposite to all you say of your friend—not good-looking, not a "chap" at all, and rather a black sheep—though, poor man, I should not say so. But you cannot imagine the provocation of his manner or the excess of his conceit. It induced a freezing sort of snappishness in oneself that was, however, utterly unavailing; it only made him more affable and jocose. And, to crown all, he shaved his head after a fever, or his doctor shaved it to tease him, or something of that sort, and he came dancing about in a little velvet skull-cap.

I think my health has been so good this year at Calcutta because Pearce Taylor was not there.

No, dearest, I never blame you for not writing. I always feel that I know you just the same as ever, and that it is not your fault if your children take up all your time. I only regret that the world should be such a very large, thick, slice of bread, and that butter should be so scarce that they should have been obliged to spread us at the two opposite ends. We should have been much happier in the same butter-boat, but I suppose it could not be helped. My side of the bread too, is turned to the fire and I am half-roasted, which, if I do not write twice to your once, is my *set off* against the claims of your children.

I have always wondered how much you liked Mrs. Fane. You mentioned her in one letter as liking her very much, and she is a good-natured little woman, but not *one of us*, is she, Pam? I think she must have felt Sir Henry's death. He was always very kind to her in his way, without putting her at her ease.

Our George has done very well in India, has he not? You know we always thought highly of him even in his comical dog days.... Now I think he has done enough, and might as well go home, but none of the people at home will hear of it, and this month's despatches have made me desperate. Moreover, I cannot stay away another year from Mary and her girls, and fifty others. I do not like anybody here, and if we try to get up a shade more intimacy with any lady, then all the others are cross, and her husband or brother wants something, and that makes a story, and so on.

William Osborne is gone with the China expedition, which is a sad loss to poor Fanny. However, I believe that will be a very short business, and that he will soon be back again. The Chinese have already begun to say they hope there will be much talkee before fightee, which does not promise much fightee. William says that at Singapore they saw quantities of little dogs fattening regularly in coops for the table, and their captain's steward was looking at them, which gave Lord Jocelyn and himself an alarm about their future dinners.

Your little picture is still such a pleasure to me. Mind you keep like it, that I may know you again. None of the children know me, which is shocking and foolish. Your most affectionate

E. E.

Lady Campbell to Miss Eden.
DUBLIN,
September 27, 1840.

Just so my darling. I am rather glad you wrote before you saw the Taylor I sent, for fear he should be a beast in spite of Edward's good word. Emmy, this other year seems harder to swallow than all the rest. But I will not touch upon it; it is too raw. There has been a talk of our asking for something in India; I thought it just probable that we might pass each other at sea! However, we should have to leave so many children they said it would not pay, and I could have hugged them. One man I can scarce bear to look at who put it into Sir Guy's head at first, and how much we were to lay by, and how charming the climate was, and how I should marry my daughters!

Yes, Sir Guy's Fanny is married and very happy. Captain Harvey is a very handsome, nice person; they have not much money at present, but that cannot be helped. Pam has been with her for the last month at Carlisle, where Fanny is quartered. Pam was very ill with ague, so I sent her to the Napiers. She comes back to me next week. I long to show her to you—not for the beauty, for she is no beauty, tho' nice-looking. But, Emmy, she is quite, quite one of us—I need not explain how pleasant, how good, how full of sense and fun. She is such a comfort to me.

The next, Georgina, is very pretty and very dear, but not so gentle and patient as Pam.

I had my sailor boy for two blessed months. This boy, Guy, came home so improved, so gentle and affectionate, and delightful from sea. I felt so thankful, as I rather feared the sea. It is a dreadful life to be the mother of a sailor; so hard to bear. Wind always to me was a sad sound, but now I can hardly help crying. All the rest are good little nice things, and I have no governess, so I have a good deal of their company more or less. We are quaking for the Brevet, but I will not entertain you with my hopes and fears, and want of pence, or what you call *Pice*, don't you?...

I like Lord Ebrington, and he seems to like you all so much. I get on much better with him than with Lord Normanby. However, he does not give dinners and balls and parties enough, and the *trade* complain. Dear Lord Morpeth is coming to dine with me to-day, and won't we talk of you? He is such a charming person, and my most particular friend. You gave him to me, you know, when you went away. Mary will have told you how we had settled I was to go over and see her. Her girls are so nice, and she herself dearer than ever, and all the better from going out more. For a little while she really ensconced herself inside the high wire nursery fender, and one saw her in the uncomfortable way in which when we were bairns you may remember we used to see the fire, never getting at it enough. I was sorry she gave up poor Grosvenor Place. I like all those old Grosvenors; I could have cried when I looked at No. 30! *Du reste*, I rather like getting old; there is wonderful repose in it; it saves one so much trouble—so much of the work done. I am so glad you are getting fat, so am I, and I combine also the grey hair which you mention George has assumed. I am very grey; fat and grey sounds like an old cat, but what does it signify? when once we meet, how young we shall feel then. Emmy, do you remember your aversion to mittens? My dear, I was in advance of my age. When I wore them, like Bacon and Galileo I appealed to posterity, and posterity made haste, and everybody wears mittens, morning, noon, and night. The only chance you have is, that they will have burnt out before you come back, and my hair too. Everybody *lisse* and banded, and they little know that George and I were the only two people that wore close heads in our day.

The Lansdownes spent a week here. She is looking well, and in much better spirits, and her countenance so much softer and gentler, that I think her more loveable than I ever knew. I never knew how much I loved her till I was with her in her grief. Louisa looking well for her, and ready to talk and be pleased. Lord Lansdowne rather older. I was wondering what made him look so well and distinguished and conversable, and I found he was set off by Lord Charlemont, who rejoices in a brown natural hair wig, which made Lord Lansdowne in his nice grey hair look quite beautiful.

I have got a nice two-year-old baby just *pour me désennuyer*; such a nice duck! The youngest after six girls. Pam says he is doomed to wear all the old bent bonnets out, and accordingly I found him in the hay with a bonnet on.

Tuesday, September 20, 1840.

I wrote all this Sunday and I must just add one word. Lord Morpeth dined here early with me and the children, and was to start by the eleven o'clock train to the packet for to sail for England to attend the Cabinet Council, *as we vulgar* imagine, upon peace or war, *rien que ça*. However, my delicacy was such I did not pump at all. He is a real good soul, and I have scruples about pumping him. Old Berkeley Square I always make a point of pumping till the handle has come off in my hand often, but very little water ever! Yours ever,

PAMELA CAMPBELL.

Miss Eden to the Countess of Buckinghamshire.

CALCUTTA,
January 15, 1841.

MY DEAREST SISTER, After a long cessation all our letters came to hand—all from September to November 4th. You had been doing your *Mimms*, which I never think sounds comfortable. Indeed, I remember seeing the place once and thinking it very melancholy, damp, and dead-leafish.

Yes, as you say, as long as Chance is alive there is a wall between Dandy and death; but then you know spaniels live longer than terriers, and at all events it would be a sort of preparation to Dandy to insinuate to him that Chance has lost his last tooth, which the faithful Jimmund, his servant, has had set in a silver ring.

You have never mentioned that you have a new clergyman of the name of Hazlewood at Greenwich. You never tell *me* anything in confidence whatever, after so many years; and after all, I don't see the use of making such a mystery of it. "But I have often observed a little spirit of nonsense and secrecy," as Mrs. Norris says, about your clergyman, that I would advise you to get rid of. Your Hazlewood (you see I know his real name) is brother to our Captain Hazlewood, commonly called Harum Scarum. Hazlewood Scarum got a letter by this last post saying: "Lady Buckinghamshire, who is a constant attendant at my church, is, I find, a sister of Lord Auckland's. You cannot imagine how much I wish to make her acquaintance. I think our mutual interests in India," etc., etc.

Probably by this time you may have seen him. Our Hazlewood is going home next week in the *Hardwick*. The wounds he received at Ghazni were very severe; and he rattles about, and dances and rides, and proposes and breaks off his engagements, and altogether he has never let himself get well, and has suffered so much from his arm lately that his general health is beginning to give way, and Doctor Drummond has ordered him home. A man who goes home on a medical certificate has his passage paid by the liberal Company, and gets £50 a year while he is in England; so that upon the whole a slight wound is not such a bad thing. I am rather on the look-out for a generous adversary who will wound me just up to the pitch of being ordered home, and having my passage paid, but not a bit more. Poor Hazlewood's is much more than that; but the voyage will probably set him up, though he will never have the use of his arm again. As he will go to Greenwich to see his brother, I have given him a line to you. It will not entail upon you more than a dinner, and he is a very good-humoured, obliging creature, and not at all vulgar. There is not the slightest chance of his spoiling the view at Eastcombe by setting that little wretched stream the Thames on fire; though I have no doubt he will try, as he always must be busy about something. He may give you a flourishing account of us, as we are all going on very well, I think.

The Admiral has made a shocking mess of China—at least he has done nothing, and the force and the ships and the money have all been wasted, leaving things just as they were a year ago. Now he has given up the Command, writing most pitiable accounts of his being in a dying state from disease of the heart, with no chance of reaching home alive; and for the last ten days we have been believing this and pitying and defending him. And now to-day George has a letter from him, written on board his son's ship, saying they were all on the way home; that he thought he had mistaken his complaint, which was now merely liver, and that he felt nearly well again. It is an unhappy bit of his career, and such weakness is rather odd in such a stern, stiff-looking man as G. Elliot.

Charles is now left sole Plenipotentiary, and if he can but keep to his own mind two days running is clever enough to do very well; but he is terribly vacillating. She wishes very much that she was with him just now, and I can fancy she might be of use in keeping him up to the mark; but she cannot go during the present monsoon, and except for the pleasure of seeing Charles again, I think she will be very sorry to leave Calcutta. Ever your most affectionate

E. E.

Miss Eden to Mr. C. Greville.

CALCUTTA,
January 17, 1841.

MY DEAR MR. GREVILLE, I am grieved you were so troubled with the gout when you wrote, as I have never been of the opinion that a fit of gout is a matter of that perfect indifference which people who are not sufferers from it claim to assert. I think you had better come out as Lord Auckland's successor, if you cannot come and visit us. Nobody has the gout in India. I suppose it is *perspired* out of them. And even General Elphinstone, who was a wretched victim to it when we met him going up to Meerut—almost the worst I ever saw—has, I hear, lost it quite during the hot season. He is going to succeed Sir W. Cotton in Afghanistan, and does not like it on account of the cold climate.... Ever yours most truly,

E. E.

Miss Eden to the Countess of Buckinghamshire.

BARRACKPORE,
February 6, 1841.

MY DEAREST SISTER, I am just come back from doing a bit of duty, so I may as well try whether writing to you will not be a bit of pleasure in this dark half-hour before dressing.

The little Nawâb of Moorshedabad has anchored his fleet of boats just in front of this house, on his way up the river home. He is the convoy of the late lamented Captain Showers, who has gone and married himself to a very plain, unpleasant young lady, and has consequently left us, and George has given him the care of this boy's education. George took the little Nawâb a drive, and I have been, with Rosina as an interpreter, to see the Begum in her Pinnace, and it strikes me that it is very lucky I was not born a Mussulmannee. I am sure if they shut me up in that fashion I should have got into a thousand scrapes, and probably some very bad ones; and moreover, I should have gone out of my mind with bore and heat. She was in the centre cabin of the Pinnace, with three or four antechambers made of curtains, so arranged that there was no possibility of her being seen when one was opened. All the jalousies of the cabin were shut, and it was so dreadfully hot that I was obliged to ask for a breath of air; and then there was such a fuss: Captain Macintosh and the boats that brought my servants requested to keep off—sentries on deck thrown into a fuss—and then when a fishing-boat came by, such a rush to shut up one wretched bit of blind which nobody could see through—and if they had, I think they would have been very much disappointed. "I am not the lovely girl I was," and the Begum, though rather pretty, is so extremely small I don't think they could see her at all without a glass. Her women were shut up in another dark cabin, and her visible attendants were all of that class (saving your presence) who are allowed to wait on Eastern ladies.

Visits to native ladies are much more amusing when I go with Rosina, than when there is a stiff secretary translating from the other side of the punkah. The Begum was delighted with some English flowers that I took her, and began asking Rosina about England, and amongst other things, she and her attendants having ascertained that it was really true that we walked out in London, wanted very much to know if we did not wear veils and loose trousers on those occasions. Rosina made them all laugh very much, and the Begum gave her £5 when we went away. I should think a laugh must be cheap at the money. I am quite sure I should have gone wrong, particularly wrong, if I had been one of these shut-up ladies, out of mere spite. It might have been difficult to contrive it, but I think I should have been a very profligate Begum. They say this little lady was. Now she is not more than twenty-six, and having lost her husband has lost her power, and is under the control of a strict mother-in-law, and her chief occupation is to *cook* for her son. She never lets anybody else cook for him for fear he should be poisoned.

CALCUTTA,
February 9, 1841.

No more decisive news from China. Charles Elliot still goes on negotiating—or as the people there call it, *no*-gotiating. The navy, army, and merchants are all equally dissatisfied. By the last letter, he declared Sir Gordon Bremer was to attack the Bogue forts the next day if the Chinese did not sign the treaty, but he has said so so often that nobody will believe it till they see it, and even when they do it is impossible not to regret that it was not done a year ago. Mrs. Elliot has rather a hard time of it, I fancy, as the society here is chiefly mercantile, and they all consider themselves ruined by all this weakness and procrastination, and the papers, too, are full of abuse. She bears it better than most people would, but fidgets about his vacillation, I suspect. She talks of sailing in about ten days.... This day twelve month how sea-sick I hope to be. Yr. most aff.

E. E.

Miss Eden to the Countess of Buckinghamshire.

CALCUTTA,
April 6, 1841.

MY DEAREST SISTER, I did not write to you last month. I daresay you never found it out, only I am so honest I tell. But I had a large arrear of friends to bring up, and as Fanny said she had written you a double letter, I thought you would not miss me if "I just stepped out for a bit."

I am sure you would pity me at this moment. Just fancy yourself trying to be fond of Dandy's successor, and in the still lower position of finding that successor refusing obstinately to be fond of you. As for ever caring for a dog as I did for poor dear Chance, the thing is impossible. I do not believe there ever was so clever a dog, and very few equally clever men; and then, after eight years of such a rambling life, we have had so many recollections in common, and he was such a well-known character in India. I had no great fancy to have another; but we are alone so many hours of the day that a pet is almost a necessity, and a Doctor Young, who is just come from England, hearing I had lost Chance, very politely sent me a little English spaniel he had brought with him.

The gentlemen all say it is a perfect beauty, with immense ears, and a short nose, and all the right things. It may be so; unluckily it is not even the kind of beauty I admire, and in all other respects I think I may safely say I never hated a small dumb beast so much in all my life. It is wild and riotous and foolish, and whines after its old master half the day; or else runs off like a mad thing, and the servants, who cannot pronounce its name, Duke, are streaming about the house after it, calling Juck, Juck! That name is its only merit. I suppose nobody ever had a dog called Juck before. Everybody says it will grow tame, but I know better. I have had it eight days, and I think in another week it will be lawful to return it to Doctor Young, and say I cannot deprive him of it—such a treasure, such a Juck!

Your account of Dandy barking at the Southwark police particularly amused us. Fanny's dog flies at all the natives who happen to have stepped out without their clothes just in that way, and George longs to murder him for it, as a dog frightens them out of their senses.

We have just had the very Chinese news that George has anticipated all along—indeed, so certainly, that two months ago he luckily sent his own orders to stop all of the convoy and fleet that C. Elliot had not dispersed. The Emperor would not even listen to that treaty, bad as it was, so now it is a declared war, and the Bogue forts have been taken, which was easily done, as the garrison all ran without firing a shot.

That was what George advised, and indeed ordered as far as he could ten months ago, when the expedition started in full strength. Now the ships are half-dispersed, half-crippled, and an immense proportion of the soldiers dead or disabled, and it is evident that Charles now does not know what to do. In the meanwhile, in his odd mad way, he had sent orders to have Chusan evacuated without waiting for a ratification of the treaty, and he has been obliged to withdraw the few soldiers that had garrisoned Hong Kong, his great hobby of an acquisition, because they were wanted on board ship. So we literally have not an inch of ground or a single thing gained by all this immense expenditure. The Chinese actually ordered us out of Chusan before they would give up one of their few prisoners, and we obeyed. The sort of fun they must make of us.

I have had a line from Mrs. Elliot, who met the news at Singapore and was much out of spirits. But George has not yet heard from Charles. It is lucky he is what he is, totally blind to his own folly, for I am sure half the men in his position would be driven to some act of desperation.

April 14.

No more tidings from Charles Elliot. William is gone off on a tiger-hunting expedition with a Mr. Larpent. It is a dreadfully hot time of the year for this sort of work, but I believe tiger-shooting is that degree of exquisite pleasure that makes up for all inconveniences, and the mere idea did him a great deal of good. He has been in one of his *meandering* states of spirits ever since the excitement of the races were over, living very much alone and looking utterly broken-hearted; but this new excitement has roused him again, and he went off quite happy with the thermometer at about 95, I suppose, out of doors.

Juck has subsided a little, but is a positive misery, and very uninteresting. I am getting on very fast with a collection of drawings and flowers, those that are not common in England. I sketch them and put in the colours, and I have hired two natives by the month who sit in the passage and paint them. I think you would rather like to see them (the drawings, not the natives), but I know what you will say—Very pretty, my dear, but they are all red and yellow. You must have had a sad want of blue flowers,—and I don't exactly know how I can contradict you. Some of the parasite plants, tho', are very beautiful. I have been gradually making a new garden in front of the house, rather in the large round chumpy line, but the size of the house requires that bold style, and by the time we go it will be very pretty, and quite ready to be destroyed by the next Lady.

Lady Amherst made a magnificent garden all round the house, which stands in the centre of what we call a huge compound. Lady William said flowers were very unwholesome, and had everything rooted out the first week. I never thought of restoring it till last year, and now it is all done very economically, and only on one side of the house, and at a considerable distance, so that the doctors can't have the conscience to object, etc. I am just finishing two little fish ponds.

All the bamboo fences will be covered with creepers after the next rains, and then, as I said, the next lady may pull them all up, and let the ground lie fallow for her successor, and so on. Whatever she may think of the garden, I am sure she ought to be obliged to me for clearing up the house. It was all left in such an untidy state. You must recollect those old looking-glasses that had been put in the ball-room by Lord Wellesley. I think they must have lost all their quicksilver when Lord Wellesley was a little boy. I sent them all to the auction last month, as we are not up to re-silvering glass in India, and they actually fetched £400; and with that I am going to have the ball-room gilt in a very elaborate manner, and I think it will be a great improvement.

We have lost Captain Hill, who succeeded Major Byrne in the management of the house and its expenses, whether ours, or the Company's. He was taken so alarming ill that he was obliged to go off to the Hills, nominally on sick leave, but I fear there is no chance of his returning. And it was all so sudden that he had no time to instruct his successor. However, Gales is a very efficient House Steward, and I am carefully educating Captain Macintosh in the Company's interests. It often strikes me that a very extravagant Governor-General might puzzle the Directors very much; he can order any expense whatever, and as it is, the establishment is enormous. Of course they can recall him when his accounts go home, but there is nobody to check him here.

They say Lord Elphinstone has been in a horrible scrape with them for his Durbar expenses—money spent on his house and furniture. They ought to think highly of my little looking-glass economy, and if they would send us out just a dozen very large looking-glasses, etc. However, I am going home, at least I hope so. I expect this will find you under a Tory Government—wretched, ill-governed creatures! The last hope of elections seems fatal, and China news will be a good grievance to have the Government out upon. I wish our successor were named. It is quite time he should be, as George wishes to see him here before we go. Do name him at once.

Ever, dearest Sister, your most affectionate

E. E.

Miss Eden to her Brother, Robert Eden.

CALCUTTA,
April 12, 1841.

MY DEAREST ROBERT, There is no particular good news to send you this time, though nothing much the reverse from India; but I think if the Opposition did not take advantage of C. Elliot's first absurd peace, they may turn the Ministry out on finding it is no peace at all, and that, moreover, he has not left himself the means of carrying on a war. There never was such a man, if he were not a positive fool. I really think he would go mad when he looks back on all he has done this year. The last act of giving up Chusan, without waiting to see if the Emperor would ratify the treaty, is the crown to all his absurdity. We have not a foot of land left of their territory, and they actually ordered the last soldier out of Chusan before they would give up their few prisoners. Everybody wonders what will be the next news. Probably, that he will prevent Sir Gordon Bremer from taking Canton, for fear it should hurt the feelings of the Chinese, and the Emperor will probably send down orders that our sailors are to wear long tails and broad hats, wink their eyes, and fan themselves, and C. Elliot will try to teach them. I don't think my national pride ever was so much hurt.

Everybody is curious to know what the orders from home are. I have a horrible fright that if the Whigs are still in, they will send out full powers to George to take the business in hand. That *might* interfere with our going home, which would be much more distressing than any national offence, and also it would be very inconvenient to him just now.

The Punjâb remains so unsettled that all the spare troops are obliged to be kept on that frontier; and then Major Todd has brought Herat into a mess, and though I think that is nearer to you than to us, it makes great difficulties in this direction. Then Singh and his army cannot get on at all. Runjeet's death has been so like the death of Alexander, and of half those great conquerors in ancient history that we used to read about, and believe in. His army was a very fine thing, and his kingdom a good kingdom while he was there to keep his one eye upon them, but the instant he died it all fell into confusion, and his soldiers have now murdered all their French (I began on a half sheet by mistake) and English officers, and are marauding wildly all over the country. It is not actually any business of ours, but it interrupts our communications with Afghanistan; and, in short, it is obvious that it might at last furnish one of those pretences for interference England delights in, and when once we begin I know (don't you?) what becomes of the country we assist—swallowed up whole.

Anyhow, I wish you would bestir yourself about our successor. It is high time he should be named; moreover, my stock of gloves is exhausted, so at all events I must come home. Do you think you could buy me instantly from Fownes a dozen of long white gloves, ditto of short, and send them off by some ship that is actually in full sail, not lying in that dockyard where Grindlay locks up all the ships.

I suppose Fanny has given you most of our private history, so I have given you this little touch of our public history. William is gone tiger-shooting. Our new doctor is, I think, a very remarkable boxer, and does not suit George at all. However, he is a good-natured man, and if he would leave off cutting little melancholy jokes and making a face like a rabbit when he laughs at them, and if he would not ask such a quantity of small questions, there would be no harm in him. Your affectionate

E. E.

Miss Eden to the Countess of Buckinghamshire.

CALCUTTA,
May 6, 1841.

MY DEAREST SISTER, Fanny means to write to you a line herself before the post goes, and indeed may probably be strong again before the express starts; but in the meanwhile I may as well begin a regular letter, as she will not be able to do much. I am convinced we are all many hundred years old, and barring that I have lost my hair, and my teeth, and my eyesight, and I rather think my hearing, and am quite yellow and probably stoop a little, I am very juvenile, and I must own never had such good health in my life.

Between ourselves, our doctor is a perfect calamity, and George had nearly yesterday made up his mind to get rid of him, but it would be a strong measure. He has taken all the pains he could about Fanny, but he is evidently an ignorant man on the subject of medicine, which is a little unlucky for a doctor, and in other respects the greatest bore I ever encountered—a sort of thing that makes one wag one's ears and stamp, he is so tiresome and slow.

What has knocked him up with George is his treatment of the natives. Nothing will induce him to take the slightest charge of the servants and their families, and he and I came to a grand blow up on the subject yesterday about a boy who had been bit by a mad dog. George wanted to get rid of him on the spot, but I thought it would be supposed he had been sent away on account of Fanny's protracted illness, which would be ruin to him in his profession, and it must wait. But Macintosh added up the case as it really stands: "The man is a brute to the natives, and I am very glad that I have hated him ever since he entered the house, and we all do the same."

Yesterday we sent for old Doctor Nicolson, the Sir H. Halford of Calcutta, whom everybody abuses and yet they all send for him, and the other doctors mind every word he says. I have no faith in him myself, except perhaps in these Indian cases, which he has seen enough of the last forty years, and at all events he has put Fanny in better spirits about herself.

Certainly the body is quite as inconsistent as the mind. I remember laughing so the first two years at people going out, even in the cold weather, with shawls on, and thinking it affectation. All the last week I have dined with two shawls on, and George with his great cloth cloak, and both of us declaring the evenings were delicious, only too chilly. I imagine the kitchen at Eastcombe would be an ice-pit in comparison. Last night at cards I asked Captain Macintosh if he had any return of ague, and he said no, but that he and Captain Hollyer were both so dreadfully cold they wanted to have the jalousies shut. The thermometer was at 79, but I was quite as shivery as they were. I hope we shall brace ourselves up on the voyage home, otherwise you will think us very tiresome and fusty.

I still think my new dog a great bore, thank you. I knew you were going to ask, and I do not suppose I am capable of an infidelity to Chance's memory, for everybody says this is a perfect treasure. I have had the promise of another, more after Chance's pattern, but it is ill, and as dogs always die in this country as soon as they are ill, it never may reach me. But, in the meanwhile, I am not obliged to attach myself to Juck. Your most affectionate

E. E.

Miss Eden to the Countess of Buckinghamshire.

CALCUTTA,
June 1, 1841.

My dearest Sister, You can hardly have the cruelty to expect a poor creature to write after three weeks of the most desperate weather ever felt in India, and no signs of a change. Even the natives are completely beat by it. The Baboos say they can't write, and the tailors can't sew, and I see the man who is pulling the punkah has a large fan in the other hand with which he is fanning himself. Even George owns to falling asleep over his work; and then the evenings are so hot we cannot drive, which is unwholesome for him. Under these circumstances it is rather difficult to write.

Fanny left a letter for you before she went. They have been gone a week to-day, and therefore ought to be at Singapore to-morrow. I heard from her on Wednesday evening when the pilot left them, just gone to sea, and she said she felt better, though the heat had been dreadful in the river, and that it was the quietest ship she had ever been in, and that William was very contented, etc.; and Sir Gordon wrote word she was in excellent spirits. If they find a ship ready to start from Singapore they may be back in less than five weeks, and at all events in six, and I am sure they will have had a blessed miss of any part of this month. I rather hope they will make a week's more delay, and go and see Penang when they are about it. Everybody says it is so beautiful.

In the meanwhile, I take it we are going to bring her and Sir Gordon and the whole ship's company into the Supreme Court, I believe, and probably transport them all. The captains of three several ships have all come storming up the river, declaring that Sir Gordon fired upon them because they did not salute his pennant quick enough to please him; and one captain has brought two *balls*, one of which passed between him and his pilot, and the other went through the cabin full of passengers. As they were arriving from England, not thinking of finding a Commodore, and certainly not expecting to find him on board a steamer tugging another ship, it is rather sharp practice firing at all; but firing loaded guns is quite a new idea. I hope it will not be proved that Fanny has been popping away out of her cabin on these unsuspecting new arrivals. Sir Gordon is always amazingly on the alert about his dignity; and having detained *The Queen* a day in order that he might attend the birthday ball, went to bed before supper. It was supposed from some jealousy about the Members of Council taking precedence of him.

I cannot think Charles Elliot and he, by clubbing all the intellect they have, will ever be a match for one Chinese, even of a very pale-coloured button, or indeed an unbuttoned Mandarin, if there is such an improper character.

Our Queen's ball was very magnificent, and, as I fondly hope it is our last, I am glad it went off so well. I *wore my diamonds!* I think that sounds well, so the particulars will remain a mystery, but they really looked very well, and George bought a beautiful row of pearls the other day which he *lends* me. We had Dost Mahomed and his sons and suite at the ball, the first time he had ever seen European ladies in their *shameless* dress; but he did not see the dancing; George took him into another room. He is a very kingly sort of person, and carries off his half-captive, half Lion position with great tact. By way of relieving George part of the evening, I asked him to play at chess, and we played game and game, which was rather a triumph, considering the native chess is not like ours, and he kept inventing new rules as we went on. I somehow think if he were not a Dost it was not quite fair.

I opine this weather is having an excellent effect on George's mind. The most opinionated Governor-General never could dream of staying another year after having been done to a turn—I may say rather overdone now, and I cannot think that he *is* thinking of it, only the letter from England frightened him. But he declares that he wrote home for a successor two months ago. Mr. Colvin, who is as anxious to go home as I am, was in his room when I went there just now, and we made an invited poke, which elicited an explicit answer that he meant to go home, barring any extraordinary accident. I do not know how there could be any accident more extraordinary or more fatal than our staying here another year, and I feel we shall go.

Whenever I am too much beat by the weather even to take a book, I find I am always thinking of packing and tin cases, and whether the railroad from Portsmouth is not a horrid conveyance; and I never dream of anything that is not purely English.

Law! Sister, there is such a gale of wind it has actually blown open a window by breaking an iron bar, and the rain is coming down like smoke, and I rather think, but cannot be sure, that I am coming to life. Of course it is not the actual rains, but they must come in a fortnight, and this is a blessing for an hour.

My new dog is a total failure. I still call him mine, but Captain Macintosh takes care of him. I have been offered another, but I know nothing will do after Chance.

Take care of Dandy and yourself. Ever your most affectionate

E. E.

Miss Eden to the Countess of Buckinghamshire.
CALCUTTA,
July 18, 1841.

MY DEAREST SISTER, At first I scorned your spiteful imputation that I had not written to you by the April mail, but upon looking back into my littel boke of dates, I found it was true, and now I only wonder how you found it out. I see that it is for some years the first month I have missed writing, and for fear the case should occur again, I strongly advise that you should seal up two or three of my old Indian letters, if you can find them; and desire Streeton to bring one in on a silver waiter at the proper time. You will be quite taken in, for I have a deep conviction that my letters have all been copies one of the other, so one on the old pattern will seem quite natural to you.

Those horrid English letters of June 4 came in yesterday. They always give me a low day, but this was worse than ever. I had made up my mind that the Whigs were to be out and the Tories naming another Governor-General. I do not now think the dissolution will help them much, but others say it may, and now they have sent out full powers to George to try and mend up that Chinese mess, and he thinks that if the Whigs stay in, that he will be obliged to stay on. However, I did nothing but cry about it yesterday, and now to-day I see it all quite differently. I don't think they will stay, nor he, nor we, and so I won't bother you about it till I see things more dispassionately. We are to have another post in before ours goes, and that will show the turn the elections are going to take, and I think—I am not sure—but I *think* I can live on in the hope of that post settling our return. I always believe for the best, and this would be such a disappointment that I have a sort of faith it *cannot* happen, and so let us talk of something else.

I am glad Hazlewood's visit was not very fatiguing. He is a good-hearted creature, and a shocking martyr to his wounds, but he has not half an idea in his head, and I rather thought it a bold thing to introduce him. But I daresay the pleasure to him was greater than the bore to you, and that is the way to balance those things. And then, all Indians dote on a live Countess. A stuffed one they would look up to, but a live one is really a treat.

How is Dandy? Zoe, my new dog, is decidedly a treasure, marked just like the lamented Chance, but smaller, and she does not interfere with my respect to his memory, as she has no talents and no temper, but is *creepmousey*, and cares for nothing and nobody but me, and requires constant petting—a familiarity Chance did not admit of. She is unluckily not used to the climate, and Brown, our coachman, who is probably disgusted at having to doctor her so often, said to me yesterday, "She is a nice little pet, ma'am, but I think the delicacy of her health will give you a great deal of trouble." Just as if it were a delicate baby.

We had a sad incident amongst the pets yesterday. Captain Thurlow was in William's room, and was looking at some of his daggers and playing with William's great bloodhound. William was called out of the room, upon which Nero laid hold of poor Captain Thurlow's nose and bit it quite through. They say he would have bit it off, if he had not been *in play*. But in the meanwhile Thurlow is bit and Nero sent away, an event that delights George, who always thought him an unsafe pet.

August 11, 1841.

Think of that being written three weeks ago, and Thurlow was at Barrackpore three weeks ago in attendance on his General, and his nose so dreadful that, though he only appeared by candle-light, and that for the first time since his accident, his poor dear nose made me so squeamish I could not touch a morsel of dinner. However, they say it will come right in time, but if it had been Thurlow's dog and William's nose, George was wondering when he should have heard the last of it.

You will see our China news, which George thinks very good as far as it goes. Charles Elliot is supposed again to have interfered too much *against* fighting, and to favour the Chinese pride as much as ever, and the Army and Navy are both as bitter against him as the merchants; but George is so thankful that our 2,000 men should have got out of the scrape of attacking 47,000 without utter destruction, that he is rather pleased. And then the million and a half of our money is a great point, the more so that he has just heard that four million and a half of dollars will be here in a week, just when money was most wanted.

I have had a long letter from Mrs. Elliot who had been at Canton before this attack, and out shopping where no English lady ever shopped before. She has picked up some curiosities of an expensive kind for George, and some smaller ones for me, and Fanny has got a boxful from an American to whom she gave a commission, and just because we want to unpack our little goods, it is a Hindu holiday and the Custom House is shut. Do the Hindu holidays annoy you much? But of course they do; we always felt alike.

Poor Mrs. Elliot has had a trying life of it lately. She seems pleased with this Canton business, and it is the best point at which Charles could meet his recall. I imagine from some letters of his which George showed me that it will not be a surprise to him, and he means to show the world, etc., how right he has been. I foresee a long life of pamphlets, don't you?

No other English post come in, but I think we have quite satisfied ourselves that the Whigs cannot stay and we shall go in February at latest. I have heard from Captain Grey, to whom I wrote to ask what accommodation he could give us in the *Endymion*. He says, smaller than the *Jupiter*, but he thinks he can take us all. We shall be fewer by Mars married; Chance, dead; and Fop, William's greyhound, also dying of old age. I wonder whether we have only been here six years. I imagine we are all dying of old age sometimes, and that we have been here the usual Indian terms of twenty-one years.

August 16, 1841.

The July post come in—the Elections all wrong, and so our going home is certain. George sends his resignation by this post, and in February we sail. God bless that dear post for bringing us such good news and so quickly. I am still an excellent Whig, but there is much pleasure in Opposition. And then the delight of going home! Good-bye, Sister; I'm coming directly. Just stop one minute while I draw my ship up your river. I really believe George is rather sorry, but he says not, and he is an honourable man. Your affectionate

E. E.

Miss Eden to the Countess of Buckinghamshire.
CALCUTTA,
September 10, 1841.

MY DEAREST SISTER, I have never felt such unwillingness to set off letter writing as this month, and it will be worse and worse and worsted for the next three, and then I shall be ready to write a line to say we are going on board, and after that I never mean to write to you again—never. I am tired of it, and besides, mean to pass the rest of my life with you. What a horrid prospect for you to find me always tugging after you with a long languid Indian story, only diversified by requests for a large fire and shut windows. I would not be you on any account. Besides, think of the obtuseness with which we shall meet each other's topics. I beg to apprise you at once that I do not remember the botanical name of any one single flower; so don't expect it. I have gone back to the old childishness of roses, wallflowers, and carnations, and beyond that I cannot charge my memory.

I have been ornamenting the garden with some stone vases that the natives make very prettily, and just at the proper moment, Fop, William's old greyhound, died, so I buried him *symmetrically* opposite to Chance, and Captain FitzGerald has put two ornamental vases over the two dogs, with a slight tendency to the funereal urn about their design for the consolation of my hurt feelings, and yet sufficiently like flower vases to deceive the Tory Governor-General, so that he cannot be spitefully tempted to pull them down again. Zoe, my new dog, is very pretty and very small, but certainly with none of the genius of her predecessor. In fact, between friends, she is rather dull, but she is such a little helpless thing that nobody can help coaxing her, and I could not expect two Chances in one life. George rather affections her, though he says he thinks a black bottle full of hot water would be quite as good as Zoe sitting on his lap, and full as lovely. Every morning in the auction papers there is a list of "Europe toys" for children, and I found one called a black cloth dog, defective, which is clearly another Zoe for sale. However, all this is only a hypocritical jest. I am very fond of her; and I assume you think that if anything happened to Dandy, you would be obliged to try a successor. One wants something of the sort.

Sir Jasper and all the Nicolls family are on the point of setting off for their march through India. Lady Nicolls has done it once before and is fully awake to its horrors, and the young ladies do not like leaving Calcutta, but Lady Nicolls looks so ill that it is lucky she is going. They are a nice English family, and will be a loss here. The married daughter from Madras arrived last week with the first grandchild. Such a hideous little baby—but they are all in such ecstasies with it. I went there this morning and found our Miss Nicolls with the thermometer at 1000, I believe, walking up and down the room with the baby, away from the punkah because they thought it made the child sneeze. The perspiration was streaming down her face, and there was old Sir Jasper in a white jacket snapping his fingers and saying, Bow, wow, wow, and then rushing back to the punkah and saying he really could not stand the heat, but perhaps the baby with her cold had better not venture near the punkah. I believe the child was boiled; it looked like it. I think I ought to be excused a few small sins for the merit of going to the Nicolls this hot day.

There is an old blind General of 98 at Barrackpore, and his wife (who is 84) has just been couched, and sees with one eye, which is the only eye they have between them, and now the old man is going to be couched, and their pet doctor is ordered off with one of the marching regiments. They applied for an exchange for the doctor, which Sir Jasper refused, and the old lady came crying about it to Barrackpore last week; but I did not think I could well ask for it. However, she wrote a moving letter yesterday, and it is so hard at 90 and 80 to be thwarted in one of the very few wishes one can form, that I took courage, and set off this morning and expounded the case to Sir Jasper, who is very good-natured, and I rather think will do what they want. Sir Henry Fane would have snapped anybody's nose right off who had asked him for any favour of the sort. It will make the old Morleys very happy. The glare was so great that I think I shall have to be couched too; but that, of course, the doctor will do gratis. My eyesight is shockingly bad—I mean even for my age—and I have a strong and decided preference for large print.

I quite forget what one does of an evening in England. Here we dine at eight and go to bed at ten, so a short game at cards after coffee fills up the time, and nobody can read by the flickering lights here. Perhaps you will play at Beg-of-my-Neighbour with me; and then we shall step out, and smell the night-blooming stock in that little round border by the breakfast-room, and listen to the nightingales, and then go to bed, and I hope you will tell the bearers not to go to sleep when they are pulling the punkah in the company-room, because that wakes me.

Dear me! I sometimes feel very English just now, but ungainly, and with an idea that you will all laugh at us. I remember so well seeing all the Lowry Coles debark at Lord de Grey's from the Cape, and they were very unlike other people, and had very odd bonnets on.

September 15.

This must go. We have had a hard-working week,—a great farewell dinner to the Nicolls, and then to attend a play which Sir Jasper bespoke, and which lasted till near one. We luckily did not go till ten, but the audience who had sat there since eight were nearly dead, and we were all horribly hard-worked. Then I have been making a sketch of Dost Mahomed and his family, and he set off this morning for the Upper Provinces, leaving me with one of his nephews unsketched. So this morning, with immense activity I got up early, and Colvin abstracted the nephew from the steamer and brought him to sit for his picture before breakfast. The nephew is very like the picture of Judas

Iscariot. They are all very Jewish, but he is a fine subject, and considering Colvin had had no breakfast, he seemed to talk Persian with wonderful animation. Ever, dearest Sister, yours most affectionately,

E. EDEN.

Miss Eden to the Countess of Buckinghamshire.
BARRACKPORE,
October 8, 1841.

MY DEAREST SISTER, It is time to be writing again. Only three, or, at most four times more. It makes me yawn and stretch, with a sort of nervous shivering—just as one used to feel as a child the morning before going to the play with the idea that by some particular mischance *that* day never would come to an end, or that the theatre would tumble down, or somebody take our box. I have those theatrical misgivings and yearnings about the next three or four months, and I wish the September post would come, just to make sure that the new Governor-General is a man of active *packing* habits. I want to go in February. They say now that going in March makes such a long voyage. I think it is rather lucky that this month's news did not go home by last month's mail. That sounds Irish, because, as you justly observe, it is not so easy to advance a month's news as it might be a month's allowance; but there is George with his predatory habits up to the ears in preparation for a Burmese war, and if that news had got home in time, the Court of Directors would probably have made a strong objection to a change of rulers at the beginning of a war.

It may still go off, but the villain who is almost a savage, has suddenly moved down to within 24 hours' distance of our territories with a horde of fifty thousand men, plenty of guns, boats, etc., and in short, he looks full of mischief, all the more that he is egged on by the Chinese. He may change his mind and take fright at the last minute, but in the meanwhile he gives just as much trouble as if he had declared war, and George has had a very busy week, ordering off regiments, taking up transports, buying stores, etc., and as usual, if a thing has to be done in a hurry, he has to *see to it* all himself. He lives in a rage with the slowness of the people whose real work it is, but by dint of *aggravating* them, he gets them through their work. I see the necessity of sending out a fresh English head of affairs, with the English constitution and habits of business, every five or six years. He keeps all the poor languid Indians moving.

George was to have come up here yesterday, but he found the Captain of the man-of-war and the Colonel of the regiment that are to start first were making out that they could not possibly sail on Monday; so he sent for them in the morning and made a row, and then asked them to dinner in the evening to keep up the impression, and got some knowledgeable people to meet them, and I suppose he will get them off in time. The Chinese news is already better since Charles and Sir Gordon came away. Sir H. Pottinger began in the right way. The Chinese Commissioner wanted to see him at Canton; he said it was the Commissioner's place to come to him at Macao. Now there is an expedition gone to Amoy. The Chinese by their proclamations seem thoroughly frightened. The General and all the Navy people seem to be in ecstasies at having somebody who will not stop all their fighting, and I should not be the least surprised if Sir H. Pottinger finished it all in six months, by merely making war in a common straightforward manner.

I suppose Fanny has told you of all Mrs. Elliot's anger, and her expectations that Charles is to have titles and governments, etc., the instant he lands in England. She is quite right, poor thing! to take his part, though foolish to announce such expectations. But the change of Ministry may be of use to him. Otherwise, there never was a man, meaning well—which I really suppose he did—who has left such a fearful character behind him with everybody but the Chinese, who profess the greatest gratitude to him, as well they may. Your most affectionate

E. E.

CHAPTER XIII

1842-1849

Miss Eden to Lady Theresa Lister.
KNIGHTSBRIDGE,
Tuesday.

MY DEAREST THERESA, I can write to no one in all the nervous flurry of these first meetings but yourself, my poor afflicted friend. Amongst all the happiness of others your hard trial haunts me, and shocked me more, much more than I can say, when I heard it at Southampton.

I had dwelt so much on seeing you, as I was told you were unaltered, and then to hear of this! I will not write more now, but even the first moments of arrival cannot pass away without my telling you how heartily I feel for you and love you.

We are all well. Your most affectionate

E. EDEN.

Miss Eden to Lady Francis Egerton.
MONTAGU HALL,
Tuesday.

MY DEAREST LADY F., I have been meaning to write to you constantly, but once caught again in the trammels of civilised life the thing was impossible.

We spent a great deal of time (very pleasantly, so there is nothing to repent of) at Penrhyn Castle. We went there for two days last Thursday week, and somehow stayed on till yesterday. Every time we talked of pursuing our Welsh researches, Colonel Pennant declared that that particular sight was one of the drives from the Castle, and there came round a jaunting-car with four great black horses, and we went off to Conway.

There was no end to the sights, besides the Castle itself, which I think one of the finest things I ever saw. The arches over the staircase looked just like so much guipure lace carved in stone. Every table and cabinet is carved either in slate, marble, or oak, till it is a curiosity of itself. I slept in the State room, an enclosed field of blue damask and carved oak. The bed, which I should imagine did not cover more than an acre and a half, is said to have cost £1500. I never had an opportunity of judging whether there was work enough for the money, having slept generally near the edge.

Old Mr. Pennant spent £28,000 a year for twelve years in building this Castle, and died just as it was finished. Everything from the Keep to the inkstand on the table was made by his own Welsh people; and I never saw a more wealthy-looking peasantry, and I suppose he spent his money well according to Miss Martineau's principles of doing good; that of getting as much work done for one's self as one's money will pay for. I daresay that is all right, but it always sounds like a suspicious system, and against all the early ideas of self-denial and alms-giving that were so carefully dinned into one; but the result in the instance of Penrhyn Castle has been highly satisfactory, and I do not really mean that he did not do a great deal of good besides. There never was a more charitable man.

The present Col. Pennant, too, seems very anxious to do all that is right, but he is oppressed, I think, by his immense wealth, and is not quite used to it yet. He seems quite wretched still for the loss of his poor little heiress of a wife. I like him for that, and also for that, having like Malvolio had greatness thrust upon him, he has not set up any of the yellow-stocking men or cross-garters Malvolio thought necessary, but is just as simple and unpretending as he was in his poor days.

We had a very large party and a pleasant one, Edwin Lascelles amongst others. What a man! If there happens to be any one day in which he does not say or do anything absolutely rude, everybody takes a fit of candour, and says: "After all, *I* like Edwin Lascelles. I think we are all wrong about him; he did not shut the drawing-room door in my face when I was coming across the hall, and if you observed, he said before he shut all the windows that he hoped nobody minded a hot room. I do not think him selfish."

We came here yesterday; rather a change from Penrhyn Castle. The house was built in the reign of Henry the Sixth, and furnished, I should suppose, by his own upholsterer, and has not been touched up since apparently. And there is a window from which Henry the Seventh escaped, and another at which Oliver Cromwell looked out, and in short, every window has its legend, but none of them have any shutters or curtains, and the doors are all *on the latch* and never shut, and the weather has turned cold, and in short, it is a relief to my feelings to say that I am bored to death and wretchedly uncomfortable, and think seriously of following Henry the Seventh's example, and of escaping out of one of the windows, to which my interesting legend will henceforth be attached.

It is very wrong, I know, to say I am so bored, but it is only to you—and I might have an illness if I did not mention it—and though it is extremely kind of them to have us here, I wish they wouldn't, and we had never meant to come. But when we were on our way yesterday to Pengwern (Lord Mostyn's) this Mr. and Lady H. Mostyn brought him over here, and then sent out letters and ordered post-horses to bring us too, and I always knew how it would be. However, it is so very dull it is almost amusing, particularly when I look at Lord Auckland, who has always declared he should like the Mostyns. Indeed, he was the only one of us who knew them, and I am happy to say that he sank into a sweet slumber after coffee, from which he was roused with difficulty at bed-time. One good of age and of hard practice in India is that one does not mind being bored so much as one did in youth, though then, to be sure, it hardly ever happened. The sediment at the bottom of the cup is decidedly thicker whenever I am reduced to swallow a spoonful; but still, I am more used to the taste of it, and as Dickens says of orange peel and water, if you make believe very much, it is not so very nasty. I am in a strong course of mutiny between them. But there is the luncheon bell happily; that is always a cheerful incident. Ever your affectionate

E. E.

Miss Eden to Lady Theresa Lewis.

BONCHURCH, 1845.

Our post goes out now about half-past one, and we have had an immensely long sermon against the poor Babylonians, who have all been dead and gone so long that I for one have quite forgiven them their little errors; but the preacher here is always having a poke at the poor sinners in the Old Testament. It can do them no good, and it does none to us, and he preaches an hour extempore, and altogether I think he had better not be so spiteful.

Our Bonchurch has been a most successful experiment, and I have not enjoyed a summer so much for the last ten years. We have a beautiful little cottage in pretty grounds of its own. The country about you know well, and I must say it is a very kind dispensation that as the wear of life takes away or deadens the interests that seem so exciting in youth, and many of which are artificial, the love of nature becomes more intense. I am quite happy with shadows and clouds passing over beautiful hills. I wish I could read Wordsworth, but the actual food itself I cannot swallow.

Fanny has certainly been very much better since she came here. She is one of the people who cannot exist without constant excitement, and then, though it makes her quite well for the time, it affects her spirits still more afterwards. She never from a child was happy in a quiet home life, though with such high spirits in society, and of course that tells more in her present state of health. When the Bingham Barings and Lady Morley were at Bonchurch for a week, she was in good spirits, and then seemed quite languid and thoroughly *cheerless*, and then all of a sudden went over to Ryde for two days, and George says walked and drove and paid visits, dined out both days, and seemed quite as well as ever, and she certainly looked all the better for it. Now again, she has sunk into a listless state, and I am afraid there will be no amusement she will care about for the rest of our stay. We have the R. Edens and 7 of their children perched on their little hill. Lady Buckinghamshire was nearly three weeks perched on hers, quite delighted with her life here. She had never before been on a railroad, nor on the sea since 1793 (when my father was Ambassador in Holland), and she left her carriage in England and rumbled about in a fly. She delights in pretty country and astonished us by her activity.

Then Maurice Drummond suddenly appeared, walking about the Island with a young Grenfell, and they took a cottage for a week at Shanklin; and it is certainly satisfactory, as Mary says, to see how innocently the young men of the present day can amuse themselves. These boys walked about 20 miles a day and were in such a fuss to keep their expenses down,—ordering 4 lb. of mutton, and cutting off wine at luncheon, and really happy in a good, joyous, young way. And they settled when they went away that they should have a pilgrimage next year to their dear Rose Cottage—such a little hole you never saw.

Maurice made no allusion to the state of his affection, but he does not seem to pine. With a little mellowing he will turn out very agreeable; he has so much natural fun. We wanted him to stay on with us, but he had not time. Your most affectionate

E. E.

Miss Eden to Lady Theresa Lewis.

EDEN LODGE,
Tuesday.

MY DEAREST THERESA, Many thanks for your long amusing letter. I do not wonder you are pleased, both with the Election itself and the manner in which it went off; and I am not at all sorry you were spared the presence of F. O'Connor. Even though he could have done no harm, I can't abide these Chartists, and hate to be convinced that they are real live people, and particularly wish that they never may come between the wind and my nobility.

Of course you will drive about in London for a few months with your carriage as it appeared in the streets of Hereford, and by the courtesy of the real member, you will be favoured with the real bouquet used on that occasion. Great attraction, immense crowds, etc.

I know nothing more of Macaulay except that he unfeignedly rejoices at an opportunity for getting out of office, an escape that he has unluckily wished to make for some time. There is of course a great struggle made to keep him, but I can imagine office must interfere materially with the pursuits and pleasures of his life.

I think Edinburgh, which affects all sorts of classical and pedantic tastes and enthusiasm, turning off one of the first orators and cleverest men of the age for a tradesman in the High Street (both men having the same politics), must feel slightly foolish now it is over. They say the prejudice against Macaulay was entirely personal; he never would listen to a word any of his constituents had to say, which is hard, considering his demands on other people's ears; but still they may look a long time before they find a member so well worth listening to. I wonder whether Cowan is agreeable.

I am really better, thank you, and able to walk about the garden. But the quiet system has answered so well in bringing back my strength, that I am willing to go on with it a little longer. It is said about Elections that the Liberal cause has gained ground, that the Government has lost ditto, which is as much as to say that four Ministers have been defeated and we have a very rough Radical Parliament. If Sir George Grey is beat, I think a fifth loss of that kind would lead to some decided change. Yesterday everybody said his success was quite certain, and as every Election has gone exactly against the assertions made in London, I presume he is beat by this time.

My Lord is very busy at Portsmouth reviewing, sailing, firing guns, surveying, giving great dinners at bad Inns, and doing everything that is most unnatural to a quiet landsman; but he seems very happy, and it is more wholesome than that eternal writing. To-morrow, he is by way of sailing to Jersey and Guernsey. I never understand men in office, and cannot catch an *aperçue* of the motive which induces them to take office or keep it; but I presume if this stormy sort of weather continues, he will hardly persist in that little dutiful party of pleasure.

We have been reading Lamartine's *Girondins*—interesting, as that eternal French Revolution always is, but most painful reading, and I do not like Lamartine's style. It is too epigrammatic and picturesque, and his sentiments drive me mad. He tries to make out that Robespierre was humane, Pétion *homme de bien*, Madame Roland virtuous, the Revolution itself glorious. It gives me a great deal of exercise in my weak health, for I throw the book away in a rage, and then have to go and fetch it again. Your ever affectionate

E. E.

Miss Eden to Lady Theresa Lewis.

ADMIRALTY,
Tuesday.

MY DEAREST THERESA, How tiresome it is that you are out of town just now! And such an unexpected blow, because we have acquired this year the right to expect to find each other in London.

To-morrow being Twelfth Day, seven of Robert's children drink tea here, and Mrs. Ward's nineteen youngest come to meet them; so I scoured London yesterday morning to secure a conjuror for their diversion, but there is an awful run on conjurors this month. Spratt of Brook Street is engaged every day till the 19th; Smith of St. James, ditto; but I worked my way steadily up from conjuror to conjuror through all that tract of land lying between No. 1 Brook Street and 32 Fleet Street; and there I finally grabbed Farley, who *says* he can pound watches into bits, and put rings in eggs and so on, though I rather doubt it. Then from Fleet Street I drove straight and madly to Kent House, determined to insist on the loan of Déjazet, and of Villiers and Thérèse too; if they were not above it; and "I tumbled from my high" when I heard you were in the country till Thursday. What can be the matter? Where is the country, and why are you there? However, if any sudden change in your plans occurs, recollect that our innocent little pleasures commence at 7 to-morrow evening.

Bowood was very agreeable. We stayed there eight days.

The Greys and Lady Harriet were in their best moods, and very pleasant. Bingham kills me, dead; he is so tiresome, that it almost amounts to an excitement. Macaulay quite wonderful, and I rather like him more for the way in which he snubs the honourable member for V. Even the last morning, when we four were breakfasting together by candle-light to come up by an early express train, he made a last good poke at him. I asked Mr. Dundas for some coffee, and he said he was shocked and he had just drunk it, upon which Macaulay said: "What with your excess and your apologies, Dundas, you put me in mind of Friday, who, when his father asked for a drop of water, began thumping his breast and saying, 'Friday, ugly dog, drank it all up.'" Mr. Dundas clearly did not like the epithet—indeed so little, that he was obliged to laugh outrageously and to say: "One of the happiest quotations, Macaulay, I have heard you make."

As a general rule, I should not recommend travelling habitually by the railroad with Mr. Macaulay. The more that machine screeches and squeals, the louder he talks; and when my whole soul is wrapped up in wonder as to whether the stoker and the guard are doing their duty, and whether several tenders and trucks are not meeting in between my shoulders, the minor details of the Thirty Years' War and of the retreat of the 10,000 Greeks lose that thrilling interest they would have in a quiet drawing-room. There is a sort of aggravation in knowing that 10,000 Greeks died ignorant of railway accidents; and there is no use in bothering any more about them, poor old souls!

Your cousins the Duff-Gordons were at Bowood. I think her anything but agreeable, but I strongly suspect that instead of our cutting her, she was quietly cutting all of us, merely because she thinks women tiresome. At least, I think there is so little good done by being rude to anybody, that I try to be civil to her, but was repulsed with immense loss. She came down to luncheon every day in a pink striped shirt, with the collar turned down over a Belcher handkerchief, a man's coat made of green plaid, and a black petticoat. Lord Grey always called her the Corsair; but she was my idea of something half-way between a German student and an English waterman, that amounts to a *débardeur*. Whatever that may be, I do not know.

London seems quite empty, the 4th Nr. of Dombey has given me infinite pleasure, and I think even you must like that school. Just Villiers's case at King's College.

I presume you are at the Grove. Love to all there—at least not all, but a selection. Your ever affectionate

E. E.

Miss Eden to Lady Theresa Lewis.

ADMIRALTY

MY DEAREST THERESA, I was not *standing out* this time for the sake of a letter; but, in the first place, I thought you were to be in town again before this, and then I have been so poorly that writing was a great exertion. It is five weeks to-morrow since I have had a breath of fresh air, and now I have taken entirely to the sofa, and do not attempt sitting up, even to meals. When I do, the second course generally consists of a fainting fit, or some little light delicacy of that sort. So now you see why I did not write; it would not have been *égayant* for your holidays. And illness always seems to me such an *immediate* visitation from God that it never frets me as many other little *travers* do, which might have been avoided by a little more sense or conduct.

Lord Auckland seems quite satisfied with the efficient state of the Navy, notwithstanding the loss of that poor *Avenger*. I saw such an interesting private letter to-day from the gunner who was saved, stating so simply his escape and difficulties, not making half the fuss that we should if the carriage had been overturned and we had had to walk half a mile home.

I do not feel alarmed by the Duke's or Lord E.'s letters, but I do not imagine they tell the French anything they did not know before, and as the English never know anything till they have been told it twenty times, it is perhaps not amiss that they should be so far frightened as to make them willing to pay for a little more protection. They would like a very efficient army and a great display of militia, but I doubt whether they will like a shilling more of income-tax.

I always keep myself in good heart by all the axioms on which we were educated, the old John Bull nonsenses—that one Englishman can beat three Frenchmen; that the French eat frogs; and the wooden walls of old England, and Britannia rules the waves, and Hearts of Oak, and *parlez voos*—all most convincing arguments to us old warriors who lived in the war times, and who went up to the nursery affecting complete insouciance, but fearing that the French would arrive just while Betty Spencer the nurse was down at supper. I quite remember those terrors in 1806; and then came all our victories, and the grand triumphs which reassured me for life. I feel a dead of certainty that before the French had collected twenty steamers, or had put twenty soldiers on board any of them, Sir Charles Napier, or somebody of that sort, would have dashed in amongst them and blown up half ships.

Still it might be as well to have a few more soldiers, if the Duke of Wellington wishes for them, nor do I much object to his writing a foolish letter. He has written a good many in his life.

I go on believing that if the use of pen and ink were denied to our public men, public affairs would get on better. Johnnie writes foolish letters, and Lord P. does not seem to have written a wise one to Greece. Lord John called here last Thursday in good spirits, and his visits are always as pleasant as they are rare. I do not mean that I blame him for their rarity; it is more surprising that he should be able ever to call at all. But as I have been so shut up for nearly a year, I have seen but little of him, and I must say a little *snatch* of him is very agreeable and refreshing. Ever, dearest Theresa, your most affectionate

E. E.

Miss Eden to her Sister, Mrs. Drummond.

January 1848.

MY DEAREST MARY, George came home yesterday—a journey from Bowood; a Cabinet yesterday afternoon; another long one this morning; and a Naval dinner which we gave yesterday.

He says Macaulay has quite recovered his spirits, and there was not a break in his conversation at Bowood. Lord John paid me a late visit yesterday, and the servants wisely let him in, though I had said not at home. But it was good-natured of him, as he was only in town for a night, to walk down because he knew I was ill. "So I told them they must let me in."

I must say that when he told me particulars of the letters that had been written to him, to the Queen, etc.—particulars he did not wish to have repeated—and of the organised conspiracy it has been to try the prerogative of the Crown, he is quite justified in any *twitness* of letters himself. It is a great pity that some of Dean Merewether's letters, and of Lord John's begging him to withdraw them, were not published. He wrote to say that if he might have Hereford, or, as he expressed it in a post-boy fashion, "If the Government gives me this turn, which is my due, there would be no objection raised to their giving Doctor Hampden the next Bishopric." So it shows the Bampton Lectures had not much to do with it.

As for the Bishop of Oxford, the odd intrigue he has been carrying on would have been hardly credible in Louis XIII.'s time in a Cardinal who hoped to be Prime Minister himself. However, I won't say what I was told not to say. But there is that to be said for our Queen and Prince, that their straightforwardness is a very great trait in their characters, and that they never deceive or join in any deceit against their Minister, but always are frank and true, and repel all intrigue against him. George thought the Prince very clever and well-informed at Windsor; and his character always comes out *honest*. I take it that he governs us really, in everything.

Somebody said to Lord John, "The Bishop of Oxford could be brought around immediately if you would only say a few words to him," and he answered, "I suppose he would, if the three words were 'Archbishop of Canterbury.'" He did not seem at all bitter against him yesterday, but said he had been made a bishop too young for such an ambitious man, and that he had taken to court intrigues in consequence.

I am so glad *Daughters* interested you. I have heard such teasing stories about that Lady Ridley—quite incredible. I am sure a few mothers' and daughters' books are wanted just to make them understand each other. If mothers would take the same pains not to hurt their children's feelings, that they do not to hurt other people's children, it would make homes much happier. They should not twit them with not marrying, or with being plain, etc., and they should enter, whether they feel it or not, into their children's tastes. The longer I live, the more I see that if the old mean to be loved by the young, and even on a selfish calculation they ought to wish it, they must think of their own young feelings and susceptibilities, and avoid all the little roughnesses from which they suffered themselves. One of the remorses of my life is not having loved my mother enough, because she was a most excellent mother; but she rather teased me, and held up other girls, and roused bad feelings of jealousy. And my father we all worshipped, though I think he was particular with us, but then it was all done with so much tact. I heard a great deal more about Mrs. Fry and her daughter, which set me thinking over all these things. Your ever affectionate

E. E.

Miss Eden to Lady Theresa Lewis.

ADMIRALTY,
Friday.

MY DEAREST THERESA, It is impossible to say anything in your favour as a correspondent, so don't expect it. But you may have other good points. I do not know that you are entirely depraved. To make an example: You might hesitate to stew a child—one of your own, perhaps. But as a constant letter-writer, you are decidedly and finally a failure. I could not imagine what had become of you, and it was a beautiful trait in my character not writing; because nothing is so tiresome as a letter about a long recovery.

I am better, but not well, and the more shame for me, for Ramsgate was charming, everything that it ought to have been, delicious weather for anybody who could not walk much, or drive at all. As it was warm enough to sit out half the day, we had a small house quite close to the sands. Not an acquaintance to disturb us. Ella and I suited each other admirably. I was not equal to company, and yet should have been sorry to drive my *young* lady to a dull life. But it is what she likes best, and she really enjoyed her quiet life, found plenty of amusement for herself, and was quite sorry when our five weeks were over. I do not know any sea place I could like better than Ramsgate; it is so dry and so cheerful, and such quantities of vessels are constantly coming in and out. There were Greek, Russian, Dutch, Swedish, Spanish and French ships in *quantities*; and the most picturesque-looking people always walking about in the shape of foreign sailors.

We came back on Monday, having a very smooth sea for our voyage, and a remarkably thick fog for our reception, which has lasted till this morning. It is fine now.

No, I cannot say I have worried my intellect much with endeavours to understand the monetary crisis. I am sorry Parliament is to meet, being well aware that a country cursed with a House of Commons never can have any liberty or prosperity; but I suppose it is unavoidable. I was rather glad the Government did something; because even if it is a losing thing, I think the country is better satisfied when the Government seems to try and help it, and it is more creditable to all parties. But it seems to me that the measure has hitherto had a good effect, and has done no harm.

May not I now allude to the "Secret of the Comedy," and wish you joy of Mr. Lewis's new office, which is one I should think he would like, and I should think you would too. It is interesting work, without being dull slavery, as many offices are.

To be sure, there never was anything like the character Lord C. is making for himself; and if he could make one for that desperate country he is trying to govern, Solomon would be a misery to him. But what a people! I quite agree with Carlyle, who says: "If the Irish were not the most degraded savages on earth, they would blush to find themselves alive at all, instead of asking for means to remain so." But everybody agrees in saying they never had such a Lord-Lieutenant before.

I always meant to tell you about your brother Montagu. Two old gentlemen were sitting near me at Ramsgate and talking of the difficulty of finding a seat at the church there, and one of them said: "It is just as bad in London. I sit under the Hon. Villiers, and what's the consequence? I never go to church because I can't get a place." The friend, who was slow, apparently said, "Ah, and it's much worse if you sit under what's called a popular preacher." "Why, sir, that's my case. The Honourable Villiers *is* a popular preacher, the most popular preacher in London, and I say that's the worst of a popular preacher, nobody ever can get in to hear him." I see Montagu preaching a splendid sermon to himself, and his congregation all sitting glowering at him because there is no room for them in church! But the idea is flattering. The most remarkable marriage in my family is W. Vansittart's. He has been ten years in India, lost his wife, has two children, on whom he settled what little money he had. His furlough was out, and now he has found a Miss Humphreys; good looking, pleasant, well brought up, thirty-four (his own age), and with *more* than £100,000, and a beautiful home in Hyde Park Gardens, who is going to marry him, settled all her fortune on him, and of course he has not now the least notion where India is, unless towards Paddington perhaps. There is another sister, much younger, if you know of any eligible young man. Your ever affectionate

E. E.

Miss Eden to Lady Theresa Lewis.
Sunday.

MY DEAR THERESA, I was quite sorry you took all that trouble in vain for me, but I had already let in Lady John and Lady Grey.... But what crowned my impossibility of speaking any more, was an extra visit from Locock. I am a beast for disliking that man, only everybody has their antipathy born with them. Some don't like cats, some frogs, and some Lococks. But he is grown so attentive, I repent, and he came on Friday of his own account, and he did not scold me for not being better, and he would not take his guinea, and was altogether full of the most agreeable negatives. I am glad to have seen a doctor once refuse a fee. I felt as if I had earned a guinea. Your ever affectionate

E. E.

Miss Eden to Lady Theresa Lewis.

ADMIRALTY, *Saturday, December 1848.*

MY DEAREST THERESA, Your letter has come in at an odd time of day, not leaving much time to answer it; but that is as well, as I cannot make out a long letter. Lady Ashburton is undoubtedly dead after twelve hours' illness; but nobody seems to know much about it, and that family always forget to advertise their own deaths, so that one keeps thinking they may recover long after they are buried. The Miss Barings went to Longleat the day after their mother's death, and the Ashburtons came to town for two nights, and then went to the Grange. I have written twice to her but have had no answer, and I never know exactly how she will take grief; but I should think she must feel all those rapid deaths of friends and relations very much.

C. Buller is such a loss to her society as well as to herself, and it will make a great difference in her parties. He is so very much missed by those who knew him well. We had seen a great deal of him this year, and it was impossible not to be fond of him—he was so amiable and good-natured and so light in hand.

I always felt Lady Ashburton would not long outlive Lord Ashburton; she never cared much for anybody else, and was just the woman to fret herself to death. Your affectionate

E. E.

Miss Eden to Lady Theresa Lewis.

Tuesday evening.

MY DEAREST THERESA, I was very glad to see your hand of write again, though you might have given a better account of yourself and Thérèse if you had wished to please. And then poor Bully! That was melancholy; but however, he has been a pleasure to you for years, and that is something, as life goes. I am glad you are up to Lord John's tricks, because in a general way that very artful young man takes you in in a manner that astonishes me, who sees through him with wonderful perspicacity, and when the Duke told me he was going to Harpton *on his way to Knowsley*, I thought he was going to try to seduce my boy Sir George from the paths of rectitude.

I wrote so much to your brother of all the Duke of Bedford said of the old statesman being of use to the young one, and the young statesman taking to the old one (words on which he rings the changes till he makes me sick), that I can't write it all over again; but by dint of positively declining to understand, and by being so intensely stupid as to ask which Lord Stanley he meant (perhaps *he* of Alderley), and by writing him short, savage notes in the intervals of the weekly luncheons he takes here, I hope I have rather enlightened that slightly damaged article—his mind. It is a good old mind, too, in its little bald shell; but Lord John had evidently persuaded him that new combination of parties was necessary, and that Lord Stanley was, as he always calls him, the young statesman of the age. William Russell has succeeded Lord John at Woburn, and had evidently snubbed the Duke about this alliance, as his tone was quite changed about it, and he was anxious to prove that the friendship began here. Your affectionate

E. E.

Miss Eden to Lady Theresa Lewis.

ADMIRALTY,
Sunday.

MY DEAREST THERESA, I may as well write a line while I can, just in the stages that intervene between the pains of my illness and the pains of my cure; the last being decidedly the worst and the most destructive; my courage has gone for pain.

How are you and yours, and what do you hear from Dublin? I have heard nothing about them since they went. London is this week entirely empty; otherwise there has always been an allowance of a visitor a day—Lord Grey, Lord Palmerston, Lord Cowper, passing through, and so on; and while Lord Auckland and Fanny were at Bowood, my sister, Mrs. Colvile, abandoned in the handsomest manner her husband and children in the wilds of Eaton Place, and came and lived here. I was very unwell at the time, and she is the quietest and best nurse in the world. Poor thing! she well may be.

The report of Lord Godolphin's marriage to Lady Laura gains ground, and though I feel it is not true, it is too amusing to dispute. Ditto, C. Greville's to Mrs. H. Baring. I see his stepchildren playfully jumping on his feet when gout is beginning. Henry Eden is so happy about his marriage, and so utterly oblivious of the fact that he is fifty, that I begin to think that is the best time for being in love. Miss Beresford has £20,000 down now, more hereafter; and as the attachment has lasted twelve years, only waiting for the cruel Uncle's consent, which was wrung from him by Henry's appointment to Woolwich, they ought to know what they are about, and luckily when they meet they seem to have liked each other better than ever. But twelve years is rather an awful gap....

Macaulay's book has unbounded success. Not a copy to be had, and everybody satisfied that *their* copy is *the* cleverest book in the world. Don't tell anybody, but I can't read it—not the fault of the book, but I can't take the trouble, and had rather leave it till I can enjoy it, if that time ever comes.

Good-bye, dearest Theresa. Love to Mrs. V. When do you come to town? How goes on your book? Yours affectionately,

E. E.

CHAPTER XIV

1849-1863

Miss Eden to Lady Campbell.
EDEN LODGE, KENSINGTON GORE,
Tuesday evening, 1849.

MY OWN DEAREST PAM, I hear to-day that you too are bereaved of what was most dear to you; and it has roused me to write, for if any one has a right to feel for and with you, through my old, deep, unchanged affection, early ties, association in happy days, and now through calamity,—it is I. Dearest, how kindly you wrote to me in my first bitter hours, when I hardly understood what comfort could mean, and yet, your warm affection did seem to comfort me, and I wish I could now say to you anything that could help you.

You have children, to love and to tend, and yet again, they may be fresh sources of anxiety. I have heard nothing but that there was a long previous illness; and though you may have had the anxiety of much watching, still I think that it is better than a sudden rending of the ties of life.... We came here Friday, but I have not been able to go out of my own room. This reminds me of you as well as of him. Your ever affectionate

E. E.

Miss Eden to Lady Theresa Lewis.
EDEN LODGE,
Saturday, December 1849.

Thank you very much, my dear old friend, for thinking of me and my sorrows in the midst of all your gladsome family, and your happy Christmas. I earnestly hope and trust you will have many as happy, and even more so as your children grow up around you, and become what you have tried to make them.

The paper-knife is beautiful, and if it were not so I should have been pleased at your thinking of me; and considering how long I have tried the patience of my friends, it is marvellous how little it has failed.

It was a twelvemonth yesterday since he left me to go to the Grange. I had got out of bed and was settled on the sofa, that he might go off with a cheerful impression of me, and we had our luncheon together; and he came in again in his fine cloak to say good-bye, and I thought how well he was looking. And that was the close of a long life of intense affection. I do not know why I should feel additionally sad as these anniversaries come round, for I never think less or more on the subject on any day. It is always there. But still this week is so burnt in on my mind that I seem to be living it all dreamily over again.

I wish at all events to be able to keep (however cold and crushed I feel myself) the power of entering into the happiness of others, and I like to think of you, dear Theresa.... Your ever affectionate

E. E.

Miss Eden to Lady Theresa Lewis.
, BROADSTAIRS,
Wednesday .

MY DEAREST THERESA ...I do not know whether you have heard of dear little Mary Drummond's marriage to Mr. Wellesley. He is a really good, sensible young man, the greatest friend her brothers and sisters have, much looked up to in his office; and though he might have been a little richer, they will not be ill off, and there is a tangible sum to settle on her, and altogether I think it is a cheerful event. Their *young* happiness will do good to all our old unhappinesses, and I think Mrs. Drummond's letters are already much more cheerful from her having all the love-making, trousseau, etc., to write about instead of her health. Little Mary is such a darling—so bright and useful and unselfish, and so buoyantly happy, that I do not see how they are to get on without her. Her letters make me feel almost youthful again. She is so thoroughly pleased with her lot in life.

Maurice and Addy are taking their holiday at Broadstairs. I had never seen them in this sort of intimate way, and I did not expect to be so pleased as I am with both of them. His manner to her is perfect—not only full of tenderness and attention, but he is very sensible in his precautions about her health, and takes great care of her in every way. She looks fearfully delicate. He is very attentive to me too, and as they came in this direction partly to see if they could be of use to me, I am glad it has all turned out so well. My health is in a very poor state, and I am obliged to give up going down to the Baths, but a cottage always has room for everything; and we are turning what is by courtesy called a Green-house, into a bath-room, opening out of my sitting-room. I like the place, and its quiet and bracing air and its busy sea. It is always covered with ships, and I do not regret the move. Your ever affectionate

E. E.

Miss Eden to Lady Dover.
BROADSTAIRS, 1851.

Your letter, dearest, was by some accident delayed on the road, and when I received it the life you were all watching so anxiously was then only to be numbered by hours, and I did not like to break in on you. Your poor sister! From my heart I grieve for her, and from the very beginning of this severe trial I have had almost daily accounts of her.

I would have written to you sooner about your own child's happiness, but I was very ill when I heard of it. It is one of the marriages that seems to please everybody, and as I do not think anybody would have been satisfied with a moderately good son-in-law for you, or a commonplace husband for Di, I am quite convinced that all that is said of Mr. Coke must be true.

I sometimes hope that when your child is married, and your poor sister can spare you, that you and Lucia might be tempted to come here for a few days. The journey is only three hours, and it is such a quiet little place to stay in. The hotel is only a little village inn. I do so long to see you.

Lord Carlisle talked of coming here for a day or two, but then I was not allowed to see anybody. I wish you would tell him with my love how much I should like to see him at any time, when he can leave his family and his public duties.

Lady Grey kindly came here on Saturday, and is gone back to-day, and I had a visit from the Ellesmeres last week, for which I had been anxiously looking, as I was obliged once to put them off, and I wanted much to see her. She is looking very thin, and is much depressed; but still it always does me good to be with her, and to see such a well-regulated Christian heart as hers. The second day she talked constantly of her boy, and as it was her own volunteering I hope the exertion may have done her good. Lord E. is particularly well. The suddenness of the poor boy's death preys on her, and much as your sister has witnessed of pain and illness, I still think that it is the sudden grief which breaks the heart-strings. It is the difference between the avalanche which crushes and the stream which swells gradually and has time to find its level. But perhaps every one that is tried finds the readiest excuse for their own especial want of resignation.

My health does not improve. They say the last attack a fortnight ago was gout in the stomach. I trust God will spare me a recurrence of such suffering, for I am grown very cowardly; but, at all events, every medical precaution has now been taken, and I am not anxious as to the result, though shamefully afraid of pain.

God bless you. Yours affectionately,

E. EDEN.

Miss Eden to Lady Theresa Lewis.

, BROADSTAIRS, 1851.

There is nothing I like so much as a letter, dearest Theresa, but I am so often unable to answer them that, of course, my correspondents are disheartened, and I cannot wonder at it. Just now a private letter is invaluable, for when I woke up after six days of agony, which cut me off even from a newspaper, I found that there had not only been various Ministries formed and destroyed, but that *The Times* had become perfectly drivelling. Its baseness and inconsistency did not shock me, and we have been brought up to that; but it writes the sort of trash that a very rheumatic old lady who had been left out of Lord John's parties might indite. It really worries me, because I cannot make out who or what it is writing for or about, or what it wants. There is no use in commenting on your letters. I am very sorry for all that is past, because I like Lord John, and he seems to have played a poor part. This last abandonment of the Papal Bill is to my mind the falsest step of all, and I think the most ruinous to his character and the country, and totally unlike him. I always keep myself up by setting down everything wrong that is *done* to the Attorney-General, and everything foolish that is *written*, to C. Greville. Quite unjust; but I have never forgiven the Attorney-General that Park history, and C. G. tried to do as much mischief as he could in *The Times* last year about foreign politics, and this year about the Pope.

Anyhow, it is an ugly state of things, and cannot last long. I heard from a person to whom Sir James Graham said it, that he would not serve *under* Lord John, but that he would under Lord Clarendon; and I cannot imagine that Lord Clarendon will not be Prime Minister before three months are over. I am afraid he is papally wrong, but I give that point up now. The Pope has beat us and taken us; and when once a thing is done there is no use in grumbling. England will be a Roman Catholic country; and I shall try and escape into Ireland (which will, of course, become Protestant and comfortable eventually), unless I fall into the hands of Pugin, who has built a nice little church and convent, with an Inquisition home to match at Ramsgate. I suppose we shall be brought out to be burnt on the day of Sanctus Carolus, for the Pope cannot do less than canonise Charles Greville.

I did not admire Lord Stanley's speech as many Whigs did; there was the old little-mindedness and grudging testimony to adversaries in it. I always think Lord Lansdowne comes out as a real, gentlemanlike, high-minded statesman on these occasions. However, I know nothing about it really, for I have not seen a human being this fortnight.

Eden Lodge had been let to what seemed an eligible tenant, a rich widow with one daughter, but three days before she was to have taken possession she said her friends had frightened her about the Exhibition. I do not suppose anybody will take it this year, which is inconvenient to me, in a pecuniary point of view; but it cannot be helped. You do not mention the children—is Villiers grown up? married? Prime Minister or what? Your book looks imposing in the advertisements.

Love to Mrs. Villiers and to Lord Clarendon when you write. Your affectionate

E. E.

Miss Eden to Lady Theresa Lewis.

EDEN LODGE, KENSINGTON GORE,
Saturday, March 1856.

MY DEAREST THERESA, Such a fascinating bullfinch! Mr. Whittaker's assortment arrived two days ago, and he brought six here this morning in small wooden prisons; and the scene was most interesting. All of them clearing their throats and pretending that they had taken cold and did not know whether they *could* sing; and all swelling into black and red balls, and then all bursting at once into different little airs; and Whittaker, who partakes of the curious idiosyncrasy which I have traced in Von der Hutten and other bird dealers, that of looking like a bullfinch and acting as such, going bowing and nodding about to each cage, till I fancied that his coat and waistcoat were all *purfled* out like bird's feathers; and I, lying on the sofa, insisting in a most stately manner that some of the birds did not bring the tune down to its proper keynote, though it was impossible I could tell, as they all sang at once. However, I chose one that sings to command (a great merit). "'Tis good to be merry and wise," and now I have him alone, I am confident you will like him. If not, the man will change him. I shall be so pleased, dearest Theresa, if he gives you even a moment's pleasure, and I am certain from sad experience that in a settled deep grief, it is wise to have these little adventitious cheerfulnesses put into the background. It is good for those who are with us, at all events. And there is something catching in the cheerfulness of animals, just as the sight of flowers is soothing.

You must find Harpton looking pretty for March, particularly if it is suffering under such a very favourable eruption of crocuses, etc., as my garden is. I never saw them in such clumps.

I have been fairly beat by Miss Yonge's new book, *The Daisy Chain*, which distresses me, as I generally delight in her stories; but if she means this Daisy Chain to be amusing, it is, unhappily, intensely tedious, and if she means it to be good, it strikes me that one of Eugène Sue's novels would do less harm to the cause of religion. The Colviles are very angry with me for not liking it; and, above all, for thinking Ethel, the heroine, the *most* disagreeable, stormy, conceited girl I ever met with. Starting with the intention of building a church out of her shilling a week—which is the great harrowing interest of all Puseyite novels; finding fault with all her neighbours; keeping a school in a stuffy room that turns everybody sick, because she cannot bear money that was raised by a bazaar by some ladies she disliked; and always saying the rudest thing she can think of because it is *her way*. I read on till I came to a point when she thought her father was going to shake her because she was ill-natured about her sister's marriage; and finding that he did not perform that operation, which he ought to have done every day of her life, I gave it up. The High Church party are all going raving mad!

That pretty Mrs. Palmer has had herself taken to a hospital as a sort of penance in illness, and has left her most excellent husband and five little children to take care of themselves. She has, moreover, taken a vow of six hours' silence every day during Lent, but will write an answer on a slate. If I were her husband I should take advantage of that vow and give her my mind for six hours at a time. She may not answer again. Ever your affectionate

E. EDEN.

Miss Eden to Lady Theresa Lewis.
Eden Lodge, Kensington Gore .

MY DEAREST THERESA, Will you tell me what I am to think about the India Bill? I believe I think with Roebuck, that it is claptrappy, and generally that it would make a mess of India, but I have not the least idea what it means, and will you tell me what effect it had?

I am still so much occupied in rearing up Sir George Lewis to be Leader of the House, that I have hardly time to write. May I ask you to make his holidays advantageous, by pointedly contradicting everything he says, or does not say, while you are at Harpton; allowing him to argue in defence of his opinions, but continue to contradict him in the pertest and most offensive manner. I am afraid, too, I must trouble you to allow him to find fault with everything you do—from ordering dinner, downwards; because, though I hope this India Bill will finish the Derbyites, still my Leader must be up to his Opposition duties. After the recess, the House will continue his education, and your domestic felicity will be more complete than ever for this little sacrifice to the public good. You are quite wrong, my dear, about Lord John. A charming individual in private life, but not fit to govern a country or lead a party. So please attend to the above directions. Your affect.

E. E.

Miss Eden to her Niece, Lena Eden.
EDEN LODGE
.

MY DEAREST LENA, It is pitch dark to-day, so that I have not been able to attempt my newspaper. I am afraid you will have to go out as a daily governess when I die, for I am spending my whole fortune in coats. Lady Georgina Bathurst's letter was very amusing, but it is clear that her friend Bennett makes himself generally odious, and that poor Mrs. Bennett suffers as much from it as she did formerly. I am sick of the High Church clergy's cant about respect for their Diocesan, etc., when they always do everything they can that is rude and disrespectful to their Bishop; and it always surprises me that a sensible woman like Georgina can be taken in by them. But she always was in extremes. In her political days she did not think it possible that a Whig soul could be saved, and may think so still....

The seagull pigeon is sitting. I am so glad I am not married to a pigeon; they are such teasing, tyrannical husbands. Yours affectionately,

E. E.

Miss Eden to Lady Theresa Lewis.
RICHMOND,
Tuesday evening .

DEAREST THERESA, Sorry you did not come; hope for better luck Thursday. I have had a *passage at arms* with old Bentley, who has dawdled over the "Auckland Correspondence" till he says it is now too late for the publication this season, and it will not appear till October; but that this is the best time for a work of fiction, and he wanted mine instantly. I wrote him a coldly savage letter, conveying all sorts of reproaches in political terms, and saying that, as of course he could not undertake a second book till he had done with the first, and as I was in a hurry, I must accept the offer of some other publisher (I have had several offers). Whereupon he rushed down here early this morning and told Lena he was "a persecuted victim," that he would bring out the *Semi-Detached* in a month, and that he must have it, etc. He offered only £250, and I really will not take less than £300. Lena told him so afterwards, and he said he dared to say that there would be no difficulty about terms if he could talk it over with you. So mind you stick to £300 and a very early publication. I really do want the money, for poor Richard Wellesley has been obliged to resign, and they are ordered to winter abroad for the winter and will have some difficulty in managing it, so I want to be able to help them.

Dear little Mary is a greater darling than ever. Ever your affectionate

E. EDEN.

Miss Eden to Lady Charlotte Greville.
CHILD'S HILL, HAMPSTEAD,
Saturday, 1859.

So like you, dearest, to think of sending that review, which I thought very flattering. Lena had already picked it up at a neighbour's house, and I am told it is a great help to a book to be reviewed by the *Globe*. A review in *The Times*, even unfavourable, is supposed by publishers to ensure a second edition, but *The Times* does not stoop to single volume novels. "Semi" has had more success than I require, and considerably more than I expected.

It gave me real pleasure to think that I had amused you. That, and a kind note from Lord Lansdowne, who said that the book had been a great amusement to him in his convalescence, gave me intense gratification. Altogether, people have been marvellously good-natured about it, and if ever I write another story, which is not very likely, I shall call it "The Good-natured World." I really do think that, though we all carp in a petty childish way at each other, that there is an immense amount of solid *bienveillance* in constant circulation; only we do not think about the kindness we meet with, till we actually want it, and then we see the amount and the value of it.

I wrote my congratulations with very great ease to the Buccleughs. That marriage seems to give universal satisfaction, and Char was in such a fidget to have her son married, that she would have put up with a very inferior article in the way of a daughter-in-law. I am more puzzled with my letters to Theresa Lewis. Lord Clarendon had cut him on account of his writings, and Theresa Lewis had never asked him to Kent House, so you see there is rather a mess to be cleared up before congratulations come out in a clear brilliant stream.

However, Lord Clarendon has been extremely amiable about it, which he was sure to be, and Thérèse was so regularly and thoroughly in love that I think T. Lewis was quite right to make no objections on the ground of poverty. After twenty-one, young people may surely choose for themselves, whether they will be rich or poor.

Do you want a perfection of a little dog to *égayer* you? Lady Ellesmere knows my little Manilla silk dog, a small bone run through a large skein of white floss silk, full of wit and affection. I feel certain it would be a happiness to you and no trouble, except that you would have to coax it fourteen hours out of the twenty-four, and then strike for thirteen hours.

Love to Lady E. Ever your affectionate

E. Eden.

The Duke of Bedford was here yesterday. He is looking very thin but in good spirits, and happily satisfied that Lord John is the best Foreign Secretary we have ever had, and a *juste milieu* between Lord Palmerston's extreme French, and Lord C.'s extreme Austrian views.

Lord Lansdowne to Miss Eden.

RICHMOND,
August 22.

MY DEAR MISS EDEN, Many thanks for your very kind letter. You will see from the date of this I have advanced a step, and tho' not quite well yet, am at least convalescent, and just in a state fully to appreciate a pleasant letter or a pleasant book; the *Semi-Detached*, innocent as it is, did indeed amuse me greatly. I only wish all people could be made half as agreeable. You have been able to hurry on a catastrophe without the assistance of one villainous couple.

I am much disposed to be seduced by your view of Napoleon III.; no man ever committed such mistakes and knew so well how to get out of them. A friend of Mme. de Staël once said to me that she had an irresistible propensity to throw her friends into the river; but that it was relying upon her skill *pour les repêcher, l'un après l'autre*. This is somewhat the case with him. He would not run so voluntarily into blunders if he did not feel confident of extricating himself. Believe me, always, affectly yours,

LANSDOWNE.

Pray read B. Osborne's speech at Liskeard. One can afford to forgive impudence when it is so amusing.

Miss Eden to Lady Theresa Lewis.

CHILD'S HILL, HAMPSTEAD,
Monday evening.

MY DEAREST THERESA, This has been a great "Semi" day, concluding with your letter which is just come; and I began the morning with four closely-written pages from Locock, who generally throws very cold water on any of my little pursuits. But he says the grandest things of "Semi," which he had read on Saturday evening, and says that a bystander would have thought him quite mad; he was screaming with laughter by himself, and that he is ashamed to add that in church next day it *would* come back to him. "It really haunts me." He was longing for Monday to read it loud to Lady L., and he says that he must, at all events, be a good judge of a confinement. *Blanche*'s lying-in is so thoroughly true.

I enclose a bit of Mary Auckland's letter, which also came to-day, and which is the third she has written about it. All the family from Wells have written in the same strain, and Robert, who is painfully punctual, was missing at breakfast the morning after "Semi" arrived; and was discovered in bed, peremptorily declining to get up till he had finished his book. We look upon this as a great compliment, as he never looks at a word. Anne Cowper is equally civil; but then these are all friends, and would say anything that would encourage me to fill up my sedentary sick life with any occupation; so any little word that you hear from strangers is more valuable as a genuine judgment.

To be sure—the luck of having you as my editress, my shield, my sword, my everything. You know everybody, and are good friends with them all.

Miss Eden to Lady Theresa Lewis.

CHILD'S HILL, HAMPSTEAD,
Monday.

MY DEAREST THERESA, The important enclosure arrived safely this morning, and I sent Ellis forthwith to get the money and pay it in at Drummond's, for fear Bentley should fail to-day. But my belief is that he is a wealthy Bentley; and he has behaved like a gentleman, and evidently is not discontented with his bargain. And so, all's well that ends well, even if it be only a Semi-Detached House.

Thank you again and again, dearest Theresa, for all the successful trouble you took. Nobody but you could have brought the affair to such a good end, and I now fondly think that between this and November you will work up the Harcourt income to £4000 a year! You made £100 out of the £25 I expected, therefore, etc., etc.

You all sound very happy at Harpton, and Lord Clarendon had given me the same account, and said how much his girls were taking to their new cousin, and how pleased they were with Thérèse's perfect happiness.

The house in Pont Street is a good idea. Thérèse will be so handy for you to fetch and carry, and it will be such a mere step for her to Kent House. I do not mean to settle yet what my little offering is to be. I want to choose it myself when I go back to town. And then I have rather set my heart on a china dessert service, but if anybody else steps in, I can easily set my heart on something else. There are so many duplicates in wedding presents; such unnecessary quantities of inkstands and cream jugs; that I think it better to wait a little and hit the spot at the end. I began life by giving my sister Mary a dessert service when she married on £900 a year, and settled in that little cottage at Neasdon; and in all their after wealth Mr. Drummond never would have any other, but went on filling up the breakages in the old pattern to the end. And so it has been my usual wedding *cadeau* since, and I gave one to J. Colvile when he went to India, and as I look on Thérèse as a niece, I should like to go jogging on in the old dessert fashion; so, if anybody consults you, say *that* is bespoke. So Mr. Harcourt may have one. But you will let me know in the course of time. The Sydney Herberts called here yesterday. They had slept at the Grenville farm and he came very good-naturedly to assure himself, he said, that I was aware of the complete success of "Semi," which seems to have taken his fancy prodigiously. He said it had become a sort of byword in London, and that if anybody talked of taking a house, the answer was, Semi-detached, of course. I have not seen him for 12 years, and he is not the least altered in looks. They were going to dine with Florence Nightingale at Hampstead, or rather at her house, for she has come quite to the last days of her useful life and is dying of disease of the heart. Every breath she draws may be heard through her closed doors, but when she can speak she still likes to talk to Mr. Herbert of soldiers' hospitals and barracks, and to suggest means of improving them. Ever your affectionate

E. EDEN.

Miss Eden to Lady Theresa Lewis.
EDEN LODGE, KENSINGTON GORE,
Saturday evening, November 1859.

MY DEAREST THERESA, Between Lena, and Lady Ribblesdale, and Eddy and Theresa, and all the maids in the house, I am mistress of every detail of the wedding, and I am so very glad that it all went off so beautifully. Lena says it is the most interesting wedding she has been at; there was so much feeling and family affection floating about; and I hear dear Thérèse looked very pretty and very pale. But it is *you*, my old dear, that I have been thinking of all day—thinking so much that I am obliged to write to get the subject off my mind. I am so sorry for you, but only just at this moment. And, after all, the wedding is not so bad as the day of proposal to the mother. Then you had nothing to look to but her going away; and now your next prospect is her coming back; and in the meanwhile you have done all in your power to secure her happiness.

God bless you, dear. This does not require an answer, but I could not resist writing, and I thought you would like to know that I was as well as could be expected; after the fatigue of being at Mrs. Harcourt's wedding this morning. I really feel as if I had been there. Your affectionate

E. EDEN.

Miss Eden to Lady Theresa Lewis.
RICHMOND,
Monday evening.

MY DEAREST THERESA, It is just bedtime, but I must write a line of warm congratulation on the advent of the grandchild and our dear Thérèse's safety; I missed the announcement in *The Times* this morning, and it was not till the middle of the day that Lena, with a railroad sort of screech, made the discovery, and then with infinite presence of mind I said, "Then Theresa cannot be come to town and I shall hear from her this evening." And so I did.

What a discovery chloroform is. By the time we are all dead and buried, I am convinced some further discovery will be made by which people will come into the world and live through it and go out of it without the slightest pain.

Don't you think that if Thérèse continues to go on as well as she has begun you will be able to drive down here? Lady Clarendon sometime ago got an order for Lena to see Strawberry Hill, but as Lena only returned from Wells on Saturday I made no use of it till to-day, and then we found Lady Waldegrave was living there. However, an imposing groom of the chambers showed us the pictures, and Lena saw the rest of the home, while I was all the time longing to ask him if he knew anything about Thérèse, but felt too low in the scale of creation to propound such a question to him.

My best love to her. Do come here. Your affectionate

E. EDEN.

Miss Eden to Lady Charlotte Greville.

EDEN LODGE, KENSINGTON GORE,
October 24 .

MY DEAREST LADY CHARLOTTE, A sudden wish has seized me to write to you—not that I have an atom of a thing to say except the old hacknied fact that I am very fond of you, and also that I heard constantly of you when I was at Richmond through your sons, and the Flahaults, and that now I do not see how I am to hear of you at all, except somebody at Hatchford (not you) will have the kindness to write to me.

Barring the loss of the view, and the drives in that beautiful park, I do not miss my Richmond so much as I expected.

There is always something intensely comfortable in home, and my own books and things, and I am very busy with a new sitting-room that I have made upstairs, by throwing two small bedrooms into one. It has made a very pretty warm room, looks clean and bright, and then there is the fun of furnishing it. It is painful to look out of the window. Those dreadful Royal Commissioners have cut down all the fine trees belonging to Gore House and are running up a blank wall 20 feet high, for their new garden.

My own trees are the only ones left in this neighbourhood, and though the blank wall is better than another row of houses staring into my garden, the general effect is that of living just outside the King's Bench Prison. I look upon a man who cuts down a large tree in London as capable of committing murder, or any other crime, and have a vague idea that the Road Murder might be traced home to Prince Albert and Lord Granville, or one of these Commissioners.

It will interest Lady Ellesmere to know that Lena has returned to her navvies, and has been greeted with the greatest warmth. Indeed, I should prefer a little more coolness in her place, as they all insist on shaking hands, and I imagine washing is a virtue they do not practise more than once a week. However, they are an interesting race, very grateful in their rough way; and the Controller and Clerk of the Works both say that there is a great improvement in their habits, and are very eager now to encourage the readings. A great deal of the work in these gardens has now passed into the hands of London bricklayers and carpenters. They steadily declined listening to Mr. Ward, the missionary, and were very rude to him.

He was very anxious Lena should try and tame them, so she began by collecting the débris of her navvies, and sitting down with them under the old tree (which they have killed of course), and some of the bricklayers gathered round and began to laugh, so she told them very quietly that they need not come out of their shed to listen to her if they did not like it, but that if they came out she could not allow any laughing at such a serious subject. And they took it very well and said they did not mean to jeer, and that if she would come to their shed, they would listen if they might smoke; and the navvies in their gentleman-like way advised her to go, and said they would go with her, and they made a path with planks and put up a sort of seat, and showed the bricklayers how the little lady, as they call her, was to be treated. And it all went well. She read them a tract called Slab Castle, which always touches them, and when she came to the chapter on the Bible, half of the bricklayers were in tears, particularly the ones who had laughed, and they conveyed her to the gate, begging she would come again, and clamorous for copies of Slab Castle—which I advise her to decline giving for the present. But they have been extremely civil and attentive since, and she has certainly heard such satisfactory accounts of her old congregation, that it is an encouragement to go on. My love to Lady or Lord E., and believe me ever, dearest, your affectionate

E. EDEN.

I hope Alice will not insist on my liking Miss Yonge's new book. It is more unintelligible than "The Daisy Chain," though not quite so tiresome. But she brings in too many people. There are four generations of one family, and her moral is quite beyond me. Those that are well brought up turn out wicked, and the worldly family produce a crop of saints. I am proud to say I am quite incapable of construing the slang she makes her ladies talk.

Miss Eden to Lady Theresa Lewis.

EDEN LODGE, KENSINGTON GORE,
Monday, December .

MY DEAREST THERESA, It is obvious that I must write and wish you and yours a happy New Year, and a great many of them, and one happier than the other; but barring that I do not see that I have anything else to say. London is so utterly empty during Christmas week, everybody thinking it right to go to somebody else's house, and it is always the most solitary week of the year to me. But I feel so comfortable in the thought that I am not passing it in bed as I have for the twelve preceding years, that it seems to me a singularly merry Christmas.

I suppose you are all rehearsing and acting. Lady Derby writes word that she hears Alice is well enough now to think of acting on the 11th, so I hope she has made great progress in health since she got home. Lady Derby gives rather a poor account of him; he gains strength so slowly, but she says that after being confined to his own room for three months, he was now able to get about the house at times....

The only two people I have seen this week have been Lord Brougham and Sir C. Wood. Lord Brougham was only in town for two nights on his way to Cannes. He is quite enthusiastic about my father's papers, and has written something about them in the *Law Review*, and he was rather good-humoured and pleasant. But on going away he always cries so much at the prospect of our not meeting again, that he leaves me in a puzzled state of low spirits. All the more, that I have not the remotest idea whether it is his death or mine that he is crying over; but he looks so well, I think it must be mine.

By the bye, your old Dean Milman came hobbling into the room on Saturday, full of abject apologies to Lena, whom he chose to suppose he had affronted, and taking great care to ignore his real grand sin of abducting the papers without asking leave. However, he came to say that he was most agreeably surprised that Mr. Hogge has done his part well, and that he and Mrs. Milman had been greatly interested, etc., which she amply confirmed. I like her very much, and she is still so handsome.... Good-bye, dearest. I did not write sooner, as I had just written to the Grove when your letter came, and as everything is public property there, this counts for a letter to Lord Clarendon as well as to you. Your affectionate

E. EDEN.

Miss Eden to her Niece, Mrs. Dickinson.

Eden Lodge, Kensington Gore.

MY DEAR MRS. DICKINSON, I am charmed with your letter, I wanted to have one from you. Dear old Longleat! I should so like to see it again. I passed so much of my youth so very happily there, and I do not think I ever attained loving anybody more than Lady Bath,—not this one—but her mother-in-law, and the daughters pay back to me the affection I had for their mother....

I suppose they told you about the Horticultural Fête? I saw and heard nothing but the crash of carriages, and linkmen went on screaming for them till nine at night. I have not heard linkmen screaming for the last thirteen years.

Yesterday Lena got leave from one of her friends working in the garden, to bring me in thro' a little obscure door into the great conservatory, which we had to ourselves, and I really could hardly believe the flowers were real, they were so unearthly beautiful, particularly the geraniums and roses, great round stools of flowers of the brightest colours. Some day I have a fancy that I shall be well enough to go down and visit you, my old pet. What a bore for you! Your aff.

E. E.

Miss Eden to Lady Theresa Lewis.

March.

MY DEAREST FRIEND, I would rather write to you myself. I am so thankful I saw and took leave of dear Mary. She wished it so much herself, and was as loving and as dear as ever. You know we had always been the greatest friends of the family, and till I went to India, we had never missed for a single day writing to each other. It was an intimacy that only two sisters nearly of an age can have, and she referred to it again on Tuesday, and told me still to be a mother to her children. They always *have* been like my own children. But I am most thankful I was able to witness such a really happy deathbed as hers, so calm, so peaceful, and her mind as entirely clear as it ever was in its best days. And to see those six tall sons, four daughters-in-law, and her three daughters all round her bed, the sons more overwhelmed even than the daughters, and she thanking them, and saying how happy they had made her, it was a scene that quite comforts me for her loss, and her poor daughters had quite the same feeling. I saw them yesterday after the case was hopeless and they were quite calm.

Dearest Theresa, I do not think it good for you just now to go through more melancholy scenes, otherwise you are one of the few I should like to see. I *depend* on you so much. Is it not strange that with my health I should have outlived my six sisters—all, except Lady Godolphin, in perfect health when I came from India? Ever, dearest, your affectionate

E. EDEN.

Miss Eden to Mrs. Dickinson.

EDEN LODGE, 1863.

I have been out only four times since I came to London. The very ordinary looking women who inhabit London at this time of year, with last year's dirty little bonnets put at the back of last year's dirty little faces, and with dirty gowns to match spread over absurd hoops, make me quite uncomfortable.

The "Semi-Attached Couple" was written in that little cottage at Ham Common. I do not exactly know who Mrs. B. was at this moment, but all our Camp ladies were always lying-in, and it is a very easy business in India.

I do not exactly see unless I turn back, and grow young again, that I shall ever visit you at Berkley,—Richmond is looked upon by doctors as an immense journey for me. I am very much pleased my book altogether amused you. I have such quantities of old letters of thanks for it, from people I had forgotten. I had a grand letter from Lord Houghton (Monckton Milnes) in praise of my pure facile English, among other things *Slang* was not invented in my day.

You are quite right to make your children's childhood happy, and as merry as possible, but please do not spoil them. Life does not spoil anybody, and so teach them early to take it as it comes—cheerfully. Your aff.

E. E.

Printed in Great Britain
by Amazon.co.uk, Ltd.,
Marston Gate.